P

ANDREW LEWIS CONN

Andrew Lewis Conn

SOFT SKULL PRESS
2003

P

ISBN: 1-887128-55-7

First Edition

Cover Design: David Janik
Interior Design: OCDesign
Editorial: Richard Nash, Sarah Groff-Palermo

Printed in Canada

Library of Congress Cataloging-in-Publication Data
Conn, Andrew Lewis.
P / by Andrew Lewis Conn.
ISBN 1-887128-55-7
1. Young men—Fiction. 2. Runaway children—Fiction.
3. City and town life—Fiction. 4. Quests (Expeditions)—Fiction.
5. Separation (Psychology)—Fiction. I. Title.
PS3603.O623P145 2003
813'.6--dc21
2003004555

SOFT SKULL PRESS
71 Bond Street
Brooklyn, NY 11217
tel.: 718 643 1599
www.softskull.com
www.pthenovel.com

To Mom and Dad

ACKNOWLEDGEMENTS

The author wishes to thank:

Jeremy Lasky for being a lifelong friend. I could not and would not have written this book in this way if I didn't know you.

Huy Dao, Michael Gurton, Philip Kang, Stephen Turbek, and Luke Wilcox for boundless friendship and inspiration.

Suleiman Osman and David Kartch: better and more supportive readers, roommates, and friends I could not have wished for during the writing of this book.

Ray Forsythe, Barbara Pflughaupt, Alan Miller, Jeff Lovari, Hillary Herskowitz, Bill Douglass, Nan Leonard, and all of our business associates at P&F Communications for being a remarkable group of coworkers and mentors.

Steve, Ruth, and Orin Conn; and Stuart, Lilly, Adam, and Susan Schwab for ceaseless love and encouragement.

Professors David Feldshuh, Don Fredericksen, Marilyn Rivchin, Ron Wilson, and Dr. Steven Shapiro, Walter Gern, and Debra Schmitt for being generous with their knowledge.

Jason Lee for explaining the significance of Pez. Anita Ruth Heitman for being a faithful and dedicated letter writer. Kate Kondell for making an important introduction.

Andrew Blauner for the three P's: patience, perseverance, and professionalism.

Richard Nash for being a brilliant and subtle editor. Soft Skull Press for seeing something good and true in my book.

Siobhan Adcock, Gabriella Aratow, Andrea Berloff, Jennifer Bristol, Sonia Canales, Fabrizio Ciapini, Drew Filus, Seth Fogelman, Alexandra Gelber, Bill Gilman, Christopher Goffard, Jennifer I. Bortolus-Goffard, Daniel Gonzalez, Gayle Goodman, Omri Green, Richard Greene, Alison Hoogerwerf, Omar Jadwat, Amy Karnchanapee, Melissa Karp, Jameel Khaja, Anita King, Josh, Ronnie, and Stephen Lasky, Ira and Lynn Liran, Rachel Natelson, Reg Oberlag, Phil Oxenstein, Chris and Shannon Reid, Mike Rhee, Andrea and Vivienne Rossi, Matthew Rutman, Charlotte and Robert Sawyer, Erica Shoemaker, Brit Till, Joy Tutela, Jaime Villamarin, Trac Vu, Thomas Edwin Ward, Harry Watson, Brendan Werner, Durand Williams, Sal Wilson, and Brian Wolk for loyalty and friendship.

St. James, whose day in the life of Dublin served as North Star through the writing of this book.

Kay Baxter for faith and courage.

Mom, Dad, and Jenn for the world.

"Books you were going to write with letters for titles.
Have you read his F? O yes, but I prefer Q.
Yes, but W is wonderful. O yes, W."

Ulysses

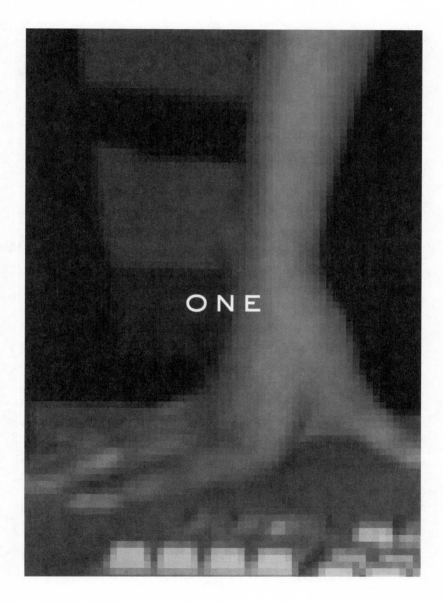

ONE

I

yes, yes, yes, O, yes, yes, yes, O

"Yes, I'm in the fuck film business."
"I thought you looked familiar."
"Yeah, well I was in a couple of videos back in the mid-eighties, so maybe you recognize me from one of those. But back to you. You seem to know your porno."
"Like I said, I grew up with four brothers—"
"—And their friends."
"And their friends, right, so yeah."
"And you don't have any problems with it?"
"As long as no one's getting hurt and everyone's getting paid, right?"
"Yeah . . ."

He was Benjamin Seymour, thirty-three, Benji the Boss in the black leather chair sitting in his office at Commercial Urban Models, where Benji the Blasphemer had been quietly cranking out adult entertainment for the past five years. And she was Allison April Pryce, Allison of Littletown, Illinois, All-American Ally of the loosefitting black leather pants, white halter-top, platform shoes, and teddy bear knapsack.

The office. Apart from the lack of receptionist and apparent cheapness of furniture, in layout the office could have doubled for a therapist's: plywood desk and bookshelves, carpet castered chair, convertible couch, architect's lamp, television set, and steel file cabinet presided over by an Ivy League degree discreetly hanging on the wall. Not neat so much as bare, in its austerity the office was still the most inviting Allison had visited all day, a long day which had taken her across the city, from the wintry-gray stateliness of the Upper East Side to the trash-strewn manginess of Alphabet City and the East Village. New to New York, a novice at job interviews, Allison attempted to answer Benjamin's questions as openly and honestly as she could as a scene from the X-rated video, *The Anal-yst*, rumbled on in the background.

O yes, I like it, I like it in the ass, O

"So you knew what this was about when you came?" Benji asked, tracing an imaginary finger round the racetrack of her mouth.
"You mean the ad?" Allison asked, squeakily readjusting herself in her hardback chair.
"Yeah, the ad."

The ad, as worded and designed by Benjamin, was definitive, industry standard:

Wanted: Female Figure Models For Immediate Placement
$150-$1,500 per diem
Eighteen-up
Legitimate, Bonded, and Licensed
COMMERCIAL URBAN MODELS
337 West 33rd St., Suite 203
Open Call June 16, 10 A.M.-6 P.M.

What was not standard about the ad was where Benji had decided to place it. Whether Benji had gone into hock spending $1,395 running an eighth-page advertisement for erotic film actresses in the *New York Review of Books* out of sarcasm, self-destructiveness, or both, even Benji could not weed out. Whether by accident or guided by some perverse sense of pride, godless, loveless, childless Benji had scheduled the open call on a Sunday, a Sunday which turned out to be not just any ordinary day of rest but Father's Day, even he could not tell. He had plenty of time to ponder these questions, however, as he wormed his way through an eight-hour parade of housewives, teachers, librarians, and bookish, middle-aged women who'd presumed "figure modeling" meant something along the lines of hand and calf flexing for nail polish or pantyhose commercials. A long summer day. Until April.

When Allison April Pryce, the twenty-eighth and final girl Benji had seen during this, his twice-yearly open call, slunk into his office, the pilot light under Benji's flagging energies immediately reignited. He had not discovered an actress this way in over two years, the de rigueur open call serving as little more than a six-month reminder that, yes, he was in fact still in business. But Benji recognized talent's smoky scent when he smelled it, and Allison's aroma positively broadcast itself.

Following the initial introductions, after she had been properly seated and the interview had begun in earnest, Benjamin noticed Allison's attention beginning to stray. Rather than maintain eye contact with him, Allison seemed more interested in greeting the ghost of her own image as it flitted about, reflected in various surfaces around the room: the dirty windowpane behind Benji's desk, the glass of water he had poured for her, the television screen, the blown glass paperweight he had purchased on vacation in Venice. If it could reflect or refract light, Allison would spend a moment or two lost in its illuminated glow.

This narcissistic propensity promised everything to Benji. He had been in the industry long enough to know that naked exhibitionism may be the only trait erotic film actors have in common: that is, they want to watch themselves, they want you to watch them, and they want to watch you watching them. A lesson learned early, when he was just sixteen entering a strip club in Queens for the first time: all the girls were watching themselves as they danced, reflected in the panels on the mirrored wall. The last thing they were interested in was the men fanning dollar bills in their garters. Even as a teenager it was apparent to Benji that the primary exchange going on in porn was a monetary one. There is, however, a protective aspect to this self-involvement, and career performers learned to cultivate it. So long as they remained wired into themselves, so long as the true source of all their pity and joy remained private, so long as they never made a genuine connection with another human being, they could never truly comprehend the damage being done to them by others. With Allison alone in the room with herself, Benji took the opportunity to study her. The face. If she wasn't quite beautiful, she missed entrance into that magic kingdom by millimeters, minuscule degrees of genetic miscalculation. But finally, Benjamin decided there was something too asymmetrical, something in too obvious a state of flux about her face for it to settle into beauty. (Because more than anything, Benji believed that at the center of beauty lays stillness.) Her hair was wild: straight strands here, kinky curlicues there, strawberry, banana, and peach colors mixed together in some exotic punch held in place with an arsenal of pins, clips, and rubber bands. Her eyes too had a similarly unsettled, roiling quality about them: an aquatic blue-green swishiness. For all the brightness of her eyes, however, there was something dull, something crosshatched and papery about her skin, an absence of that bewitching feminine glow that, like a benevolent Medusa's stare, can freeze a man in mid-sentence. Scanning her epidermal damage, Benji was confident this was nothing a citric acid fruit peel, an Asian pearl cream, and a couple of visits to a tanning salon couldn't remedy. Besides, she had something that outshined the dullness of her complexion. The girl had flesh appeal. Looking at her, you could almost taste the sea salt of her skin, imagine yourself picking leaves and gooseberries from her tangle of hair, drinking milk and honey from the golden valley between her thighs . . . She passed the bar. She gave Benji a hard on.

Just one look down at those apologetically sagging, bathetically bunched-up black leather pants, however, and Benji's hopes all but extinguished themselves. The pants were all wrong, a terrible mistake. And so, despite Allison's pug-nosed, goyishe good looks, despite her pert breasts, despite the easy, uncomplicated winsomeness of her smile, despite her open, unstudied manner, despite the tight parentheses of her taut behind, and, most important in Benji's profession, despite her possession of a fifteen-year-old's face atop the body of a twenty-year-old, yes, despite all these resplendent gifts, Benji, on the evidence of those loose leather pants, decided Ms. Pryce might not have the stuff for smut.

Points for effort, Benji thought, but leather pants are a strict measure of bravado. If you have the moxie to wear them—to own them, to have entered the boutique with the intention of buying them—you better go all the way and pour yourself into a pair two sizes too small. Benji, for his part, did not wear, had never worn, did not own, nor had ever owned a pair of leather pants. During a film shoot once, Anita Cox, an aging industry veteran who'd studied fashion for a semester or two at FIT, took a look at Benji's duds and commented disdainfully that the clothes we choose to wear each morning is the most aesthetic decision many of us are likely to make all day. (In fairness, Anita was wearing a pair of stiletto heels, a spiked dog's collar, and a strap-on dildo when she made the comment.)

While the statement stuck with Benji, it did little to change his two uniforms, which rotated respectively between a pair of dark brown, wide whale corduroys which he wore with zip-up fifties style cabana boy shirts, and outdated eighties Adidas jogging suits. (All accessorized, regardless of season, with a white v-neck T-shirt and black-and-white canvas high top Chuck Taylor Converse All Stars.) If the corduroys, with their crenellated topography worn and thinning at the kneecaps, spoke of a certain workmanlike integrity to Benji, the glossy eighties jump suits reminded him of better days, that is, when Benji himself once shined, that is, when Benji loved a girl named Penelope, and Penelope he.

Yes, those simple, commodious costumes spoke of a great deal of integrity to Benjamin. And integrity was important to Benji. What else was important to him? Certainly not his looks. He was no longer pretty, for one. In the eighties, a man could be merrily out of shape—and that was cool—but this was no longer the case. On a recent visit to the beaches of Coney Island, Benji found himself awash in a homoerotic whirlpool of oiled, hairless, washboard-stomached men. As part of the fallout of feminism, it seemed that suddenly the nexus of human sexuality had relocated, jumped gender from distaff T&A to the male abdomen. Follicles had been violated. Softness had yielded to hardness. Maternal curves had been trounced by masculine rigidity. Where did this anatomical diaspora leave Benji?

Tall and broad-shouldered, Benji had the look of a once superior athlete gone to seed, the suggestion of ropy musculature hiding beneath a furtive layer of flab. Only Benji had never been athletic. The roll of fat he had been accumulating round his mid-section was a holdover from high school, and he wore it as a badge of honor. Only gay men, models, and career women work out more than three times a week anyway, Benji assured himself as he stood—broad, naked, and baboon-like—before the bathroom mirror, alone with the knowledge that his days before the pornographer's camera were over. Not that he had lost interest in sex. The contrary. It was just that sex—the waters he once daily drank from, sweetly swam in—wasn't something he just did, it was something he did with Penelope. Penelope Pigeon, his pretty Penny.

Pennywise, he had shrunk an inch in height and added an inch in width for every year she had been gone, a development greeted with much alarm. It wasn't that the middle aged spread took him by surprise exactly so much as it was occurring much earlier than expected. Everything about him had bloomed, everything about him had swollen: waist, ankles, wrists, neck. His testicles too had begun to enlarge and sag in their prune-like pouch (looking more and more to Benji's considerable delight like the plum-sized balls of his father from memory long ago). His toes now swelled before rain. Rather than lose hair, he simply grew more of it, in all the wrong places. His facial and eyebrow hairs grew tougher, more bristly. Sheaves of the stuff wrapped around his knuckles like wreaths. Worse, the twenty-year war he'd waged against shoulder and back hair had finally been forfeited as armies of soft quills materialized and made their rapid advance across the mountains and crags of his flesh. And so, physically, in his thirty-third year, Benjamin Seymour, broke, with the great tragedy of his life already behind him (marriage, failed), one parent dead (mother, cancer), and another ensconced in a retirement community (father, FL), found himself both shrinking and expanding simultaneously. He had become irrevocably squatter, thicker, boxier. Alone, surrounded by machinery, reviewing the latest hardcore release, he often thought, a few more years like this and I'll begin to take on the dimensions of a television set.

Although he had chosen pornography as his profession, he often worried about the sensibility of his career choice. (And worrying was something that came naturally to Benji, having mastered its precepts in childhood.) Benjamin's place in the industry was a curious one: fixed yet tangential, historic but negligible, at once well-known figure and minor operator. The final holdout in the East Coast/West Coast porno wars, Benji had seen it all and was still holding tight to his little spot on 33rd and Ninth. Even after the old Jews had packed it up and left for LA, even after the Pigeon had flown the coop, even after the incident at the New Purity, even after two of the actors in his stable, Ana Rexia and Roy G. Biv, had been shot and knifed outside their apartments in Brooklyn and the East Village, even after the suicide, Benji was still there, banging away, hanging his hopes on the Aristotelian unities.

Alone among his peers, Benji remembered and longed for the days when New York was the bustling hub of the industry, when the industry cared about good lighting, proficient acting, and intelligent stories, when those stories were shot on film, and those films shown across the country in the-aters numbering a thousand strong. Although economics dictated that Benji too revert to shooting solely on videotape, that only fueled his sense of outrage. Benji entered the industry just in time to witness the fuck film, which had once seemed something noble and indelible—as indelible as the light that etched itself onto a film strip's silver emulsion—degenerate into the plastic impermanence, the electronic blip and buzz of video. Benji'd had enough. He wanted out. But like a puzzled penis, Benji, who dreamed of escape, who longed for some sort of transcendence, recognized how firmly rooted to his spot he really was. Some sleepless nights Benji wondered how much fight was left in him; how long it takes an Angry Young Man—gone unfortified, uncossetted by good love and good work—to resign himself to failure and calcify into a Bitter Old Man? Perhaps it was happening. Perhaps it had happened already.

* * *

"Why don't you tell me why you want to get into the business."
"Well, basically, I've just always been really confident with my body, y'know."
"Uh huh."
"And I've been dancing nights for the past couple of months, and I know from some of the other girls that you could make a lot more money danc-ing if you do a few of these."
"That's right. That's true. Erotic actresses can pull down some pretty good money on the road as headliners. That's true. So it's mostly a money thing?"
"Well . . . yeah."

The trick was to break them down during the interview, to not let it go beyond this point, to send them home with their tails between their legs but their genitals intact. Who were these women? The men Benjamin could understand: he did after all, briefly count himself among their ranks, and there was always that neat sexual double standard as alibi. Besides, there were fewer of them. The industry's leading men were career players who stayed on the scene for decades, their penises as reliable and omnipresent pornographic fixtures as Claude Raines and Peter Lorre were to Hollywood pictures of the forties. But the women? Who were they? They couldn't all be the child molested, the drug addicted, the runawayed, could they? Once Benji tried to make a list of all the women he had known—personally—in the ten years he had worked in the industry. He stopped counting at 3,281. Presumably, each of them had histories, hopes, skills apart from boa-mouth, apple-bob, and akimbo-spread. Presumably, each of them had mothers . . . Yeah, the trick was to call their bluff and send them packing.

"You like to fuck?"

"You mean right now?"

"No, you don't fuck to get the job, you fuck after you get the job. Simple question: you like fucking, yes or no?"

"Yeah, most of the time."

"You married, have a boyfriend?"

"Boyfriend."

"Well then do yourself a favor, go home and ask him to teach you how to type, 'cause I don't need it. I don't need it. Does he even know you're here?"

"Yeah."

"Yeah? And how's he feel about that?"

"Larry? Larry wants me to go for it, y'know. I mean, we've watched a lot of these movies together and Larry's really helped me come a long way in terms of y'know, getting me in touch with my body."

"Well, goody for him then. Listen, tell you what, how 'bout we give Larry a call right now and ask him what he thinks about this," Benji said, picking up the phone receiver and pointing it toward the video monitor where Luke Warm coolly withdrew and ejaculated into the platinum hair of Bea Smirch. "'Cause the last thing I need is some angry boyfriend motherfucker hanging round the set giving my people a hard time. Y'understand?"

O, you're a filthy little bitch, aren't you? Filthy . . . Little . . . Bitch. Well, you're just stuffed full of cock now aren't you?

"Look, we talked about it after one of the girls showed me the ad at work. He wants me to try it."

With that, Benji cradled the phone and spastically reached for his Mickey Mouse Pez dispenser. His desk was littered with them, the characters standing upright like martinets: Charlie Brown, Snoopy, Lucy, Superman,

Spiderman, Captain America, Darth Vader, C3PO, Storm Trooper, Wonder Woman, Garfield, Batman, the Incredible Hulk, Casper the Friendly Ghost. Off to the side, separated from and regally presiding over the rest, was the Disney gang: Minnie, Donald, Daisy, Pluto, Goofy, and of course, Benji's favorite, Mickey Mouse, the fastidiously white-gloved Wildean king rat. The special holiday editions—Santa, jack-o-lantern, ghost, witch, Easter Bunny—Benji kept in his bottom desk drawer, bringing them out only when seasonally appropriate. (Where's the Moses Pez? The Yul Brynner Pez? The Burning Bush Pez? Where's the Herman the Fucking Chanukah Candle Pez? Benji thought, shamefacedly reloading his Santa each Christmas.)

He loved Pez. A traditionalist, Benji had been collecting the dispensers since childhood. He even thought of using Cherry Pez as his nom de porn when he entered the industry in the early eighties. A few years back, as part of the Pez Renaissance, in addition to the reissued collectors editions, and oversize Pez piggy banks, and the Swarovski crystal version, the manufacturers of Pez in Orange, Connecticut, (by way of Vienna, Austria, seventy years ago; the name Pez having derived from "Pfefferminz," the German word for peppermint), introduced an automated version of the Pez dispenser, an electronic, ashtray-sized obelisk that, at the push of a button, dispensed a single, tooth-shaped candy. This technological advance was conspicuously absent from Benji's otherwise definitive collection. Why? Because who needed a battery operated Pez? Everyone knew Pez were negligible as candy but indispensable as dispensers. Put simply, Pez were fun—kicky, twisted fun. And more than that, Pez offered a priceless lesson in the surprises of violence and beauty the world holds for us, because each time you wanted one, you had to split your favorite cartoon character's head open and eat its brains, which always, magically, took the form of candy. Candy. He popped one in his mouth.

Now suck it! Suck it, suck it, suck it, suck it!

She reminded him of her. There was no getting around it. And not in the usual way that anything, anytime, anywhere—a song, a movie, a change in the weather—reminded him of her. No, there was something about this Allison April Pryce, something direct and open and vulnerable at the center of her face that struck a familiar, pained key. Or maybe it was the eye. Penelope, of the mercurially fluid face (a wise-child face that could look, alternately 12, 21, 39, 45, 63, 80 with the slightest shift in light, the faintest change of expression) was in possession of a brilliant flaw. A Picasso flaw. An imperfection that pinned everything around it down and held her face in jewel-like precision. One of Penelope's eyes was permanently closed more than the other, the left one—perpetually, alluringly lidded at half-mast. So it was the right with Allison. And Benji, staring at that eye, was once again reminded, painfully, of everything he had, of everything he had lost. Penelope. Penelope Catherine Pigeon. The Pollyanna of Porn. Penny, Penny, Penny, Penny. Penny.

"O, Benji," she said to him once when they were kids together up at school, in the cool springtime pudding of Ithaca's fairy tale gorges, on a black and purploid moonless night, "tell me something. Tell me you'll love me forever."
To which blustery Benji bristled, "C'mon. How many stupid twenty-year-olds say that to each other?"
"Then say something original, say something smart," Penelope pleaded.
"Aw, they're just words," he said, submerging his hands in the stinging cold water.
"Yes, but we have only words to play with."

Yes, we have only words to play with, so use them big boy and get her out of here. Quick! Chase her out of the office if you have to, just get her the hell out of here.

* * *

"Y'ever been molested?" asked Benji, bending the arm of the aluminum architect's lamp so its hot 120 watt bulb shined directly in her face, illuminating its imperfections.
"What does that—"
"—It has everything to do with it. Didn't you read the fine print, Only Sexual Cripples Need Apply! You think normal people get into this business?"
"Stop yelling at me. Look, I just thought this could be an easy way to make some extra money dancing."
"Easy!? Lemme ask you something, have you thought about this for a second?"

"Like I said—"

"What're you going to do ten years from now when your kid brings home a magazine with a picture of you with a candlestick shoved up your ass and says, 'Mommy, what's this?' You gonna tell him, 'Billy, that's when mommy was an actress. I got to play the part of the Menorah?'"

"Jesus!"

"No, Yahweh. I mean, look, you're young, you're cute, you think this is a good idea now, but you do this once, you do this once," he said, raising a finger biblically, patriarchically, for emphasis, "and you're through. There's nothing else you can do. Persona non grata, understand? And I don't need that. I don't need anymore Ophelias in my life. I don't have time for that."

"All I want—"

"Okay, so let's say you do enter the industry. Understand, there're maybe forty, fifty performers total make a decent living at this. Forty or fifty total. And they're all out on the West Coast, 'cause that's where the shit gets made."

"Well I'd be willing to—"

"—And then let's say you do start making some money at it, most girls have careers last like three, four years, tops. Why? Because the stroke artists get bored very easily. Very fucking easily. So it's a constant turnover, constant turnover, constant demand for new faces, for bigger tits, for blonder hair. So in the end we're talking total lifetime earnings of maybe, maybe fifty, sixty thousand dollars. Fifty, sixty thousand dollars! For what? For nothing! For nothing! So basically, you've thrown it all away, thrown your life away. For nothing. And you know what? I don't need it. I don't need that shit. I don't need any more ghosts, I got ghosts of my own already. So my suggestion is to go home to Larry and Billy and find your-self a normal job," and here Benji, catching his breath with a huff and a puff, reached under his desk and brought up last Sunday's *New York Times* Help Wanted section. "Here," Benji said, "take mine."

Allison looked down at the pages, which may as well have been written in cuneiform. BA, BS, CPA, CPO, MBA, NPV, SAP. Degrees she never received for skills she'd never master for experience she'd never gain for jobs she'd never have. She looked up again, away from the various entice-ments of her image, and stared directly at Benjamin.

"Look," Allison began, "I need a job. I need a job where experience isn't required that'll pay more than six dollars an hour. I have a beautiful body that I work hard at and I'm proud of, so if it's all the same to you, I really would like to give it a try."

After a frozen moment of incomprehensibility, a moment that reminded Benji of lunchroom stare down contests from childhood, stare downs that invariably erupted into giggling fits accompanied by streams of cafeteria-issued milk running down nostrils, Benjamin removed a wilted employee questionnaire form from the left hand drawer of his desk and somberly passed it to the girl sitting across from him.

*　*　*

It started with loops: short, 16- and 8mm black-and-white films dating back to the silent film era that guys would stand around watching at stag parties. Then, in the sixties came the influx of porn from Sweden and Denmark: curious films featuring strapping young blonde mountain climber types fornicating between discourses on the virtues and deficiencies of Marxism. Then, after the dark ages of the assassinations, the hose and the bomb, Nixon and Vietnam; after the country awoke from its collective torpor, came the mid-seventies, the American Renaissance of Porn. Halcyon days: a flood of high quality films, reviews in *Variety*, the *Hollywood Reporter*, and the mainstream press, klieg lights and cement footprints outside the Golden Bowl theatre in Hollywood, former Campbell's Soup girl and *Leave Me to Beaver* star Michelle Vault on the cover of *Esquire*, movies with real stories and legitimate actors, creamy Hollywood lighting, craft food service spreads, costume and prop departments, sound stages, entire days spent shooting just dialogue scenes, even some films shot on 35mm, the Italian leather of film stocks.

And the money! The money, the money, the money. So much money in those days. It was all virgin territory, undiscovered country. These pioneers—the Milton Minegolds and Johnny Bloodstones and Leslie Goulds—these were the Paul Bunyans and John Henrys of the adult entertainment industry, pick-axing their way across this last, great American frontier. Like a ghetto kid carving out his first crack corner, like a Native American Indian given a patch of tax-free reservation land upon which to build a casino, these guys learned as they went, were mercilessly capitalist, and forged a multi-billion dollar a year industry out of nothing more than the rumbling of their guts and the metronome tick of their pricks. Looking up to the sky or down at the gravesite, these good boys, yeshiva bruchas all, knew their fathers would be neither embarrassed nor ashamed at their success. The contrary, they'd be proud. These ragmen's sons were making a product people wanted, and wasn't that what the dream was all about, wasn't that the distinctly American dream of success, whether it was butter and eggs, or horseshoes, or schmattes, or smut? Two generations and millionaires! They weren't disgracing their fathers, they were honoring them, as Milton Minegold made resoundingly clear in his poignant, musical, Semitic sex spectacular *Diddler on the Roof*.

Back then, in the early seventies, a feature could be made for as little as $15,000 and could return a profit upwards of a million. That's how Milton first got into the business. Already in his late thirties, Milton was an accountant, a CPA, an attaché case–carrying Willy Loman, a bearded, balding B'nai B'rith pisher, until, in 1966, working on Frisk Fendelson's tax returns, he saw how much money Frisk was trafficking through his tiny little storefront operation on 43rd and Ninth in Times Square. And what did Frisk's magic closet consist of? Eight little booths, each showing a two minute loop for a quarter a pop, each pulling in just over ten thousand dollars a year. And the kicker was, there was no new product. "I'm showing the same film now for three years, Milty!" Frisk would complain, helplessly shaking his head back and forth, palms open to the universe in a pose of supplication, "But they keep coming back. They keep coming back."

In 1976, Sony released the first VCR for consumers. By 1985, the industry had completely converted to videotape, a conversion that turned a negligible trenchcoat market into a four-and-a-half-billion dollar a year fantasia. As Milton Minegold put it to Benji that very first day they met, quoting Lee Strasberg's Hyman Roth in *The Godfather, Part II*: "Benji-boy, we're gonna be bigger than U.S. Steel." And he was right. He was right: video brought the product into people's homes, thereby forming a bizarre alliance between the lonely masturbating monk and the adventuresome copulating couple, an ungodly magic kingdom opening its all-encompassing arms to welcome the curious, the celibate, the lonely, the shy, the family man, and the pervert. By 1985, X-rated films accounted for more than one-fifth of all video sales in America.

But then the amateurs figured it out. They figured it out so quickly. If you could get the VCR clock to stop blinking "12:00 A.M.," you too, could make a porno. In the early eighties, essentially anyone with a video camera, five bucks for a tape, and the ability to convince others to have sex for public consumption could reinvent themselves as a moviemaker, a Scorsese of smut. And they did. They did. Because videos could be made so quickly, so cheaply, because the market was now flooded with an overabundance of product, because the rules of competition mercilessly dictated everyone reduce operating costs to the same static level of demi-competence, video effectively marked the end of high production values, and the beginning of an artistic credo of non-actors with bad skin and dirty feet having poorly lit, up-against-the-bathroom-wall style sex. And so, video, which began by promising a pornotopia, in reality marked an aesthetic regression as severe and uncompromising as demanding a composer to write an entire opera for the fiddle, or commissioning an author to write a novel without use of the letter *e*, or forcing a painter to render a landscape in a single color.

In place of storytelling, video gave birth to a two-headed hydra, genre twins that could be made on the quick and cheap: compilation and gonzo video. Random samplings of sex scenes culled together from other videos—one intermissionless scene rammed up against another without the slightest concession toward plot or character—compilation videos marked a return to the hit-and-run dynamics of loops, only compilations came packaged in two, three, four, and six-hour wrist-bruising installments. The stranger and more experimental gonzo video, on the other hand, drew inspiration from the cinema verité school of the sixties and the groundbreaking documentary work of such film artists as the Maysles brothers and D. A. Pennebaker. In gonzo, the cameraman/protagonist exists solely to seek out sex. A soiled scavenger, he searches anonymous apartments, scours the streets, prowls the gutters, predictably stumbling upon sex's netherworld at every turn, like Alice gone spinning down the rabbit hole. The trick of the genre, the element that leant it its strangely resonant sense of audience identification, was that the cameraman, who breathes the very air of sex, gets close enough to smell its fumes, but is never invited to the party. Thus, he exists in a weirdly heightened funk, a perpetual state of pre-ejaculatory frenzy. And it's precisely this strange, unlikely empathetic form of surrogate brotherhood between filmmaker and viewer that accounted for gonzo's position as the industry's leading genre of the nineties. And it was a particularly hardcore gonzo video, *The Anal-yst, Peeping Tom, Volume 14*, that Benji chose to play during open calls in an attempt to scare away the uninitiated, the ill-informed, the foolishly curious.

O, you like it in the ass. You like it in the ass, don't you? Yeah, look how that ass of yours just swallows that dick right up.

* * *

"So after you fill out this form, we'll take some photos and see where we're at," said Benji, standing up and passing the piece of paper across the desk to Allison.
"Could you just ask me the questions?"
"What?"
"It's just, I hate taking tests."
"This isn't a test."
"I just hate answering questions like that on paper."
"Are y'illiterate?"
"No."
"Dyslexic?"
"No."
"But you want I should give it to you orally?"
"Look, I'm not illiterate, I just hate test situations. I'd do better if we do it out loud."
"All right, fine. Age?"
"Twenty-three."
"Aren't you a little young to be twenty-three?" Benji asked, duly writing down the answer.
"Nope. Next question."
"Height?"
"Five-foot four."
"Weight?"
"One fifteen."
"Measurements?"
"I'm not exactly sure. I think they're something like 30, 25, 32."
"Hair Color?"

"Auburn."

"Do the collars match the cuffs?"

"What?"

"Do the curtains match the carpets?"

"I don't understand."

"Your pubic hair? Does it match the color of the hair on your head?"

"Yeah, it's real."

"Good. Who was the first president of the United States?"

"George Washington."

"Good. Okay, now it asks, in your own words, to write a little paragraph about why you want to enter the business."

"Well, I always wanted to pose for a magazine."

"Lemme guess, from the time you discovered your daddy's *Playboy* in his sock drawer when you were twelve, right?"

"He kept them in the garage."

"Textbook," Benji said, decapitating his Mickey, sucking out a sugar pellet and triumphantly crunching down.

"There's one photo I always think of. I forget the name of the girl, but she's in like a white dress or a nightgown, only it's sheer, and she's by a lake or a pool or in the woods or something, and her hair is soaking wet and it's dripping onto the dress and you can see right through it. And she always looked so sexy and clean. I always wanted to be in a picture like that."

"Wants to be . . . girl . . . in white dress. Okay. Yeah . . . that's about a paragraph," said Benji, frantically transcribing. "I bet we can find you something like that."

"Good, but I'm not ready to do the hard stuff yet, okay?"

"That's okay. That's all right at the start. Some girls do all right just dancing and doing stills and box covers. But you already knew that when you came in, or we wouldn't be here talking. All right, now it says to list what you will and won't do."

"Well, I don't think I'd ever kill anyone."

"No, no, no, not like that. What you will and won't do sexually."

"O, well I guess I'd have to see who it's with before I know what I'd be comfortable doing."

"You suck cock?"

"Uh, yes."

"You consider yourself wise in the ways of cocksucking?"

"Yeah, I guess so."

"A?"

"What?"

"Anal?"

"No . . . Once. A few times. It hurt."

"Shouldn't hurt. Ever been with a woman?"

"Just messing around with my friend when we were kids."

"Goody. Ever fuck a black guy?"

"What does that have to do with anything?"

"Well, Ally, you'll find that porno's a racial utopia. The only place left in America keeping Dr. King's flame burning bright. BNW?"

"What?"

"Black 'n' white?"

"No."

"But you have nothing against it?"

"I don't think so."

"Good. You believe Oswald acted alone?"

"Who?"

"Lee Harvey Oswald. Guy shot Kennedy."

"Yeah, I'm pretty sure he did it by himself."

"Okay. This part's like a grid that asks you to check off which of your body parts are pierced: ears, nose, eyebrow, chin, tongue, navel, nipples, labia, clitoral hood."

"Just my ears. The left one's pierced three times."

"Tattoos?"

"None."

"Ear . . . three times," Benji said, scribbling. "So lemme get this straight, you really think Oswald acted alone?"

* * *

Following the questionnaire, Benji escorted Allison down the hall to the second of Commercial Urban Models' two rooms, the editing suite, where Troy Marcus, CUM's twenty-four-year-old black cameraman-cum-assistant, was busy cutting and adding wah-wah pedal sound effects to their latest video, *Where's the Meese? The Meese Commission, Volume III*, one in a series of poly-porn videos that included such popular titles as *Of Meese and Men: The Meese Commission, Volume I*, and *I'll Show You Mine If You Show Me Meese, The Meese Commission, Volume II*.

In the editing suite were situated two 17" video monitors, two beta decks, two $3/4$" decks, one $1/2$" VHS deck, a video effects board, a soundboard, an equalizer, a DAT machine, a microphone, a boom box, and several stacks of marble-covered composition notebooks, tapes, and CDs. Between the hushed quiet, the tangles of electrical cords, and the sepulchral, single spot halogen lighting, the space had the eerie feel of the Reptile Room at the Bronx Zoo.

To prevent the equipment from getting overheated and frying, air conditioners were kept on constant full blast in this room during the summer months. The climate apparently didn't seem to bother Troy, however, who spent most of his time in this room and liked to brag to Benji that he was in fact, "a cold blooded snake motherfucker."

In the cold room, as Benji watched, Troy placed Allison on a stool covered with a thin white drape, and asked her to undress so he could take some Polaroids. It was at this point that Benji, who was always more concerned with how women looked in reproduction (photograph, film, video, memory) than in reality, excused himself to sit on a stool of his own.

* * *

His afternoon shit. His first of the day, and he had been looking forward to it. (Perhaps that's the true mark of adulthood, Benji thought, looking forward to things you once hated doing as a kid: shitting, bathing, reading, sleeping.) CUM shared a large men's bathroom with the other businesses on the second floor of 337 West 33rd Street which included: Gordon Norman, Immigration Lawyer, a nervous, hunched, twitchy fellow who couldn't have weighed more than 110 pounds; Realty Bites, a small real estate agency staffed by a rotating collection of young kids just out of college (two of whom, Carrie Lasky and Jeremy Jameson, Benjamin had proudly raided a couple of years back and baptized Connie Lingus and Jeremiah Jism); and Gurgles, a small baby products wholesaler specializing in bibs, rattlers, and nipples (all of which had come in handy in Benji's line of work).
Somnambularly, Benji walked down the long white hallway accented in wedding cake yellows and pinks. Entering the bathroom, he took stock of the familiar military bluegray inventory: six stalls, five urinals, four sinks,

three hot air hand dryers, two paper towel dispensers, one flickering row of fluorescent lights. Why did Benjamin always take it as a good omen when no one was in the bathroom and all the stall doors were ajar? (Could it be because Benji had once been discovered there late one night shooting after hours by the very surprised, very Spanish, very pregnant cleaning lady, Pilar, and had to hustle using his seven word Spanish vocabulary—hola, mañana, miercoles, muerta, dinero, tequila, adios—to keep himself from getting evicted?)

Benjamin undid his belt and squatted. Adjusting to the warm seat, Benji remembered being eight years old on a shopping trip to Macy's with his mom and how his mother, the good woman, afraid to leave him by himself, brought him with her into the ladies bathroom. There he stood and waited, young, sweating, and alone, as his mother entered a stall and lowered her pantyhose. Never before or since had Benjamin felt himself so acutely asexual as he did that day, meeting the curious stares of women who looked him up and down only to complacently return to the bathroom mirror to continue applying their make up. Although only eight at the time Benji had already developed an interest in girls, and, fascinated by the differences he perceived between the sexes, took encyclopedic note of everything he heard and saw: an aluminum tampon dispenser (Pez!) stuck to the wall, the peculiar absence of urinals, the mellifluous, taut-sounding laser tones of women micturating and how different it all was from the familiar water pistol dribble and squirt of men. But most of all, he was amazed that women shit (his mother shit?), an act he had always taken to be a distinctly masculine activity. For women he pictured something more delicate, birdlike. As he imagined it, perhaps once a month, they would sit on a large sofa and, as they read back issues of *Cosmopolitan* and ate cucumber sandwiches, a pink egg would slowly emerge from their mouths. But those sounds and smells were proof—Proof!—and he was determined to get out of there to tell the tale.

Suddenly, a man entered the stall next to him, causing Benji to tense up. Was the man (whom, from the high polish shoes and chalk striped pants cuffs, Benji assumed to be Gordon Norman) here to shit, smoke, or jerk off? That his feet were facing the toilet and not the door seemed to eliminate the first possibility. Then Benji heard the crumpling of plastic, foil, and paper, the Zippo's dependable "click," and following a wheezily prolonged pause, smelled the smoke. Now the questions began in earnest for

Benji. The guy's in here to relax, to enjoy himself, to have a cigarette break in a no-smoking building. But I'm in here to shit. What do I do? Wait until he leaves? Squeeze slowly, or push it out with supreme evacuatory force? Fuck this! Why'm I arguing propriety over this shyster cocksucker?! I'm a fucking pornographer, I shovel shit down people's throats for a living! Benji thought, squeezing violently until a vein drew a ghostly exclamation point down the center of his forehead.

After blacking out on the bowl for a moment, Benji, regrouping, reflected on how strange it was that he knew how to operate a movie camera, could explain the difference between VHS, Beta, and $^3/_4$" video format, could approximate the correct candlelight measure of a room to within half a stop of a light meter, yet couldn't explain how his body takes a shit. Shit. He had shit. His body had just taken a shit. What kind of shit was it? A loose larval load that follows a heavy night of Irish drinking? A forlorn pebble? A bran-filled angry porcupine? It was none of those. Rather, a respectable worm. How did Benji know? Because he stood up and looked. Benji only half-kiddingly believed that you could divide people scatologically into two groups: the type of person who looks at their excrement in the toilet and the type who doesn't. (He once wondered if the same experiment could be made using pornography as the agent, and concluded that yes, it could.) Benjamin found cleaving humanity into these two halves supremely edifying and often used it as a litmus test for personality. Intuitive examples from the worlds of politics, movies, and literature:

George Bush: flush.
Bill Clinton: look.
Charlton Heston: flush.
Marlon Brando: look.
Tom Wolfe: flush.
Norman Mailer: look (perhaps even smell, perhaps even feel).

That the groups so clearly divided themselves along liberal (look) and conservative (flush) lines was of great interest to Benjamin. It helped explain a lot. Benji's brother, father, and mother were all flushers, while Penelope, God bless her, was definitely a looker. Benji, a waffler, was caught stubbornly in between.

* * *

After Allison had (unabashedly) de-robed, Troy took her measurements (30", 25", 33"), and then, using a standard Polaroid camera, took a series of three photographs (back-to-camera-looking-over-the-shoulder, full-face-bust-sticking-out-arms-behind-back, close-up-smiling-face). The cold steel of the stool conducted through the thin drapery, causing Allison's skin to prickle. This in turn caused a slightly pained expression to pass over Allison's face, an expression which Troy felt made her look all the more alluring. "She's got talent, B," Troy tersely reported as the two examined the shots from Benji's office while Allison re-robed in the other room. Looking over the three Polaroids, Benji had no choice but to agree.

She had it all. The youth, the body, the terra firma upon which mansions of plastic surgery could be constructed, and a face that looked like it had never said the word, let alone seen, let alone begged for "cock." He could see what the next six months, the next year would bring for her, and he wished she had never stepped foot in his office. He looked at the photos of her, looked at her with the wildest of wide eyes, eyes that held the strangest expression, eyes that looked not so much shocked by what they saw as shocked to find themselves floating in this particular face, staring out at this particular life, eyes treated for severe nearsightedness by his gay brother, Jerry the ophthalmologist out on Long Island, eyes that made a living spotting latent talent like this. Studying the photographs of her visage, Benjamin once again came face to face with the central conundrum of his adult existence: Are they in porn because they look like that or do they look like that because they're in porn? The answer, Benji decided, like the answer to all the other big questions, is: both, and, wrong question stupid.

* * *

"That's neat," Allison said, once they had re-situated themselves in the office. She was referring to a framed poem, an acrostic, hanging to the right of Benji's bookcase. In calligraphy, red, on a small piece of faded paper, read:

> Belief is never far from fright:
> Einstein, Darwin, Brothers Wright.
> Newton split the prism's white
> Just to shame our sense of sight?

An honest Penny, burning bright;
Mnemosyne's wings bring second flight.
In dreams we'll walk again some night,
Nearer, nearer to the light.

"Yeah someone gave it to me," Benjamin said. "Look, before you make up your mind, I want to show you something."

And with this, Benji removed his ever-more-sizable girth from behind his desk and fumbled through a stack of videocassettes on the bookshelf behind him. Past the musical take-offs that were the bread and butter of CatchPenny Productions (*Breast Side Story*, *Jesus Christ Superschlong*, *Joseph and the Amazing Technicolor Dildo*, *A Slutty Thing Happened on the Way to the Orgy*, *The Jiz*, *Crease*), past the James Bond knock-offs (*Cock-To-Pussy*, *For Her Thighs Only*, *Dr. No Means Yes*), past the movie homages (*The Joy Suck Club*, *E.T.: The Extra Testicle*, *Pulp Friction*, *RoboCock*, *A Star is Porn*, *Splendor In The Ass*, *Tits A Wonderful Life*, *Woodfellas*, *The Sperminator*, *Schindler's Fist*), and finally, past their last film together, the award-winning *Lawrence Of A Labia* (filmed expensively on location in Morocco with Benji, Penelope, and Wally the Camel), his fingers flew. Past all that shared history, their crazy quilt, he thumbed to a worn and withered tape entitled *Cali Does California*, upon which, in small green type was printed, "Watch Cali Pigeon take on 131 horny guys in the world's biggest gang bang! A Scylla & Charybdis Production."

Milton Minegold. Green gimlet-eyed Milton. Milton, the great green dancing devil. Shaking, Benji struggled to get the red videotape out of its worn cardboard box, then popped it into the VCR. Taking a deep breath before pressing "Play," Benjamin reflected how pornography is like that first blast of winter cold: always shocking, and always exactly the same.

The tape remained cued: 1:14:37 into the production, the grand finale, as horny guy number 131, the special surprise guest, out of retirement and in an unprecedented appearance, emerged naked and jiggling from behind the camera to cap things off. The image flickered to life and there he was, all 250 pounds of him, all sixty-three years of him, every pinky-ringed finger of him, each black, white, and gray hirsute hair of him, a jolly fat man jumping from behind the camera, stripped, glistening, and smiling, to pump Penelope from behind. That is, Benji's one and only wife, his one and only love, his one and only Penny. Penelope, Pigeon-holed.

"O, but I would never do a gang bang video," Allison assured him as Benji stood basking in the television's reflected puke-green glow. And so, at the end of six months, April Showers, née Allison Pryce, following a full battery of dermabrasion, liposuction, 350 cc saline breast augmentation (incisions through the armpits: no scars), teeth whitening, and Mohawk-strip pudendum shaving, had posed for eighteen videocassette box covers at $500 a box, and appeared in twelve hard-core adult films at $750 a scene. (Titles which included the undinist videos *Yellow River*, *Yellow Peril*, and *Urine Nation*, as well as the anal-themed features *Anal Allies*, *Anal Island*, *Anal Agony*, *Anal Depressive*, and *Daddy, Take My Temperature, All In The Family, Part I*). Teamed with May Flowers, April Showers also co-starred in the twin Thanksgiving Holiday releases, *Pilgrim's Pussy* and *Basting the Turkey*.

After eight months, April had a fan club boasting some 10,000 members nationwide ($25 membership fee), three web sites, five 900 number sex phone lines ($3.50 a minute), and a mail order catalogue which sold ladies undergarments ($50-$195), lotions ($8-$29.95), lubricants (same), custom-made video fantasies ($300-$2,500), and molded plastic vaginas ($69.96). Around the time of her one-year anniversary in the industry, having just turned twenty-four, April took the triple crown of Best New Starlet, Best Facial Cum Shot, and Best Simulated Anal Rape (for the video *Anal Food Cake*) from the X-Rated Society of Film Critics at their annual awards ceremony in Las Vegas, Nevada. The following year, April moved out to Los Angeles to live out her final days as a drug addict under the hot California sun.

* * *

"I think I recognize her," Allison said, fixing her gaze on the girl. "That's Penelope Pigeon, right?"
"Yeah," Benji said, "after she'd changed her name to Cali."
"Wait, didn't she like, die a few years ago?"
"Yes," Benji replied quietly, "she did."

2

He was alone. Troy had left to go home to Coney Island at a quarter to seven and, after Benji supplied her with the appropriate information for a box cover shoot taking place the following day over at Pete Profitt's, Allison, now on the payroll, left as well. He looked out the window: an unpleasant day: the sky the color of cream soda. Some nights, when he was feeling particularly lazy or despondent, Benji slept right there in the office, on a ratty fold-out mattress he kept in the utility closet, or in his chair, or on the floor. Tonight, though, he had some errands to run, so he picked up the photos of Allison, pocketed the Pez, locked the place up, and left.

Hitting the street, Benji considered the mugwump quality of the neighborhood; how the area just around Penn Station and Madison Square Garden had no real identity. At once too far uptown to still be considered part of Chelsea and too far south to be enslaved to Midtown's corporate crunch, this strip of blocks was one of the only patches left in the city with an absence of geographic personality. Correspondingly, it was devoid of a neat little moniker like SoHo, TriBeCa, Hell's Kitchen, Inwood, the Village. Like Benji himself, the area was floating, in exile, caught stubbornly in-between, which is precisely why Benji had chosen it as his place of business and residence.

Over the years, Benji had managed to winnow the entire sphere of his existence to a ten-block radius, a radius whose end points were marked by his office on West 33rd and his home at 214 West 30th, with his (rarely used) gym, drug store, video store, and most of the take-out restaurants he frequented lying somewhere in between. Rather than feel claustrophobically curtailed by this narrowing of life's possibilities, like a turtle moving slowly back and forth across its cage, the very predictability of this daily pattern came as a great comfort to Benji.

It was Sunday, so he visited The Great Wall of China on West 33rd for his usual plastic-bagged take-out order of half a fried chicken, carton of pork fried rice, and a can of Dr. Brown's Original Cream Soda. (Welcome to Chinese Restaurant. Please try your Nice Chinese Food with Chobsticks the traditional and typical of Chinese glorious history and cultural.) Then, on to Rite Aid, on 24th and 8th where, pennysaver flyer in hand, after picking up a one pound jar of macadamia nuts (for some reason he had inexplicable, wild cravings for the Hawaiian delicacy lately), he combed the aisles for a family-sized thirty-two ounce tub of Jergen's Aloe Enriched Advanced Therapy Lotion. Benji suffered from neither something as minor as an irritating patch of dry skin, nor as serious as an Updikean case of psoriasis. No, after eighteen years of experimenting with everything from ketchup to peanut butter, from Tide to tofu, from handfuls of peach preserves to mom's mink coat, Benji had landed upon Jergen's Lotion as the ideal masturbatory lubricant.

Before Penelope had rescued him, Benji had been an incessant masturbator. At Cornell, in the beginning of Freshman year, living with three other boys in a room meant for two and forced into sharing the dorm's unisex communal bathroom, in an attempt to remake himself as a brave and beautiful young man, Benji had seriously attempted giving up his most beloved practice. A three-month ordeal, marking a happy return of wet dreams, ensued, until, finally, Benji stumbled upon an empty, private, specially equipped handicapped bathroom in the lobby of an adjacent dormitory. With trumpets blaring, he jacked himself off standing up, his first conscious orgasm in a quarter year, and when it was over, his member had the shiny-smooth look of a new born baby seal, his gobby ejaculate as thick and rich as buttermilk.

After that, Benji couldn't leave himself alone. College! All that nature! All that fecundity! All that ripe flesh busting at the seams! Benji thought, squirting his seed into one of the pocket Kleenexes he kept on his person at all times. Where did he shoot loads from? The stacks of Uris Library,

Jansen's dining hall, Fuertes Observatory, professor's homes, in vacant rooms of the most respected and well-endowed buildings on campus, off bridges, into the gorges, even once, silently, during class. (But never did he manage the ultimate feat, to unload atop Cornell's clock tower into the hilly countryside below.) After a while, he even started quietly jerking off on the top bunk of his bed, with the other boys in the room sitting at their desks late at night studying. He didn't care. Three, four, five, six times a day he would blast into his baby blue blanket, forming a Jackson Pollock-like canvas of no small artistic merit.

Had anyone ever had such a strange masturbation history as he? Jerking off was surely one of the three ritualized topics of conversation open to young men (the other two being sports and women, topics of conversation young Benji had precious little to contribute to), and after listening to hundreds of hours of joshing confession, Benji was confident he had lived through the most absurd experiences any male had ever had alone with his privates, including an operatic cycle of death and rebirth unlike any he'd ever heard.

Once, during junior year, living with three other boys in an apartment off campus in College Town, Benji was awakened in the middle of the night with a painful erection. Too lazy to make the trip down the hall to the bathroom, instead Benji searched his room for a suitable lubricant, eventually landing upon an unopened bottle of Vidal Sassoon shampoo. After slathering his shaft in the sticky stuff, he quickly brought himself off, and then, paralyzed, fell asleep. The following morning he was shocked to find that the shampoo had dried, encrusting itself over his prized puppet, and refused to come off. In fact, so many layers of transparent gunk had solidified over him overnight, there was no feeling left in it. That morning, he stood in the shower for forty minutes, causing himself to be late for class, scouring away with Ajax and Brillo pad, but the thing was irrevocably trapped, painfully encased.

He had little choice but to continue his day, business as usual. What else could he do? Go to the school nurse and explain what happened, as she strapped him down, put on a pair of goggles, and went at him with a laser beam? Benji flew into a panic, mercilessly scraping the thing in the bathroom between classes, washing it under scalding hot water, praying to God to free him from bondage. (If you release my cock, I promise never to touch it again. And next year in Jerusalem!) For three painful days this went on, days in which urination was rendered a ritual akin to passing a few precious burning drops of gasoline. Until, finally, on the third day, something miraculous happened.

At home, alone, behind a locked door, snake-like, the thing began to peel. For two hours, Benji sat under a hot lamp and watched in silent astonishment as layer after layer of dried shampoo and dead skin magically lifted from his wounded and weary putz. At the end of the ordeal, it looked pink and pristine, as if he'd just been issued a spanking new model. It was one of the proudest moments of his life. "I am become death incarnate! I am the phoenix that doth rise from his own ashes!" Benji exclaimed, immediately bringing himself off, twice, in quick succession, in front of a full-length mirror. (For the whole event meant he hadn't come in three days.) He was the Gilgamesh of jerking off.

Combing the aisles for the lotion, he was reminded of how many of these strange products had become familiar to him in the years he had spent with her. How many lotions, creams, ointments, hair products, women's products had she used? How many had he purchased for her? With her? Rubbed on her? Applied to her? Pulled out of her? List, list, O, list: Ponds Cold Cream, St. Ives Alpha-Hydroxy, Dove $1/4$ Moisturizing Beauty Bar, Caress Moisturizing Body Wash, White Rain Shampoo, Henna, Noxema, Tiger Balm, Covergirl Ultimate Finish Liquid Powder Make Up, Oxy Balance Deep Action Night Formula, Neutrogena Sensitive Skin Moisturizer, Playtex Gentle Glide Odor Absorbing Non-Deodorant, Always Pantyliners, Dry Idea, Suave, Lady Speed Stick, Smooth Rounded Tip Cardboard Applicator Tampons. To be a lotion folded into the very fabric of her flesh! To be a trusted tampon! To feel every faint follicle! O, to be one of those!

In the years they were together, he had possessed her in every way imaginable, but it was never enough. One penis wasn't enough. One tongue, one anus, two arms and legs, ten fingers and toes seemed painfully inadequate for the job. He wished they could have wrapped around each other, engulfing each other like happy amoebas; wished his body could have been covered with millions of micro-follicles he could have plunged into her every pore; wished he could have turned her inside out and made love to her very organs, her slippery liver, her proudly pumping pancreas, her

laughing lungs, her sweetly beating heart. He wished he could have physically eaten her, devoured her whole and experienced the sensation of
passing her through him, first sliding down his esophagus, then splashing
around his stomach, onto the small intestine, through the large, and out
his anus. These holes, these glands, these protuberances marked a terrible
conspiracy. If love is simply a reward, a reward for being brave with another, why won't the body alter to conform to the experience? Why? It was
never enough for them. It was never enough.

"That's it?" asked Maria the salesgirl.
"You carry Pez refills?"
"Pez? Watchoo mean, the candy?"
"Yeah."
"No."
"Just the nuts and the Jergen's then."

* * *

Siren Home Video, located on West 31st Street between 8th and 9th, is
where Benji had been going to keep himself abreast of changes in the
industry for the past five years. In exchange for the occasional in-store
autographing session, Siren's Indian owner, Omar, pretty much gave Benji
the run of the place: freebies, three-night rentals, reserved tapes, the
works. For the others it was $3.50 a night, no exceptions. Brown beaded
curtains parted, baptizing his body, as Benji entered the store. Ahead, up
by the counter he spotted a middle-aged gray-haired man in a starched
blue and white pilot's uniform trying to make a deal:

"But I'm only going to get to watch it once. That's my point. I'm flying in.
Landing. Going to the hotel. Spending the night. Then flying back anoth-
er twelve hours. What I'm saying is, even if I wanted to I can't return the
tape until Thursday," the pilot desperately explained.
"Sir, if you keep the tape for three nights I have to charge you for three
nights."
"You can't work something out with me here?"
"Sir, I have to run a business," said Omar. "You keep the tape three nights
I have to charge three nights."

"Yeah, all right, all right," sighed the pilot, handing over two quarters tightly wrapped in a ten dollar bill and greedily laying hands on the tape.
"Hey Omar, how's it hanging?" asked Benji, breaking the tension.
"Down to my knees, Mr. Seymour, down to my knees."
"Down to your knees? Waddaya doing working here then, we oughta put you in movies. Hey man, you got any good P for me today?" Benji asked, "P" being his preferred shorthand for pornography.
"Very hot stuff, Mr. Seymour," Omar said, conspiratorially pulling a red videotape of *The Island of Dr. Fellatio* up from behind the counter as if it were an illegal prescription drug. "Very hot stuff, indeed."

Benji examined the blurb on the back of the box. Hacking a path through the thick jungle of verbiage (Join Dr. Fellatio in his search for fresh-faced sluts who luv to suck cock!) Benji translated the story as follows: the lonely Dr. F., living in exile on an unnamed tropical island, invites T. Bone, a documentary filmmaker, to videotape his experiments, experiments in which the doctor successfully creates a race of genetic superwomen, superwomen, who, after sucking the good doctor dry, take over the island, reclaiming it a Sapphic paradise. Despite the uncomfortable Riefenstahlian overtones, the video seemed a not unclever combination of some of the best hardcore had to offer: movie satire, gonzo, and hot lesbo action. A good choice then.

"Yeah, that's the stuff," Benji said, passing the tape back to Omar. "Hold that for me will you, I'm just gonna take a quick look around the place."

He liked coming here. It was the equivalent of a local bar, where the faces were familiar and he was the reigning neighborhood celebrity. And, like in a local bar, there were lessons of compassion and tenderness to be had along with the squalor. Sometimes guys, respectable looking men in business suits and briefcases, would approach the cash register with stacks of eight, nine, ten tapes, and Omar, a decent and responsible proprietor, would subtly rebuke them in lilting Indian tones, "Do you think you can watch all of those in just two days, sir?" More important than turning a tidy profit, Omar, who just five years before had been a practicing physician in Bangladesh, prided himself on reminding his patrons to abuse themselves responsibly.

Duuuuuh, duh, duh, duh, duh, duuuuuh, duh

Wafting through the aisles, Benji experienced the strange sensation whereby he found himself floating after a song, a song that seemed to be rising up from inside of him, until he realized it had been playing around him all along. Chasing it down, Benji consciously caught up to the song's climax:

> Someday girl I don't know when
> We're gonna get to that place
> Where we really wanna go
> And we'll walk in the sun.
> But till then tramps like us
> Baby we were born to run

"Born to Run." Chariot race song. She had sung it to him once, incomprehensibly, in French. "We'll walk in the sun, Benji," she had promised him then. "We'll walk in the sun." The sun. Le soleil.

A Springsteen fan, years later Benji had gotten hold of a bootleg import in which the Boss, now in his mid-forties, played a solo acoustic version of the song. In its slowed tempo and the aged, textured gravel of the singer's voice, Benji felt that the meaning of the song had changed in twenty years; that this most archetypal, propulsive of rock songs about rebellion and escape had come to mean something different, something ineffable, hinting, Benji felt, of an older man looking back at his younger self and wishing for home. It was one of the most beautiful things he had ever heard.

As the song fluttered away, Benji continued jostling between the aisles, between men cemented in front of their selections. The video boxes, bathed in a puke-green fluorescent haze, were categorized by genre: Classic, Gonzo, Gang Bang, Anal, Lesbian, Bondage, Pro-Am. Then, there were the shelves dedicated to fetish videos: hair fetish videos (*Hair to Please!*), foot fetish videos (*Ped-O-Feelia*), coprophilia videos (*Shit Eating Grin*), pregnancy fetish videos (*Something's In the Oven, Ready To Drop, Part I*), food fetish videos (*Someone's in the Kitchen with Vagina*), obesity videos (*The Fat Lady Swings!*), granny videos (*Generation Gap*), midget fetish videos (*Small Packages*), menstruation fetish videos (*Bloody Good Time*), wrestling fetish videos (*No Holes Barred*), cunnilingus fetish videos (*Eating at the Y*), Asian fetish videos (*Chinese Box*), Russian Literature fetish videos (*Dopplebanger*). There were even cigarette fetish videos, videos featuring an hour-and-a-half of naked girls doing little more than smoking. There were high heel fetish videos of women going into department stores to try on shoes. There were videos of women doing nothing but blowing up brightly colored balloon animals. Toward the back of the store were several shelves organized by director: Benji had a shelf, Milton had one, as did Leslie Gould, and Johnny Bloodstone. Off to the side, there was even a shelf featuring some of the newly emerging women directors: Epiphany McIntosh, Vivian Darkbloom, and Winnow Screenlad.

Bopping along toward the front of the store, myopic Benji tried envisioning the place seen through the eyes of an impressionist painter. What was their idea? That forms don't exist, just light? Light on objects. Only color and light, thought Benji, allowing his vision to go slack and color and light to dictate until the place swirled, recasting itself as a turn-of-the-century music store. Shaggy men hunched over video boxes became elegantly suited gentlemen pondering musical programs. Colored condoms became the picks of lutes and guitars, tubes of lubricant became reeds, multi-pronged vibrators burst into row after row of polished wind flutes and clarinets, sex magazines rearranged their stunted mechanics into the mathematical infinity of musical annotation, handcuffs became tambourines, blow up dolls froze and calcified into three-holed woodwind instruments. For a moment, everything was color and light . . .

"*Dr. Fellatio?*" asked Omar, breaking the spell. Yeah, *Dr. Fellatio* it would be. As Omar placed the tape in a plain brown paper bag and sealed it with a piece of scotch tape, a threatening looking black man approached the counter. The man, who wore a blue and orange Mets cap, a Mickey Mouse T-shirt, a Band-Aid covering the entirety of his left eyebrow, an inconsistent beard, and the eyes of a failed rapist, stood just inches from Benji's face, staring at him. Benji froze.

"Yo, motherfucka thinks he can go unrecognizable 'n shit. Man, I know you. You Benjamin Seymour. Man, I seen your dick!"
"Great. That's great," Benjamin said, laying hands on *Fellatio.*
"Yo, back in the day, homeboy could move! Homeboy kicking it old-school style, pumping much pussy! None of that faggot-ass ass-fucking bullshit like they all into now. Hey Benji-man, answer me dis, why you stop making movies wit dat girl, da Penny girl?"

Benji considered the question for a moment.

"I never did," Benji said, tapping a finger to his cranium.

"Yo, homeboy's a comedian 'n shit. No, for real, funnyman, why you stop making movies together?"

"No reason. She went to California, and got into the whole LA thing, and I stayed here."

"That's right. That's right. Keeping it real in NYC. Ah-ight my brother," he said, holding his hand out for Benji to slap, or punch, or kiss, or put a dollar into.

"Keep on fucking."

* * *

He was holding three bags now, the food, the lotion, and the pinot. ("Pinot" being Benji's favored term for that rare piece of pornography that demands to be pored over and lovingly savored like a fine wine.) He shifted the bundles from hand to hand, experimenting with different levels of comfort. It was still warm out, and he could feel the sweat trickling down his sides. By this point in the day, every day, he felt his entire body covered in filth, a filmy mixture of sweat and dirt and moisture you just couldn't escape from if you lived in the city. Bags of garbage were roasting on the sidewalk, so Benji would have to wait until he was inside to see if the smell was him (in him, on him, of him), or the street.

"What time is it?" asked an elderly prune-faced woman, leaning out her ground floor apartment window. Every day Benji passed her, and every day the question was the same. She might as well have been a parrot. Besides the annoyance of the question came the added realization that this time-less eighty-five-year-old (Fifty more years of this!) was probably paying $25 a month for her rent controlled apartment as opposed to the $1,075 Benji paid for his.

"Excuse me, sir. What time is it?"

"It's about 8:15," Benji said, strenuously conferring with his Swatch.

"At night?"

"At night."

"And what month is it?"

"June. June 16th."

"June 16th. And what day is it?"

"Sunday."

And then she pieced it all together and repeated it, trying to commit the information to memory, "Eight fifteen in the evening on Sunday, June 16th. Thank you. Thank you very much. God bless you. I'll pray for you," she said, beaming.

"It's just the time, ma'am."

"O, God bless you."

What time is it?! You live for eighty-five years and that's the best question you can come up with? What time is it? Time to ask a better fucking question, that's what. Entering the lobby with a thud, it occurred to Benji that maybe she knew the time already. Maybe she knew it all along. Perhaps this was simply the last topic of conversation left open to her. Or maybe the opposite, maybe this was her wise woman's way of reminding her neighbors, busy New Yorkers all, that time is not a limitless commodity, a commodity that could be parsed, or traded, or bought, or bargained with. Her way of telling us that time is infinite, and you don't fuck around with the infinite. Time. The mystery train we're forced to book passage on which promises to move forward while forever plunging into the past. Time. Benji didn't believe in it.

He opened his apartment door, took a step in, and inhaled deeply. Yeah, it's me, he thought. He opened a window. If Benjamin's apartment was just this side of squalid, it was quietly redeemed by a modest but sure sense of style: a nice set of speakers, a surprisingly erudite library, a cactus plant in bloom on the windowsill, and a small fish tank which held Nestor, a baby turtle Benji had purchased illegally from a man in Chinatown, who had carried the critter around in a filthy bucket.

Benji dropped a few dried brown shrimp into the tank where Nestor was sleeping on his back, his yellow underside covered in a diseased-looking slime. Benji had tried bringing Nestor to the office once, but Troy had warned him against it. "I'm happy you got a pet, Benji, but if you keep him here, I'm afraid I'll step on him," Troy warned. "Don't worry about it Troy, I'm going to keep him in a tank," Benji reassured. "No, no, no. Benjamin, you misunderstand me. If you keep him here, I will step on him. A turtle's not a pet, Benjamin. A turtle's a bug with a shell." So, Benji planted him on his desk at home. When purchasing the tank, Benji made sure that proportionally the animal didn't have more room than himself. Which he only thought was fair. Likewise, Benji ensured that the animal live in a similar state of crippling isolation. Nestor, like his master, had not had a mate in many a moon.

Benji spent most of his time in his apartment in the living room. For some reason, he never got around to fixing up the bedroom, a small space in which chipped paint, a wheezy radiator, and a large unmade bed, precariously leaning on a paralyzed leg, held court. If the bedroom was devoid of color and life, though, the rest of the apartment was not: considering he was on the third floor, the living room received a surprisingly good amount of light; his collection of CDs and tapes was grand and eclectic, alphabetically ranging from Miles Davis to Maria Callas, from the Beastie Boys to the Beatles, from Led Zeppelin to Ludwig Van; he had a few glossy coffee table books from some art history courses he had taken up at Cornell sprinkled about, and a big, untitled Jackson Pollock print (America? Mushroom cloud? Delphic oracle?) hanging (exploding?) over his couch.

Although he didn't cook, and never really used the small eat-in kitchen, Benji always kept the table neatly set for three. Putting the crinkly packages down and looking around the place, Benji couldn't help but think, this is it, this is my life, my one and only life, and I'm blowing it. For at least the last five years Benji felt alert and clever enough to find amusement in his daily failings and humiliations, but too passive to actively engage his situation, to take a stake in what was happening to him. Some mornings, upon waking, he had to remind himself who he was, remember the identity he'd built up around himself—an identity as arbitrary as any other—and painfully pull it on, like a child's glove. It hadn't always been so. He remembered being in love, remembered love as the fuse that set everything else aglow. Me. And me now. He spread some old newspaper out over his little rug and opened the styrofoam-packaged chicken. Tearing into the mealy meat, he sadly acknowledged he was an outcast from life's feast.

After eating and wiping his greasy fingers clean, he unwrapped the Jergen's, spread Allison's photos out along the rug, and popped in the tape. Reclining, he clutched the remote with his left hand, fast forwarding through the red and white FBI warning and phone sex ads, while, with his right, he pulled down the worn elastic waistband of his pants. This was his favorite part of the magic show, the accordion-like expansion and diminution which never ceased to amaze and delight him. Fully upright, his penis measured six and one eighth inches from stern to prow, and had the width of a good blues harmonica. A not immodest size, it was still, by all accounts, the smallest member ever to be featured in porn. At present, it measured about an inch and a quarter, curled as it was, asleep in a fetal position. Benji, a doting parent, was careful not to wake his little lamb.

First, he spit a nice globule of saliva into his hand, then, he squirted a few dollops of cream into his palm. His baby rustled awake, so he playfully teased the hairs on its underside. His little lamb laughed in response, dipping its cycloptic head playfully from side to side. That was his cue: he quickly lathered himself up, gently tugging at the gray warm elephant flesh. The sound was something they both always enjoyed, a squishy-squirmy sound that provided a surprisingly accurate facsimile of the swish and suck of a woman's innards.

The trick these days—having not had actual sex in three years—was to surround himself with as much pornographic material as possible, and then, at the crucial moment of inevitability, pull up a Penny memory from the permanent file, the permanent file being Benji's term for all of the erotic ephemera he had accumulated over the years. A mental topography across whose rolling pastures women of all ethnicities, languages, and ages were invited to roam, the permanent file had organized itself with precisely moments like this in mind. Since, during masturbation, it was extremely rare for one image or scenario to carry him through from beginning to end—since Benji's masturbatory ritual usually started strong on plot but quickly degenerated into a miasmic morphing of faces and limbs akin to the special effects used to animate the liquid steel villain in *Terminator 2*—it was almost always necessary for Benji to continuously flip through his erotic Rolodex for something exciting enough to keep the festivities going. It was crucial, therefore, to keep a repository of images, scents, and memories at the ready, a well-endowed bank from which he could afford to make easy withdrawals. However, since holdings once held in high erotic esteem would invariably plummet in value, and since the rare errant image—a little boy, his mother, Ethel Merman belting out "Anything You Can Do, I Can Do Better"—would occasionally attempt a hostile take-over during moments of mid-masturbatory panic, Benji was obliged to carefully manage and maintain the file, to update, to prune, to expand his portfolio at every turn. If there were fluctuations in this mental marketplace, however, the Penny fund existed alone, above the rest, a blue chip, the IBM of Benji's erotic exchange.

On the television screen, Dr. Fellatio was conducting all sorts of experiments on Model I for the benefit of his videographer, T. Bone. The doctor explained that Model I represented a recent advance, a new, lightweight model, the voluminousness of whose hollows the doctor would now test with a variety of dildonic devices. . . Although the pinot looked pretty interesting, tapes never really did it for him, serving as little more than erotic white noise for Benji's endeavors, orchestral accompaniment to the theatre of Benji's memory. He closed his eyes and began.

It started slowly: images of his first *Playboy*, his first *Penthouse*, his first *National Geographic* with a bare-breasted black woman carrying a basket of laundry on her head; his first glimpse of a girl's panties in elementary school (plain white panties still the best); *Babe, the Farmer's Daughter*, the first porno he watched with his brother Jerry; a teacher in high school whose visible panty line had driven him wild; an FIT girl he saw in the street that very morning (permanent file?); his first girlfriend, Stacey, a bright and clever girl who sucked cock ambitiously, like she was being graded on it; a girl he noticed walking in Central Park the other day walking in cut-off jeans shorts, shorts torn just below the buttocks, twin tears which looked like eyes blinking open and closed, open and closed, open and closed as she sauntered away in the summertime heat (permanent file!); April, looking in that photograph so much like Penny. Penny. The palpebral flutter of Penny's face during orgasm, caught, frozen, and etched onto the magic lantern of his memory.

He was beating it steadily now, rhythmically, to the beat of an internal metronome, faster, faster, faster. The phone rang. Faster, faster, faster.
The phone rang again. Faster, faster, faster. Click.

"You've reached the answering machine. Leave a message after the tone."
Beep.
"Benjamin, this is Dad. Listen, when you get a chance, give a call, it'd be good to talk."
For a moment, the sound of his father's voice, increasingly weaker but

louder too, to compensate for the hearing loss he attributed to the world around him, caused Benji to freeze. But he would not be deterred. Opening his eyes, Benji quickly squirted a few more streams of goo into his hand, adding it to the thickly coagulating coat. It was surging through him now, he could feel it, orgasmic inevitability was close at hand, just a few seconds more would put him over. It was time to dig deep into the Penny file, that endless, indestructible reservoir of memories, words, sights, smells, tastes, and touch wherein not a single preposition is spared: in Penny, on Penny, behind Penny, atop Penny, astride Penny, below Penny, above Penny, all over Penny, all over Penny, all over Penny! He broke and splatted.

For an astral moment, everything was flashbulbs and paisleys, magician's smoke and the Cartesian grid. Then, the tears came. Lately, inexplicably, Benji began to cry after orgasm. The physical sensation was unlike crying, his diaphragm and breathing were still under control, but he would tear up and come to moments later in that familiar, post-lachrymose haze. Doubly wet, Benji slowly recovered himself and opened his eyes. He considered his ejaculate, archipelagically streaked across his belly, a sight he always found strangely reassuring. His shyly receding shaft was now coated in a thick pudding of saliva, Jergen's, and come. A few moments longer and the semen would cool off, lose its gelatin-like consistency, and dribble down the side of his belly.

He thought of lifting himself out of this position, of getting a rag or a sock or a paper towel and wiping himself clean, but he just couldn't move. Trying to locate the feeling in his legs, for a brief, terror-stricken moment, he felt paralyzed, but then, he happily reassured himself that he wasn't paralyzed, just lazy. He found his feet and put them back on, remembered his hands and fingers and pulled them back onto his arms like gloves, recognized his skull, lying on the other side of the room, and screwed that back onto his neck like a light bulb. He was going to fall asleep right there with the lights on and the porno playing, cemented in his own dribbling ooze in the middle of the living room floor like a little boy.

When he was a boy and couldn't sleep, tossing and turning in bed with all that energy because there was so much to see and do and everything was so goddamned fantastic, rather than counting sheep, he would try to pinpoint the exact moment when sleep came, isolate the moment when the cocoon of consciousness split open and the butterfly of dreams came fluttering out. He could never do it, of course. By the time he was asleep, he was no longer conscious. Besides, he had no trouble falling asleep now. Sleep was the reward for making it through another day.

The phone started ringing again, and Benji, drowsily drifting away, struggled to incorporate its ugly sound into the rhythm of his oncoming sleep; to syncopate his breathing to it, to use its dissonant chords as the aural basis for a dream (spy dismantling bomb, church bells ringing, the wings of angels . . .). He didn't care who was calling, since there was no one he cared to speak to. A woman's voice:

"Hello, I'm trying to reach Benjamin Seymour. My name is Peggy Poshlust, and this may sound like a strange request, but, I'm a publicity agent, and there's an important matter I'd like to discuss with you on behalf of one of my clients. Anyway, call and we'll chat. My cell phone number is 323-389-6017. Thanks. And O, I apologize for calling you at home."

Home. Whose home? O, my home. This is my home. He even managed to whisper the word to himself three times aloud: Home. Home. Home. This couldn't really be his home could it? Home? Where was home? Was home on Avenue J in Brooklyn where he'd spent his childhood? Was home here, amidst the porno tapes and hand lotions? Was home even a place? No. Entering sleep's furry embrace, Benji fuzzily acknowledged the only thing he ever considered home was in a girl's arms, many years a go a way a long a lass a love in

3

Ithaca. A princedom by the sea. Cayuga Lake. 1985. Cornell. A hallway.
Sitting. Her. The girl he'd spotted outside of Ollie's as he stood in line
waiting for his soup. He had seen her before, and on all of those occasions
she had been alone, which, on a campus twenty thousand strong, intrigued
him. She? She was here. Sitting in the hallway. A raspberry beret. A camel
hair coat. Rosy-cheeked. Her face. Look smart. Look down. Just come from
the European Novel. Flushed, Benji glanced at the page:

> A girl. A strange and beautiful seabird. Long slender bare legs.
> Her thighs. Featherings of soft white down. Soft and slight,
> slight and soft. But her long fair hair was girlish: and girlish,
> and touched with the wonder of mortal beauty, her face.

"You like it?"
"Huh? O, yeah, it's okay."
"Je m'appelle Penelope. Et tu?" she asked, extending a long, white-fin-
gered hand.
"What?"
"Please don't make this hard for me. I feel like I'm behind already.
"Je m'appelle Penelope. Et tu?"
"I'm sorry, I don't understand."

No need. Unnecessary. Lived there. Live there. Tonight, we'll sleep,
begged Benji, badgering his two-tiered consciousness. If even in moments

of repose, Penny was the lode-star subject of all his pain and joy, when conscious Benji could attempt to suppress or, at the very least, lend a measure of architectural coherence to his memories of her. But at night, with the protective curtain of consciousness drawn and the dark providing a terrifying blank screen upon which to project the magic lantern of memory, he was utterly defenseless. A remembered look, a smell, a touch, patches of dialogue, all replayed themselves through the night fog like favorite television reruns. Piece by piece, jockeying against each other they locked into position, forcing themselves on him in their nightly attempt to reconstruct and solve the riddle, the tortured jigsaw puzzle that was them. Only he knew it would never be solved, and so morning after morning, after daylight broke and the pieces were sent scattering away, he would be left alone to start again.

Junior year. Kingsley Roth, one of Benji's apartment mates, a short, balding, bespectacled boy of no small wit and charm, tries to encourage Benji to date, to get out more. Although something of a bookworm, girls are interested in him, and, as Kingsley points out, "they're easy marks in college, Benji. Trust me on this. Once we graduate, it's a whole different ballgame: money, cars, career. Fucking's going to come with a lot more provisos attached. The market currency's gonna change, bubee, so you better get yours while the getting's free." A creature of pure id, women-wise, Kingsley, a Napoleonic five-foot-four, did quite well for himself, winning girls over through sheer force of avidity. "A ridiculous name, a ridiculous height, I don't care if they look at it as a mercy fuck or not. They think I'm a homunculus? Good, fuck 'em. They know the only way to shake me is by sleeping with me."

Sleep with me. Yes, sleep.

A French and Art History double major. A transfer student from Beaver College. A date.

"When?"
"This Friday."
"Who with?"
"You don't know her. She's new. A transfer student."
"The Pigeon chick?!"
"Yeah, why, you know her?"

"O, baby! Rumor has it she gets down."

"Meaning?"

"Benji, look at her. She's the type of girl who double majors in Women's Studies and sucking cock. Look, this is obviously a chick who does stuff, and if you play your cards right, she's gonna do stuff to you, Benjamin. To you!"

And she did. He had (fumblingly) lost his virginity two summers before, but this was a different, more intricate, well-lit affair. She would teach him things. Sex. Coitus. Fucking. This was waiting for him at night, every night. How do people get through the day, every day, knowing this is there, is theirs? The experience of having an honest-to-god steady girl-friend leant his daily activities a subterranean charge. He felt as if he'd joined a secret society: was suddenly fluent in Sanskrit: was given insider information on eighties Wall Street: had just been issued a special government dispensation to vacation in Cuba. Fucking. The unreality of fucking. If you thought about it too much, it made no sense at all: like a simple word you've seen a thousand times before that, after being typed out, you stare at a moment too long.

"I need me some happy," she'd say, bursting into his room.

"Okey dokey, smoky," he'd respond, her mouth already engulfing his. And soon, his favorite view of her, the image of her that burned holes in the fabric of his memory: Crotch-shot: Benji below: On her back: Full flat face. Happy. Laughing.

"Benji, my faithful lap dog," she'd murmur, as Benji, inly moaning inly dying, close enough to breathe her air, covered her.

"I'm the scuba diver, baby. I go down, down, down."

Down? Stay Down. Undercover? Eyes closed? Good boy. Okey dokey smoky.

"Look, it's a Penji," she'd say as they walked arm-in-arm across the Art's Quad in midwinter, their shadows comingling across blankets of snow.

"Hello, Benelope."

"Nice to meet you Penjamin."

And with a tug, the two were one, rolling in the soft fluffy stuff.

Soft, fluffy, hypoallergenic, sweet, lonely, lovely pillow.

Here they are leaving a movie theatre after seeing *The Fly*, a deeply romantic film disguised as another Cronenberg gross-out.

"We have so much to be thankful for, Benji."

"Like what?"

"Like we're not a fly."

Fly. Imagine flying. Over great fields and castles and moats.

Penny sleeping. Light falling across her in Venetian stripes. Penny eating chocolate and drinking port. Penny reading Plath's complaint to his Portnoy. Red-fingered Penny parsing a pomegranate.

Pomegranate, pomegranate, pomegranate, pome

She had strange and wonderful ways of reading books. In order, as she put it, "to crack the conspiracy of the book's code." Although she assiduously eschewed lit theory, she had developed unique ways of attacking texts: she would read them from back to front: she would read only every second or third page: she would read only the dialogue: she would read in rondo form (like in elementary school when half the class is singing "merrily, merrily, merrily, merrily, life is but a dream," while the other half struggles to concentrate on "row, row, row your boat"): she would get halfway through a book and begin again, from page one, while continuing to make her way through from the center.

She learned like no one else he ever knew. Everything had to be deeply felt. She didn't learn to memorize or to score good grades, but to expand, like a helium balloon. The only way for knowledge to have any impact on her was for her to personally relate it to her experience, for her to feel the knowledge entering her almost physically. She would study say, Marxism in a political theory class, or Duchamp in a modern art survey course, and would look at Benjamin and ask plaintively, helplessly, "Am I a Marxist?" or "Am I a Dadaist?"

Am I asleep? Am I asleep?

"My boy's in looooove," said Kingsley through Cheshire cat teeth after just two weeks.

"C'mon, lay off man."

"Buddy, lemme explain something to you," Kingsley began, inhaling dramatically. "You wanted the ten. You waited for the ten. You got the ten. But you gotta be like me. You gotta be smart. You gotta forget about the ten. Everyone wants the ten. I want the ten but I'm happy with two fives. Some weekends, I settle for five twos."

"What are you talking about man?"

"Ever play cards with a five-year-old, Benji? It's impossible to win. You know why? Because they're constantly changing the rules on you. Aces are wild. Okay. Now deuces are wild. Okay. Now one eyed jacks. Okay, now all the red cards are wild. What I'm saying is you can't win because there're no rules. And how you gonna win a game with no rules? How you gonna win a game with no rules, Benjamin? And that's the situation you're in now. Beauty creates its own rules, bubee, and you're in love with a beautiful woman. Forget it, your days of peacefulness are over."

Nights too.

There she is sitting on his bed, naked, reading a psychology book.

"I got you something," Benji said, unsheathing a six-inch-wide colored lollipop shaped in the provocative personage of Daisy Duck, the high-heeled Disney vamp who most reminded him of her.

"Neat," she said, unhinging her jaw as if she were a boa ready to take in a suckling pig.

"I have a question to ask you."

Pop!

"You know, right?"

"Know what?"

"What you do to us? To me?"

"What do you mean?" she asked, licking her lolly.

"The effect you have on us."

"O, I dunno."

Lick. Lick. Lick.

"But you know, right?"

"Well, it's not like I'm trying. I mean, it's not like I'm conscious of it or anything."

Suck. Suck. Slurp. Slllpppp.

"But you know we know?"

Nod.

"Okay. So when did you know?"

Shrug.

"Come on you nasty little self-monitor. When?"

Crunch! went Daisy.

"O, I don't know. When I was twelve, I guess. Thirteen."

"That young?"

"Yeah."

"How'd you know?"

"I got this job after school at this haircutting place."

"And?"

"Well, my job was to wash people's hair. Just wash people's hair. I did it a couple of hours every day after school. This was in Arizona. All the women had beehives and bright red lipstick and smoked cigarettes. It made me feel grown up. I worked for tips."

"Yeah, I bet."

She hit his arm.

"And. . . ?"

"And after a while, I started noticing the men were giving me tips like five and ten dollars."

"So?"

"A haircut's only eight."

"O."

"And then these balding guys started requesting to get a shampoo before their cuts, which was like, totally unnecessary."

"Uh huh."

His cock was waltzing in her hand.

"And then guys would start coming in, without appointments or anything, with their cars double-parked outside with their families waiting, and come in and ask for just a rinse."

"That's right, rinse it, baby. Rinse it!"

Sleep!

His cock curled up against her cheek like a seashell.

A princedom by the sea.

He remembered following her across campus one day, inadvertently find-ing himself trailing her as she made her way to the sculpting studio. She seemed less a girl than an impressionistic painting let loose: gold light following her across grass, trees, buildings. A magical moment, Benji thought, one that must be akin to a parent watching their baby sleep. Unwatched, he watched Penny the blue-jeaned pixie stroll along with that improbably tomboyish gait of hers, plucking a leaf off a lucky tree, twirling it at her side. Happy. Alone.

Following, Benji noticed the size of the tree she had stolen from. Benji must have passed the tree a thousand times before on his way to class, but today, its size and woodenness and scratchiness stripped away from its surroundings and pulled into focus, the tree was suddenly remade into itself. A tree. He looked ahead at her, moving over a bed of grass, grass whose whiskers whispered to each other in delight at the anticipation of her approach. Grass. Grass is green. He remembered how it was so, how there was no other color for grass possibly to be. And suddenly, the world was his. In Technicolor! In Cinemascope! In Panavision!

Hiding behind a limestone wall, sweating, keeping a safe distance of a hundred yards or so, it was still unreal to him, unreal that this figure, this entity separate from him but of him, was a person and not some specter conjured up from a dream: unreal that she had ever, ever made love to him: unreal that, in all likelihood, she would make love to him tonight. He continued watching her form, keeping distanced pace with that wide, silken walk of hers. He noted how, as she strolled, her i's became v's became t's. He pressed to commit the moment to memory. The experiment (Is she as enchanted, as natural, as unselfconscious unwatched as watched?) completed; its conclusion reached. (Yes.)

What time is it? Midnight hour? Later? Wee small hour? Sinatra? Any day now.

"Let's play catch," she said one sunny Sunday toward the end of senior year.
"You know if you don't hand in your French paper, you're not gonna graduate."
"But it's so nice out, let's play catch," Penelope protested.
"But I haven't any balls," Benji objected.
"C'mon sweetie."

Catch. Catch is a game where an object is thrown between partners. The object preferably being a ball. A ball being something round. An edgeless round for the satisfaction of the grip. A good grip to prevent injury and insure the circular, contiguous nature of the game. Catch, a peculiar game, since well-behaved experience teaches us that objects are meant to be placed or moved, not thrown. To throw being an activity that connotes a measure of violence. Only, catch is a game of tenderness. Catch.

"We'll use my book," she said, once they were firmly planted outside, giving the dog-eared paperback a hefty hurl. Watching the book breeze through the balmy air, its pages aflutter like wings, Benji loved her for reinventing the world for him. He caught the volume and tossed it back as she loudly struggled to recite the lyrics of popular American rock songs in French. A book in flight. A world for her to re-name. The very is-ness and such-ness of things in transit in her good and tender hands.

"Catch!"

Catch some sleep. Treasure but keep hidden. Push back. Away. Resist. Nogreengoldstayaway.

The Greek House. Senior year. May. Rain.
"WhatcanIgetchahon?" the waitress asked, posed before a blue and white Grecian seaport mural.
"I'll have three scrambled eggs, hash browns, toast, strawberry jam, coffee, and a big orange juice," rapacious Penny replied.
"And I'll have a chicken parm hero and a Coke."
"Thanks," the waitress said, collecting their menus and turning around as Penelope's foot, magnet-like, re-inserted itself in the warm spot under Benji's balls.

"An existential order," a voice, emanating from the adjacent booth behind an outspread *Wall Street Journal* said. "The chicken and the egg. . . " the newspaper continued, slowly lowering itself to reveal first the short-spackled hair, followed by the deeply creased brow, then knotty nose, neatly trimmed beard, discreet gold-chained Chai, open shirt, and chunky gold watch. But the Rome all roads of this stranger's face led to were his eyes: shocking deep-set green flashing jewels that reverberated off a corresponding emerald pinky ring.

"So the chicken is lying next to the egg in bed, looking angry as hell," the stranger began. "Meanwhile the egg is smoking a cigarette, looking self-satisfied. After a while, the chicken turns to the egg and says, 'Well, I guess that answers that question.'"

Penelope laughed.
Benjamin smiled, not getting it.

"Excuse me, I don't mean to interrupt," the stranger said, neatly folding his paper and sliding his formidable heft to the edge of his seat, the better to get closer to the couple, "but didn't I spot the two of you at the theater last night?"

The previous evening at Willard Straight Hall there had been a presentation of student films from Theatre Arts 377, Fundamentals of 16mm Filmmaking. Like most undergraduate film programs, it was a long, dull affair, with a few dollops of originality and wit for nourishment. The usual suspects—a feminist film (Look at me, I'm a woman!), a film about coming out (Look at me, I suck dick!), and a film about the student-director who doesn't know what film to make (Look at me, I've seen $8^1/_2$!)—were all accounted for. With just three days before his final project was due and nothing to show for it, panicky Benji simply asked Penny to stand in front of the camera, keeping her face neatly cropped out of the shot, and as a Bach harpsichord concerto played in the background, encircled her body from neck to toe until the film magazine expired. A valentine.

Although Benji was the one who'd enrolled in the filmmaking class, it was Penny who was the real movie lover. It was she who explained to Benji that film finally has very little to do with people, characters, or stories. Rather, film is a chronicle of light, the merciless, simple story of light falling on surfaces. ("It's all about light Benji. Just keep an eye on the light," she'd implore during shooting.) She had grasped this concept intuitively, because her very presence itself seemed infused with light. No matter what time of day or night it was, no matter where the sun or the moon hung in relation to her, no matter how dark the room, she was always perfectly, perpetually lit, from the inside. A forties femme fatale streaking through a shimmering world of surfaces, she was always camera ready.

What Benji had not asked for, and was surprised by, was Penny's reaction to the filming. Perhaps impressed with her boyfriend's easy facility with the camera, perhaps aroused by the prospective permanence of sixteen millimeter, perhaps numbed by the Bolex's dumb hum, Penny began to undress as Benji's camera circumscribed her. A three-minute handheld single shot black-and-white film, shot on Kodak reversal stock, for the coup de grâce Benji had handpainted every frame with a light blue felt-tipped pen, handpainted each of those four thousand three hundred and twenty frames, leaving Penny's breasts and neck and legs in silky black-and-white while coloring the surrounding room an aquatic sea-blue-swirl. *Blue Movie* he called it, and it had been gaspingly heralded the hit of the evening.

"The screening?" the stranger asked.
"Yeah, we were there," Benji replied suspiciously.
"Yes, my son was showing a film. I'm Gabriel's father, Milton. Milton Minegold," he said, extending a Nosferatu-like hand.
"I liked Gabriel's film a lot," Benji offered.
"Gabriel's film was a piece of shit," said Minegold.

Gabriel was an odd, gawky, beak-nosed kid. A serious, pale-faced, painfully shy boy, Benjamin had a hard time imagining him the product of the robustly tan extrovert now sitting across from him. A hard worker and a loner, based on the two or three conversations he'd had with him, Benji couldn't tell if Gabriel was merely overly-dedicated or seriously self-loathing. What he did know was that the boy was a prize-winning astrophysicist who had a job operating the chimes inside Cornell's beloved clock tower, the university's symbol, its beacon, its pride. One of seven people on campus who knew how to operate the clock's chimes, having worked in the tower for three years, Gabriel was also one of only four people in possession of their own set of keys to the clock tower. In fact, rumor had Gabriel spending most of his time in the tower's innards, a rumor his short film, *The Hours and Chimes*, did little to dispel.

"Most student films are pretentious pieces of shit anyway, why should my son's be any different . . . Which was yours?" Milton mined.
"*Blue Movie*," Penny proudly proffered, "Benji wrote it and directed it and I starred in it."
"And you would be?"
"Penelope. Penelope Pigeon," she said, extending a gentle greasy hand.
"Penelope Pigeon. Huh. I hope I don't embarrass you by saying so but you look just like my youngest daughter. She's eighteen. And you

would be . . . ?"

"Twenty-one."

"Twenty-one! Perfect! Penelope and . . . Benji?" he asked, pointing, his hand cocked like a pistol.

"Benjamin Seymour," he said, wrapping his hands around a glass of water.

"Penelope Pigeon and Benjamin Seymour. Hah! Lovely film. You tinted the frames yourself?"

"Yes."

"Lovely film."

The food arrived. Manfully, Benji took a big bite out of his epic hero, burning and searing the roof of his mouth, as Penelope languidly licked a swipe of jam off her butter knife.

"You know film is going the way of the dinosaur, kids," said Milton, navigating a crust of toast over the dead sea of egg yolk, bacon and sausage fat coagulating on his plate. "Soon it'll all be video. Digital. Once that happens, anyone'll be able to make a movie. True artistic democracy. Then, we'll be bigger than U.S. Steel." He took a big drink of milk, leaving a few drops to curdle in the thickets of his beard. "You from New York, Benjamin?"

"Yes," boasted Benji the Brooklyn Boy.

"And you?"

"I'm moving there after graduation," Penelope said, squeezing Benji's hand above the table while tightening the ball of her foot below.

"O, I see. Well, here's my card," Milton said, extending it through a long white fingered hand with nails filed into sharp points. "When you get settled in New York, if you're serious about the motion picture business, give Papa Bear a call." And then, deftly reaching his hand past his barely-concealed holster, Milton removed his billfold from his inside jacket pocket, dropped two twenties on the table, and added, "Ruth, this should take care of everything."

As she turned around, Benji, reading the waitress' nametag, sheepishly realized that after four years of nameless good service, the woman had magically transformed herself into Ruth. Ruth.

"Thanks, Milty. Come again," she said with a smile

"O, you know I will," Milton chortled. Then, redirecting his attention, "See you kids in New York," and, with a cape-like flourish of his long black leather coat, he was gone. Benji examined the card, which read, in green:

Milton Minegold - President & CEO
Scylla & Charybdis Productions*
Motion Pictures
666 5th Avenue, Suite 515
New York, New York 10103
212-946-2040
*By Appointment Only

"Ground control to Major Tom, what was that all about?" Penelope asked after the air had settled.
"I don't know. I guess he's for real. Look, he's got a card and everything," Benji said, passing it to Penny who sat smiling broadly.
"Movies. Benjiiiiiiiiiiiii, we can be in movieeeeeeeeeeees."

Act I, scene v. Look, a ghost . . .

"Gabriel, hi this is Benji. Benjamin Seymour, from film class."
"Yes, hello Benjamin, how can I help you?"
"Well, I wanted to talk with you about your dad—"
"Benjamin, are you calling from a public or a private telephone?"
"I'm in my apartment."
"Good. This conversation is now over. Meet me at the base of the clock tower at twelve midnight tonight. Goodbye."
Click. When Benjamin re-dialed, there was no answer.

For Benji, college had come down to a decision between Cornell University and Duke. Imagining a complete, Thoreau-like transformation, Benjamin opted for the former. He dreamed of the sports he would take up: fishing, hiking, cross country skiing, rock climbing: imagined rugged camping expeditions in upstate New York's wooded regions: pictured himself emerging from deepest forests with Davy Crockett coonskin cap, utility vest, and work boots, bowie knife clenched between teeth, rounder of bicep, deeper of voice, straighter of walk, with a full growth of facial hair. None of this happened, of course. For eight months of the year the place was inadmissibly cold, and socially, the Greeks ruled the scene. But on nights like this, walking through campus alone in the cold brisk spring-time, he luxuriated in the correctness of his decision. And, despite his natural resistance to nature, on nights like this it was impossible for some communion not to occur, impossible for fresh sounds and sensations not to enter and enlarge his range of experience and response: the damp crunch of salad as he walked over dewy grass: the prickly feel of gossamer cobwebs falling across his face: the spotlight of the moon marking his path, looking not so much spherical in nature as an irregular patch torn through a black curtain, hinting at the luminescence that lay behind. Happy, he began to whistle.

Reaching the clocktower a few moments early, he was greeted by the skinny, bristly-headed hunchback Gabriel, who stood nervously munching pumpkin seeds from a brown paper bag.

"Thank you for agreeing to meet me," Gabriel whispered.
"No problem."
"We'll speak inside."

With a creak, Gabriel unlocked the heavy wooden doors and the two began to climb the tower's 161 steps. Slightly asthmatic in youth, Benji tried double and even triple-climbing steps, but this only winded him more quickly. Climbing. Echoes of footsteps. The first plateau of the tower's innards: the yellowing, jaundiced reverse side of the clock-face. The set of a forties film noir with Gabriel casting long Max Schreck shadows on the wall. Higher. The chimes: a rig and pulley system in which the chimesmaster stands partially suspended, marionette-like, between the upper ten wooden levers which he controls with his arms, and the lower nine which he controls with his legs. Higher still. A steep spiral staircase. The top. Anticipating another step, Benji landed on his left foot, full force. Open air. Night. Black rudderless night.

It was markedly colder and windier at the top, and Benjamin, never a great fan of heights, took up a post equidistant from all sides of the ledge, pressing the backs of his Converse sneakers against the cold stone wall. Aloft. The wind. Viewed from above, the traffic lights of downtown Ithaca twinkled dully, blinking on-and-off like the bulbed strings of a Christmas tree. And beyond that, the winedark water of Lake Cayuga, its calm waves illuminated by the bright bulb of the moon like dancing silver coins. Ithaca.

A woodcut drawing out of a gothic horror book: a feudal kingdom: a plagued fiefdom. A misty cloud passed over the moon like a veil, casting everything in inky darkness.

"Y'know, this is my first time up here."
"That right?"
"Believe that? Four years of this place, and this is my first time here."
"Largest set of chimes in North America," Gabriel offered proudly. And he was proud. Perhaps one hundred people in total had known the deeply physical satisfaction of being a Cornell chimesmaster, of being in control of the tower's nineteen bells, of the exertion it involved of both hands and both feet to make the clock sing. The chimes were automatically rigged to go off every half-hour, but the creative part of being a chimesmaster involved playing songs, and figuring out new ones to add to the tower's repertoire, songs that would match the spirit of the day. Cornell's alma mater, "Far Above Cayuga's Waters" for registration and graduation, "Jingle Bells" for Christmas, Darth Vader's imperial march from *The Empire Strikes Back* during finals week, those were the perennial favorites. But for Gabriel, the best melody to play, the most rigorous, the one that even Twilo Juergens, master chimesmaster, admitted was the gauntlet of chimesmanship, was, in a cakewalk, Nino Rota's theme to *The Godfather*.

"I always wanted to bring my girlfriend up here."
"You should. The tower's open every day."
"That's not exactly what I had in mind."
"O."

At that moment a butterfly passed between them.

Bong! Bong! Bong!

"Hear that! Feel that in your lungs?" begged Gabriel, the pale vampire.
"Yes," Benji said, reeling from the booming proximity of the sound and laying both hands behind him on the cold gothic wall for support. After a moment's deep reverberation, the chimes stilled themselves.
"I love it up here," Gabriel said, bringing forth a small red telescope, mounting it on a tripod and extending its legs. "It's much better than down there. Y'know, I used to think that college was a psych experiment being implemented by the government."

"Wa?"

"Figure it out. Take a control group of a few thousand bright, middle-class kids, bring them out to the woods, isolate them from the rest of society, cut them off from parental guidance and adult supervision, induce sleep deprivation, surround them with every synthetic substance known to man and watch 'em cook. Waddaya think's gonna happen?"

"I don't know."

"Benjamin, look down there. Waddaya see?" he asked, pointing, leaning dangerously beyond the ledge.

"West Campus."

"West Campus, yes. And what do you think is going on in those dormitories on West Campus right now?"

"I don't know. Kids studying, watching television."

"Wrong. Y'know what's going on down there Benjamin? Fucking. Raw animal fucking. The one great lesson my father taught me: it's all about the fucking. No matter how much money, no matter how much brains, no matter how thick the patina of good manners and etiquette and charity and kindness, don't be fooled. In the end, it's all about the fucking."

Bong! Bong! Bong!

"Listen, Gabe, if you don't mind me saying so, this is all getting a little weird."

"You called me, Benjamin. Don't forget that. All right, why were you asking me about my father?"

"Well, we met and—"

"You met him? Where?"

"Here."

"He was here?"

"I think he still is. . . Penny and I had breakfast with him this morning and—"

"You had breakfast with him?" Gabriel demanded, clutching both of Benji's arms with his hands, pulling him close enough for Benji to trace the thin blue veins of his winged nostrils.

"Well, no, we didn't arrange it or anything. Penny and I were at the diner, the Greek House. He recognized us from the screening last night."

"He's here," Gabriel whispered disbelievingly. He released Benji from his grip, moved to the parapet and looked silently out onto the land.

"He said he came to see your film. I thought you knew he was here. He gave me this," said Benji, flummoxed, presenting the card. "He told us we should contact him when we get back to New York . . . You really didn't know he was here?"

Bong! Bong! Bong!

"I haven't spoken to my father in seven years," Gabriel said, taking a deep breath. Slowly, he turned around. In the moonlight his skin was as white and flawless and smooth as a porcelain bowl. The dark circles under his eyes looked like smudges left behind from a leaking fountain pen. He lifted the card from Benji and, shakily, examined it. "Motion Pictures, huh? That's what he's calling them these days? And I suppose you want to know what kind of motion pictures he makes, right? That's why you called me in the first place, right? That's the million dollar question, isn't it Benjamin? The man gives you his card tells you to call him when you get to the city, you want to know if he's legitimate, right? Are the motion pictures he makes legitimate? Well, let me put it to you this way: is he legitimate after he lands my mother in a mental hospital? Is he legitimate after my sister catches a glimpse of one of his films and gets it in her thirteen-year-old head to give up her virginity to a thirty-seven-year-old auto mechanic? Is he legitimate after I have to spend my nights up here 'cause I can't sleep for the rage? Man gives you his card says call him you wanna know what kind of films he makes. Do I have to spell it out for you, Seymour? Do I have to draw you a fucking map? I presume you already know the biology, dating that pug-nosed little girlfriend of yours. You wanna know what kind of films he makes? Fuck films, Seymour! My father makes fuck films! The cocksucking motherfucking motherfucker makes fuck films!"

BONG!

"My father."

BONG!

"My father."

BONG!

"My father . . ."

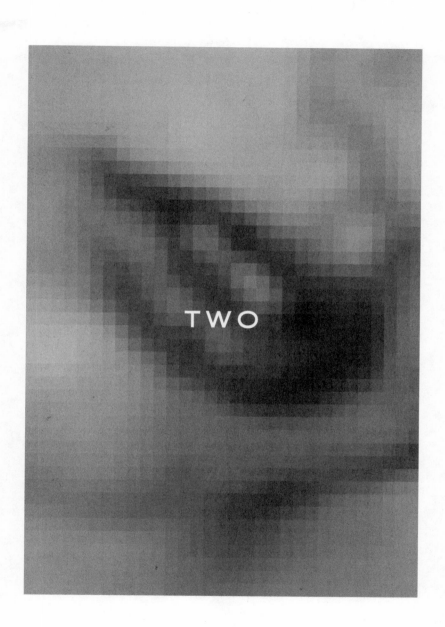

TWO

4

Stephanie Welland ate with little relish her morning breakfast of bran muffin, sliced banana, and fresh-squeezed orange juice. She liked unhealthy, poorly spelled cereals best: Froot Loops, Count Chocula, Cap'n Crunch, Kix, Trix. Most of all she liked the sandy residue left on the bottom of the bowl. Sandy sugar milk: her favorite part.

Those things which she wanted but could not have were very much in her thoughts as she moved about the kitchen softly, quietly arranging her mother's breakfast the way she liked it: vitamin shake (thinly stirred), smiling sunburst grapefruit (neatly halved), whole wheat pita bread (lightly toasted). She sat at the table alone. Waiting. Still not out. On the bike. *It's a good thing I got that thing. Otherwise, I'd fall apart! I never have time to go to the gym anymore.*

"Mom!"
"Just a sec hon, I'm still changing."

Stephanie occupied the lonely moment by mashing a dollop of imitation butter spread into the fibrous foodstuff, making it look as if she had nibbled at it. It's lonely here. Maybe a cat to liven up the place? Why not a cat? Something to take care of. A kitten. She split one of her banana slices in three, along its natural seams. Then, in a swoosh: a dark pinstripe pants suit, a smart butterfly pin, a thick leather bag. Pretty. Determined. Not quite yet forty. Mom. She sits.

"Stephanie?"

"—Finn!"

"Fine. Finn. I don't expect to be home until late tonight. So here, here's some money," Ms. Katherine Welland said, handing her daughter two twenty dollar bills. "You can pick up some nice fresh pasta at Dean & DeLuca's on the way home or order Chinese if you like. Carol's going to be coming by around six. I should be home around nine thirty or ten. O, you made breakfast."

Breakfast. A command? A description? Yes, things break fast. Break fast and mend slow. Mother? Don't know. Still can't tell.

"Mom?"

"Yes honey?"

"Do you think it's true that some women can have it all?"

"That's a strange question to ask," Ms. Welland answered, weightily consulting her grapefruit.

"One of your magazine covers asked it. Do you think it's true?"

"O, I don't know Finn," Ms. Welland began. "People sometimes use words in tricky ways."

"Hm."

"What are you reading at school these days?"

"*Hamlet*."

"Really? Isn't that pretty advanced for fourth grade?"

"Just words," Finn responded, none too much in the sun. "I've been reading it on my own."

"What'd I do to deserve such a smart kid?"

A kiss. Atop the head. Mother?

"C'mon," Ms. Welland said, taking a first and final bite of her bread, "we'll be late."

Entering the elevator. The thirteenth floor. A prison. Complete with guards at the door.

"Here, don't forget the key," her mother said, pressing the bronzed coolness into her hand once they were entombed in the chamber. Finn looked into her palm. The key. To an abandoned kingdom.

"So, are you looking forward to your birthday?"

"No, not really."

"Don't be so glum, Finn. I know it's sad to say goodbye to nine, but ten'll be a great year."

"It's not a number I'm sad to see go."

Her mother put her attaché case down and flattened the lapels of her pants suit. "I still haven't been able to get hold of your father, but I spoke with Susan a few days ago and she said he might be able to make it sometime in August."

The news was met with silence.

The doors opened magically, mightily, onto an imposing black lacquered lobby. As always happened when they were running late, Finn's mother walked quickly ahead of her, cutting a swath for her young daughter to follow. Passing the mirror. Bright clothes. Book bag. Pleated skirt. Tights. Terrible, sensible shoes. Straight fine brown hair. Smart pleasant girl. Me. As she and others see me.

"Good morning Ms. Welland. Morning Stephanie."

A guard in uniform. A uniform for me, she, and he.

"Finn!"

"It's her new nickname," her mother explained.

"Okay. Morning Finn."

"Good morning, Rinaldo."

"Rinaldo, I'm running a little late, would you do me a favor and catch a cab for her?"

"Sure thing Ms. Welland."

"Thanks." Turning. "Okay. So you're all set: you have the key and the money and your bookbag. Thanks again for breakfast, honey, that was really very sweet of you. Sorry I have to run but there's a very important deposition I have to take this morning that I can't be late for. I'll see you around nine or ten," she said, leaving the words hanging in the air behind her as she disappeared.

Outside. Light. Sun on skin. Nothing better. Building from below. A tower for a princess.

"So, summer vacation's coming up pretty soon, huh?" Rinaldo smalltalked.

"Next Friday."

"Friday, wow. Planning anything special?"

"Mom has me signed up for camp, but I don't want to go."

"Really? The summer I was a camp counselor I had the time of my life. Besides, July and August, the city gets so hot, everyone gets crazy."

"Pretty shitty city."

"Yeah, okay, you could say that," Jose's face said, swallowing its smile. "Here we go," the doorman continued as a cab pulled up to the door. Yellow carriages between prisons.

"The Brearley School, 610 East 83rd," the porter commanded. "See you later Finn."

It happened today as it happened every other. In the rearview window Jose got smaller and smaller and smaller until he disappeared as the cab pulled away from their building on 67th and Columbus Avenue, found the main vein, and cut through the park. Looking out the window, Finn watched as people streamed by in a blur: an endless, multicolored flag. Since New York never stopped moving, Finn felt the only way to hop aboard its spinning carousel was to be in a state of perpetual motion herself, as if her own quickened pulse, calibrated to match that of the city's blinkered streets, would stroboscopically cancel each other out, calming one another into a trance-like state of temporary passivity.

"Faster, please."

"That's 83rd and York, right?"

"No, he made a mistake. West Third and Broadway. Class trip today."

"All right," said the cabby, who, with bursting forearms, executed a perfect U-turn.

In the backseat, once the driver's eyes were averted, Finn changed out of her starched prep school uniform and into her hooded black sweatshirt and jeans. Morning clothes. Eighth day. Must remember to intercept mail and erase messages from the machine. Checks them at noon and three. And don't forget to call Tobey with the pneumonia update. She consulted with her wrist. Minnie Mouse watch I have to wear. Traffic through the park. They built this park. How did they do that?

Sometimes Finn would stare at something, something simple and small like a nail or a napkin or a piece of gum or a straw, and marvel over the fact that somewhere there must be a factory where this stuff is made, a person whose job it is to count the straws, another who pulls tissue paper over each of them like gloves, another in charge of laying on the stripes, another who puts them in boxes, another who drives them away in trucks. Things. The wonder of a world of things made. A park. Where there was no park. She leaned her head out the cab window. The sun. She closed her eyes. So warm. Desert Island Day. Dad's idea. Hooky once a month for the three of them. What movie was playing the last time? *Planet of the Apes*. Mom in the candy store: *you can pick anything you want, but only one. You can only choose one.* Tough decision between Twizzlers and Rolo. Picked Twizzlers because you can bite off the ends and use it as a straw. Back home they opened all the windows and spread the big bedspread out across the living room floor. The big blanket: the island. The surrounding carpet: a crocodile-infested moat. Stranded. No one allowed on or off all day. Everything they needed spread out at the start: bread and olives, oranges and almonds, cheese and salami, red and yellow wine, frozen grapes and iced tea, paper and crayons, newspapers and magazines, toys and remote controls. A cool breeze came in from the window. Mom's lap like the cool side of the pillow. Dad's hand warm as tea. So happy.

"That'll be $8.75," the cabby said, rocking the vehicle to a halt.
Finn scrunched up her school uniform and squeezed it into her bookbag as she pulled a crumpled bill from the skirt pocket.
"C'I have ten back, please," she asked, pressing the twenty dollar bill into his palm. His callused hand was three times the size of hers.

Third street. Ten. Thirteen. Unlucky number. Even the elevator skips it. But Sara's planning to celebrate it. Different religions. I'll be ten next week. Ten times round the sun. Dad won't be coming. A long way away. Never been to England. Not sure I want to go. Ten. Double digits. Probably won't get out of double digits alive. Ten. Then eleven. Then twelve after that. Things to look forward to: breasts (developed), menstruation (achieved), first kiss (stolen), virginity (lost), marriage (postponed, suffered through, dissolved).

Deep in thought, Finn started out for Washington Square Park. A native New Yorker, Finn had an uncanny sense of how the city was laid out, intuiting behind its design its regal, chess-like divisions. If she sensed the outer boroughs were looked down upon and ignored by people in her mother's class as a consolation prize for those who didn't really belong in the city—

lifelong commuters humping their way back and forth to work each day on the F and D trains—then the Upper East Side, with its museums and private schools and doorman-lined avenues was the opposite: the heart of the city where the old money lay. The streets were stately, the architecture grand, engraved, and gargoyled, the buildings neatly stacked together like books on library shelves. The Upper West Side, where Finn lived in single-parented-latch-keyed-splendor, was more nouveau riche in feel. The architecture looked like giant stereo speakers; all sleek and black and personality-deprived rectangles of glass and steel shooting up into the clouds, deforming the skyline. The Upper West Side was a younger, more GAPified, Body Shopped terrain. Midtown scared her. Those streets didn't breathe properly. Nowhere than in the nexus from 34th Street to 56th did you feel more acutely aware of the city's unrelenting congested grid. Everything about those blocks was about direction, purpose, movement. As for anything past 86th and Madison or 92nd and Broadway, besides one trip to Columbia University (her mother's law school alma mater) and another to the Cloisters, that half of the city simply didn't exist for her. No, downtown is where she liked to go. There was something invitingly European about the arched entranceway into Washington Square Park, something lonely and romantic and sad about walking along Washington Mews or down Soho's rain-drenched cobblestone streets. Downtown made it easy for Finn to lose herself, to imagine she was in France in the twenties: a street performer, a young poet, a modern dancer, a painter's muse. Besides, down here, shopkeepers didn't look twice at a young girl quietly moping around record shops and used bookstores at ten-thirty in the morning on a schoolday. Today would be her eighth day of successfully playing hooky, and it was time to celebrate. Time to get high.

Where is Dime Bag Man? She remembered being surprised at the packaging. Neat little zip-lock bags, the kind of bags you might keep a pair of earrings in on the bottom of a tin of Band-Aids when you went away on vacation. He walked through the park indiscriminately asking people, chanting really, *Smoke, smoke, smoke?* And she had been touched that his casual lack of discernment had landed upon her, like the time a tourist once asked her for subway directions and her knowledge made her feel very grown-up indeed. *Smoke, smoke, smoke?* She had never intended to try marijuana at so early an age, but seven days ago, she had, and it had been a revelation.

Not knowing how to properly roll a joint, she had wasted most of her first ten dollar purchase and spent a good deal of the early afternoon searching out her man. When she finally found him, and relayed to him what had happened, he chuckled to himself lightly before slipping her a readymade from his black leather vest. At home that night she practiced her technique with oregano, parsley, and dried basil, using sheets of loose-leaf paper she carefully cut into strips for rolling paper. (When her mother asked her later in the week, in the midst of preparing a late-night omelet dinner, what had happened to all the spices in her spice rack, the bright and clever girl was ready with, *I made an extra spicy Boboli!*) By mid-week, she was a pro: rolling doobees that were as tight and well-packed as Cuban cigars; slow burning, leafy beauties. She found the process relaxing, and it was time to put her skill to good use.

Smoke, smoke, smoke? Yes, yes, yes! A green ten dollar bill with your name on it, buddy. High. I want to be high! Remember the tree with the red leaves? A man approached and picked one. I closed my eyes: the tree is going to bleed to death! But look, there it is. Still hanging in there. Remember the fly that landed on your arm and stayed there, feasting away at dead skin and sweat. You could feel every hair his legs touched. Lightly, lightly. But you didn't shoo him away. No, instead you brought your arm close to your face, slowly, closely, and stared him down. Big black orbs. Revealed nothing. That's all he left you with, the mystery of his blankness. But that was something. O, I want to be high! Dime Bag Man where are you? Too early. Time to kill. Rolling paper I can buy.

She walked along Broadway for a bit, ducking into the first newspaper tobacco shop she could find. The trick is to be cool. Be cool, baby, be cool. Look around, like you don't know they're kept behind the counter. Pez dispensers. Peculiar product. Gum. Some still 25¢. 5¢ a stick. Still a good buy. Remember when Cheez Doodles were 25¢ a bag? Now they're 50¢. Getting old. Packs of gumdrops, licorice, and jelly candy. Two for a dollar. Probably stale. Sucking candies. Grape, cherry, lemon, lime. Tastes like sugar. Not like fruit. Like nothing at all. Like the peaches and pears in canned fruit cocktail. Same but for the color. Cheez and crackers with the little red utensil. Bring you into the process. Spread the cheez product evenly across each cracker? Make sandwiches? Or eat the crackers first and save all the cheez for the end to scoop up on the stick and eat all at once? Choices. Decisions. Paralysis. Enough stalling. She approached the man at the counter.

"Do you have any rolling paper?"
"Rolling paper?" asked the grizzly cashier in disbelief. "Just Big Bambú. But I can't sell em t'ya."
Play dumb.
"Why not? It's just paper."
"Y'dun unnerstand. I can get in a lotta trouble selling ese t'ya."
"It's for my dad."
"Well tell im ee can come down ere an buy em en."
"He can't. He's sick."
"Well ee shouldn't be smoking if ee's sick."
"He's not sick like that. I mean he's really, really sick. Cancer of the pancreas. He says smoking's the only thing that makes him feel better."
"Here," the man said, flicking the pack across the counter as if it had just delivered him an electrical shock. "Just take em an get outta here."

Trés cool, Finn thought, laying claim to the package. Thin as a book of matches. Thinner. She examined the packaging. Made in Spain. Thirty-three leaves. She slipped open the slipcase. NOT INTENDED FOR SALE TO MINORS - ORDER YOUR BAMBÚ T-SHIRT TODAY.

Finn moved over to the stacks of newspapers where she was assaulted by twin paternal headlines from the *Post* and the *News*. FOR DADDY. ONE FOR DAD: JORDAN'S FATHER'S DAY GIFT: NBA TITLE. Father's Day yesterday. Card sent. No word yet. Sentimental or funny? Card selection always a binary choice. She had labored over the decision for days before settling on a comedic card. *This Father's Day, I decided to give you something I knew would be difficult to find.* Open onto an anonymous bug-eyed cartoon kid holding a remote control. Ha ha ha. A mistake? Maybe he didn't get it. Or maybe he didn't get it that way, either. Not much of a television watcher anyway. She averted her eyes and quickly found the *Times*. Check the weather. Late Edition: New York: Today: Partly sunny, a thundershower. High 85°. Thundershower. Damn. Maybe not a good day to runaway.

She abandoned the newspapers in favor of the magazine rack. Monday. Magazine day. Mom always excited to get her magazines. Especially the *New Yorker*. Says it always makes her feel smarter for reading it. A short

Mexican man was hunched over in front of her using a box-cutter to slice the twine binding together bundles of fresh glossies. *New York* magazine: RENTS GET RIDICULOUS. The *New Yorker*: Two male sailors kissing in Times Square, bent at the knees (famous WWII photo?) *Newsweek*: RED ALERT. *Time*: AMERICA'S 25 MOST INFLUENTIAL PEOPLE. *Premiere*: Tom Cruise. *Entertainment Weekly*: Nicolas Cage and Sean Connery. Orange powdered faces with deep soulful eyes. Staring out. At whom? Deep in the movie magazine section she came across a copy of *Teen Idol* magazine and liberated it from the rack. Will I be interested in this in a few years? Michelangelo Virelle. Cover boy. New but familiar face. ON DECK FOR STARDOM. Mom mentioned something about him once. Her firm? She flipped through the pages until she reached a full page, black-and-white shot of Michelangelo, topless, his longish hair blown out around him like a cone of cotton candy. She examined his face. Smooth, hairless chin. Probably never shaves. Razor's sweet buzzing music. Smooth butterscotch skin. Alcohol smell. Shoe polish. Sweaty t-shirts. Neck ties. Tennis rackets. Shoe trees. Chunky watches. Dad.

She pulled at the strings of her black hooded jersey and continued moving along. *Rolling Stone*. Lollapalooza. Lots of faces. Only one I recognize is the bald-headed Pumpkin. All in black. Like he's out of a fairy tale. Frog boy becomes a prince. Music sounds that way, too. *Mellon Collie and The Infinite Sadness*. Neat name. What's that song I like?

>   The world is a vampire
>   Come to draaaaaaiiiiiiiin

She stared up at the rows of woman's magazines. *Cosmopolitan*: THE SECRET THAT CAN ENSLAVE YOUR MAN AND MAKE HIM YOURS FOR LIFE. HOW LONG SHOULD YOU WAIT BEFORE HAVING SEX WITH YOUR NEW FLAME. WHAT COSMETIC SURGERY CAN (AND CAN'T) DO FOR YOUNG WOMEN. *Seventeen*. Liv Tyler. Cat's eyes. Wet gluey lips. She passed a finger over her own and parted them thinly, running a forefinger between the underside of her lip and fragile, porcelain teeth. Dumb look but sexy. *Vogue*. Kate Moss. On all fours in the grass. Another cat. Will I ever look like that?

She moved deeper into the store, into the adult section. *Playboy*, *Penthouse*, *Hustler*, and then the hard-core stuff, sealed in cellophane wrappers, *Beaver Damn!*, *Lickety Split!*, *Hard Boiled Dick*. She had seen pornographic magazines before, in her father's desk, and some of the older girls had brought one to school once and shown it off in the courtyard during recess, but the naked adult body still elicited reactions of shock and delight in her. Not like cats at all, like gorillas, orangutans. All that hair! So much sexier with clothes on. Don't men know? She stood before *Beaver Damn!* staring at a heroic picture of a big blonde with pendulous breasts who sat staring straight out, spread-eagled, her pierced labia pulled back like a web, and considered her own undeveloped body: her concave chest and small nipples, her hairless crotch and spindly legs. Must get tiring holding those up all day. Bras must be restricting. Expensive, too. All that stuff from Victoria's Secret and no one to see her in them. She buries them under the day-to-day underwear. Sad. And getting your period. Vinegary smell. Squishy feeling all day. Must be bad. I don't want mine. Maybe better to be a boy. No.

"Hey kid get away from there! You wanna shut me down! Get the hell outta here!"

Maybe he will be back. She cut across Broadway, down Mercer—past the Angelika Film Center (*Stealing Beauty*, *Switchblade Sisters*, *Welcome to the Dollhouse*, *Dead Man*, *I Shot Andy Warhol*), past the NYU gymnasium, past her favorite used book store where just last week she had exchanged her social studies textbook for a worn and ratty Nietzsche primer—and cut across Bleecker Street. She looked down as she walked. In the street, pieces of colored glass were pressed into the asphalt like tile mosaics. Coca Cola green. Bottled Coke the best. Cold peppermint checkerboard taste. Could use one right now. Bottled water? Why pay for it? New York has the best water anyway. Evian: naive spelled backwards. Secrets in words. Hidden meanings.

In the street, shining dully atop a heap of garbage, sat an old broken black manual typewriter. He worked on one of those. Clackety clack clack. The sound from dad's office. But the words never came out that way, did they? Years ago, he showed her the keyboard's three magic words: QWERTYUIOP, ASDFGHJKL, ZXCVBNM from which all others are made. *Those three words are all you need, kiddo.* He liked showing off his typing skills to her, transcribing their conversations as they talked together, staring at her the whole time, never once lifting his eyes off her. Before his departure, he had collected the scraps of typed conversation and made her a present of them. Faulty m and c keys. She looked to the ground.

> Step on a crack
> Break the bitch's back
> Step on a line
> My father is a swine

Newspaper man. The crime was committed by the newspaper man with the typewriter in the study. Walking along the Brooklyn Promenade once, aloft on his shoulders, he told her to look, look how the skyline looks like a typewriter, a typewriter whose keys are stuck in various states of depression.

A month after the divorce the dreams began. Through an openwindowed cityscape it appeared to her, slowly, wholly, drifting toward her, a black and alabaster form taking hold through shymisty clouds. Smiling. She had read somewhere that prehistoric people painted bison on cave walls to conquer the thing they feared: that art began as a simple defense against fear. With shaking hands she removed her recently purchased philosophy book from her backpack, flipped to an empty back page and began a poem, her first:

> With vampire smiles
> And grinning teeth

Smoke, smoke, smoke. To walk to buy to smoke to fly. She remembered a week ago how a group of skateboard kids had been practicing, using the shell in the center of Washington Square Park as a rink. They left their boom box blasting the Pumpkin's vampire song and, as the drug took hold, she closed her eyes. Swooning, as she listened to the music she began isolating each instrument, separating bass from percussion from guitar from keyboard from lead vocal from back-up: six songs simultaneously spinning round her like strands of DNA, entrancing her. Opening her eyes, it felt as if hours upon hours had passed. A hidden world of sound, color, and light, peeled back and revealed for just ten dollars. Ten.

Back in the park, she sat down on an empty bench. She put her bookbag down on the grass beside her. A lone cloud passed over the sun, slowly, wholly, shadowing everything in deeper shades of green and brown. I am lonely here. I am quiet here alone. Sad too. Behind. Perhaps there is some-one. A messenger. She turned her face over a shoulder. No one. An empty place save for a bird, silently moving and moving silently: a bird alone: a silent animal.

5

BONGS BEGAT BELLS

Alarm clock. Dammit! What's in those things makes that fucking screeching noise? Stiff neck. Shitty sleep. Deep diving? No. Pebble skipping. Swim toward the surface. Closer. Closer. Closer. Awake!

DREAMS?

None.

DRIED SEMEN?

Some. He picked the scabby flakes off his stomach and chest, being careful not to tug the hairs. He had slept through the night in a jarring position: Picasso's Egyptian'd whore: a Saul Bass movie poster cutout: a murder victim police outline. Massaging his taut-tight neck, he imagined his obituary.

BENJAMIN SEYMOUR, PORNOGRAPHER, FOUND DEAD IN APARTMENT

Benjamin "Benji" Seymour, pornographer, thirty-three, was found dead in his apartment yesterday. The writer/director of over 350 erotic motion pictures, Mr. Seymour, who early in his career regularly appeared in films alongside his ex-wife Penelope Catherine Pigeon, proved among the most popular hardcore erotic filmmakers of the late eighties and early nineties. Summing up a brilliant career, adult film veteran Anita Cox had this to say about Mr. Seymour's untimely passing, "The world has lost a champion woodsman, a master cocksmith."

NOT AUTO-EROTIC ASPHYXIATION, CORONER

The victim of what was first believed to be auto-erotic asphyxiation but was later revealed by the coroner's report to be a lethal overdose of laziness, sloth, and lack of ambition combined with an inclination toward morbid depression, a tendency to live in the past, and an over-reliance on Pez candies, Mr. Seymour was discovered alone in his apartment, approximately three days after his death, naked and semen-encrusted in a fetal position on the living room floor.

ALWAYS SMELLED BAD, NEIGHBOR

Neighbors were first alerted to Mr. Seymour's death due to the rank stench emanating from his third-story apartment. "At first I didn't think anything of it," an unidentified elderly neighbor said, asking for the time. "He always smelled pretty bad."

"DAD" FIRST WORD

Mr. Seymour's first word, upon looking into his soiled diaper, reported to be "Dad!" To the end, Mr. Seymour championed the bowel movement as an act of the highest artistic order. "To me defecation is the high point of one's day, as well as the sincerest form of creative expression man can aspire to."

CORNELL, GOOD PLACE TO MASTURBATE

Mr. Seymour's masturbation history began in earnest in Ithaca, New York, where, as an underachieving undergraduate, he led a triumphant campaign of compulsive self-abuse across the Cornell University campus. "A good place to masturbate," Mr. Seymour would later advise youngsters eager for college advice.

ITHACA ALSO BIRTHPLACE OF "SEXUAL HARASSMENT"

Ironically, the first reported use of the term "sexual harassment" occurred in Ithaca, New York, at a 1975 conference in which a group of feminists held a "Speak-Out On Sexual Harassment" on behalf of Carmita Wood, a forty-four-year-old employee of Cornell University.

WOULD WOOD IF SHE COULD?

Mr. Seymour, upon hearing the story, was heard to exclaim, "Carmita Wood—now that's a porn star name if I ever heard one!"

ENCHANTED, IMPOSSIBLE

In the fall semester of his junior year, Mr. Seymour met and fell in love with Penelope Catherine Pigeon. Together they entered the adult film industry under the tutelage of Milton Minegold. The love of Mr. Seymour's life, Ms. Pigeon would later prove to be something of an Achilles heel for Mr. Seymour. An enchanted and impossible person, Ms. Pigeon was loved by Mr. Seymour nonetheless, until the end of his days, more than anything he had ever seen or imagined on earth, or hoped for anywhere else.

AMBIGUOUS?

Very.

LIGHT

On several occasions, Ms. Pigeon was known to ask Mr. Seymour imploringly, "What is the light?" Mr. Seymour, who had no idea what she was talking about, had no response.

PERPLEXED BY PUSSY

Although he led a successful life as a pornographer, to his final days Mr. Seymour remained troubled by the heterosexual act in all of its (limited) varieties. At age thirteen, the creatively gifted Mr. Seymour tried his hand at poetry, producing the following:

> *Asked Benji the dog*
> *Lapping up at his dish*
> *'Tis stranger than a flower*
> *That smells like a fish?*

LAWRENCE OF A LABIA, TOP FILM

Lawrence Of A Labia, the 1990 film Mr. Seymour wrote, directed, and starred in alongside Ms. Pigeon, is considered by many to be his magnum opus and one of the finest adult films ever made. Although perhaps sexually outshone in the picture by Wally, a dromedary camel, Mr. Seymour had this to say about *A Labia*: "I'm very proud of that film. Besides the sand, it was the best professional experience of my life. It just goes to show: it all starts with the script."

SURVIVED BY TURTLE, PLACE SETTINGS, HAND LOTION

Mr. Seymour is survived by his homosexual brother, Jerry the Ophthalmologist out on Long Island, his father Art (who had been nervously preparing for the deaths of his wife and two sons since his wedding day and their respective births), the ghost of his wife Penelope, an aborted fetus, several boarded-up porno theatres in New York City's Times Square district, a three-day-late videocassette rental, Nestor, a salmonella-stricken turtle, a dining room place setting for three, and thirty-one ounces of Jergen's hand lotion.

"SEE YOU IN HELL," SAYS MILTON

Mr. Minegold, father figure, mentor, and later nemesis of Mr. Seymour, is said to be eagerly awaiting Mr. Seymour's appearance in the ninth circle of hell.

REVERIE BEGETS REALITY

Enough. New day. Here. Be here now. And so, without really knowing how, Benji managed to pull himself into the present, shower, dress, forget to put in his contact lenses, pocket his Pez, exit and lock up his apartment, purchase the *Times* at a newsstand, and currently found himself walking down sleepy gray morning streets.

WEATHER: PARTLY SUNNY, A THUNDERSHOWER

A lone cloud passed over the sun, slowly, wholly, shadowing the street in a darker shade of gray. Looks like a hot one, thought Benji in black. Why always black? Gets hot. Black conducts? Reflects? Refracts? No, absorbs. What time is it? 10:25. Real job I would've been up two, three hours ago. Wow. Remember that publishing gig summers in college? Dress down Fridays. Same work different clothes. No sense at all.

SHORTAGE OF FOOD SUPPLIES NOTED

Benji put a hand in his corduroy pants pocket and felt around. I need Pez refills, he thought, snapping his empty dispenser.

LONG DISTANCE CARRIER

Entering the editing suite of Commercial Urban Models, Benji came upon Troy, unexpectedly engaged in an intimate telephone conversation:

"Yeah . . . yeah, uh huh? Uh huh? What are you wearing? That sounds niiiiiiiice . . . Look, baby, Daddy loves you but he's got bid-ness to tend to," said Troy, quickly cradling the phone.

"Who was that?" asked Benji.

"Sales call. Wanted us to change our long distance. You got a call this morning, too. Some lady," Troy said, passing a scrawled yellow message pad note to Benji. "Real polished sounding voice."

WHILE YOU WERE OUT

TIME: 9:45 A.M., Mon, 6/17
TO: Big Boss-man
FROM: Peggy Potluck?
OF: Fuller & Grand on 50th & 8th
RE: to sked appt.
PHONE: 975-3021

"Huh. She called me at home last night too. She say what she want?"

"Said she wanted to suck your dick for a dollar. You holding out on me boss-man?"

"No. You know my heart belongs to P."

"Benji-man, you need to get out more."

SEE MORE OF LIFE

5' 11" 195 lb., brwn hr, bl eyes, Jewish,
Ivy League educated failure. Interests
include long walks along moonlit
hores, museums, film, theatre, sodomy.
Photo a must.

DEWEY, CHEETAM, AND HOWE

"We're busted," Benji began, examining the message.

"What're you talking about?"

"Tax fraud."

Most of Commercial Urban Model's business came via phone and mail order, where the potential for fraud is very great. It worked like this: when someone orders an item over the phone with a credit card, when the bill comes from the credit card company all one has to do is say that they never ordered the item, that they know nothing about the transaction, and won't pay for it unless the creditor can provide them with a written record containing their signature. Since such a record cannot be produced, the creditor credits the cardholder's account and debits the merchant's account. These transactions are called charge-backs and account for any-where from three to five percent of phone and mail order sales.

Benji had figured out a way to reverse the situation and actually make a profit doing so. During particularly hard times, Benji would make up six-teen-digit credit card numbers and attempt to charge the holders for a sin-gle pornographic videotape, tapes he invariably would never send. He would spend hours running different combinations and permutations until one of them checked through the credit card machine. What Benji was counting on was that when Mr. or Mrs. Cardholder received their month-ly Visa bill with an unexpected charge of $29.95 for *Lesbo Bikini Beach: Where The Boys Aren't*, they'd be too embarrassed to call their bank to can-cel the charge. And it worked. As his production slate had fallen off, this practice had kept Benji in the black.

"We're fucked," Benji said, nonchalantly resigning himself to fate. "If it's not the credit card scam, we used a minor by mistake. I can't see any other reason why we'd be getting calls from lawyer bitches. Either way we're busted."

LIST, LIST, O LIST

"Recyclable or not recyclable?" Troy asked, presenting Benji with an empty yogurt container and a welcome opportunity to change the subject. "I dunno, not recyclable," Benji distractedly guessed.
"Wrong. Recyclable," Troy said, adding the words "yogurt container" to his most recent list: THINGS I DIDN'T THINK I COULD RECYCLE BUT REALLY CAN.

As his workload had diminished at Commercial Urban Models, rather than seek other employment, steadfastly loyal Troy had instead become something of a compulsive listmaker. Recent lists included: THINGS I CAN DO WHEN BENJI IS AWAY FROM THE OFFICE ("no. 3: switch long distance carrier, engage operator in small talk"), TOP TEN THINGS YOU ALWAYS SEE IN A PORNO ("No. 2: women walking up stairs"), and WAYS TO ECONOMIZE AROUND THE OFFICE ("No. 8: separate two-ply toilet tissue before wiping").

Troy made lists constantly, incessantly. Even more than editing films, he considered listmaking his life's work. He wouldn't go to sleep at night without first typing up and printing out a list of reminders of things to do the following day. (Reminders which often included such hygienic minu-tia as "shave" and "pick scab.") More than mere fastidiousness, these lists made Troy feel purposeful, especially given the lack of things to do at work. And there was no more satisfying occasion in his day than crossing off an item from his personal list of things to do. (Oftentimes "make list" would take pride of place on newly minted lists so that at least one task could be consigned to immediate oblivion.)

EXCITING NEW FALL LINE-UP

"You watching this?" Troy asked, referring to the television humming peripherally in the background.
"What?" asked Benji, distractedly scrambling together five crusty purple Pez from dirty corners of the soundboard.
"Some talk show. Mother and daughter. Haven't seen each other in three years. Daughter ran away to Cali to become an actress, ended up in porn."
"Yeah? Turn it up," Benji said, simultaneously reloading Mickey, placing his weight on a nearby stool and turning his attention to the

DEUS EX MACHINA

32" STEREO REMOTE COLOR TV W/2 TUNER PIP SEQ FRONT SURROUND SOUND COMB FILTER NITEVISION UNIVERSAL REMOTE 10-AV JACK PACK INCLUDING 2-S-VHS JACKS PARENTAL CONTROL A/V INPUT JACKS 10 WATT SOUND SYS-TEM WITH DBX NOISE REDUCTION FOR GREAT STEREO RECEP-

TION DIGITAL COMB FILTER FOR CLEAR PICTURE

IN MEDIAS RES

"I love Brad! I love his big f——— c— and I love f——— him on camera and I love making f— films and I'm gonna keep doing these forever and there's nothing you can f——— do about it!"

SECOND PERSON TRANSPORTATIVE FEMININE
IN THE EXCLAMATORY

"You go girl!" triple-snapped an audience member.
"YOU B——! YOU S—!"
Bleeped another.

THE MOUTHS OF BABES

"She has the right to claim her own sexuality!" declared a twenty-year-old girl in a highpitchedmiddleclassliberalartsexperimentingwithlesbianism accent.

THE STARR CHAMBER

Just three seconds of watching and Benji was reminded why he had given up on television. Thin sprayed Alexander Starr—of the double-breasted pinstripe, polka-dot tie, rimless spectacles, and sprayed-stiff bouffant—was handsome and thin, but not handsome enough to offend the populace. He was television handsome, that is, handsome without the animating beauty of intelligence, handsome without possessing troubling depths of character. (For, as old film noirs teach us, really good looks hurt.)

A meaningless institution, a signifier of nothing, Starr, following a three year stint as Mr. Philips, the wacky next-door neighbor on the popular network sitcom *Spilt Milk*, had been granted his own daytime talk show, the eponymously named *Starr Chamber*. The format was always the same.

Up and down the aisles with his magic wand he stalked, an emotional thermometer physically registering every nuance of his audience's empathy and disdain: stiffly upright posture for the old ladies in the audience, slacker-slouch for the kids, head conspiratorially tilted to the side for the blacks.

Everything Starr did, every mannequin's pose he struck, every whip and curdle of his creamy voice, every raised eyebrow and half-smile was practiced, polished, oiled, smooth: smoothed and oiled by the fill lights and pancake makeup and sighs and laughs emanating from his studio audience: oiled and smoothed by the very electrons fluctuating in the space between him and the camera, electrons driven wild by hot studio lights and the crush of bodies, electrons that showered the camera lens, that drove through cables, across switchboards, over wires, out antennas, off satellites, and into television sets in homes across the republic. A creature of pure television, Starr seemed to gain his very sustenance this way, electromagnetically, as if he were a rubber-suited Japanese monster. Coarse, hairy Benji sat there in appalled astonishment. He couldn't imagine this creature living in the same world as he, the world of subways and newsprint and curdled milk and grime, couldn't imagine this man taking the train in the morning, smearing his fingers with morning newspaper, tentatively sniffing the milk to see if it had gone bad.

YES, EVERYONE GETS ONE

"Who is this fucking clown?" Benji demanded. "What's the story these days, everyone gets one? You get a television just for showing up?"
"Yeah, that's right," Troy began, beginning a new list (WHY BENJI HATES ALEXANDER STARR). "Everyone gets one."

ZEITGEIST DENIED

"Now some people would say, Alexander, why are you doing another show on pornography. It's exploitation, it's titillation, it's just for ratings, etcetera, etcetera, etcetera. Well, think what you may, but that's not it. I think you're a fascinating person Missy. And you know what, you're gonna help us today, Missy. Missy, today you're gonna help us put our finger on the pulse of the zeitgeist."

"Wait, I told the man in the room before I came out there's certain things I wouldn't do on television."

"Okay, let's roll tape."

TEE PEE

"We obviously can't show this to our viewers at home, but, and forgive me for being crude, but it would appear that Ms. Missy is surrounded by and is, um, servicing three men at once. Describe what we're seeing here, Missy."

"That's called a Tee Pee," Missy provided helpfully.

"A Tee Pee?"

"Triple penetration."

TRI-PARTITE MAN-GOD, INVOKED

"O, God!" Missy's mother Mrs. Marple cried as she watched the video monitor from the stage.

"What? What are you feeling right now, Mrs. Marple? Madam? Our viewers want to know?" Starr asked, racing down the aisle to prod the matriarch with his microphone.

"I believe God will provide and lead my baby out of this wilderness of confusion and sin," Mrs. Marple said through broken sobs.

"Jesus fucking Christ!" Benji exclaimed, slapping his right hand against his forehead in a successful attempt to lead a few hundred thousand brain cells to a happy death. "Why do these chromosome cases always have to bring God into it? If they really believed in God, the first thing they'd know about his program is that what he's fundamentally against more than anything else is boredom. Read the Bible lady! Homeboy likes to fuck shit up!"

GOD: THE THEORY

"So wait, you believe in God?" Troy asked, excitedly beginning a new list (WHY BENJI BELIEVES!).

"God's just a word. But it's what's behind the word that counts, the thing the word signifies, the things that can't be expressed in words."

"Yeah, but you still didn't answer the question."

"Do I believe in God? Well, I believe enough to think there're still things left in His dominion worth sinning against. I believe enough to know that sometimes transgression is the highest form of tribute you can pay Him."

TRANSGRESSION IN THE HOUSE OF CHRISTENDOM

In the spring of his sophomore year, Benji spent a semester studying abroad in Rome, Italy, the highlight of the excursion proving to be Benji's masturbating in a bathroom stall atop the roof of St. Peter's Church, the holiest locus in all Christendom. The first blasphemy in a life full of blasphemies, explanations for this seminal moment of transgression include:

CIVILIZATION

It was a salute to Rome's pagan past.

CELEBRATION

After two days in Italy, astounded by yellow and gold table wines and pastas and sauces and gelato and hissing espresso machines and polyester and silk and sandals and fragrance and ruins and rock and motor scooters and bluegreen Mediterranean seas and bloodred Mediterranean suns, confronted by this ceaseless parade of beauty, there was no alternative, nothing left to do but offer sacrifice, a small, heartfelt tribute to everything lush and luscious on God's good earth.

CEREBRATION

If the act did not exist, fiction would make it so, for everything imaginable is human, and fiction is the realm in which all will be played out.

(OVER) COMPENSATION

The act was self-consciously performed: the Nice Jewish Boy From Brooklyn asking, *How bad can I be?* in an arena where he knew the Gods would be listening.

RATIONALIZATION: JUSTIFICATION

It was blasphemy, plain and simple. And an inspired bit of blasphemy at that, for if in theory the central tenets of Christ were, on the one hand, a coolly pre-socialistic belief that wealth and materialism are not the answer, and, on the other, an overriding spirit of acceptance and love, then in practice, His church was, as Benji saw it, surely one of the richest, most corrupt, intolerant institutions on earth, one whose entire existence was predicated on the denial of the basic fact of animal fucking.

Traveling through Italy, bombarded by the iconography of Christendom, Benji was never more conscious of his status as a Jew. He had always fashioned himself an outsider, and perhaps even courted the role, but now, abroad at last, he was angered that the position may have been to some extent historically preordained for him.

A long-time Charlton Heston fan, Benji had seen *The Agony and the Ecstasy* just before crossing the Atlantic and pledged to himself to track down as much of Michelangelo's work as he could. Visiting the San Pietro in Vincoli the day after landing in Rome, once inside the darkened church Benji was disgusted to find that he had to put a 500 lire coin into a machine that resembled a parking meter in order to illuminate the master's Moses (a Moses that, besides an inexplicable set of horns, looked remarkably like Charlton Heston in *The Ten Commandments*). The next day, he was appalled to find stands selling Kodak film and souvenir tchotchkes inside the halls of the Vatican.

Worse, traveling through Florence some weeks later, Benji had visited the Academia, where Michelangelo's David loomed from above in all his ill-proportioned splendor. From some angles confident, from some hesitant, from some pensive, what struck Benji most about the sculpture (beside the expressive malleability of his mask), was that this magnificent Jewish specimen, this pinnacle of Hebraic heroism, this Semite stud looked decidedly Italian, and worse still, was uncircumcised! In silence and disbelief, Benji stood before the famous cold marble cock and pledged to take action.

BAPTIZATION: EJACULATION VIA MASTURBATION, SANS LUBRICATION

On the third day, He had risen, and lassoing streams of goo from the head of his proudly circumcised prick, Benji was comforted by the certainty that Christ—the scrappy insurrectionist Jew—had, along with divinity, come equipped with a Jewish sense of humor. Give unto Caesar that which is Caesar's, Benji thought to himself as he treated the St. Peter's stall to a seminal moment.

REALIZATION: TRIVIALIZATON

While all of these explanations remain possibilities, the reality of the situation was this: in churches across Italy Benji watched helplessly as Kingsley Roth, his multilingual warty toad of a roommate, scored with dark-haired babushka after dark-haired babushka. Benji's masturbation then was an act of hopelessness disguised as a challenge: his sad, shy attempt to out-fillip Roth.

BENJI IS A DOG

"O, God. O, God," The woman cried, weeping into Starr's thickly padded shoulder.
"I love making these movies mom! And I'm gonna keep on making them! I'm a big f——— star and there's nothing you can do about it!"
"O-o God . . ."
"She doesn't get it does she? This is God. She's staring into the face of God. You wanna know if I believe in God? Yeah, I do, 'cause I see Him everywhere. It's recognizing Him where you wouldn't think to look, that's the trick. A woman staggering away from a gang bang video to fight for another day—that's God. A gaper the size of a silver dollar—that's God.

God is a shout in the street. I see God everywhere, Troy. I see God every time I take a crap."

THE AGE OF ABSURDITY

"That's some pretty heavy shit," Troy marveled.

"Yeah, well I watch this shit and I'm convinced that God must be dead because I refuse to believe that God would make anyone so fucking stupid! And lemme tell you something, if God is dead, we're truly living in the age of absurdity, and there're no stakes left and everything's fucked!"

FASHION TREND NOTED

"Okay, we're going to go to a commercial," Alexander crooned. "But we'll be right back to hear what the experts have to say about Missy, her mom, and America's war on pornography, after this." "Hey Benji," Troy asked as the camera craned across the audience, landing on a black woman in a tank-top whose exposed right shoulder was decorated with a Mercedes Benz emblem. "When did everyone start getting tattoos?"

"I don't know," Benji answered. "Used to be only sailors, convicts, and circus freaks had 'em. Used to be advertising was something you'd only see on television, billboards, or magazines. Then people started wearing shirts with logos on them. Now I guess you just tattoo the ad right on your body. Progress."

"Yeah," Troy yawned.

HYPNOGOGUES, WE

"Keeping you up? Y'know in college, in film class I learned this word. It's called hypnogogic. The hypnogogic state. It refers to the moment between sleep and awake, that floating moment of suspension between sleep and wakefulness. I always thought that word describes the way things are now better than anything else. With everything we have to do, with all the information coming at us, we're anesthetized: work-weary: sleep-deprived: numb. We've become a nation of hypnogogues. A hypnogogic culture."

CLIMAX, THE FRAGRANCE

Wispily, a commercial materialized on the screen. As some ersatz-classical music played in the background, five or six androgynous, undulating bodies languorously writhed in creamy black-and-white. Then, a heavily accented Aryan girl, a sylphid gamine, looked directly into the camera and asked in Germanic tones of high seriousness, "Are you ready for Climax?" "What is this shit?" demanded Benji, throwing his rolled up newspaper at the television screen with a whack! "At least porno's up front about who's fucking whom."

ALEXANDER STARR, PUNSTER

"Okay, we're back. Today we're talking about pornography and feminism," singsonged Starr, on-camera and alive once more. "We've already seen first hand how pornography can destroy, demolish, and decimate a normal American household in the case of Missy and Mrs. Marple. Now it's time to look at the issue through the eyes of the experts. Now some feminists would argue that there's no difference between men and women, that the only difference between us resides in a single tiny little chromosome. Well, speaking as a man, I think there's a vas deferens between men and women," Starr said, smiling into the camera conspiratorially. "A vas deferens. And to discuss some of those differences with us, I'd like to introduce the first of today's experts. She's the author of *Pornography and Rape: Theory and Practice*, and *The Myth of Consensual Intercourse*, please welcome radical lesbian feminist Corrine Dwarfkin."

ENTER THE DWARFKIN

And there she was: a lumbering three hundred pound pentadactyl monster, a frowning, sexless woman dressed in blue overalls and flats, topped with a seventies-style fro, her angry, unhappy mouth lending her the expression of a person condemned to carry a small turd beneath her nose through eternity.
"Now that's my idea of a fucking bull dyke," Troy marveled.

POPULARITY OF LESBIAN-THEMED VIDEOS, EXPLAINED

Watching her take the stage, Benji was reminded of the battles of '88, when Dwarfkin successfully campaigned to close three X-rated movie theaters in Times Square and unsuccessfully lobbied for the introduction of a new zoning bill that would have pushed most of the sex shops to the outskirts of Queens and Staten Island. That year Benji had taken the liberty of naming a couple of lesbian videos in her honor including *Corrine Dwarfkin's Box Lunch* and *Corrine Dwarfkin's All You Can Eat At The Y*.

"Benji, why do you think lesbian videos are so popular with straight men?" Troy asked, transcribing.
"I think it has to do with this idea some people have that there's no such thing as a true lesbian. In other words the guy watching envisions that once he were to enter the picture with his big hard cock the two women would just immediately drop everything and start fucking him instead."
"No, I think it's simpler than that," said Troy, pen suspended in midair, considering this explanation for a moment. "Instead of one naked woman, there's two. Math, Benjamin. Math."

THE MYTH OF CONSENSUAL INTERCOURSE, EXPLAINED

"Before we continue, just to get us up to speed, why don't you explain to our audience the basic premise of your book?" Starr prodded the Dwarfkin.
"Yes. In capsule form, my thesis is that heterosexual intercourse is the pure, distilled expression of men's contempt for women. Throughout history, men have used intercourse to exploit, occupy, invade, degrade, and colonize the female body. And, since the world is a patriarchy ruled by men who fundamentally hate women, no act of intercourse between men and women can ever be viewed as truly consensual."

THE VIOLATION OF THE SOCKET

"Why do I get the feeling no one asked her to the prom?" Benji chuckled unhappily, simultaneously leaning into the television screen and massaging his still stiff neck. "Hey Troy, how many feminists does it take to screw in a light bulb?"
"How many?"

"Two. One to screw it in, the other to discuss the violation of the socket."

ENTER THE ANAGRAM

"And now to help us look at the issue from the inside, she's the writer-director of over one hundred pornographic feminist videos including *Renaissance Whore*, please help me in welcoming Ms. Winnow Screenlad."

And there she was: a strong tall woman, tall and strong across the shoulders and back, the kind of woman one refers to as handsome. In the equine length of her face and the musky olive of her complexion, in the dusky smoke of her almond eyes and the mellifluousness of her voice, in her gallows humor and the depth of her laughter, she could have passed for Benji's long-lost sister.

"It looks like Nixon-Kennedy up there," Troy marveled.

WHERE'S THE MEESE?

"In their 1986 report," Starr began, "Attorney General Edwin Meese's Commission on Pornography reported that they believed the use of pornography is addictive and progressive, and that pornography perpetuates the so-called 'rape myth.'"

"Correct," the Dwarfkin corroborated, "The Meese commission bravely established that pornography is the theory and rape the practice."

"But the Meese commission was a puppet show, it can't be taken seriously," Screenlad rebutted. "First, it represents a direct contradiction of the 1970 President's Commission on Obscenity and Pornography which concluded that there's no evidence demonstrating a causal relationship between sexually explicit material and sex crimes."

"Yes, but the nature of pornography has changed dramatically over the last two decades. It's become progressively more derogatory, violent, and fetishistic in nature," the Dwarfkin countered.

"Well, that may be true, but we need to keep a few things in mind. First, if you read the Meese commission in its entirety—which I did, God help me, all one thousand pages of it—the first thing that leaps out at you is that their thesis is predicated on a wild contradiction. That is, while the members of the commission were apparently unaffected by spending an entire year wading in the worst of pornographic waters, they remain convinced that the average American would be transformed into a criminal or deviant by his or her encounters with the same material. Next, the language of the report made it clear that the commission was patently against the explicit depiction of sex in general. They found sexual representation of any stripe offensive and harmful in and of itself. But finally, Corrine, it surprises me that you, as a lesbian and an avowed feminist, would choose to align yourself on this issue with the conservative right, the same group that would deny you your right to an abortion."

"I'd never allow a man to impregnate me," the Dwarfkin offered.

"Regardless, the Meese commission was a puritanical charade. The tone of the report made it clear: the commission wasn't antipornography so much as antiwoman. It wasn't pornography the commission was afraid of so much as the idea of sexualized women in general. The commission, which in all its one thousand pages, didn't bother to recommend a platform of sex education, was more concerned with censoring sexual depictions than with eliminating violence against women."

"But even if I agree with you that the Meese Commission's report was deeply, deeply flawed," the Dwarfkin demurred, "the fact remains that pornography is inherently harmful. It exists to subjugate, violate, and objectify women."

EROTIC, QUIXOTIC

"You want to attribute the inequality of women in society to dirty pictures? Pornography's an industry like any other. It's about money! It's a waste of your time!"

CORRINE DWARFKIN, FEMINIHILIST

"How can you make these films and consider yourself a feminist?!"

"Wait a sec—"

"How can you use these women in films—"

"Wait—"

"Ladies, please!"

"You're not a feminist!"

"I never said I was a feminist."

WINNOW SCREENLAD, SEXIST

"Please, ladies, I know this is a hot topic, but let's try to ask and answer questions in an orderly manner," Alexander refereed. "Ms. Screenlad, you've just been accused of being a feminist."
"As a rule, I find being labeled undesirable. But," Screenlad said, catching her breath and holding it for a regal pause, "if I had to label myself, I suppose I would label myself a sexist."
"A sexist?"
"Yes, a sexist. I'm not a feminist and I'm certainly not a masculinist. So, yes, if I had to choose, I'd call myself a sexist. Because I believe in the differences between the sexes. And I believe in sex."

PORNOTOPIA, A PRINCEDOM BY THE SEA

"Yes, there are aspects of the industry I find distasteful, and you don't find them in my films, which are predominantly women-centered and focus on women's pleasure," Screenlad began, gaining composure. "As someone who's worked in the sex industry for close to a decade, let me shoot down some myths. Not every woman who works in the sex industry is underage, not every woman in the sex industry is a drug addict or has been sexually abused. In fact, I think what a radical feminist like yourself would fear more than anything is a beautiful young woman getting up here and saying, 'I'm not a drug user and I wasn't molested as a child. I'm a sex worker and I enjoy it, and I feel less exploited doing this than working in a McDonald's for five dollars an hour or being ogled by my boss in a secretary pool.'"
"And we'll be back after this!"

WORLD WIDE WASTE OF TIME

As the picture faded to video black, on the bottom of the screen in discrete white letters appeared the show's website address: www.starrchamber.com.

"Ever check it out?" Benji asked.

"Yeah."

"What they got in there?"

"Starr's bio . . . chat rooms . . . clips of fights that've broken out on the show . . . um, that time Starr got an on-air ass-lift by the Nazi plastic surgeon, lots of unexpurgated titty shit, and some T-shirts and stuff you can buy."

"Huh. You have an account at home?"

"Benji, we have our own website."

"O, yeah."

"Benji, if you were any more out of it, you'd back up into it."

THE GREAT AMERICAN LONELY

At that moment, a loud beeping noise dopplered through the room, interrupting the conversation. For a moment, the pair couldn't tell whether the sound was emanating from the phone, the fax, the television, the fire alarm, the clock radio, the VCR, the microwave, the computer modem, or Troy's cellular. Synaptically rifling through the "sound=machine" file of his short-term memory, Troy robotically answered the phone:

"Hello, Commercial Urban Models . . . I told you baby, Daddy's already happy with his long distance carrier. O.K. baby, Daddy's gotta go now . . ."

"I don't know," Benji began, clinging to the thread of conversation, "Technology promises to speed everything up, to make everything faster and more efficient, but I think it creates the opposite effect. If you're plugged in all the time, if you're available all the time, don't you end up filling your life with clutter, don't you end up devaluing those connections?"

"Yeah, but don't you think it's cool how the net can bring like-minded folk together. Like every day I check this website for hot prison bitches, and my special e-ladyfriend LaTonya's getting out in three months—"

"So what? You can play chess with a stranger in Malaysia? You can put your time in on the flight simulator? In the end you're just home alone staring at a computer screen."

AMERICA, A PORNOCRATIC REPUBLIC

"And you know who's to blame? We are."

"Huh?"

"Pinot and technology. Pornography leads and technology follows. Print, movies, video, the internet: technology always advances as a way of pollinating porn. You think the printing press was invented because Gutenberg wanted to give Bibles to his friends for Christmas? No, man, he invented it to spread dirty pictures. Technology is to porn what cigarettes are to nicotine: that is, a delivery system."

"Huh."

"Think about it. The only websites that post a profit are porn-related. And the boom economy everyone keeps talking about is being driven by all these overvalued internet stocks. And America's the economic leader of the world. So, in certain important respects, porn powers the globe."

THE FIRST TIME

"Hey Benji, you remember the first time you watched pinot?" Troy asked wistfully.

"Baby, you always remember your first."

MORT DAY

In late March of 1976 Benji's uncle on his father's side, Mort, had decided, for reasons unknown to all, that after twenty-two years of marriage, he was calling it quits with his wife. Unbeknownst to Mort, it was decreed that April 3rd, 1976 would be Conference On Mort Day, during which Mort's six brothers and two sisters would drive or fly down to Jersey and convene on poor, timid, arthritic, balding, disheveled Mort, in order to convince him for the sake of Esther, for the sake of the children, for the sake of tradition (Tradition!) to hang in there, just hang in there.

To Jerry and Benji what mattered most was neither their uncle's split with his wife, nor their father's palpable rage as he shouted at his brother over the phone. No, what mattered most was that their parents would be away for a night: a rare and solemn window of opportunity for the boys to engage in some form of transgression, an opportunity that Jerry, bright and clever Jerry, was determined to take full advantage of.

Jerry had heard from friends about mail order catalogues that delivered 16mm pornographic film strips to your home in discrete brown paper packages for thirty dollars. The details remained sketchy in Benji's mind, but, after forking over fifteen dollars of Chanukah gelt to Jerry he was repeatedly assured, "Not to worry."

OFT PROCLAIMS THE MAN

Benji remembered what he was wearing that night. His favorite pair of blue jeans. Size twenty. A normal boy's size. This after two years of shopping in over-sized boy's clothing stores, clothing stores with names like "Mom's Big Boy" and "Big Little Fella" and "Huskies" on 13th Avenue in the Hasidic Jewish section of Brooklyn, of being made to stand on small, shaky wooden platforms in the center of stores like a performing seal and lift his shirt while bearded, stale-smelling salesmen wrapped yellow tape measures round his swollen smooth pink girth. But, now, after six months of dieting, twelve-year-old Benji was in fighting trim. And better, having proven himself an enthusiastic if clumsy third baseman, his jeans were even a little threaded, a little mud-encrusted, a little packed with dust, a little decorated with the patriotic rips and tears of the all-American crazy.

What else was Benji wearing? Black-and-white Converse sneakers, which were falling to pieces, the rubber sole of the left foot barely holding onto the threading of the shoe body. But Benji refused to trade them for another pair. The summer before, on the bus going home from his final day of camp, Sheila McPetry, a little blonde girl Benji had a crush on, had embroidered a little design around the sole of his left shoe using a black ballpoint pen. To Benji, the mysteries of the universe, the secrets of the Cabala, the riddle of the sphinx, the music of the spheres were contained in the lines and squiggles and loops of the girl's design. And more than that, the shoe held erotic promise for Benji, promise that with camp just three months away, he would see Sheila again. (He didn't. And never would again.)

T&A WITH M.M.

Benji also wore a Mickey Mouse T-shirt. His favorite one, the shirt featured Mickey at his most iconographic with embossed, clear plastic eye pouches in which circular black irises were free to bounce around. When Benji walked, the jiggling irises leant Mickey's face a crude animation, but, in these next few moments, Mickey's eyes, like Benji's, were glued straight ahead. Steely-nerved in anticipation of committing his first illicit adult act, unblinking Benji remained frozen, and Mickey matched him in concentration.

First Jerry insisted on making both of them drinks from their parent's stash of booze. (Theirs being a Jewish household, this was no small trick, as most of the liquor bottles had unbroken seals.) Not knowing the proper ratio of vodka to orange juice that goes into a screwdriver—and loving the word "screwdriver" too much to abandon the project—Jerry estimated 50:50 and poured the drinks by the mugful. (Leading Benji to spend a good part of the night vomiting, vomiting not so much from the alcohol as the cup of Listerine he had gargled with and then swallowed in panic as his parents made their way up the front porch steps some twelve hours ahead of schedule.)

After a toast, they brought the dusty projector up from the basement, cleared a place for it on the living room coffee table, plugged it in, drew the blinds, threaded the film through the gate, and began.

BABE, THE FARMER'S DAUGHTER

The projector was a rattling 16mm number on which Benji's parents watched films of their wedding every anniversary and argued, with equal passion, over food and disease. (Death and the Viennese Table: They were chocolate eclairs! No, Napoleons! He died of kidney failure! No, it was gout!) The summer before, Benji's father, practicing his newfangled golf swing in anticipation of a business convention in Arizona, had accidentally torn the screen in two, so the boys were forced to project the film against the living room wall, with parts of the black-and-white image curving across books, sliding over mantles, contaminating family heirlooms with its feathery touch.

The name of the silent short was *Babe, The Farmer's Daughter*, and, in the days prior to the exhibition, the name alone—which the brothers had invoked as an incantation, a talisman, a shibboleth—had driven Benji dizzy with lust, the notion of a girl growing up on a farm in the American heartland knee-deep in hay and cowshit being as extravagantly exotic to him as a Tahitian topless.

For all that, Benji knew nothing of sex. When he thought of a girl he liked, he imagined kissing her, or braiding her hair, or giving her candy, or if he really, really liked her, maybe one day marrying her. Sex didn't exist as a mystery to Benji so much as a void the existence of which he remained blissfully unaware.

The picture flickered to life, and there she was: Babe, the befreckled blonde farmer's daughter milking a cow, a dungareed princess on a toad-stool. Every so often there would be a cut to her hand wrapped around one of the cow's udders, then a shot of Babe concentrating hard, then a cut back to her hand in the same position, this time stroking a cock. This went on for several minutes until a mustachioed cowpoke entered the hayloft and there was an abrupt cut to full penetration.

HORSE MANURE

"She was only a farmer's daughter," Jerry commented, "but all the horse men knew her."

GUNCH

"What's that, Jerry?" Benji asked, tugging at his brother's sleeve during an extreme close-up of Babe's shaved pudendum. "It looks like a turkey giz-zard."
"That," Jerry said solemnly, "is gunch."

FLASHFORWARD

"You remember when your brother came out?" Troy asked hesitantly, familiar with the story.

"Yeah, I was in college."

"Did you suspect it?"

"I think so."

"How'd you take it?"

"I don't remember."

FLASHBACK: YEP, I'M GAY

"Hey Benji."

"Jer, man, 'sup?"

"I have something important to tell you, and I want you to know you're the first person I'm coming to with this."

"Okay. Shoot."

"Jerry's gay."

Pause.

"Hello. You still there?"

"Yeah."

"Did you hear what I said? I said Jerry's gay. Your brother's gay. Jerry's gay. Don't you have anything to say about that?"

"Why are you talking about yourself in the third person?"

THEORY AND PRACTICE

"It's just so obvious to me," the Dwarfkin demanded, snapping Benji back into the present. "Pornography incites men to violence toward women."

"Like there was no rape in the world before pornography," Screenlad countered. "The antiporn crusaders are always so quick to whip out rape statistics, but just imagine what the rape statistics would be without porn."

"Just answer the question! Do you or do you not believe that pornography incites violence against women?"

JAPS, BLACKS

"No I do not. To give an example from another culture: Japanese films and animé are notorious for their depiction of bondage and rape, usually of teenage girls, and yet Japan has one of the lowest rates of rape of any industrialized country in the world. Why? Because the Japanese view eroticized rape in films as a cathartic valve for the expression of unacceptable behavior. Conversely, why are African Americans, Black Americans, who are among the lowest consumers of porn in this country, so over-represented among those arrested and convicted of rape? It's not from watching porn. Maybe it has something to do with an economically disenfranchised minority asserting a sense of masculinity and aggression in a misguided way. Violence against women has little or nothing to do with pornography, at least as far as the Japanese and Black American communities are concerned."

FLASHBACK, PART II: INTERVIEW WITH THE PORNOGRAPHER

"You look pretty skinny to wanna go into porn. You must be packing some heat then, right? 'Cause that's what they want to see. Down south. The racist motherfuckers. Miscegenation's what they want. It's wild. That's the shit that sells. Up north it's guys named Cohen want to see Mary Jo take it in the ass, down south it's Babe the farmer's daughter stuffed full of big black cock."

Young Troy Marcus sat silently across from Benjamin Seymour, the man he had first seen in *Lawrence of A Labia*, the film that had changed his life. Troy was a first-year graduate student at NYU's Tisch School of the Arts when he'd seen the film and decided on the spot to seek out this man, his Lawrence, for employment. Made toward the end of his association with Penny, in *A Labia* Benji had already gone to seed, had already started showing nascent signs of paunch, but there was such tenderness, such latent equipoise to his lovemaking, such poignancy in his strained unathleticism: it was clear that these two sex performers were deeply, passionately in love. Troy had never seen anything like it.

"No you don't understand, I don't wanna—"
"What you don't do straight?" Benji asked.
"No, no, no," Troy answered, catching his breath. "I don't want to be in the movies, I want to get into production."
"Production? This is a casting call buddy!"
"I know that but I want to help you. Behind the scenes. Shooting. Editing.

Sound. I'm about to graduate NYU."

"And you wanna go into pinot?"

"Look, I'm not interested in making hood movies, or playing step-n-fetch getting coffee for people on the set."

"Lemme get this straight, you're about to graduate the top film school in the country and you wanna go into pinot? Why?"

Troy thought hard, and answered honestly.

"Because pinot can't hurt you, and pinot never says no."

"You're hired."

PORNO: A THEORY IN FOUR PARTS

"There are four major reasons why I support pornography and think it's necessary for the health of society," Screenlad explained. "First, pornography shows what people will do for money, and that, especially in a capitalist culture, is endlessly instructive."

"That's really glib!" roared the Dwarfkin, burning with rage and dyspepsia.

"Maybe not. Why is it that former Communist countries such as Czechoslovakia are such hotbeds of pornography these days? One could argue it's because sexuality is the one aspect of life that even Communist regimes couldn't control.

"The next reason has to do with pornography and the role of the artist in society. Why has so much of the greatest, most adventurous, most ground-breaking art of this century been originally shouted down with cries of obscenity? The intersection between art and pornography is endlessly fascinating and will always remain so, because if the artist does his work honestly, he's bound to offend certain members of society."

"Those are all very well-positioned intellectual ideas, but you still haven't addressed the actual imagery of pornography: women forced to shove broom handles and guns up their v———, women spread out like slabs of meat in front of the camera for the pleasure of men."

"What I've never been able to understand about the feminist argument against pornography is that you're saying you're fighting for the rights of women to do what they want with their bodies, but then turn around and say, 'No, I don't approve of that.' How is taking away that choice, or condemning that choice, any worse than siding with the right to lifers?"

"Because pornography as it exists in this country is explicitly antiwoman! It's the theory of every hateful stereotype of women put into practice solely for the pleasure of hateful misogynists."

"Okay, look, does pornography subjugate, humiliate, and objectify women? Yes, some of it does. Perhaps even most of it does. But to try to eliminate pornography would suggest that violence, subjugation, and objectification don't exist in sex. And our experience teaches us that that's simply not the case. Violence, subjugation, objectification—even humiliation—those elements are a part of sex. They may not always be a part of sex, they may not be the most important part, or the best part, or the healthiest part, but they are a part, perhaps as important a part of the mix as tenderness and compassion. And if those elements are just one tenth of one percent of the mix, they deserve to be accounted for. You can't politicize fantasy. You shouldn't try."

The credits began to roll over Screenlad's pleasant pale-oak face. The audience was applauding.

"But finally, what porn shows, rather poignantly I feel, is the limitations of the human experience. I think people are drawn to porn because they feel it can offer them a glimpse of what they think they're missing, some hidden erotic world, but—and I'm saying this as someone who makes and loves porn—if you watch the stuff for more than five minutes, what you discover is how circumscribed it all is. In the end, you're dealing with a finite number of protuberances and orifices. Put plainly, there's only so much you can do with a p—— and a v——. And so, pornography becomes a rather poignant expression of the human limitations we're all condemned to."

LOVE CONNECTION AT 11:30

The credits continued to roll over electronic synthesizer music as the picture cut to Mrs. Marple's face from earlier in the program, weeping in slow motion.

"Show's over?"

"Yup."

"That's it, huh?"

"Yup."

"What's on next?"

"*Love Connection*."

"*Love Connection*, huh?"

"Yup."

"Turn that shit off."

THEORY OF RELATIVITY

"It's only television, Benji."

"Yeah, and people only spend half their waking lives watching it. Troy, we just watched fucking *Medea*. A family destroyed for our delectation, and then—Bam!—onto *Love Connection*. Only it's all the same. It's all fun and games."

"Slow down doggy."

"We're crippling our capacity for a normal emotional existence. Look, okay, you're watching the evening news and they show some footage of firefights in Beirut or some starving kid with flies buzzing around his head in Africa, then they cut to Michael Jordan scoring forty-seven points during the playoffs, then to Hurricane Hannah brewing off the coast of the Philippines, then to the weekend box office grosses for Mission: Impossible, then to a McDonald's commercial about some octogenarian who's finally found peace and happiness slinging greasy fries for kids. Only the commercial's rigged to elicit as much of a reaction as the atrocities. More of a reaction! More of a reaction! I've cried over some of those commercials! And I know I'm being manipulated, I know I'm being conned, but I care more about the McDonald's guy than the starving kid in Africa! Why? Because everything's relative. Because it's all coming at us so fast all you can do is hope your circuitry is still capable of producing a normal response, so you're actually relieved when the copywriting cocksuckers are able to get a rise out of you."

EVERYTHING IS A HEADLINE

"Y'ever look at the paper on a slow news day? It's the same fucking size as on election day! Why? Because everything's a headline. Newspapers, magazines, books, movies, phones, faxes, the internet, there's so much information coming at us every second per second screaming for our attention, it's impossible to interpret how we should engage ourselves emotionally, morally, intellectually. Our wires are crossed. Our circuitry is blown. We're losing it. We're losing our capacity to feel, to have a normal human response to things. And for what? All in the name of better, faster, more.

Look at this crap! Look!" he gasped, picking the newspaper from off the floor, rolling it up again, and hurling it at Chuck Woolery. "There is no love connection!" Benji said desperately, a single tear hanging from each eye like drapery.

"You got mail," announced a disembodied voice from Troy's Compaq.

"What's that?" asked Benji, alarmed.

"PC," Troy said.

PC?

"Fuck PC!," Benji exclaimed. "That's not a movement. You're gonna tell me some eighteen-year-old Wesleyan student getting upset because her professor calls her girl instead of woman makes for a friggin' movement?! Martin Luther King getting sprayed with a fire hose—now that's a movement! Kids getting stoned to Jimi Hendrix and fucking on the grass at Woodstock—that's a movement! Feminism? Everyone knows feminism's just for rich white bitches anyway. They want business suits and laptops? Fuck 'em, let 'em have it. But multiculturalism? Political correctness? Who are these things for anyway? I mean, the only thing that makes PC interesting is how it shows a jaded society's wish to reinstate some kind of sense of fragility, of propriety, however fake. But since when did this country become so polite? You're gonna tell me after the sexual revolution, after the assassinations, after Vietnam and Watergate, you're gonna tell me there's still someone out there capable of being shocked by a word? PC only exists because those words don't mean anything any more."

"NIGGER"

"Even the word nigger is in quotes. Hey Troy, hear any good 'nigger' jokes lately?" Benji asked, holding up two fingers on each hand, Nixon-on-the-tarmac-style, to frame the offending word. "What do five niggers call a white guy?"

"They'd call him 'coach' wouldn't they Jew-man?"

"Yeah, that's right. Look, all I'm saying is, once the word nigger is ironized, italicized, inoculated, we've moved into some pretty heavy shit."

BENJAMIN SEYMOUR, POET

"Benji, you're a poet and you don't know it."

BENJAMIN SEYMOUR, PONTIFICATOR OF CUNT

"I'm no poet, baby. I'm a cuntificator."

TALK BEGETS PLOT

"All right, enough talk," Benji said, crumpling the phone message in his hand and lifting his heft off the stool.
"Time for some plot," he said, and with that, was out the door.

6

Food. What would Pez taste like if I just let one dissolve in my mouth? Just let it rest on the tongue. Mix with saliva. Acidic juices. How long would it last? Benji removed a Pez from his Mickey Mouse dispenser and began the experiment, the same one he had been unable to see to fruition in all his years of eating hard candies. Lollipops, peppermint twists, butterscotch drops, red and green striped candy canes, menthol throat lozenges: nothing was immune to the ferocious work ethic of Benji's teeth. Not even freezing ice cream scoops could escape the ferocious chomp and chew of his all-consuming jaw.

I'm hungry, thought Benji, crunching down. What to eat? Hot day. Sweating already. Maybe just a drink. Iced coffee? Hm. No. Caffeine and sugar. Bad mix. Tears through the system. Gives me the shits. Haven't gone yet today. Better eat first. Balance things out. Eat you. I'm going to eat you. Tent of love. Pit of excrement. Close biologically. Funny when you think about it. I'm hungry. Find something along the way. Fuller and Grand. 50th between 8th and 9th. Not too far.

Peggy Potluck? Pockmark? Queer name, Benji thought. First thing we do, let's kill all the lawyers. What is it she wants? Fraud? Zoning law? Eviction? Bankruptcy? Worse. Underage girl. Arrest. Trial. Conviction. Jail. Small room like now. Bells, books, and buggery. The comforts of home. Probably best to call first, but I hate getting bad news by phone. Just hate the phone. Only half a conversation. Especially with people you don't know.

Need to see. The eyes. The hands. Better in person. To see.

A well-coiffed man in a gray flannel suit passed before him, voraciously tearing into a gyro sandwich wrapped in aluminum foil, careful to protect his suit and tie from twin dripping streams of tahini sauce and meat juices spackling the street. Ariadne's thread. Minotaur meat. Comes in a loaf. No bones. How? Packed? Compressed? Mixture of meats. Could be anything. Dead cat? Cover with lettuce, tomato, and onion, can't tell the difference. Shh. No one will know. Benji stood before the sandwich stand for a moment, examining its contents. Grilled crosshatched chicken breasts stacked by the dozen. Cubes of coal-black beef on skewers. Toasted piles of pita bread. Buckets filled with green and white sauce. Black-encrusted grease-grill. Flies circling round garlicky billows of smoke heat. No. Too hot for meat. Just lays there, worming its way through your tubes. Something cool. Light. A salad? Pizza. Original Ray's. Who's Ray? Who the fuck is Ray? Second, third, and fourth generation Ray, all searching for the original. Century after century, branch after branch of the family tree combing the city looking for the original pizza-slinger. Not even real pizza. Too doughy. Italian pizza more delicate. Like matzo. Cracker thin. Pizza in Rome with hardboiled egg and bacon and goat cheese. Hmm. Light yellow table wine. So sweet it doesn't even hit you until you get up to leave. Strong black coffee. Olives. Mint gelato with whipped cream. Hot Mediterranean sun. Hands on the Parthenon at night. Cool, cool stone. Western Civ. Italy. He stood before a pizza store on the corner of 33rd and 8th. Ices? Rainbow, cherry, lemon, orange, coconut, piña colada. None of them taste like fruit. Like Life Savors. Tastes like sugar, all of them.

He continued walking up Eighth Avenue, behind the back of Penn Station, past the subway entrance for the A,C, or E. City beneath the city. Bunion hurts. Could take it. Haven't in a while. Be faster. Don't know it well enough though. Terrible sense of direction. Just terrible. Fell asleep that time ended up in Queens. And tokens are so easy to lose. Maybe one day computer'll do that too. Charge it. Put it on my card. Card for every-thing: driver's license, bank account, social security card, credit card, gym card, why not the subway? Life history on a card. Good for first dates. Let's not talk about my childhood, here's my card.

"Jesus is coming," said a smiling, clean-shaven, orange-shirted young man; distributing fliers a few feet from him, the young man both blocked his path and broke his line of thought.

"What's that?"

"Jesus is coming," the young man said, suddenly thrusting a flyer into Benji's hand. Benji stopped in his tracks for a moment and looked at the flyer, a piece of yellow paper featuring a familiar personage, arms out-stretched, with rays of light emanating from his thorny crown. Superimposed over the image were the words:

Jesus Is Coming!
Are You Ready?

"Well you tell him if he can come twice in five minutes I got a job wait-ing for him when he gets here," said Benji, crunching the flyer up into a tight little ball and tossing it down the street with the practiced form of a professional bowler.

"Jesus loves you!"

"Thanks, Christer," Benji said over his shoulder, continuing his march.

"Jesus loves you!"

Sneaky bastard. Didn't even see him coming. What makes someone do that? Hand out flyers like that on the street? Money? Nothing else to do? Jew for Jesus? What's that other word for them again? O yeah, Christian. Kathie Lee Epstein. Or does he really believe? Imagine believing in some-thing like that. Jesus Christ. Jesus loves you. Jesus loves you. Jesus loves me. Fucking slut. Nothing against the man. Actually like him. Even see some resemblances. Hung out with hookers and lepers. Jewish. Worked with his hands. Rough relationship with dad. By all accounts a good guy. All that two thousand years ago and we're still carrying on about it. This must have all been country back then. Hilly countryside. Farms. Indians? Do they go back that far? Two thousand years since Christ climbed the cross. Must be a terrible end. Naked, tacked-up, outstretched S/M pose. The sun, the birds. Alone. Cold up there at night too, I'll bet, on high. Maybe that's why Christianity caught on the way it did: God in pain like the rest of us. Betrayed by a friend. Sad. Really simple when you think about it. Two thousand years of it. No, not really. Two years ahead? Behind? Christian calendar all screwed up. Jewish one too. Chinese too. Time. Gotta at least give Him that. A damn good timekeeper. A second's just a second, no matter what you do. And it always takes a year to move around the sun. Clockwork. But people mess it up. Like daylight's savings.

Where does the hour go? Who gets it? Didn't Einstein prove that time folds back on itself at the speed of light? Maybe that's why memories hit you so fast. Mind traveling backward. Time travel. Wait. Isn't that? Boarded up? The place where? The last time?

After Benji and Penny knew it was finished, after they were no longer living together and she started making movies with other people, after the bank accounts had been separated and closed, Benji had decided to take her, for their final meal together, to the famous five-star restaurant Brulée. And she had agreed. It was a self-conscious bit of myth-making on his part, but Benji, who had an abiding belief in the power of kind gestures, also believed in embellishing memories with the framing devices of theatre even in the instant of their occurrence.

It had been some time since he had worn a suit, his one and only suit being a sleek black double-breasted number he had purchased on sale at Today's Man the night before his mother's funeral three years before. In the space between then and now, his belly had gone a bit slacker, his legs grown a bit fuller, his stature slunk a bit smaller, but, freshly shaved, with the top jacket button fastened and his hair combed back, Benji surprised himself with how handsome he could manage to make himself. And that was part of the bargain: if he was self-conscious about making memories, he demanded he look the part.

Brulée was booked solid two, three, even four months in advance, but Benji, sensing that the end was inevitable and desirous of a strong curtain, had booked the reservation three months before they'd split. He'd been subconsciously planning the breakup around their lunch reservation, and when it all came down, everything happened right on schedule.

Barrels of fresh apples aligned the hallway vestibule, giving the place the thick-fresh scent of a tree house. A hollowed tree. A land of elves. Benji gave his name, took a seat by the bar, and waited, smoothing out his tie and tugging at his sleeves so an inch, inch-and-a-half of linen would show. In the years they had been together, had he ever taken her out formally? Had they ever shared a bottle of wine in a restaurant together? And yet look at her, look at her as she enters the hall, pale and thin and a bit clumsy with the door but still beautiful, still radiant, still a source of light. Still his girl. Are they in porn because they look like that or do they look like that because they're in porn? The question was rendered moot by her appearance in that hallway, an appearance consisting of a slim black velvet dress, conservative heels, and pearl necklace. A society swan out to lunch. A Capote chick.

If the invitation to the restaurant was a generous gesture, it was also one not devoid of provocation. In the weeks leading up to the date, Benji was a bit worried that Penny would show up in a glittery sequined mini, or in a tank top, stretch pants, knee-high boots, and riding crop. For if Penny was someone who read biographies of Liv Ullmann and Maya Deren and Miles Davis, she was also someone who remained completely oblivious to the changing winds of pop culture: the hot new band, the top spots in the Hamptons, let alone which three or four five-star restaurants in the city in which it was impossible to secure reservations. But her appearance surprised him. If implicit in Benji's choice of restaurant was the challenge, "this could have been our life together; a life of fresh apples, and French restaurants, and string quartets," Penny's outfit and matching poise announced, "Benji, this could have been me."

"Two kids playing dress-up," Benji said, surprising her from behind with a hand on her arm.
"O, I didn't see you."
"You look lovely," he said, retracting.
"I wanted to look nice for you," she said, reclaiming his hand and squeezing it gently. "Smells like France," she added, picking an Eden-ripe apple from one of the barrels and placing it on the windowsill opposite.
"Let's eat."

Prix Fixe Gustacheon Menu

Chilled tomato gelée with peeky-toe crab meat topped with avocado
Endive Salad
Spanish mackerel with tiny potatoes, baby leeks, and caviar
Sockeye salmon with coral cream
Pan-seared tuna wrapped in black truffles and country bacon
Squab stuffed with foie gras and forcemeat served on a bed of spinach with chanterelles
Fresh blueberries served warm with vanilla bean ice cream
Napoleon of coconut and pineapple topped with rum-raisin ice cream

Tart verbena ice cream melting slowly across an apricot tartlet
Milk chocolate tart
Dark cake filled with lemon mousse

And that wasn't all. To begin this last supper, first, compliments of the chef, came an hors d'oeuvre of baby quiche with crabmeat and gorgonzola cheese. Small scoops of lemon, cantaloupe, and grapefruit sorbet with fresh mint leaves were served between courses as palette cleansers, and upon arrival of the check, following a dessert of complex, near-mathematical density, came a three-tiered silver tray of cookies, chocolates, marzipan, and mints served with twin flutes of pear grappa. A monstrous meal. An assault of food, one that grew more elaborately orchestrated, cross-referential, and contrapuntal as the afternoon progressed.

And the service: a new set of silverware for every course, removed and replaced invisibly, as if by telekinesis; an elfin waiter whose job it was to circle round the restaurant discretely scraping crumbs off tables using a funneled pen-sized instrument. And the light! You simply didn't know a ground floor restaurant in New York City was capable of capturing and projecting light this way. Only they weren't in New York, Benji thought, as he looked first to the left of him, then to the right, taking it all in, memorizing every detail of the place. They were somewhere else entirely. They were existing inside a memory.

"Mmmmmm. Tastes good," Penny said, splitting a steaming slice of walnut bread in two and plastering butter in its smoking slit.
"Real butter," she said, running her tongue over a glistening finger. And in that gesture the full force of her reasserted itself and he was reminded of everything: the moral power of her naturalness, the depths of her sensuality, the unaffected physical candor which was so alien to him. His wife. His ex-wife. He took a drink of water to force things down.

He remembered once up in Ithaca she had bought a pack of gum. Big Red because that was the school nickname. Nothing exceptional in that, except that mundane gestures, under the steady guidance of her gaze and hands and tongue, could take on the contours of erotic ritual nonpareil. First, she unwrapped the outside, plastic-coated package using two fingers and clenched teeth. Then, she withdrew an erect, aluminum-covered piece of gum, which she held for a moment between beestung, red, jelly-wet lips, leaving it to hang precariously in a manner not unlike Jean-Paul Belmondo's sublime way with a cigarette in *Breathless*. Next, in one unbroken gesture, she peeled the aluminum armor away and slid the slice of gum into her mouth, folding it over itself with her tongue, forcing the helpless hostage to go somersaulting into its new home, her happy mouth. Everything she did was touched by the same spirit of blissfully unaffected sensuality. Even when she started making porn, somehow, strangely, none of it ever seemed dirty. All Benji could do was watch and record, watch and record, watch and record.

"To the end," he said, lifting a glass.

She looked up from her plate into him. It was the first time she had looked him in the eyes in months, and he was surprised to find them neither bloodshot nor dilated nor tear-filled, but clear. Clear and translucent as the day he had met her, when she was just a girl. His girl. A girl honest and open and unprotected, a girl equipped with the sensitivity and cruelty of a child, a girl who invited you to look at her, and look at her, and look at her, to look into her, to look through her, to devour her, to fuck her, to penetrate her, and to never understand her, to never get to the end of her. He hated her.

"To the end," she said, raising a glass.
They drank.
"I made something for you," she said, and with shaky hands, presented him with a paper scroll, tied together with red ribbon:

> **B**elief is never far from fright:
> **E**instein, Darwin, Brothers Wright;
> **N**ewton split the prism's white
> **J**ust to shame our sense of sight?
> **A**n honest Penny, burning bright;
> **M**nemosyne's wings bring second flight.
> **I**n dreams we'll walk again some night,
> **N**earer, nearer to the light.

"Thanks."
"I wrote it for you."
"It's good. It's really good. Thank you."

"Read it. I wrote it for you."
"I know. Thank you. I always loved your handwriting, you know that?"
She shook her head. An invisible waiter cleared the crumbs from the table
as she wiped the almostnotears from her face. The salad arrived.

"So what's your plan now?"
"I was thinking about trying L.A."
"L.A. as in the new Jerusalem of the Apocalypse?"
"Milton says there's work out there. He says that's where all the work is
now."
"You don't drive."
"They have people for that, Benji . . . you can come."
"And what? Be your chauffeur? Wait in the car when you go to work? I
think I'll stay here, thanks."

Benji, immediately regretting what he said, turned to his salad, a salad that
resembled a plate of freshly mowed lawn, and looking down, began
crunching away. Penelope meanwhile gently removed her wedding ring
(or what the couple had always referred to as her wedding ring: a simple
silver band), and placed it to the side of the table. Then she drizzled olive
oil around the perimeter of her salad plate and ran the first two fingers of
her right hand over the edge. Then she rubbed her two slick fingers against
the outer ridge of her thumb. Silently she moved her chair closer to Benji,
and without engaging his face, slithered her oiled hand beneath the table.
Benji put his fork down.

"What're you doing?"
"Keep eating," she said, lifting her wine glass with her available hand and
nonchalantly taking a sip.
His one good suit.
"Miss me?"
"Yeah."
"You gonna miss me?" she asked through closed lips and averted eyes.
"Yeah."
 "You scared?"
"Yup."
"I don't know what I'm gonna do without you," she exhaled.
"Don't, they're watching," he said, turning away from her as she applied
more pressure.

"Let 'em watch, Benji. Just you and me right, Benji? Just you and me."

Placing both hands above the table, she finished her glass of wine. Then she wiped her hands, placed her ring back on her finger, rose from the table on unsteady legs, and excused herself. He was alone.

"Garçon," Benji snapped. "Napkin!"

He looked around the place. In the corner, off to the side, he spotted a family of three. Mother. Father. Son. On the floor under the boy's chair he spotted a rolled up scroll sitting atop a program. June. Graduation day? A son. Something to impart. Leave behind. Your face in his. He looked at the man. A suit. A tie. A work-lined face. Gray hair. Was it worth it? It must be. How had she explained it to him? Three months. A father for three months. Didn't even know it was there. Didn't even get to hear its heartbeat. He looked from the opposite table down at his hands, which were trembling. Terrible nails. Cuticles too. Bad habit. Embarrassing. Gotta stop biting them. He polished off his glass of wine. Penny returned to the table, sat across from him, and smiled.

CLOSED FOR RENOVATIONS. Good, thought Benji, forcing his frozen legs into motion. He passed the boarded up restaurant and quickly crossed the street. A skinny pigeon pecked a crumb from an overturned garbage can. Such ugly birds. Stupid, gray, and mean. Fitting animal for the city. And their beady-eyed cousins marching along the subway tracks underneath. Rats. Eat anything. The more rotten the better.

He passed an open-air fish market and peeked inside. Strange sour-pungent smell. Sea smells salt-fresh, but fish smell like rot. Clams on the half-shell. Squishy, fishgluey slime. Said to be an aphrodisiac. Can't see it. Penny loved those. Just slurped them down one after another on the beach at Coney Island and never got sick. Such a wide variety of colors from the sea. Silvergreen and graysilver and purples and grays and oranges and gold. Flounder and bass and orange roughy. Shrimp served with the head. Beady black eyes on ice. All you can eat. Crabs. Funny walk. Approach everything sideways. Walking crabwise through life. Lobster served whole. Thrown into the boiling pot. Never knew what hit him. At least pour in a shot of vodka or something so the poor thing dies with a smile on its face. Keep things loose. Who wants to eat a tensed-up animal? Shock-tight muscles. Lobster in the shell I like. Work for your food. Get to see how the thing works. Joints. Claws. Set up compartmentally, like armor. Get to wear a baby's bib. Make a mess. Swordfish and tuna steak. Meaty fish. Chewy thick tasty skin. Tuna sandwiches on white Wonder bread, celery and carrot sticks and a container of apple juice in the red construction worker's lunchbox. Childhood favorite. Wouldn't mind a tuna sandwich now. No one makes it the way I like, though. Mom made it best. Just enough mayo to hold it together. Too much mayo's no good. Thick heavy yolk paste. Clogs up the tubing.

He turned down 8th Avenue at 45th Street past a few boarded up Broadway theaters. Frankie and Johnnie's steakhouse. White delivery truck outside with wide open doors. Slab after slab of blood-drained red, purple, and white sides of marbled meat, hanging on hooks, stamped purple. Flies buzzing around. Burly man in a pinkstained apron heaving one heavy carcass after another out the truck down cellar stairs. Must be unpleasant hugging all that dead flesh all day, the smell rubbing off on you. Up and down, up and down. Hundreds of steaks. Hundred and hundreds of cows munching grass in a field no more. Where? The West? Chicago? What difference does it make. Killed. The slaughterhouse. The charnel house. Larry at Med school. Brought me to the dissecting room once to see the cadaver he'd been working on all semester. Said it'd changed his view of things. Didn't know what he meant. Wanted to see for myself. Cold room. Thick formaldehyde smell. Older man. Stubble. Bristly chalk-white skin. Flayed open at the chest, stomach, and legs. Expression didn't seem to mind. Invited me to look. Looked much the same. Meat. Bodies stacked in a chemical cold room, table after table. The camps. The ovens. Piling them in. Just meat, must've thought. No, not today. Shake it off, Benji thought, pressing ahead.

Suddenly, a man in a business suit violently cut Benji off, swooshing down the street on rollerblades while carrying on a conversation on his cell phone. Cocksucker! Urban fucking deer! Motherfucker! You go outside to get away from phones. Saw a restaurant once where they had phones at the tables, so you could speak to people sitting next to you. Telephone ringing. Worst sound in the world. That and alarm clocks. Blips, beeps, and bongs polluting the world with violence. And rollerblades are no better. Blading. Make a cult of movement. Faster, faster, faster. Make a religion of speed. If I had a religion, it would be all about slowness.

Slowing down, on 46th and Broadway, Benji passed a salad bar/grocery store and stepped inside. $4.95 per $1/2$ pound. Plastic containers. Plastic forks and spoons. Hate eating on plastic. Shouldn't eat on plastic. Degrading to the food. Stone, ivory, or porcelain is best. Hot in here. Aluminum trays under heat lamps. A whole turkey, its carcass half-exposed. Meat. Trays of brisket in brown onion gravy. Ham with pineapple slices. Corned beef with apricot glaze. Corned beef and cabbage. Briny pickled meat. Dozens of hardboiled eggs floating in cloudy water. Crab-cucumber sushi coated in sesame seeds. Loose fried chicken pieces. Everything better fried. I'll have a deep fried plate, please. Gooey barbecue chicken wings. Sesame chicken. Chicken salad. Chicken with linguini. Spinach fettuccine with broccoli. Greek salad with crumbs of feta cheese and black olives. Croutons and saltines. Slices of tomato, cucumber, and red and yellow pepper. Hummus and chick peas. I ate some bad hummus and now I falafel. Ha ha ha. Grapes. Melon slices and orange sunbursts. Chunks of cantaloupe and pineapple. Scoops of cottage cheese. Loose watery rice pudding. Burnt bread pudding with cinnamon and raisins. Bread. Rolls. Crackers. Croutons. Bubbling black cauldrons of yellowthick pea soup, thin noodle soup, and vegetable barley.

"Hey, could you zap this for me, the cheese's not really melted," asked a young blonde woman in a black pantsuit, passing her clear plastic container of dried out macaroni and cheese across the delicatessen counter to a kinky-haired mustachioed man who tossed it into a microwave. Ten seconds later, he passed it back, the container oozing yellow-orange oil and vapor smoke. First we nuke Japan, now we're nuking the food, Benji thought, defensively backing away from the bubbling plate of cheese. What's that expression about food getting too far away from love? Fast food. Everything's so fast. Slow it down. Slow it down. Slow. Redbrickbaked in the sun. Cows grazing. Plants growing. Fresh water running. Bees buzzing from flower to flower.

He thought of taking a small plastic container and making himself a salad, then looked at the long line at the front of the store and thought the better of it. Behind the cashier, decoratively pinned to the wall like butterflies, were all the currencies of the world: American one, two, five, ten, and twenty dollar bills. French francs, Austrian schillings, Italian lira, Russian rubles, South African rands, Czech crowns, British pounds, Spanish pesetas, German deutsche marks, Greek drachmas, Mexican pesos. Crinkly paper. Gold and silver threads. Numbers. Filigree. Portraits of faces and buildings. Money. War. Industry. The history of nations. No. Art. Art is the history of nations. I study politics and war so my sons may one day study music and art. Didn't John Adams say that? Something like it. Well, if he didn't say it, he should have. By way of confirmation, the cash register opened with a triumphant *Ping!* Benji could feel his pores opening up and pinpricks of sweat begin to materialize on his forehead and freshly shaved cheeks. Too hot in here, he thought, exiting the store.

On the next block Benji entered a florid pink and white stationary store where he combed the greeting card aisles for a (belated) card for his father, Art, not in heaven. Birthday. Anniversary. Condolence. Friendship. Get Well. Brother. Sister. Father. Daughter. Mother. Son. Father's Day. Half-empty. Damn. Hate cards, Benji thought, opening one after another. Mandatory impersonal gesture. On the inside of a card featuring a black-and-white photograph of a father and son in a fishing boat: *For a Whale of a Dad!* Ya hardy har har. Never took me fishing the sonofabitch. *For Father's Day, I decided to get you the perfect gift.* Open. *But you already have me!* Another. *This Father's Day, I decided to give you something I knew would be difficult to find.* Open onto a bug-eyed cartoon child holding a remote control. Terror. Funny isn't working. In desperation, Benji moved down the line to the serious blue and white pastel cards, cards he had always intended on holding off purchasing for his father until Alzheimer's was through with him: *Father, I do not say it often enough . . . but thank you for so ill preparing me for the intellectual, moral, and philosophical challenges the world had lying in wait. Once a year, all is forgiven, cocksucker, as symbolized by the platitudes expressed in this two dollar card. So Happy Father's Day, Dad, to the biggest mutha of them all.* Fuck it, I'll call, thought Benji, fleeing.

Here. 50th between 8th and 9th. Intimidating building. 25 stories? 30? Taller? No sense of direction, height, or depth perception without my contacts, Benji thought. Is this the office building with the courtyard round back? Yes. He walked to the center of the block into a tile-laden, tree-lined piazza, a splash of sun hitting him full force like a spotlight. What time is it? 12:15. Early for lunch and yet the courtyard was abustle with human traffic: smokers huddled in doorways passing lighters between them like samizdat; business women making calls on cellphones, messengers exiting the building's main entrance, fumbling with combination locks, wrapping bicycle chains around their hips, and riding off like modern day cowboys.

Hot dog vendor. Parve. Kosher. Glatt kosher. Brought to you by Rabbi Joey Glatt of Bensonhurst. Kosher for Passover. Pesach. Dad's Haggadah book. Out of the land of Egypt into the house of bondage. Gefilte fish swimming in cans of mucous-jelly. Haroseth. Manishevitz. Elijah's cup. The drunken ghost. Matzo. Unhappy, unleavened bread. Depressed. Matzo desserts like sand-bricks. Makes you reexperience the suffering, all right. Next year in Jerusalem!

Hot dog. Hot sausage. Pretzel. Knish. Cold soda. Iced tea. Cold water. Frozade. FrozFruit. King Cone. Cherry Garcia. Peace Pop. Hot dog. Dog? Sacred in some cultures. Bad name for food though. Read somewhere that without preservatives and coloring they'd be turnip white. Government allows certain number of cockroach pieces and rat hairs in each one. Only one cockroach in this one boys, send it back. Kept in vats by the thousands. Thousands of cold white hot dogs in cool vats at night for the roaches and the rats to get at. Shot through with preservatives and colors, boiled in dishwater, and served on a chewy bun with ketchup and cabbage. Mm.

"Lemme get a knish, no mustard, and, you have cream soda?"
"Dr. Brown's."
"Yeah, good, lemme get a can of cream soda and a King Cone."

He paid the man an even five dollars, took hold of his lunch, walked over to a bench, set aside his rock solid frozen ice cream, unwrapped the aluminum foil from the knish, popped open the can of soda (satisfying sound), and began to eat. Coney Island knish. Peculiar shape. Trapezoid? Rhomboid? Always a few grains of sand trapped inside. Fresh from the beach the summer before. Nathan's hot dogs has the best french fries. Served with that little red trident fork. Real potato taste. French fries. Queer idea. Fry potato slices in boiling oil. Medieval torture. Poor potato. "Any change buddy?" asked a homeless man, eyeing Benji's knish. "No," Benji said, staring into the large, filthy-black pores of the man's nose. "No change from the hot dog guy, huh?" asked the man with thin stale breath.
"Nope."
"Can't cha help me get something ta eat?"
"Sorry," Benji said, rubbing two quarters together in his pocket like cricket's legs.

"Thanks, have a good day, buddy."
"Yup."

Must be a hard life. Demeaning. The ones that do okay with it always have a shtick. Sing a little. Dance a little. Gangrenous leg they can show. People expect to be entertained for their money. Only give to the ones that make them laugh. What's the greatest nation on earth? Donation. Support the United Negro Pizza Fund. Unicef. Sally Struthers. Starving African babies with the distended bellies of the over-fed. Visual contradiction. Over there. Look. A girl. She's young. Waiting for someone? No shoes on. Bare dirty feet. Just enjoying the day? No. Looks sad. Her clothes. Black like me. What's that book beside her? Can't see from here. Benji removed the wrapper from his ice cream cone and bit down, directing a small chiseled bit with his tongue toward a dead, capped, root-canaled tooth in the back of the left-hand side of his mouth. Vanilla, Benji thought, consciously comparing the taste of the ice cream to the vanilla cream soda he had just polished off. Pudding, cream soda, ice cream. All made with vanilla. Just different texture, Benji thought, violently pressing his tongue toward the roof of his mouth in an effort to get the frozen crystals to melt faster. Like what's the difference between tomato juice, tomato soup, ketchup, and tomato sauce? No difference. Just texture. Texture. Happiness and sadness? Nothing good or bad but thinking makes it so. Like this fucking ice cream cone.

"Help me," the little girl said, wriggling her dirty bare feet at a couple of suits who briskly passed her by, "I have no mun-eeeeeeeee."

Cute little white girl must be bad for business. Smartest bum I ever saw was on the F train. Just asked for a quarter. No song and dance. No explanation, no Vietnam or Drug Rehab or House Burned Down or AIDS. Just gimme a quarter. Gimme a quarter. All I want's a quarter. Surely you got a quarter. Be thankful for that quarter you got. And sure enough, he'd score two or three quarters per subway car. 75¢ a minute. $45.00 an hour. $360.00 per union day. Not fucking bad. Not bad at all. All that free soup, too. No benefits though. Medical.

"Help me. I have no mun-eeeeeeeeeee."

With no luck getting the King to soften up, Benji rose from his spot on the stone bench, crunched the aluminum foil into a ball, and deposited both it and the empty soda can in a wire garbage can. Reaching the girl, using the same hand in which he held the ice cream, he dropped a shiny quarter into her cup.

"Thank you," the girl said, rattling the coin around in her cup, and staring at the cone as Benji removed something from his pocket.

"That's cool," the girl offered when Benji produced his Pez dispenser. "Where'd you get it?" she asked inquisitively, twisting her wrist around so he could see the face of her Minnie Mouse watch.

"Family heirloom," Benji replied, removing a crumbling piece of purple candy from the Pez dispenser with his teeth and snapping it shut. Philosophically noting the title of her book, Benji handed the girl his troublesome dessert, then slouched away toward the office building doors.

7

Kevin Malloy's legs stood stock still as he stood his ground, refusing to be swayed.

"The millennium is coming."

"Fuck you."

"God bless you."

"Go to hell."

"Jesus loves you."

Most days he averaged three to five flyers a minute, depending on his location and the time of day. And most of those ended up in the gutter or in embarrassed garbage cans a few blocks away. But it didn't matter. Eye contact. The trick was eye contact. If he could catch their eyes and hold them, even for a moment, he had a chance.

"Jesus Is Coming! Are you ready?"

The catch phrases, repeated rapidly, over and over, thousands upon thousands of times a day sometimes blurred together in long train-trails of words: aryooredeetooexcepjeesuscriesasyorpersnalsavyor? But Kevin believed those words. Even delivered by rote, he believed. He believed.

It hadn't always been so. Just six years ago. Six years. Hair shaved within a sixteenth of an inch. Fucking with the black kids the next neighborhood over. Fucking girls outside on the grass and in the backs of borrowed cars in the parking lot at the beach. Knee-high leather Clockwork Orange shit kickers. Butterfly knife. Swastika tattoo I thought looked cool. Selling dime bags to junior high school kids. Sleeping in cars. Up all night. Asleep all day. Or no sleep at all. Crystal meth, up three days at a clip. Messed up that kid's leg pretty bad back in '90. Didn't know shit. Didn't know shit.

Arizona. Seattle. Williamsburg. Caught. Still only seventeen so it wasn't so bad. Brooklyn House of D. Started reading cause there was nothing else to do. First just car and wrestling magazines cause there was nothing else around. Then WWII history books. Some fucked up shit. Scraped at that tattoo, scraped it, just kept scraping at the fucker till it drew blood. Gouged the fucking thing out told people it was a car accident, I didn't care. Crazy kid. Crazy fucking kid. Six years ago. Just six years. Six years. Father McNally listened. Really listened. Maybe the first person in my life. Kind man. Kind open face.

"You know Kevin, you've really come a remarkably long way from when I first met you."
"Thank you, sir."
"And I only hope that some of the spiritual issues we've talked about together have played a part in that change, and that you recognize that."
"I think I do, sir."
"Kevin, if you approach Him with a fully open heart, God provides for the regeneration of the soul. You could even say at times He encourages our foibles so long as we choose to learn from them. Are you ready to make a change Kevin?"
"Yes, sir, I am."
"Are you ready to accept the lord Jesus Christ as your personal savior?"
"Yes, sir."
"And allow Him into your heart? Are you ready to make that change, Kevin? Are you ready?"

* * *

Finn planted herself outside her mother's office building at 50th Street and Eighth Avenue, carefully removed her size four black Reebok sneakers, and placed them at her side. She peeled off her white cotton socks and stared at her naked feet. Strange. Feet. Flanks. Long, flat, and fair. At right angles from the rest of a person. Only place on the body where all the cables show.

She looked up. How many people must work in there? Wonder what she's doing now? Finn wondered, removing a thick paperback book from her bag. Or what's going on in class? Gotta check the answering machine, don't forget. The mail, too. And call Tobey with the pneumonia update.

Finn looked up from her feet to the Technicolor parade passing before her at twenty-four frames per second. So much going on in the world every second per second. In color! In stereo! So many people. And all the people before that. A whole other city stood here once. And one behind that. All those stories. Lives. Interlocking. Too much to think about. Perhaps the sensory deprived are better off. A clearer picture of things. Still. Distilled.

She closed her eyes and mouth and held her nose tight. She breathed out, puffing up her cheeks and clogging her ears. Blackness. World without sight or sound. World without end. Helen Keller moment. Spelled out words on the palm of her hand. Letter by letter. And still she managed to write books. Word known to all men? The flower she never touched. And me? When?

She opened her eyes to the clink of a coin, tossed at the foot of her feet. A quarter. For her. She thought on this peculiarity for a moment. She looked around. Near her, just a few feet away, a crushed cardboard coffee cup had just missed a wire garbage can. Finn reached for it, wiping its milky scum clinging rim with her shirt sleeve. Blue and white Greek fresco. Three kinds of columns. Doric, Corinthian, and Ironic. I've seen homeless people use these. I am homeless too.

* * *

"Jesus is coming," said Kevin, making and holding eye contact with a compassionate-looking man.
"What's that?" asked the man, approaching warily.

"Jesus is coming," Kevin repeated, grabbing hold of the man's hand and shoving a spiky piece of paper into his startled palm.

Jesus Is Coming!
Are You Ready?

"Well you tell him if he can come twice in five minutes I got a job waiting for him when he gets here," said the passerby as he crunched the yellow flyer up into a tight little ball and tossed it down the street where it bobbled and bounced before making a decisive left on Eighth.

* * *

"Benjamin Seymour? That dog still around?" marveled pockmarked Pete Profitt, adjusting a lightstand.
"Yeah. He said you were the best cover photographer in the business."
"Benji the bullshitter," Pete said, laughing. "Whatchoo got there?"
"Just some flyer a kid was handing out downstairs."
"You can put that down over there, honey. Okay . . . undress."

And so, for the second time in as many days, Allison April Pryce found herself standing bare before a stranger's eyes.

"Okay," said Pete, espying Allison's naked form through the viewfinder. "You got a nice figure on you but you need some work done on your tits." Click! "I'm gonna give you the name of a doctor, a surgeon, Dr. Meltzer, that I want you to see." Click! "Nice guy. Reasonable. Handsome too, in an Ashkenazi kinda way. Fix you up nice if you do the right things." Click! "Then you come back in a coupla weeks, we'll shoot some box covers."

* * *

Michelangelo Virelle awoke amidst piles of pillows and blankets, and stretched his feline body over the expanse of his canopied, king-sized bed. I haven't been laid in days, he thought, juggling his balls. Easier getting laid when I was a struggling actor, at least that had some romantic cachet. Now, it's work work work . . . Lawyers, handlers, photo shoots, interviewers yammering on about my boring fucking childhood, trying to find a good angle—the pool hall interview, the driving through the Midwest in a red convertible interview, the fifth grade classroom interview . . .

He slunk out of bed and approached the full-length mirror. He ran a hand over his stubble-free cheeks and chin. He practiced pouty facial expressions for his photo shoot with *Details* happening later in the day. There is something slinky, pale, and androgynous about me, he thought, mentally quoting a recent article in *Teen Idol* magazine and pursing his lips, Mick Jagger style. In another era, he'd have been lucky to be cast as Cary Grant's bellhop, Jimmy Cagney's newspaper boy, canon fodder in an Errol Flynn pirate movie. But this was the nineties: slinky, pale androgyny was in.

Michelangelo Virelle—so named because his hippie mother, Rainbow, backpacking through Europe, prematurely spilled the great boy out of her just hours after standing beneath the vaulted ceiling—was about to lose his life. Or rather, he was about to exchange his life for a newer, better one. Celebrity was in the offing, and in no small measure. Following the usually MAW (model, actor, whatever) shuffle of waiting tables, playing Biff in dinner theatre productions of *Death of a Salesman*, and the occasional soft-core bluejeans, T-shirt, and rugby print ad, Michelangelo got his big break chewing gum in a national MintySquirt commercial. From there it was just two months auditioning before landing a spot on the sitcom *Spilt Milk*, in which he guest-starred for six or seven episodes as Evan, the impish squirrel of a homeless boy who taught the Chestersons a thing or two about life, love, and the true meaning of family. Then came *Zeppelin* to fly him away to his new life.

A blimp two years in the making, *Zeppelin*—a romantic epic about a pair of star-crossed, ill-fated lovers on board the Hindenburg, as painstakingly recreated and destroyed by the film's egomaniacal auteur, Clem Sullivan— was already the stuff of Hollywood legend. Having gone a year over schedule and tens of millions of dollars over budget, the film was rumored to be something of a Hollywood guillotine—heads were ready to roll—but, finally poised to premiere after months of delays, the picture suddenly found the press back-peddling, heralding it a great film in the tradition of

D. W. Griffith, even conferring upon *Zeppelin* in hushed tones the term reserved for that most rarefied and respected of Hollywood product—Academy Award material. And word had it Michelangelo's beguiling lead performance as Johnny Belfast would thrust him to the forefront of his generation of actors. The *Vanity Fair* Young Hollywood issue group cover photo had been shot and approved. The girls were already clamoring for him in Tokyo.

Soon everyone will know this face, Michelangelo thought to himself, twisting his noncommittal expression into a thin smile as he went to work on a whitehead on his chin. He looked around the richly appointed room. Peggy told me if I trash the room I have a pretty good shot at making Liz Smith. But it's such a pretty room. And I'm not mad at anyone. Maybe something small. A vase.

He searched the room for a vase, preferably small, finally finding one on a marble table next to the toilet in the bathroom. He bent over and stared at the sculpture, which was perfectly black and clean, like the monolith in *2001*. In it, Michelangelo could fathom his own smoky reflection. That's what people want from art nowadays isn't it, Michelangelo thought. You don't want it to tell you something new, you want to see yourself staring back.

He pulled his pajama drawstring tight around his bony waist, ran a hand over his white, goose-pimpled flesh, picked the vase up off the table, exited the bathroom, opened the balcony doors, and stepped outside. He looked down at the pedestrians marching along in rows like ants. New York seemed to have grown more populous since he was in the city three years ago, scraping bottom. That was some stupid shit I got mixed up with back then. Stupid. Stupid shit. Kind of thing that comes back and bites you in the ass and I shouldn't have done it and I should have fucking known better. *Santa's Little Helper*. What the fuck was that?! What was the name I used? Dan Deer? Dilly Dally? Didn't even have an arc to the character. All I know is Peggy better fucking take care of it. How bad would that fucking suck to have fifteen minutes and a hundred dollars fuck everything up. Stallone did it. Madonna had done it. Vanessa Williams in Penthouse. Eddie with the transvestite. Just driving her home, officer. Didn't hurt any of their careers. Fuck. Fuck. Fuck. Fuck. Fuck. Now he was mad. He looked down at the string of people bounding along below. No, can't throw it out the window. Might hit somebody. Like that guy across the street. Frozen in front of that boarded up building like a mime. I hated doing mime in acting class. So many of those exercises were such bullshit. Who needs acting class, just keep your eyes open for all the crazy fuckers the world has to offer you'll be fine.

He brought the vase back inside, placed it gently on the bathroom table, and sat on the toilet. Maybe just nudge it a little, he thought, exerting a minor pressure with his pinky finger. Tell housekeeping it was an accident, drop two twenties on the floor Sonny Corleone-style, have Peggy embellish it for the tabs, make the papers, save the room, everyone wins, he told himself, looking away, pressing a little harder. Gentle . . . gentle . . . gentle . . .

Pprrrruummpalalalalalala!

The vase hit the tile floor where it treated itself to a crippled moment of wobbly indecision before righting itself, unbroken.

Plexiglass! Damn!

* * *

Each Monday morning Omar Sadjawa looked forward to his weekly UPS shipment of toys. In today's parcel were a selection of Veggie Vibes, twelve-inch vibrators in the shape of carrots, cucumbers, and corncobs which Omar dutifully removed from their big cardboard box (being sure to pick up and dispose of the packing popcorn that went scuttling across the floor) and arranged behind the glass counter at the front of the store. Then, in a heavy black marker, he fashioned a block letter sign imploring customers:

PLEASE DO NOT PLAY WITH THE MERCHANDISE

He knew when he came to America six years before that his medical degree would be useless here, and so, Omar Sadjawa, brother of seven, father of three, husband of one, at the no-longer-young age of thirty-nine, had been forced to begin again. He had considered driving a cab, like his cousin Jamal, but Omar didn't like to drive and wasn't confident enough with the city's geography. Besides, a New York City medallion cost something like $125,000, and Omar wanted to test things out first before financially committing himself to a lengthy stay. Worse, in early 1990, the *New York Post* rated being a cabby the single most dangerous occupation in New York, a job more dangerous than being a cop, and, sure enough, within months of the article's appearance, Jamal had been shot. It turned out to be just a superficial neck wound, but with blood loss, twelve stitches, and an overnight stay in the hospital, it was still enough to wipe out Jamal's entire (insurance-less) savings.

And so, after befriending a video wholesaler known cryptically as The Sheik who sold Indian immigrants hundreds of overstocked pornographic videos at cost—generally meaning three dollars or less—Omar opened Siren Home Video. To its advantage, the place was relatively quiet and Omar could usually find time in the afternoons to read and study behind the counter. He wasn't particularly abashed by what he did for a living, either. If he had no real interest in pornography as such, he felt the films, in their gynecological detail and comprehensive anal probes, actually held some educational value for him. And his clientele was, for the most part, more conservative and mild-mannered than one might expect. Sure, he got his share of OTB losers and garbage sloughed off from 42nd Street, but most of his customers were businessmen on their way home from work or horny college kids home on break. Truth is, you'd attract a rougher clientele at the neighborhood Burger King.

Omar didn't have to keep the place too clean, either. Something of a neat-freak, Omar intuited almost immediately that if the place were too spic-and-span, too antiseptic, it might actually drive customers away. Before opening the store, Omar scoured Times Square in an attempt to discern the look and layout of the classic smut shop. (And the smell, for most pornography stores have a palatable urine scent.) What he quickly discovered was that all the places looked the same: harsh fluorescent lighting, white walls, contraceptives and toys strewn in clear plastic tubs and remainder bins in the front, and tapes stacked everywhere: in racks, in stands, on shelves, on the floor, tapes everywhere christened in dirt, dust, and fingerprints, presided over by an unused wicker broom lounging in the corner. A faithful student, Omar decided to let research dictate the limits of the store's cleanliness, and so Siren was kept neat if not necessarily clean. Which was perhaps the point. The people who patronized these places didn't want to feel clean, they wanted to feel sullied.

Omar looked down at his book: *Arco MCAT Supercourse*. If Mike is on a train traveling west at 65 m.p.h. and Jonathan is on a train traveling east at 55.5 m.p.h., and the two trains depart 225 miles from each other at 10:30 A.M. and 11:15 A.M., respectively, what does this have to do with my wanting to practice medicine in America?

"How ya doin' today Omar?"
"Very well, sir, very well, and you?" Omar asked, solicitously closing his book.
"Good. Good. Can't complain. How's this one?" the man asked, passing an empty videocassette box over the counter.
"Hot stuff, very hot stuff, indeed," Omar replied, offering his standard response to such a question.
"You need my card?"
"No, that's fine," Omar said, turning around to retrieve the tape.

There were no membership cards at Siren Home Video: everyone had to either put a deposit down or leave an impression of their credit card. But Omar didn't enforce the rules all that strictly with the regulars, the familiar faces, like Larry Gelber, a forty-five-year-old divorced Madison Square Garden security guard who lived in Hoboken, New Jersey. The tape Gelber had selected was from a newfangled genre called "talk-back" videos. In talk-back, all but the male performers' genitals were concealed behind sheets and drapery, while the women—fully exposed—went to work, addressing the camera directly as if talking to the home viewer: "You fucking pervert! You like watching pretty young girls sucking cock, don't you?! Don't you, you sick, pathetic scum!"

Omar brought the man's selection, *Confessions of a Cock Junky*, up to the front of the store, where he took the man's money, made change, put the fire engine red cassette in a plain brown paper bag, and taped it closed.

The store was empty. Careful not to crease its pages, Omar gently placed his book behind the counter. He looked around. Mine. All of it. The tapes, the toys, the light fixtures, all of it: mine. From a discolored manila folder

Omar removed an $8^1/_2$ x 11 inch card stock sign which read, "Giuliani for Mayor," located the tape dispenser from the supply cabinet, and stepped out from behind the counter to look for an appropriate spot to hang the sign. At that moment, Roy, a regular wearing a blue and orange Mets cap, a Mickey Mouse T-shirt, a Band-Aid covering the entirety of his left eyebrow, an inconsistent beard, and the eyes of a failed rapist, entered the establishment.

"Yo Omar man, w'sup?"
"Very good. Very good, sir."
"Ah-ight. Ah-ight. Keepin' it real."

If Roy was a regular, a regular whose loyal patronage meant hundreds of dollars of business a year (dollars that were invariably torn, worn-thin, soaking wet, and/or patched together with tape), Omar had no taste for the man. Roy frequented the place too often to suggest much of a life outside it, and he had been known to scare off customers with his cold, fish-eyed stare. After three years of acquaintanceship, Omar still had no idea what Roy did for a living. "Cops. I watch cops. For the gub-ment," Roy answered once years ago, and the question had never been broached again.

"You got any new ATM's for me today my man?" Roy asked, "ATM" being an acronym for "ass-to-mouth," an industry term and Roy's latest fetish of choice.
"Try Milo's *Mediterranean Mystery*. I believe there may be some in there," Omar said, instinctively directing Roy toward the back of the store.
"Ah-ight. Ah-ight."

While Roy occupied himself with his search, Omar took the opportunity to find a spot for the poster near the counter. Quickly, he began taping it up.

"Aw, fuck that eye-tie muthafucka," Roy said, spotting the sign over his stack of six selections.
"He's doing a good job. He's a good man. He's cleaning up the city."
"Naw, man. Dinkins, baby. Dinkins," Roy said, taking a provocative step forward.
"Dinkins! Dinkins did nothing! Crown Heights? He let the city burn!"
"Man, Crown Heights! Fuck dat! Dinkins was one honest New York soul

brotha muthafucka."

Gripping the tape dispenser, Omar took a precautious step back behind the counter.

"Giuliani? Man, Giuliani's one Il Duce fascist muthafucka. I'm tellin' you, two-three years time, muthafucka'll close all y'all up, drive all y'all back to India, take away all my muthafuckin' tapes. And then what? Then what?! I'm tellin' you, you heard it here first, so watch out, baby! Watch out!"

At that moment, a gust of wind blew the store doors open, sending a cyclonic stream of paper, plastic, and detritus wafting through the store, ripping the Giuliani poster from its stronghold on the wall, and sending the veggie vibes tumbling over one another like dominoes before exiting the store, violently slamming the doors behind it. Like an animated exclamation point, the gust of wind stood spinning before the store, humming forebodingly, before disseminating in a quiet burst of calm, leaving behind a triumphant yellow paper flyer, a throwaway, a crumpled ball, which, after dizzily reclaiming its bearings, stared Roy and Omar into a peaceful moment's reconciliation before continuing its journey southward along Eighth.

* * *

Precariously, a pigeon pecked around Finn's sacred circle. What ugly birds, Finn thought, skinny, gray, and mean.

Clink!

Our city bird, with their dead, unblinking eyes. Rats with wings. Fanged vampire birds. Imagine if the streets were filled with falcons or peacocks or eagles. Elevate our endeavors. How much happier we'd be.

Clink!

She looked up at the office building. Today. I'll do it today. Takes her lunch at noon. If she spots me, I won't go, Finn thought, another dime jumping into her cup. If she passes me by, so be it.

* * *

In a Rite Aid on the corner of 32nd and Eighth, Maria Canales rung up another family-sized, sixty-four ounce jar of Jergen's hand lotion and a sixteen ounce jar of premium Hawaiian macadamia nuts as the same familiar song pumped through the loudspeaker system for the fourth time that day. If I hear that friggin' song one more time I swear to God I'm gonna lose my shit, Maria thought, tapping her foot to the music in spite of herself.

"$7.61."
"I think I have exact change . . . yup, there you go, Maria."
"Thankscomeagain."

Hate it when they call me by name. Like they know me 'n shit. Muthafuckas. Just reading off my nametag. They think they can get all familiar or get cute with me. They don't know me. Muthafuckas. What's up with the skin cream and the macadamia nuts all the sudden, anyway?

Outside a crumpled yellow paper flyer, a throwaway, sailing southward, stopped in front of the store and, in spite of itself, danced to "The Macarena" before continuing down Eighth Avenue.

* * *

Standing stock silent still in the hallway outside the presidential suite of the James B. Madison Hotel, Jules Ozrick looked to the future. Staring at himself in the hallway mirror, shaved, Armani-clad, six-foot-four-inch, 235-pound Jules Ozrick, Jules the accountant's son, Jules the Grade-A student, Jules the overgrown gentle giant who as a child would direct cockroaches toward paper cups and release them out onto the street rather than smash them into oblivion under the soles of his pneumatic Nikes, Jules Ozrick was forced to acknowledge a dirty secret: he was the sweet-voiced product of too much mother love.

Born in Compton to dreams of bandana warfare, Jules had proven too clumsy for the Bloods (What choo trippin' over nigga!), too articulate for the Crips (What choo talkin' 'bout nigga!). In fact, Jules proved an embarrassment to big black men everywhere. He couldn't dance, he couldn't play basketball, he'd never slept with a white woman, his nether regions were proportionally assigned. A guidance counselor trapped in the body of a legbreaker, in desperation Jules had invented a past for himself, an alternate history, a counterlife as convoluted and filigreed as Monte Cristo's, an imaginary rap sheet which included breaking and entering, extortion, arson, assault, manslaughter, bootlegging, tax evasion . . .

Lucky for Jules then that young Negroes with appealingly variegated criminal records had become the elite Hollywood accouterment of choice. Everyone wanted one. And so Jules, with no qualifications to speak of, had been hired by Big Brotha Bodyguards to protect an ivory-faced young sitcom actor from throngs of howling, acne-stained prepubescents. Apart from a few mall appearances where folded-armed Jules got to test his stuff as a physical guru staring down queues of dewy thirteen-year-olds, mostly the job consisted of sitting in Lincoln Town Cars or standing outside large hotel rooms like this one. And waiting. . .

But Jules had dreams. As yet unsigned rap artist Crown'd Jewels, Jules had dreams of sequined superstardom of his own. . . dreams of Al Pacino saying hello to his little friend in *Scarface* . . . dreams of omnipotent, Quincy Jones-like impresarioship . . . dreams of "Nigga Luv":

> Black Panthers, King Jr., and Malcolm X
> The year's 1997 and we all 'bout sex
> Got bitches in da crib
> Green in da safe
> Got my gangstas and homies
> They on da case
> Got Uzis, Smith & Wessons, and my .45 Glock
> But I'm a pacifist muthafucka
> Like Mahatma-Gat!
>
> (chorus)
>
> Nigga Luv
> Nigga nigga nigga nigga nigga
> Nigga Luv
> 'Cause I'm a nigga talkin' bout
> Nigga Luv
> Nigga nigga nigga nigga nigga

Nigga Luv
'Cause I'm a nigga

Every morning on my travels
I thank the Lord
That the bitches in my stable
Bark like a dog
Yeah, lollin' and trollin'
That's the way they be
Shaft is the dick
Played by Richard Roundtree
Yeah ladies all around me
They shake that rump
They know Crown'd Jewels love them long time
Ain't no two-pump chump!

(chorus)

Nigga Luv
Nigga nigga nigga nigga nigga
Nigga Luv
'Cause I'm a nigga talkin' 'bout
Nigga Luv
Nigga nigga nigga nigga nigga
Nigga Luv
'Cause I'm a nigga

Diamonds, silver
Twenty-four carat
Bunnies hoppin' all around me
'Cause I'm a wascally wabbit
Miami, Chicago, the Rio Grande
Ladies suckin' on my joint
Jammy in da hand
Ebonic, Teutonic
It don't matter to me
When da bitches gather round
My twelve inches of glee

(chorus)

Nigga Luv
Nigga nigga nigga nigga nigga
Nigga Luv
'Cause I'm a nigga talkin' 'bout
Nigga Luv
Nigga nigga nigga nigga nigga
Nigga Luv
'Cause I'm a nigga, that's right
Stone. Cold. Black.

Snapping Jules from his reverie, bronzed, barechested, berobed Michelangelo Virelle, redfaced with anger, flew out of his suite into the hall.

"Jules, are you particularly busy right now?"
"No."
"There's something I need you to take care of."
"Okay."
"And Jules?"
"Yes."
"There may be some nastiness involved."
"Nastiness?"
"Yes."

* * *

"Thank you," Finn said, as the man dropped a shiny quarter into her cup. "That's cool," she added as he produced a Mickey Mouse Pez dispenser from his pocket with the same hand that held an alluring King Cone ice cream. In an act of solidarity, her first of the day, Finn twisted her arm around so the man could see her Minnie Mouse wristwatch, previously, considered a source of immaturity and shame. "Where'd you get it?"
"Family heirloom," the man replied, vampirically sucking Mickey's neck, coming up with one half a purple pellet, and in a surprise gesture of generosity, handing Finn the ice cream before walking away.

Score! Finn thought, twisting the ice cream cone around to avoid the incriminating bite mark. Would have liked talking with him a little more. Interesting face. Guess they don't want to talk to the homeless. Just give them money. Maybe give them money so they don't have to talk to them. Sleeping in the same clothes. Peeing in alleyways. Bathing in public toilets. All the same, kind of disheveled looking to be heading into mom's building, no? A messenger perhaps. Sad eyes. Finn continued scanning the courtyard. Mom always takes lunch at twelve noon. Twelve noon on the dot. If you don't set the precedent, you'll never leave your desk. Finn looked down at her watch again, adjusting its faulty band. 12:17. Too late. Too late. As she watched the anonymous man enter her mother's office building, Finn pulled her socks up over her fair feet and slipped back into her shoes.

* * *

Every Monday Troy rummaged through CUM's stash of videocassettes, looking to recycle old tape. He did this because business was slow and it gave him something to do, and he did it because business was slow and there was no money to spend on fresh tape. Embarrassed, he kept the practice hidden from Benji, Benji the Big Boss Man, Benji the Broke. Besides, since videotape was the language through which the two of them communicated their love for one another, it gave Troy an opportunity to review their shared history, to catalogue their own private jukebox. He popped in an anonymous, unlabeled tape, hit play, and was hit with an extreme close-up of a woman's vulva being spread apart by an anonymous hand wearing chalk white surgical gloves. After a moment, Holiday Inn synthesizer lounge music came on, and in bright, pixilated video red, the word "Gynotopia" materialized over the image.

Gynotopia was a series of tapes dating from the mid-eighties: each a half-hour long, each consisting of an extended gynecological exam properly performed with stirrups, speculum, and flashlight. And that's all they were. While you never saw the woman's face, the series supposedly featured some of the hottest pussies in porn. "They're the easiest things in the world to make, and the cost-to-profit margin's incredible," Benji explained. "Just shoot the crack."

Troy remembered when he was fourteen, the first time he touched a girl. He didn't know what to expect and the slipperiness, the moistness had surprised him. The resistance did, too, as if the girl was fighting to close herself, heal herself over finger and cock. "Pussy. What's up with that?" he mock-boasted to friends over forties on the corner stoop in Coney Island, trying to mask his discomfort. "Watchoo mean?" his older brother A.J. asked. "It's like a piece of origami!" he pleaded. "Y'ever look a pussy in the eye? Anyone ever do that to me, I want you to drag my ass to the hospital."

He continued staring. Pussy. P. God's unfinished bid-ness. He couldn't figure out why he should be attracted to it. Troy continued watching *Gynotopia*. He tried but found himself unable to recognize whose vagina it belonged to. This one we'll keep, he thought, ejecting the tape and pressing it to his lips. Still warm. Next. The image flicked to life. A little boy (or a young man combed and dressed to look like a little boy) sitting on Santa's lap.

"And what do you want for Christmas this year?" Santa said, squirming around for position.
"A reindeer."
"Ho ho ho, you're in luck!" said Santa, slipping his member out of his red felt coat.
"What's that?"
"A reindeer," he said, pointing to his bursting red head, "But it's not just any reindeer. It's Rudolf! Rudolf the Red Nosed Reindeer!"
"O."
"Go ahead, pet him," Santa said, making his prick bounce up-and-down appreciatively. "And you know what Rudolf does when it's not Christmastime?"
"No?"
"He hibernates. When Rudolf's done helping Santa deliver all the presents, he likes to rest in a nice, dark cave."
"O."
Santa began to pull the boy's pants down around his ankles.
"This looks like a nice cave," Santa said, fingering the little boy's asshole. "Is that a nice cozy-comfy cave?"
"Uh huh."
"Is it okay if Rudolf explores for awhile?"
"Um . . . okay."

Santa's Little Helper. Raw jungle faggotry. Troy remembered filming it in Gurgles' display room during the tail end of the early nineties gay porn boom. Benji thought there was money to be made in that market and, glazed over following Penny's disappearance, Troy thought Benji would have filmed anything. And so it came to pass with Benji nonchalantly sitting around the set popping Pez and crunching Cheez Doodles as Santa fucked three boys in the ass while a pair of elves working on an assembly line fashioned dozens of red and green holiday dildos. Troy remembered it proving difficult to find a pair of midgets interested in being in a gay pornographic film, but they'd done it. In Florida visiting his father, Benji had discovered Stumpy the Magic Dwarf, a hyperactive midget who had just failed to gain entry into Ringling Bros.' Clown College in Sarasota, and Stumpy in turn convinced his partner, the tragically named Larry Little, to appear in the film in a black leather S/M mask. New frontiers were being conquered, new professional relationships were being forged, and Benji was pleased until shooting began, at which point Stumpy unexpectedly began pulling colored handkerchiefs and pigeons and balls of fire out of his pants while giving head to Santa. ("Quit the pratfalls Stumpy and suck it!" was Benji's concise, Otto Preminger-esque direction.) For Santa, they hired Milo Pipe, Milo the twenty-year, twelve-inch industry veteran who'd fuck fucking anything. "If it has a depression, I wanna leave an impression," was Milo's motto, and he stuck to it. And for the kid they got some cute, green, Midwestern acting student named Dil Doe.

When it was over, they didn't talk about it. But Troy remembered it all. The day, the time, the surprise erection he found crawling toward his belly during filming. More than anything else, he remembered the smell. Even though the men cleaned themselves out with enemas before appearing on-camera, and—unlike in straight—everyone wore rubbers and even latex gloves, it smelled foul, oniony, like stink, like damp underarm hair, like steam rooms, like ass, like shit. Troy had to admit it though: faggots knew their way around fucking. Even the midgets knew what it was all about. Fucking faggots.

At that moment, the phone rang, startling Troy out of his erection.

"This CUM?" a muffled voice asked.

"Yeah, who's this?" Troy asked.

"West Coast P rules, muthafucka. Remember that!"

Troy quickly hung up the phone, and, flustered, simultaneously pressed

play and record, turning the master copy of *Santa's Little Helper* to electronic snow as the buzzer rang, alerting him to the presence of an unexpected guest.

* * *

Knish tasted good, thought Benji, sloshing his tongue around in the space
between his underlip and teeth. And it was good of you to give that girl
your ice cream, thought Benji the Munificent, feeling fuller and grand as
he walked up the slightly steep incline to the office building entrance.
Reminds me of walking uphill in Ithaca. Simply could not do it without
being self-conscious, without looking like a total dork. Wonder how the
gay guys pull it off in San Francisco, struggling to flirt up and down hills
all day.

He reached the doors and attentively held them open for a pair of ladies
in business suits who smiled at him. Nothing. Nothing at all. Just a
moment's kindness, ma'am, thought Benji the Benevolent, monitoring the
longed-for crease in their business suits as they walked in front of him. Not
even an inconvenience and it can make a person's day. Benji remembered
wanting to be a doorman as a kid, his logic being there was no better way
to meet people. What better job could there be? Liminal space. Portal
between coming and going. And, as gatekeeper, you have that moment's
authority. Troll under the bridge.

He remembered as a child holding doors open for his family everywhere,
anytime they went anywhere. "Million dollar tip, please," he'd say, standing guard at the front door, holding his hand out as his mother passed.
"There you are," she'd say, smiling, placing the imaginary tariff in his
hand.

"Tip . . ?" he'd ask his brother, bracing himself for the inevitable punch on
the arm. "Million billion dollar tip, sir," he'd ask his father as he passed.
"Price went up fast," his father would say, mussing his son's hair, holding
Benji's small hand in his own. "Inflation," Benji would reply, proud to
know the grown-up word, shaking his hand loose from the indignity and
saluting manfully. Childhood. Doors that open only once. Childhood!

* * *

Hector Lopez, arms heavy with packages, rang the ground floor apartment buzzer at 214 West 30th Street.

"C'mon. C'mon," he murmured to himself, beads of sweat bursting across his stoic forehead.
"Yes?"
"Hello, Mrs. Fitzpatrick. It's Hector. From Meals On Wheels."
"O, I don't know about that . . ."
"Your grandson Alfred is with me."
"Alfred? O, I haven't seen you in so long," she said through the intercom, buzzing.

One of the joys, the real pleasures of being a Meals On Wheels volunteer for Hector was that some of the people on his daily route had Alzheimer's and didn't recognize him from one day to the next, so they were always surprised by the unexpected company and delighted with the fresh food and milk and bread. Not like work. Not like work at all.

A night janitor at Pace University downtown, the volunteer hours cut into Hector's sleep time, and, inattentive to paperwork and tax write-offs, he actually ended up losing money on the deal with gas and parking meters and such, but it was worth it. Seeing those crinkly prune faces scrunch up into smiles made it worth it. And some of these women—even the old lady smells of mildewed laundry hanging in apartments and crusty newspapers yellowing in stacks in the hallways—reminded Hector of his own mother, who'd died in a nursing home just three years before.

"Look what we got for you today, Mrs. Fitzpatrick!" Hector said, removing a styrofoam container from a brown paper bag and lifting its steamy lid.
"We got some bread, we got some plain roasted chicken—the way you like it without the skin—we got some mashed potatoes with a little bit of margarine, we got some, what do you call them? Some greens, some string beans, snap peas. We got some milk, some juice, and a thing of Jell-O for dessert."
"O, you brought food!"
"Now I want you to be a good girl and polish everything off, all right? And

I'll be back Wednesday, okay?" Hector said, placing dull plastic utensils before her followed by two gentle hands on her soft shoulders.

"And don't forget to lock the door behind me."

"O, boy," Mrs. Fitzpatrick said, picking the plastic fork up with shaky fingers.

"Looking good, kid-o," Hector said, passing the ancient grandfather clock, frozen with a stroke on 6:17.

"Honey?"

"Yes, doll?"

"What time is it?"

* * *

At 12:18 P.M., on Monday, June 17, a benevolent black-vested drug dealer received a message on his pager to clear out of Washington Square as two police officers entered the park on the southwest side. In a candy store on Tenth Street, the grizzly owner shifted his impressive heft from behind the counter to take stock of his Monday morning delivery of magazines only to screamingly discover he had been short-changed. On 42nd and Broadway, a man swooshing down the street on rollerblades, clicked his cell phone to call waiting to learn he had just made six point seven million dollars paper profit on an internet IPO. On 45th Street and Seventh Avenue, a gray haired cabby with bursting forearms drove past a big bald-headed black man in an Armani suit in favor of a goateed white man dressed in a T-shirt and jeans. In his dressing room at 40 Rockefeller Plaza, Alexander Starr (née, Alex Stein) sat with a cold towel draped across his porous, make-up weary forehead as he checked the stock market pages of *The New York Times*. Downstairs, (anagramatized) Winnow Screenlad and (feminihilist) Corrine Dwarfkin inconspicuously shared a cab home together (for they were lovers). In the 62nd floor ladies room of Fuller & Grand, Ms. Kate Welland sat in a bathroom stall, crying lightly, without quite knowing why. Downstairs, her daughter Finn abandoned her successful begging post and began walking through the business-busy streets of Times Square, seeking out a Mickey Mouse Pez dispenser. In a strip mall out on Long Island, Benji's gay brother, Jerry, the ophthalmologist, stood behind the counter of Seymour Glasses trying to convince a crying twelve-year-old girl that, yes, the frames he was fitting her for made her look pretty, sophisticated. In

Orlando, Florida, at Estate Beth Shalom, retirement home, Art Seymour sat by the phone, lamenting the fact that he had received Father's Day wishes the night before from one, but not both, of his two sons. In California, in the Eternal Valley Memorial Park and Mortuary, a uniformed groundskeeper carefully tended to a small, inconspicuous looking tombstone marked P.C.P. And in New York City, a crumpled throwaway, a yellow paper flyer crunched into a tight little ball, skipped lightly down the street, sailing southward, until it stopped before a decrepit apartment building at 214 West 30th Street, looked up, bowed in silent homage, straightened itself out, considered the steaming sewer grating percolating below, and, after a moment's contemplation, jumped in.

8

In silence, the elevator doors opened onto a reception area of oak and glass where Benji was silently greeted by a smiling white-haired receptionist whose trapezoidal desk surrounded her on all sides, pinning her to her spot like a frog on a dissection tray. The space was silent and empty, but Benji, popping his ears, realized that real estate at this high altitude doesn't lie fallow. In fact, the receptionist suggested nothing to Benji but a mole, a mole whose surface appearance only hints at the busy, deeply deep network of tributaries rooting it in place. He approached, his black corduroy pants making swishing sounds as his legs rubbed against each other.

"I'm here for Peggy Poshlust."
Seen those initials before.
"I could sign for her."
Thinks I'm a messenger.
"No, I have an appointment."
Look like a bike messenger.
"Your name?"
Porno-man.
"Benjamin. Benjamin Seymour."

The receptionist picked up one of the three phones on her desk, dialed, and, covering the receiver with a ring-covered hand asked, "And what time is your appointment scheduled for, Mr. Seymour?"
"We didn't really set an exact time."

She cradled the phone.

"But you do have an appointment?"

"I have this," Benji said, smoothing out Troy's yellow buck slip on the cold marble counter:

> WHILE YOU WERE OUT
> TIME: 9:45 A.M., Mon, 6/17
> TO: Big Boss-man
> FROM: Peggy Potluck?
> OF: Fuller & Grand on 50th & 8th
> RE: to sked appt
> PHONE: 975-3021

"And you would be the Big Boss-man?"

"Yes, that's correct."

"Why don't you have a seat and we'll see if we can't get Ms. Poshlust on the phone."

"Thank you."

Benji swished over to the couch. Used to love that sound as a boy. In winter sometimes it seemed the cold froze everything. Sound included. All except the sound of those corduroy pants slicing a swath through the silence. Bet burglars don't wear them. Good idea for a mystery story. Kleptomaniac college professor identified by the sound of his swishy cords and tweeds. Hm. I'll never write it.

Not much of a basketball fan, Benji lightly perused the covers of the *Post* and *News*. FOR DADDY. ONE FOR DAD: JORDAN'S FATHER'S DAY GIFT: NBA TITLE. Gotta call dad. Don't forget, he thought, easing his way into the thick black leather couch, a magisterial couch whose every curve and buckle suggested to Benji's body the attributes of warmth, protection, and comfort. You are safe here, the couch stated implicitly, expertly exerting its soothing tantric force on neurotic muscles and ruined joints; our laws will help you, guide you, protect you, all for the low, low price of just $250 an hour. A bargain. He fixed his gaze on the double glass doors just to the right of the receptionist's desk and tried picturing what lay beyond. He imagined the doors swinging open as in a Busby Berkeley musical to reveal row after row of smiling, monocled, martini-sipping, tuxedo-wearing young lawyers tap dancing on black-and-white checkered floors as the women lawyers and paralegals, sheathed in diaphanous robes of justice, stripped down to bathing suits and dived one by one into a giant gavel-shaped swimming pool for the big underwater number. But this of course was not reality.

The reality of the place was this: behind the receptionist's desk lay twelve corner offices for the senior partners, fifty-seven offices for junior partners, one hundred and forty offices for associates, two hundred and three cubicle stations for executive assistants and paralegals, a cleaning/janitorial staff of thirty seven, a mailroom staff of nineteen, and a computer maintenance department of twelve. One flight below were conference rooms and the records and billing department. Below that was the copy center, human resources department, and day care center. Lower still was the subsidized cafeteria (whose Wednesday lunch special, the chicken cordon bleu with string beans, was a perennial favorite), a small executive gym where lawyers read reports while doing laps on treadmills and stationary bicycles or took a dip in the (Esther Williams–sized) lap pool, and an ancient law library complete with two creaking wooden ladders you could wheel around the stacks on rollers.

Benji leaned further back, deeper into the couch's fleshy depths. If the hierarchy of the operation was as fixed as the tree diagrams that prefaced children's books of Greek mythology, the office was correspondingly mounted on a God-like perch. The sixty-second floor. Not the twenty-second or thirty-second, or even forty-second. No, it needed to be aloft. To believe in the foundation of its myth, Fuller & Grand needed to leave the very notion of foundation far behind. Psychologically, it worked. Clients were secretly pleased to find themselves having to switch elevator banks on the twenty-first floor, comforted to discover clouds clinging to the sides of buildings ten stories below, to spot oxygen-starved pigeons, dizzy with vertigo, struggle to make it to their lawyer's office window, only to nose-dive to the earth below like Japanese fighter pilots in World War II movies. Gazing out beyond the blazing glass wall Benji thought, you used to have to build pyramids, ziggurats, wonders of the world to get this close to divination. But no more. Money. Money is the new godliness. Perhaps always been so. From this vantage point, from above, packed together and flattened out, the city looked like a Fisher Price play set, a map you could fold, a microchip you could hold in your hand. From up here, with the summer sun bleaching everything out to the same tepid white, the New

York City skyline looked less a big apple than an egg, an egg that could be imminently cracked. For the city's young lawyers, as for the gods, perspective was everything.

Through door, stage left, enters: a woman in a dark pinstripe pants suit, a smart butterfly pin. Pretty. Determined. Not quite yet 40.

"You have a package for Peggy?"

Poise, baby. Poise.

"No, we've been playing telephone tag for a couple of days, and I don't carry a cell phone, so I thought maybe we'd have better luck in person."

Ivy League, baby.

Her eyebrows considered this for a moment.

"And you are?"

Porno-man.

"Benjamin. Benjamin Seymour."

No recognition.

"And you have business with Peggy on the West Coast?" she asked.

No idea what she's talking about.

"Yes, that's correct. Peggy said I could reach her here while she's in town."

"Okay," she nodded. "I'm Kate Welland," she continued, extending a corroborating hand. "Peggy's been working out of my office while she's in town. Why don't you come with me."

All along the hallways were vents: vents in the ceiling, vents lining the floors, artificial apple blossom pine urine air percolating through the place as if they were so high up the cabin pressure needed to be regulated. They passed through hallways, hallways where work was happening, serious work you needed good posture and a good wardrobe to accomplish. Work you had to dress up for. Mental heavy lifting so rigorous your very fingers suffered from the torqued strain, begging the invention of bifurcated keyboards. Behind these office doors, deals were being made, contracts were being signed, estates were being divided, affairs were being consummated, harassment suits were being filed. Trailing behind her, Benji breathed in the minty fresh air of power, the fresh-scented, apple-blossomed, oak-paneled, halogen-lit fumes of power. He was in the halls of mission control, a New York City power center—his first—and he couldn't help but feel the energy of that knowledge infect his stride.

They passed the pantry. Water cooler. Coffee brewing. An interracial basket of cookies on the counter. A selection of teas whose names sounded suspiciously like psychological disorders (Earl Grey, Mellifluous Mint, Wild Berry Blast, Raspberry Zinger!, Quiet Chamomile) laid out in a fan. Porcelain mugs with slogans like "Number 1 Dad," and "Thenk!" and Far Side cartoons imprinted on their sides. Bustle. Commotion. Food. Movement. Work. This is work. This is what most people think of as work. And not a naked girl in sight!

Personally, he preferred Gordan Norman's style of law, Gordon Norman who had an office on the same floor as CUM, Gordan Norman with his crumbling yellow face, mustard-stained tie, nicotine-smudged fingers, and shameless subway advertising. (When you have just one call to make, dial 1-800-SHYSTER.) A couple of years ago, after Gordan found out exactly what type of business Benji was in, he confronted him one afternoon at the urinal. "If any of these Jesse Helms cocksuckers give you a hard time, I swear to God I'll wrap the First Amendment round their necks so tight they won't be able to fucking breathe." They hadn't spoken after that, and in the years since Benji's relationship to the law had pretty much been limited to the occasional late night episode of *Hill Street Blues*. But here? What brings him here? Peggy Poshlust? Who is she and what does she want?

"Peggy's been operating out of our offices this week. We do a lot of work with her agency out in L.A. You said you had a package for her?"
Benji stopped in midstride and looked at the woman's face askance. While the mascara of her right eye was perfectly applied, her left eye was some-what smudged and bloodshot, giving her the blurry look of a woman just emerging from a crying jag. Benji felt a surge of blood shoot to his penis.
"No, an appointment."
"That's right. I'm sorry, I'm a little distracted."
"Busy day?"
She took a deep breath before pressing on.
"Always."
"Know what you mean."

They walked straight ahead, they made lefts, they made rights, they dou-bled back, they nearly collided with a black kid ditty-bopping behind a mail cart.
"Got some string so I can find my way out?" Benji asked.

"I know, it takes a little getting used to," she said, committing them to a sharp right angle. "Here we are."

Entering her office, she motioned for him to take the seat across from her, checked off a paper on her desk, then read and crumpled a Post-It note hanging on her phone.

"Ow!"

"What's wrong?"

"Papercut. Will you excuse me for a minute," she asked, leaving.

He was alone. He exhaled. As he had not done so since meeting her, it felt good, more reward than reflex. He looked around. All that oak. Oak desk. Oak table. Oak chairs. Oak book cases. Nothing makes you feel your failure like oak. Sitting in the richly appointed office, Benji measured the weight of her oak-filled success against his own plastic failure. But Benji didn't blame life for this. He considered life neither cheap nor cruel. Nor was he narcissistic enough to believe life would single him out for any special brand of cruelty. The contrary, at moments like this, Benji recognized what could only be called life's generosity. Life could be surpassingly generous at times, and one of the things it could be generous about is failure. For if it's true that life exists as a series of tests, it's also true that life offers all kinds of opportunities to fail. And at so many different things! One can fail as a husband, a father, a son, a lover, a friend, a businessman, an artist, a third baseman, a tax accountant. One's health could fail. One's will could fail. One could die of heart failure. Fail till you get it right, that was the world's secret message. Fail till you're a complete, total, well-rounded failure. So much in the world remains unknowable, at least this one thing you'll get to know intimately. A dedicated apprentice of failure, Benji looked forward to the luxurious expansiveness of his adult mastery. And he knew he wouldn't have to press for it either. Even without tempting things, life had a way of delivering failure regularly, like mail. And if you were one of the lucky ones, or perhaps just patient enough, life would occasionally throw you an epic, life-flattening failure, delivered to winners at random like Publisher's Clearinghouse envelopes.

Lessons in failure: In junior high school, Benji had a math professor, Mr. Rosenberg, an enormous, muscular Hasidic Jew with a beard the thickness of an Eskimo's coat. A let's-get-down-to-business type, Mr. Rosenberg was a teacher who never endeared himself much to his students. A teacher whose beard hid too much of his face for intimacy, he affected an unnatural air of casualness through the rolled-up sleeves of his starched white shirts, but could never relax into true camaraderie with his students. If his kids knew he was a good teacher, and respected him for that, they didn't exactly like him. And he engaged in one practice that all of his students felt particularly unfair. After grading exams, Mr. Rosenberg would call out each student's name for him to come pick up his paper. Only, if the grade were ninety or above, he would also announce the student's grade. This meant that if you didn't break that sacred barrier, if you weren't included in that week's honor roll—you would have to make the long walk from your desk to Mr. Rosenberg—he of the biblical forearms and biblical forebears—with your head hung low. Which meant that even if you came close—even if you received a perfectly respectable grade in the high eighties—you were grouped with the others, the underachievers, the slackers, the neighborhood kids from bad families who didn't care. You experienced what they felt—you were them—and that failure by proxy was the worst thing in the world.

Of course, most failures aren't so public in nature. Most failures happen quietly, unspectacularly, and their effects are cumulative. Most of the time failure doesn't reveal itself in a moment but wraps around you over a lifetime, adding heaviness to your step until one day you recognize you've been wearing failure on your face all along, that your failures have decorated your breast like the medallions of an army general's coat, that they've stripped away what's best in you, like rain peeling away the layers of a freshly painted house.

The day is only four hours old and I haven't failed at anything yet, Benji thought, congratulating himself. A day. Life is made up of many days, day after day. It's so easy to let go. Of life. Life makes it easy. To slip on the existential banana peel and go flying. Each day regrouping after sleep, remembering who you are, reclaiming who you're supposed to be, held onto yourself through thin veils of memories, dreams, reflections. A wispy mental fabric. Life. One life is all. One body. One. Who's stopping me from being someone else today? Here. Now. An architect, an Egyptian astronomer, a Russian prince, a Renaissance knight.

He looked up. Diplomas on the wall. A phone on the desk, another on the bookshelf behind. Weighty blue looseleaf casebooks. Chronology documents grouped in three-inch black binders. *Oxford English Dictionary*. Ayn

Rand's *Atlas Shrugged* slumped in a corner. Pair of worn sneakers by the closet. Today's edition of *New York Law Journal*, koosh ball, brass lamp, kaleidoscope, and framed family photos scattered across the desk. I could do it, Benji thought. I could be a lawyer. What would I need? Rimless glasses, suspenders, polka-dot tie, shoe trees, law degree. Then: the oak, the desk, the casebooks, everything: mine. Her: out the window. Me: Esquire.

She re-entered.
"O, hello!" exclaimed Benji the dreamy defenestrator.

It was the first chance he really had to look at her, and in the interim, she seemed to have reapplied her mascara, as each lash was now as fine and pronounced as the nib of a quill pen dipped in ink. Too bad, thought Benji. In the right circumstances, there's something blowzy and sexy about a woman who's been crying. He watched her features settle into calm, as if she were a Polaroid photo in middevelopment. She's pretty, he thought.

As she sat down, Benji caught a glimpse of a large mole positioned just on the underside of her left calf. Easing into her chair, she subtly but not unconsciously shifted the mole away from him toward invisibility, and Benji knew he had her. Benji loved doing this—sniffing out the hidden nexus of a woman's sexuality, and he found it easier to accomplish than most, because his nose knew to go where others feared to sniff. With Penny, it was her eye. The large eye of a feathered bird or goldfish, opened wide and languidly hung with too much lidding, as if upholstered by an overzealous draper. That's what made her sexy, no matter what new color her hair was or how many cc's of silicone she injected herself with. An eye that lazily took in the world around her, an eye that reveled in the secret knowledge of just how close sexiness lies to sleepiness. And with this woman, Kate Welland, Benji predicted it was this mole, at once too big and tactile to be peddled off as a birthmark, that lay at the center of her awareness of her physical self. The mole bespoke of wildness, tenderness, adventure, chances taken, mistakes made, just-passed youth and encroaching middle-age-dom, hidden mysteries of the body, the secret language of kisses, Arabian nights. His guess was this third nipple caused her a great deal of pleasure and shame.

Good legs. A James Bond pair of legs, thought Benji, continuing to catalogue her sexual inventory. Benji long thought you could judge a woman physically in one of four ways. A woman could be pretty, beautiful, cute, or sexy. She could be one of them, or some of them, or none of them, but only rarely all of them. And then there was what Benji referred to as the slut coefficient, the prism through which all other characteristics were refracted. A measurement more hypothetical than actual, the slut coefficient was the index by which one imagined a woman's sexual effectiveness/comfort level in relation to: blood-red lipstick, thong panties, black leather pants, miniskirts, fishnet stockings, belly chains, four inch platform heels, unnatural acts performed publicly on bananas . . .

However, the slut coefficient, once a profound measurement, was in danger of being knocked into irrelevance by recent trends in fashion. To Benji's mind, women's fashion in the 1990s—at least in the major cities—was simply out of control. Outfits that once would have embarrassed Pigalle streetwalkers were now being proudly paraded by every gum-chewing fourteen-year-old in malls across the country. And not just kids. Everyone was dressing this way. It wasn't some outgrowth of the slut feminism of the mid-eighties as championed by Madonna and her hordes of teenage underwear-as-outerwear wearing clones. It wasn't political. There was nothing ironic or po-mo about it. No. Suddenly slut fashion was fashion and there was no explaining it. If it could be cleaved, clung to, heaved, or separated we were in business. The upside of it was that professional working women now dressed like whores. The downside was all the unfortunate auxiliary corollaries the slut coefficient, when improperly applied, had given rise to, public embarrassments such as "camel toe" (the bunching up of labia major and minor as outlined and viewed through stretch pants and jeans) and "ROWG" (acronym for "Right-Outfit-Wrong-Girl"). However, since Benji trusted that trends swung in a pendulous manner, he believed a return to conservative dress was inevitable, and looked forward to the sunny day when simple flower print summer dresses, pom-pom socks, and plain embroidered white cotton panties would be sexiest of all.

As she studied some document or other, subtly moving her lips along like a child as she read, Benji sensed a ferocious intelligence at work, a rapaciousness that existed just a degree or two shy of the sexual, a nature he guessed could be steered in the direction of the nether realm with just the gentlest bit of prodding. He continued looking at her. On his index, she stacked up thus:

Pretty: 8.
Beautiful: 7.
Cute: 3.
Sexy: variable, 3-9.
*Slut coefficient: hard to read.

But this is not what excited Benji. What excited him was the prospect of real breasts (real!). Cellulite dimples! Pliable flesh! One-inch heels! The beginnings of laugh lines around the mouth! Woman! He was in the office of a woman! A woman with a diploma, a past, a family, a kid! Stretch marks! A post-feminist, post-modern, post-orgasmic woman! Woman! She looked up from her papers, remembered she was not alone in the room, and smiled up at him from under arched eyebrows. Cat. She looks like a cat. Mama cat.

He felt a cold splash of sweat sweep across his face, felt trickles of sweat sled down his sides. With a Mont Blanc pen, she began writing something on a college-ruled yellow legal pad, and Benji was quickly relieved. Nail-biter like me. Really filthy nails, even worse than mine, he thought, examining her wracked cuticles as she wrote. Wonder what her modus operandi is? Does she set aside a certain time every day, or find herself doing it inadvertently? Does she nibble at them in the morning or at night? At home or in the office? Is the habit a holdover from adolescence or a new-found discovery? Does she sensualize the act, first dipping saliva-wet fingers into packets of sugar or salt before going to work on them? Is she a salt person or a sugar person? Does she incorporate food into her fucking? Has she ever given a honey blow job? Hand dipped a cock in chocolate? Sucked an Altoid during oral sex? . . .

She looked up again and smiled, somewhat nervously, not knowing how to keep him occupied, not realizing he was happily occupied already. He looked down at his own nails. Ravaged coastlines, each of them. Neurotic solidarity. Some found nail-biting a miserable, squalid habit, but not Benji. The contrary, Benji long thought that nail-biting showed a familiarity, a lack of disgust about the body and its capacity for uncontrollable, weed-like fecundity, and he sought out the habit in others. In fact, nailbiting formed a cornerstone of his daily communion, a Eucharist made up of the regular sampling of products from his factory of flesh. He coughed up and swallowed mothballs of phlegm, gouged at his nose and munched the crunchy kernels, bit his nails to the bloody quick. Besides lovingly staring at his own feces, he was known on occasion to dip a diffident pinky into silvery seminal pools and bring the clammy puddles to his lips in cinnamony seaweed strings; he ate waxy crumbs off the pillowed heads of Q-tips; rolled burst beads of pus between forefinger and thumb, and let the salty stuff dissolve on his tongue like cotton candy; and, at every opportunity, sucked vampirishly at his own bloody leaks.

To him, it was all about self-maintenance, about shamelessly familiarizing himself with all aspects of the body until there was nothing left for him to scandalize. Of course, these were all lessons learned from Penny. He remembered the first time they had taken a shower together after sex. There she stood, under the bare light of a naked bulb, bending over in the shower, shamelessly spreading her cheeks and letting the warm water cascade down the crack of her ass as Benji stood, penis hung at helpless half-mast, mouth slung open in slack-jawed amazement. Of course. Or course! Assholes are dirty. Assholes are dirty and Penelope wants hers to be clean. As clean as . . . well, as clean as a penny. A shiny new penny you're tempted to lick. This was cleanliness ground zero, Benji thought, watching her administer to herself in the toilet like a cat licking its coat. Clean asshole, shaved legs and armpits, shorn fingernails and toes, plucked eyebrows, makeup, lipstick, powder, puff, and bam—ready to go! No shame. No shame. That was the great lesson she had taught him, and he was comforted by the hint that this sophisticated lawyer lady might swim in the same streams of effluvia as he.

The Barrister?, The Litigator?, thought Benji, trying on different nom de porn for her. He halfheartedly envisioned some titles (*Litigation Lickin' Good, Oral Arguments, Cumpensatory Damages, Pounding the Gavel*) before settling on *Judge Welland's Sex Court*, a groundbreaking series in which real-life couples aired their sexual grievances before the honorable Judge Welland, who would sentence them accordingly:

"Your ah-na, y'know we used to do it a lot—in the car, at her mutha's, in the movie theater—but now, ever since we married, not so much no more."
"Your honor, if my husband wasn't such a drunk, lazy bum, maybe I'd feel a little better inclined to him when I get home at night—"
"Enough!" Judge Welland would demand, sternly pounding her gavel, "I

sentence you to give your husband head during every broadcast game of *Sunday Night Football.*"

"Your honor!'

"Don't talk with your mouth full! And you!" she'd say, ferociously turning on the husband, "I sentence you to eat your wife's pussy every afternoon during *Oprah.*"

"But your ah-na, I ain't never done that before—"

"Well, once you get past the smell you got it licked! Bailiff! Handcuffs! To the dungeon!"

"So you said you're a photographer?"

"Yes, photography."

Pornography.

"Must be a pleasure, being an artist, being able to work in those clothes," she said, not the least bit condescendingly.

"Yes, I was thinking the same thing."

No clothes. No clothes.

"Well, Peggy's been meeting with a bunch of people while she's in New York, I have a hard time keeping track of her. All those handlers and publicists and press days. It seems like actors can't make a move without signing a release form. It's interesting stuff, but entertainment law's a bit of a stretch for me."

"I know what you mean."

No idea what she's talking about.

"So you're going to be taking some photos of Michelangelo then?" she asked, passing a head shot Benji's way.

"Yes," said Benji the Bluffer.

Cute kid, Benji thought, examining the photograph. Looks familiar. Actors. Punk ass tools. He passed the photo back to Ms. Welland.

"I'm very much looking forward to working with him," Benji said, withdrawing his hand and accidentally knocking out of position a stately silver diptych framing two photos. The first featured Kate, in a big blue mommy sweatshirt, alongside a clean-shaven, slick-back-haired gentleman in a blue oxford pinstripe shirt—all teeth and eyes and velly, velly British—and a little girl. They all looked smiling and happy. The second photo was a close up of the same little girl, a year or two down the road, presumably a school portrait as she appeared magically suspended in front of a blue silkscreen of sky. Benji looked at Ms. Welland's left hand, iris-ing in on her ring finger. A thin band of flesh near the knuckle, slighter paler than the rest. Denuded. Divorced.

"This one yours?"
Looks like her.
"Yes. She'll be ten next week."
"Congratulations."
Mazel tov!
"Thanks."
"Ten, huh? Must be something at that age?"
Four years she'll be sucking cock.
"Yeah, she's a handful, all right."
Looks like the derelict downstairs. Could be twins the two of them. Doubles. Tale of Two Titties.
The phone rang.
"Excuse me for a minute."
Suckitsuckitsuckitsuckit
"No, I never received the card the class made."
Her: over the desk. Me: to the hilt.
"No, not as far as I'm aware."
Me: from behind. Her: continue call.
"Pneumonia?!"
Me: sucking her mole. Her: toe job.
"No, that's impossible."
Me: on the floor. Her: cowgirl.
"Pneumonia? No Finn, I mean Stephanie's never had pneumonia."
Me: in the ass. Her: nasty girl.
"Ms. Royster, yes this is Kate Welland."
Me: Iceberg Slim. Her: Marlene D.
"No, not as far as I'm aware—'"
Me: over her: over us.
"Yes, every day—"
Me: home alone. Her: permanent file.
"Okay, I will. Thanks. Bye."

She cradled the phone slowly.
"Is everything okay?" asked Benji solicitously, thinking salaciously.
"I just received the strangest call. My daughter's school just called to tell

me she hasn't been to class in two weeks."

She dialed another number as Benji pulled his chair in closer to examine the photograph of the little girl, his erection hitting a cruel corner of desk. Her. It's her.

"Excuse me," Benji interloped.

She held up a finger to silence him.

"No, no, listen to me—"

"Shh, just a minute."

And then on the answering machine Ms. Welland heard the following two messages: "Mom, this is Finn. I'm running away." Beep. And then another: "Mom. It's Finn again. I forgot. Don't look for me, okay?"

"O my God."

"Listen to me will you, I saw your daughter downstairs—"

She hung up.

"When?"

"Like five minutes ago, right before I came up here."

* * *

Outside, the courtyard was even more packed, hot, and sweaty than before. The hot dog vendor had switched to the shady side of the street, making room for a souvlaki/gyro cart that pumped fresh, foggy dark clouds of chicken, sausage, and lamb product into the air.

"Where was she?"

"There. Over there. She was sitting on the grass."

"Was she with anyone, children her own age, someone older?"

"No, she was alone."

"What was she doing?"

"I think she was begging."

"What do you mean 'begging'?"

"Well, she had one of those coffee cups that homeless people sometimes use, and she looked pretty bedraggled, not like in the photograph."

"She wasn't in her school uniform?"

"No."

"But you're sure it was her?"

"I think so. Let me try to remember what else."

"C'mon, c'mon!"

"Uh, I think she was reading Nietzsche."

"O, Christ. Finn!"

Ms. Welland burst into tears and staggered away from him, wandering around the courtyard, asking anyone who'd listen if they'd seen a little ten-year-old girl. After a while she returned to where Benji was standing. "You had her and you let her go!"

"I didn't know she was yours."

"You see a ten year old in the street and you don't think anything of it? You see a little girl begging in the street and what did you do?"

"I gave her an ice cream."

"You gave her an ice cream?!"

She burst into tears again, instinctively leaning into the stranger's frame to mask her face, wipe her tears, and feel the support of another human body.

Her face. Her hand. My shoulder.

Benji couldn't help but enjoy the moment. Physical closeness. His right leg went partly numb with pins and needles, so he shifted his weight to the left. Ms. Welland mistakenly took this change in body language as a cue to his discomfort and awkwardly disentangled herself from him. Benji stared at her fallen face. This is pain, he thought. This is what another person's pain looks like. Pain. Not my own. A mother's pain—and men just don't have the faces for that kind of tragedy. Benji felt himself, for the first time in months—years perhaps—thrust into immediacy. Jammed into the present. He liked it.

He held her shoulders, gently pushed her away from him and, with shaking hands, released her. Then, clutching his Pez dispenser for support, Benji the Benumbed, Benji the Bumbler, Benji the Benighted, Benji the Big Boss Man, Benji in Black, Benji the Brave, Benji the Baritone said softly, gallantly, mustering as much masculine force as he could into his quiet voice, "Ms. Welland . . . if she's out there . . . I'll find her . . . and bring her to you."

9

But first a crap. Searching for a public toilet, Benji thought there are certain things you shouldn't do with heavy bowels, and starting a search party was one of them. Contemplating the brick of a knish currently traversing the winding road of his lower intestine, Benji remembered how he wasn't a fan of lovemaking on a full stomach. Penny was. More than anything she liked to fill herself with bread and wine and rub her round belly, taut as a steel drum, as Benji slid into her. In that moment, in the roundness of her imagined pregnancy, they made a family.

He remembered sucking on one of her roast beef–tasting tampons once, sucking her swampy thickness right out of the thing, with her following, sucking on it herself, confirming his culinary judgment. He remembered licking her salt-skinned shoulder after it had turned raw in the sun, blistered, and peeled. He remembered her giving him a blow job in the bathroom, with him standing over her as she took a crap. Why zip up? he thought to himself when it was over, similar to the rational he used for not making his bed each morning, I'm only going to use it later anyway.

Benji walked along 50th Street down Eighth Avenue, the thin red letters of Radio City Music Hall's marquee visible in the distance a few blocks ahead. What do I do if I find her? Benji thought. Why did I say I'd look for her again? Her face. What's Hecuba to him or he to Hecuba? Benji asked himself, following behind a young woman whose tight hip-hugger jeans and midriff tank top revealed a tattoo of comedy and tragedy masks intertwined at the base of her spine. True, Benji thought, watching admiringly as each expression took renewed precedence with every step. Excrement makes us comic. Had Hamlet announced he needed to take a crap in the middle of everything, the whole show would have come tumbling down.

"Girls, girls, girls," chanted a middle-aged man in a stained red doorman's uniform outside of a ruined strip club named Bare Elegance. "Look no further. Girls, girls, girls. Look no further." Yes, I agree. What was the last thing she said? Words. No, wrong girl. Pez. She dug the dispenser. Smart girl. Where would I go if I was looking for a Mickey? Only one place around here, Benji thought, as he turned the corner onto Broadway, thrusting himself into Manhattan's neon pinball machine.

Times Square. Used to think it was Times Squared. MC squared. Relativity. Everything's relative. Perpetual daylight. Time bends. Times Square. Why's it named that? *Times* offices? Must be. Crush of bodies, Benji thought, giving his stride over to the speed of pedestrian traffic, wondering if he let himself go and held out his arms if he'd be able to simply body surf all the way down to the Disney Store. Honking horns. Steaming manholes. Hell just below. So many people. Hell is other people. Heaven, too. Everyone probably missing somebody. Lawyers, businessmen, garbagemen, hot dog guys, street vendors. Like this guy. Gold and leather bands in a suitcase. Wanna buy a watch, wanna buy a watch? Crone at a card table. Palm read. $5. Old world scarves a nice touch. Astrology. She believed in it. Space. Time of birth. Chart it out. No less reasonable than anything else. Homeless man in a doorway. Outthrust arm. "One penny to feed the homeless. One penny to make a difference. One penny to help another human being." Didn't smell him coming. Passing him, approaching newsstand. Good stuff hanging on the side, wrapped in plastic for easy cleaning. All the P that's fit to print. Old cover photos? No. Not her. Not today. No P is good P.

* * *

In early March of 1991, Penny disappeared. Instead of her baby face on the side of pink and white milk cartons, Benji would spot her open mouth and gaping holes in the latest edition of *Adult Industry News*, would spot her, under a variety of names, gracing the box covers of video compilations. "Benji-boy, I don't know what to tell you. I don't know where she is," Milton reported from California when Benji called, and the industry echoed Milton's response. The story with the production companies was always the same. "That was Penelope Pigeon, no way! Nah, man, no one knew that was her. We all thought she was just some B-girl."

Missing. What a terrible place to be. A spooked mansion of many rooms, a temporal landscape where hope and resignation vie for attention like the competing strings of a harp, missing raises the question of exactly who has disappeared and who's been left behind. In the initial waiting period, wandering through streets aglow with liminality, Benji felt like a survivor walking through ruins, surveying the topography of his own emotional Hiroshima. Then, slowly, as hope of her return gave way to the reality that no, she wasn't coming back, his world seemed robbed of color, drained of multichrome until the entirety of New York settled into a brittle yellowing landscape, like a faded newspaper photo discovered in a scrapbook.

Missing. Benji tried to romanticize the word with images of itinerant lives of hobos, of jumping trains, of sleeping in boxcars, of eating beans from the can, of the American tradition of odd-jobs and cross-country X's, of life on the lam. Awake at night, he thought of how even lying still we carry some of that movement, that turmoil around with us. Traveling though mausoleums of darkness, Benji thought of consciousness as a train, a night train you book passage on and can push as hard and fast as you're willing to go: past changing seasons and falling leaves, past frozen seas and hills like white elephants, past Fellini clowns and Dylan's tambourine man, past Mondrian grids and Picasso's blue guitar picker, past figures out of your past, through memory, dream, and reflection toward some divine stillness. And what awaits you there? Knowledge? Wisdom? Peace? No. Exhaustion, as Benji discovered one morning when, upon waking, he just couldn't get out of bed. He couldn't even formulate a sentence. Burrowing deeper and deeper into the wilderness of exhaustion, "You're sleeping," his unconscious would alert him, and up he'd shoot, insomnia snatched from the jaws of sleep. All he could do was close his eyes, peer his head out the train compartment window and read, in big block letters: "EXHAUSTION TERMINUS."

"It's a beautiful day outside, Benji, why don't we go out," Troy pleaded in the early days of Penny's disappearance.

"Uggghhh."

"Get some sushi—"

"Aaawwwrrrhhh."

"Go to Scores."

"Gggrrraaahhh."

And he would cry. Cry as his business and his world went to hell. And then laugh, predicting Penny's own barbed reaction to the maudlin, womanly side of his personality. "Now that I'm gone you see me all the time, don't you? As if you saw me clearly once—just once—when we were together," she'd say, slowly forming the words, in that careful, brutal way of hers. "Get over it poet-boy," she'd say, striking a Camel Light like some black-eyed '50s Dead End Kid.

But that wasn't enough for Benji. Imagined dialogues weren't enough. Depleted bank accounts weren't enough. Sleeping fourteen-hour days wasn't good enough. The longer it went on, the more adroit he became at stoking the fires of his emotional furnace. He experienced emotional combinations that—like an Olympic gymnast landing in a split after executing a triple vault—he had previously considered impossible. Pain and exhilaration. Humor and masochism. Terror and joy. Squalor and expansiveness. Often in flashes, one after another. Until one day, the pain, which had once been so acute, which had threatened to black out everything else, like the moon made large and eclipsing the sun, became ritualized. He was punching a clock: waking up, spreading himself out on the rack, enduring, and then returning to sleep. This was his job, what he had, what he could do, what he'd become. And on clear days he recognized if he gave that up—the pain, the longing—he just might cease to exist.

This must be what doctors refer to as the phantom limb, Benji thought, bereft, groping for her form in bed next to him on Sunday mornings, longing for her hip which once fit so precisely, so tenderly into the groove of his waist. It was as if some evil scientist had taken away an element necessary to keep the periodic table of his survival in balance; as if sweet oxygen had been sucked out of his atmosphere. He even found himself gasping for air, re-experiencing the asthma he thought he had matured out of. Temporarily, Benji's adolescent bronchial dilator replaced his Pez dispenser as right hip pocket accessory of choice.

There he is, not long ago, frozen on a subway platform, in the street, in a movie theatre, rendered paralyzed by an eye lidded like hers, a calf, a sliver of arm glimpsed from behind, as if given the impetus and creative license he could fashion her together out of parts. Sometimes he'd even venture to tap an anonymous woman on the shoulder to verify her very un-Penny-ness, only to have her look into his fallen, forlorn face, and— having never seen such depths of emotion writ large across the visage of a member of the masculine sex—immediately invite him home to cook for him, to clean for him, to iron his weary trousers, to cuddle the wounded puppy that was Benji, who, after opening his mouth for a silent scream that never came, would abstain. He was married, he would say. Married to a ghost.

It was around this time that Benji, who'd kept in pretty good shape after college, switched to an all-caffeine, all-sugar diet. He drank two liters of Coca-Cola a day. He visited Hershey Park in Pennsylvania to purchase blocks of chocolate on the cheap. He licked layers of salt off potato-chipped fingers. He swallowed Swedish fish by the tank-full. He ate whole fried chickens by the bucket. He gorged on gallons of ice cream. He began taking up take-out Chinese food in earnest, drawn not so much to the food's addictive starchiness as to the fortune cookies that finished each meal, fortune cookies which told him: "Obsession is not the truth of love," and "You are a kind and generous soul," and "You are a popular person with many admirers," and "You will travel far and wide."

And why not believe a cookie? How is a fortune pulled from a fried piece of dough any less legitimate, any less a product of fate than the people who form the sitcom cast of your life, the family DNA straps you into, careers gathered from coincidence? How is a fortune cookie any less real than the advice given to you your entire life from parents and siblings and teachers and friends and lovers and enemies and your own fractured, mosaic self?

At least the cookie tastes sweet.

* * *

"Benny, now's your chance," Jerry said, that first night Benji stayed with him in Westchester in April '91.

"Wa?"

"Your chance to start again," Jerry upbeated. "To start your life again. To remake yourself as a professional. To live a professional life. To make use of that $100,000 degree of yours."

"Jerry, just because Penny's gone . . ."

"Listen Benny, I liked Penny."

"You never liked Penny. You never even knew Penny."

"Look, you got mixed up with a hot piece of tail. I can understand that. I do understand that. First three years after I came out I fucked everything in sight. But to throw everything away. To throw everything away. Benny, you just gotta adjust your thinking on this one. Remember what you said to me when I came out?"

"Stop talking about yourself in the third person."

"No. You said, this isn't a tragedy, this is an opportunity."

"I never said that."

"You did say it, and it was the kindest thing anyone around me was saying."

"Never said it."

"And that's what I'm telling you tonight. This is not a tragedy, it's an opportunity. An opportunity to change your life, to turn it all around. Dad thinks so too."

"Dad thinks I work in advertising."

"Bullshit. Dad knows. He won't talk to you about it but he knows."

"Dad doesn't know. Waddaya mean dad knows?"

Lawrence, Jerry's long-time, live-in lover, a bald, black, suspender-sporting lawyer, had entered the room while the brothers were talking and was now curled up like a cat—slinky, long, and content—at Jerry's baronial knee with Jerry tenderly stroking his silvery pate.

"I know dad knows 'cause we talked about it. I know 'cause he saw one of your films. I know 'cause you broke his heart and you don't even know it, you stupid sonofabitch. I know 'cause if losing mom to the Big C and having a fag for a son wasn't enough to kill the old man off, having a pornographer in the family just might do the trick. I know 'cause you're throwing it all away and killing Dad in the process over this crazy broad!"

* * *

The last few months in particular had been torturous, with Benji waiting by windows like a soldier's wife. He'd spend the days cleaning, cataloguing new powders and pills as they made their phosphorescent presence known in new corners of the house. It was all new. The drugs were new, the food was new (instant mashed potatoes and Hi-C orange drink), the accessories were new (a red and blue plastic Superman lunchbox whose thermos held twin syringes, balloons, spoons, and a little plastic baggie filled with cotton balls), the terminology was new ("the drip," of cocaine as it leaves an aspirin slide down the back of your throat; the tooth-fairy-ish "freeze" of a dot of powder placed on the tip of the tongue).

To make himself useful, some days he would go to the main branch of the New York public library at 42nd Street and position himself in the great hall in a jacket and tie, to research different drugs in pharmacology textbooks to discern how each of them worked in an attempt to remove them from the sphere of plastic baggies and triple scales and swarthy long-haired men with guns and goatees into the realm of antiseptic hospital hallways, of science, of medicine, of Freud. (Cocaine: a colorless or white crystalline narcotic alkaloid, $C_{17}H_{21}NO_4$, extracted from coca leaves and used medically as a local anesthetic. He copied the definition down in one of the marble-covered composition notebooks he kept journals in as a child and stared at the word. Letters and numbers! Extracted from coca leaves! Used as an anesthetic! Credibility! Mastery!)

When it came to narcotics, Benji had always preferred to wade in the shallow end of the pool. His experience with drugs had been limited to a semester or two worth of tokes up at school, with the happy leaf rendering him alternately manic and incapacitated. If, during his manic marijuana moments he was known to frequent the Japanese joint out on Route 13 and smear green wasabi paste by the spoonful onto shiny pieces of sushi until tears burst from his eyes (a practice invariably followed by week-long fever dreams of melting Dali landscapes), during quieter moments, he was known to silently stare at a corner of the room, contemplate a crack in the wall, a patch of poster, the crenellated cap of a bottle of beer, and drift off into the warmest sleep he had ever known. Since Benji was convinced that his experiences on pot were the equivalent of a lesser man's experiences with psychedelics, he never felt the urge to venture through those glutinous doors of perception and so never went near wild mushrooms or tabs of paper decorated with purple spaceships and dancing Grateful Dead teddy bears. The idea of cocaine in particular turned him off: there was a metallic thrust to the powder, a technological edge to the razor-on-glass scratchiness he didn't entirely trust, and besides, his nose was an orifice he took special pride in keeping clean. (If, according to Freud, other children traditionally passed from the oral to the anal onto the genital stage, Benji was sure he'd passed through a nasal period somewhere along the way.) But fearful of Penny flying away on powdered wings, he tried it, once, against his better judgment, as an experiment, to see if it would somehow realign them, keep them in tune. When he finally did snort the stuff, with Penny in a fuzzy blur sitting beside him, it reminded him of drinking pot after pot of espresso the night before his big art history exam during his Italian semester abroad. Wired. It made him feel wired. That, and it made his nose tingle with frostbite. And it gave him a three-hour erection.

But it was no use. He was no longer reaching her. Their satellites had stopped orbiting each other. Staring into her vacant, raccoon-eyed face, pleading, confessing his everlasting love for her, he was greeted with a distant laugh, a chuckle, a shrug of recognition. But these were symbols of something gone, road signs to the razed, magic bridge you need to cross to reach another person, that fairy tale bridge people move toward in all directions, in all earnestness, but very rarely reach.

Penny.

* * *

Sleep. What is sleep? What's it for? Necessity of dramatic structure? Separate days. Beginning. Middle. End. Benji knew he was sleeping, knew he was firmly lodged in the hypnogogic state between sleep and awake, the state he could access through drowsiness, reverie, or narcotics, the state he spent most of his time in. And for a somnambular moment, New York was his. Sifting through the city's glittering kaleidoscope, waltzing through the bubbling afternoon heat, Midtown formed a fantastic summer dreamscape, his own personal movie set: the people jockeying through the streets extras hired from central casting, the near collisions of cab and pedestrian the expert orchestrations of stunt men, the buildings and cream soda-colored sky a scrim borrowed from a movie musical. All the trees fake. The sun a giant bulb.

Finn. He would find her. This he would do. That looks like Finn, he thought, pursuing a girl from behind. So she's black? So she's seventeen? So she's wheeling a baby stroller in front of her? What the hell difference does it make? Liberal lawyer lady can live with it. Make her a hero around the office. No. Yolanda won't do. Must find Finn!

* * *

"This has to stop," he announced one morning-night when she staggered home three hours late.
"Benjiiiiii," she sang, pulling her black dress up over her head.
"Penny, listen to me."
"Benji, Benji, Benji, Benji," underclothes falling from her, feathery, as she made her way to bed. "Benji, Benji, Benji," she said lowly, arriving next to him, reaching for his hand, running it over her.
"O, Benji."
"No, don't do that. Please don't do that," he said softly, removing her gentle, learned hand. "Don't use it like that."

The room, the pastoral expanse they had spent so many afternoons, mornings, and nights in, by the light of candles and the warmth of wine and the heat of bodies, had taken on the ghastly green tincture of a horror movie. It seemed smaller than before.

Penny wasn't one to talk much in bed. She believed that words—the duplicitous double agents—had mischievous ways of changing allegiances in midflight, of turning the serious comical, the sexy manipulative, the true false. She didn't trust them at all. "What if I use the wrong one?" she'd ask Benji, whom she likewise trained in erotic silence. But this time he spoke. He'd replay the words of that night to himself innumerable times. If only he'd been clever. If only he'd been smart. If only he'd said X instead of Y. If only Penny had been a little less Penny.

"I can't keep doing this," he began. Poet.

"Benji. Benji. Benjiiiiii."

"Listen to me. Look at me. I can't do this anymore. Do you understand?"

"Come here," she said, laughing, but when he lifted her face to him, he saw she was crying, weeping, her face streaming wet, crunched up in a Guernica mask.

"Please come here," she cried, following him, flopping herself off the bed like a ragdoll, making a desperate grab for his feet.

"What? These? You want these? Here!" he said, unbuckling his shoes and throwing them at her. She scrambled after them across the floor, clinging, clawing, holding them to her face.

"Benji, Benji, Benji, Benji, Benji," she cried, hugging the shoes, speaking to them, caressing the leather as if it were his skin.

And then he smelled it. Shit. The smell of shit. Her shit. She'd shit herself.

"Benji, please don't go."

But he was out the door.

* * *

It was months and months later, after Benji had stopped watching the news, had stopped reading the obituaries (for Penny's parents, owners of a successful model toy plane company, came from money), had stopped calling hospitals, that Benji, who always hated the phone, stopped answering his calls. Since he had also grown into the habit of leaving his telephone ringer off and his answering machine on mute, it was not until the day after it was recorded that he noticed the flashing red light and received the following message: "Benji this is Penny. I think I'm married. I'm all fucked up and I'm not sure but I've got a ring and Papa Bear's with me and I think we're married."

* * *

A subterranean cultural footnote that preceded the gangsta rap deaths of Tupac Shakur and Biggie Smalls were the no less sanguinary East

Coast/West Coast porn wars of the early nineties. A direct outgrowth of Milton Minegold's move to Los Angeles, the P-wars pitted the intellectual, literary efforts of the old school New York Jewry against the cheaply made gonzo product coming out of the emergent California hardbody surfer circuit.

In 1989 Milton made the decision to move out West. His marriage had failed—for obvious reasons—his son Gabriel had killed himself—spectacularly, by hurling himself from the clock tower of Cornell University—his daughter Jessica had converted to Catholicism and was helping to build a dam in Ecuador, and Milton was ready for a change. Most important though, Milton wanted a tan.

"Benji-boy, I want to die in the sun."

"What about the show?" Benji asked.

"Fuck the show. There's no money in public access."

A program of such underground notoriety that no less a personage than Howard Stern appeared one sunny day to thank Milton for his influence, for being the shining star of inspiration he was, *Milton's Midnight Menagerie* was something of a New York institution. Each episode began the same way. After a Johnny Carson drumroll, an Ed McMahon voice announced in tones of deep show-biz seriousness, "Coming to you live from beneath the Bijou Bowling Alley in Poughkeepsie, New Jersey, ladies and gentlemen, please welcome certified public accountant, cultural gadfly, pundit, writer, actor, director, and spoiler of women . . . Mr. Milton Minegold."

As part of the city's public broadcasting licensing agreement, New York City cable affiliates had been forced to allot an hour of public airtime for every hour they sold commercially, and Milton, always ahead of the loop, was one of the first people smart enough to see the hidden potential in free broadcasting. *Milton's Midnight Menagerie*, a public access show he'd been televising for twenty years, featured interviews with porn stars, plugs for Milton's latest films and magazines, call-ins, and heated political debates on topics of the day (for Milton was nothing if not an informed member of the citizenry.) For all that, the show was perhaps best known for "Milton's Motherfuckers," the splenetic segment that ended each episode, in which Milton lashed out against enemies both real and imagined. Hitler, Nixon, Spiro Agnew, J. Edgar Hoover, McCarthy, Reagan, Mussolini, George Steinbrenner, his ex-wife Marion, all came under the emerald-eyed gleam of Milton's wrath. "Tonight let me explain to you why Tricky Dick is an irredeemable cocksucker," began one memorable segment, on the eve of the release of some more of the 37th President's secret tapes.

Most of the recipients of Milton's rants weren't so lofty. Milton came out of the generation of Jewish-American men convinced that someone was always trying to put one over on them. That was the organizing principal of his personality: to take offense, to gauge slights, to register the precise measurement of insults. And to get there first: to weigh perceived threats and counterattack before the first salvo was launched. A lost patrol in search of a fight, his helmet forever pitched for battle, what Milton relished more than anything were the momentary flashes of command that attended his interactions with people in the service industries, and anyone else whose station in life fell beneath his own. Bossing around toll collectors, cleaners, garbagemen, maids, mailmen, messengers, delivery boys, and waitresses made Milton feel like a big shot, and better yet, provided him with bellwether launch pads for his flights of animus, for if one of them didn't meet Milton's lofty standards of professionalism (or failed to give him a receipt, or flirt with him, or laugh at one of his corny jokes), they were doomed. Milton would not hesitate to call over the waitress' manager and ream her out in front of him until she cried; he had no problem sending back the food or the shirts; no qualms finding the name of the president of such-and-such a company and writing scathing, pages-long letters of complaint explaining why the gentleman's company was worthless, his workers incompetent, his product crap; there was never any delay in his storming out of restaurants, stores, theaters, and shops after making a stink. He liked making a stink. Milton came out of the generation of men that felt there was a right way of doing things and a wrong way, and that if you averted your eyes from that line for a moment, the winds of indifference would blur it away. All of which masked the sad truth: behind the outrageous camouflage of his profession, beside the weekly televised spittoon granted his bile, Milton was just another sixty-year-old alta cocker kvetching about life's indignities, protecting his small patch of pride from the daily humiliations that made life worth living.

One time, years ago, when Gabriel was just a boy, Milton was in the living room doing the taxes of one of his friends when the doorbell rang with a pizza delivery. Distracted, Milton handed Gabriel a ten dollar bill, instructing his son to pay the nine dollars for the pizza and tip the delivery boy fifty cents. When the delivery boy couldn't make change on the tip, Gabriel, flummoxed, told him to keep the ten. The difference only amounted to two quarters, fifty cents, but when Gabriel returned to the living room without any change and reported to his father what had happened, Milton hit the roof. To Milton, it wasn't a question of money. (More than anything, Milton hated the popular anti-Semitic associations of Jews with stinginess; cringed at terms like "cheap Jew," "Shylock," and "Jew-ing" someone down; and went out of his way to be generous with family, friends, and business associates.) No, to Milton, it was a matter of principle. "Son, I understand what you did, it wasn't your fault, but it's that man's job to have change. He has to be able to make change. That's what he does." Milton very calmly asked his friend to go home, then he pulled on his parka and his furry Trotsky winter hat, and marched the half-mile in the snow to the pizza joint (as the car was in the garage being fitted for snow tires), where he waited patiently in one of the bright red booths for half an hour for the return of Carlos, the five-foot-four Mexican delivery boy. "You the cheap little fuck lied to my kid?" He asked Carlos, whose cheeks were bright red from the cold. For a moment, Carlos thought the man had been sent from INS. "You the sonofabitch try to cheat my kid? Huh?! You try to steal from my kid brown-man! Gimme those fucking quarters before I beat them out of you!"

And so it went with the television show: "Tonight's motherfucker is that waitress at the Nebraska Diner on Cropsey Avenue in Brooklyn who wouldn't bring me a second basket of rolls like I asked . . ." began a typical performance, or, "Tonight's motherfucker is Mike Segundo, manager of the Potamkin auto dealership in East Rutherford, New Jersey. In your ad you promised a free, deluxe Totes umbrella with every test drive, but by the time I got there, your guy said all the umbrellas were gone. Potamkin, you broke the sacred circle of trust! You'll pay for this! You'll pay for this Potamkin! Potamkin you fucked me and you must stop it!"

For all his pettiness however, litigation brought out the poet in Milton, who, after being acquitted on obscenity charges for the fifth time in two decades, but having been sentenced to four days and three nights in jail for absentmindedly bringing a loaded gun with him to court, rose to the occasion to deliver perhaps his greatest performance, an operatic aria of Caruso-esque proportions, an obscenity-laced diatribe directed at legendary Manhattan District Attorney Robert Morgenthau, an old fashioned spiel that left even longtime viewers dizzy.

"Tonight's motherfucker is Manhattan DA Robert Morgenthau. This cocksucker, he tried to get me when I started back in '68, he came after me again in '73, and '78, and then in '84 during the Bonzo regime. And now he comes after me again. And you know what, this fucking sperm-sucker's never gonna get me 'cause what he doesn't understand is that there's a phantom America out there the Founding Father's knew would need protecting, that there's an invisible republic where it's gonna be Thomas Jefferson, Sally Hemings, Lenny Bruce, Miles Davis, and me sitting at the dais on Bar Mitzvah day," he went on, wagging his gnarled, arthritic fingers at the camera. "Okay, I'm not a smart man—I've been married twenty-six years to prove it—to bring a loaded gun to court is not a smart move, I'll admit that. But to lock me up for four days! To put me in the Tombs with the animals! To put me in the Tombs! Morgenthau you'll pay for this! You'll pay for this Morgenthau! But this guy's old, he's older than dirt. He's so old he's rotting, he's like a rotting piece of lumber! And he doesn't like me. Well, I'm not too crazy about you either, Morgenthau. So from now on, every show we're gonna run the DA's number and I want all of you watching to call this turd-sniffer and tell him Milton's minions will see you in hell! I'll see you in hell, Morgenthau! I hope you choke on my sperm next time! Timmy, run the number. Run the home number, Timmy. Timmy, put the number up. Morgenthau," he'd say, crazed, grinning his death mask into the camera as the Manhattan District Attorney's home phone number flashed across his face, "this is just the beginning!"

Once Milton moved the *Menagerie*—which for twenty years had provided a phlegmatic platform for the New York industry—that was it. As unofficial New York ringleader, Milton offered everyone a chance to make a break for the West. And most took it. Those who didn't paid the price. One old-timer, Johnny Bloodstone, who had gone legitimate years before but hung around the fringes of the industry as something of an unofficial advisor and consigliere to Milton, had pleaded with Milton to stay in New York. But Milton wouldn't be swayed. A few weeks after the exodus Johnny was found keeled over in his favorite restaurant in Little Italy, face down in a plate of shrimp carbonara, victim of a stomach-churning bout of cryptosporidiosis that landed him in a hospital room (or more accurately, the bathroom of his hospital room) for weeks. Milo Pipe, who lived in Queens and chose to stay in New York with his wife and kids, was pushed onto the subway tracks one morning during rush hour just as an oncoming F train was pulling into the station. Sliding between the tracks, just barely escaping both the train's crushing weight and the third rail's electric charge, Milo remained there, pinned for several long minutes amidst puddles of tar and piss, until the six-ton dragon precariously passed overhead. Later that week, an electrical fire occurred on the set of one of Benji's shoots when, following standard equipment checks, an inky movie light inexplicably exploded, leaving two of the most loyal actors in Benji's stable, Ana Rexia and Roy G. Biv, with isolated first and second degree burns. That same night, Ana was held up at gunpoint outside her apartment in Brooklyn and Roy was stabbed in a back alley in the East Village.

But Benji himself was never physically threatened. Benji and Penny had been Milton's surrogate kids for the past few years, and Milton knew of the heartbreak Benji had endured when Penny left. He wouldn't bring Benji any bodily harm. No, Milton was going to smoke him out. An inhabitant of a rent-controlled Manhattan apartment he swore they'd carry him out of in a box, a lover of junk food, uninterested in clothes, someone whose only real fiscal vices were glossy art books and Bob Dylan bootlegs collected at record shows (his favorites being the definitive, unofficial six-CD volume of *The Basement Tapes,* and the legendary 1966 tour of England culminating in the Royal Albert Hall show and cries of "Judas!"), Benji never considered finances much of a problem. In fact, he didn't consider finances much at all, his relationship with money having always been one of peaceful if respectful coexistence—akin to an aunt you're not crazy about whose stubbly cheek you graze with a kiss come holiday time.

As if to reinforce Benji's abstract relationship with money, these days banks—with their rows and rows of black lacquered ATMs—were looking more and more like video game arcades. Indeed, Benji looked upon his daily ATM account statement with all the competitive disinterest of a pinball machine score. (They even called it your "pin" number, he thought.) "I lost today's game," he'd think to himself, or, after an unexpected tax refund check, "I'm ahead today. All time high!"

But now money was starting to turn its (limited) affections away from him. The market was drying up. Benji Bar Mitzvah bonds were being cashed. As his movies were knocked into oblivion by shelves full of cheaper, more explicit product shot on video, the idea of hanging his hopes on film seemed more and more unfeasible, more and more ludicrous.

Benji loved shooting on film. He remembered standing around waiting for Milton on the day of his first shoot—a $50,000 mega-production entitled *Blow White and the Seven Whores*—and realizing how, as the trucks pulled up to the warehouse one after another, he had never seen such a concentration of natural resources before. As crates of metal, plastic, wood, aluminum, cables, wires, costumes, props, pipes, gels, makeup, and food made their way off the trucks, Benji couldn't help but think, "What is all this stuff?" He would soon learn.

Since most pinot productions couldn't afford more than one or two grips, when the actors weren't performing they were expected to haul equipment and props, lay down pipes of PVC tubing and push dollies during tricky tracking shots, pop open and close spiky metal tripod stands, and warn everyone on set to avert their eyes before switching on the lights. Something of a cross between art and construction work, Benji found the physical exertion of filmmaking supremely satisfying. And then, after the picture had been developed and synched and the work print returned to him on reels, he was treated to the opposite experience, as the brawny work of back muscles yielded to the fine work of fingertips. "This is where the picture comes back to you, where you get to re-establish your personal relationship to it," Milton explained, loading a bacon-thin film strip through flatbed spools the day he gave Benji his first editing lesson in a suite off 47th and Ninth. This was the part Benji loved most: making meaning out of the juxtaposition of sound and picture, cutting on movement, prolonging and compressing scenes for maximum erotic impact. Benji loved handling film, loved the lace curtain delicacy of it, loved the tactile, artisan craftsmanship that went into the process. He loved the tools: the razors and markers and tape and gloves: practical arts and crafts stuff which seemed to him to be the very opposite of film technology. He loved the hours of monastic solitude spent in editing rooms surrounded by hanging threads of film. (He even resisted switching over to the Avid, the digital editing system that had revolutionized the film industry in the late eighties, for that reason.) And he was a quick study. After two or three films, Milton made Benji chief editor of Scylla & Charybdis Productions. If he didn't consider himself an artist exactly, Benji's technical know-how made him feel, at the very least, highly skilled.

And that craftsmanship, the strain that went into the filmmaking found its way into the fucking. If the performers had to stop every time a shot was completed, if they needed to rearrange themselves and restart every time cameras and lights were repositioned, this also meant they became practiced in the Zen virtues of patience and endurance (which is the beginning of intimacy, even love). One of the saddest things about video was how easily its indiscriminate cheapness, its technological egalitarianism, leant itself to speed and detachment. The lock-and-load mentality of a five dollar video shot quickly with natural light incited jackhammer, oil rig sex, which in turn led to the apotheosis of the form, the Shirley Jackson free-for-alls known as gang-bang videos. While Benji looked on these developments with disgust, it was no use. Resist as he did, Benji no longer had the financial wherewithal to tie his aspirations with 16mm string. After Milton moved out West, Benji never shot on film again.

* * *

If the New York City skyline—with its arrogant vault of pointed buildings piercing the starless sky like needles in a pincushion—tells us everything we need to know about the city's character, then California's woozy sky—with its high, high dome the psychedelic reds and oranges of a hippie girl's dress—is equally instructive. Benji hated L.A. He hated its warmth. He hated its hipness. He hated its assorted jellybean feel. He hated driving. He hated how a sprawling suburb with a few tall buildings had the nerve to pass itself off as a city. He hated the way people looked one another in the eye as they walked along Venice Beach instead of fixating on the ground (as decades of New York distrust had taught him they are supposed to). He hated the almost imperceptible shift in one's personal space, which crushes in a few inches closer in the California sun. He hated the way every time he ordered a sandwich he had to remember to tell the waiter to hold the avocado. And his hatred was compounded by another fact: Benji was a geographical idiot. Geography being the blind spot in his general good knowledge, growing up Benji often mistook cities for states and vice versa, generally giving the cities precedence: "Illinois is in Chicago right?" he'd ask his father, or, "California is the capital of Los Angeles." If even in his native New York, laid out in its anal-retentive grid, Benji preferred mental landmarks to street signs, he was a mess out West.

Moreover, Benji disapproved of the Californication videos he saw. They all looked the same. The settings: palatial residences with wall-to-wall white carpeting, black leather couches, an absence of bookshelves, and an abundance of bigscreen TVs. The actresses: stoned surfer chicks with tattoos, body piercings, and the enthusiasm of barstools, or indestructible Slavic blondes looking to fuck their way to a visa. The actors: young, tan, smooth-muscled virtuosos with the short, compact builds of middleweight high school wrestlers. The plots: anything that would get the gang close to the pool.

Gone was the body hair, the swarthiness, the dirty sock reality principle he so loved about the New York scene. And maybe that was it, the disappearance of the reality principle, that curdled Benji's enjoyment. The L.A. videos didn't feel real. They didn't seem authentic. They looked like what a lifelong New Yorker's idea of sex by the pool might be like. The idea of Milton's minions in Los Angeles—with their vampirish hatreds and prejudices and Hebraic gloom laid out to shrivel and burn in the naked California sun—just didn't feel right. But, if the fit was all wrong, like Michael Corleone moving the family to Vegas at the beginning of *The Godfather, Part II*, it still had some sleazy charm to recommend it. And like Michael Corleone in that same film, Milton knew no empire was complete without a compound.

There were all sorts of rumors circling around The Wonderland Mansion, Milton's hideaway. And not the usual run-of-the-mill mirrored ceiling coke and orgy stuff of Hollywood lore, but rumors of underground tunnels, of dungeons, of outdoor swimming pools filled with Chopin vodka, of gynecological chairs decorating the living room, of white girls sold into slavery. For all that, the place proved impossible to locate, impossible even to verify its existence. Some pegged it a smallish house off the Ventura Freeway at the Van Nuys Boulevard, others swore it was a hotel in San Francisco, while others had it for a hacienda as far away as Colorado Springs.

If the Wonderland Mansion existed then in a terrain somewhere between the fantastic and the real, everyone knew you could always catch Milton at the New Purity Restaurant, the popular, family-style eatery he had opened in the Valley his first year in L.A. If the New Purity came off as a diner for squares, a restaurant where families, truckers, and vacationers could feel happy and safe amidst the flapjacks, mashed potatoes, and lumberjack specials, Milton delighted in the knowledge that there was usually a fuck film or two being shot on the premises (in the kitchen, the storage room, the toilet) and signs in the windows which read cryptically, gnomically, "We Have Crabs!", "Fresh Meat & Chops!", "Eat Fish, Live Longer!", and "Girl Wanted!"

Though the standard fare at the New Purity was of the cheeseburger/chocolate shake/Greek salad variety, diners, upon speaking a special, regularly changing password, were led downstairs to a separate dining room and given an alternative menu featuring the house specialty and Milton's favorite: glatt kosher Chinese food. This secret lair, dubbed Milton's Paradise Regained, served as a nightmare landscape of Milton's cultural and culinary id, resplendent as it was in garish red and green velvet, dragon-head lanterns, bamboo tables and chairs, gold-plated mezuzahs, enormous Passover plates, and blue-and-white Israeli flags. The voices of Tony Bennett, Frank Sinatra, and Perry Como mingled with the mellifluous ting! of Japanese wind chimes and the soothing sounds of freshly running streams supplied by a small, indoor waterfall. And the food: General Sharon Chicken, Netanyahu Noodles, and Gaza Strip Beef with Broccoli competed with steaming pots of London broil in ketchup and onion soup mix ladled out over beds of sticky brown rice; Dr. Brown's Original Cream Soda was served alongside bouquets of imitation fantailed butterfly shrimp; scoops of chopped liver, stacks of rye bread, and cubes of kuggel smuggled themselves onto flaming PuPu Platters already loaded with kosher spring rolls, beef skewers, fried wontons, and pineapple chunks. It was all cobbled together. It was in terribly poor taste. It was a huge hit.

More than serving good food at a reasonable price, beyond being the den of a notorious pornographer, the New Purity became known for its secret exotic pan-cultural cuisine, and, more specifically, for a grace note which combined the best of Zionist and Oriental tradition: Milton's specially inscribed misfortune cookies. "You're killing your parents!" one would read, slowly pulling a message from its innocuous-looking shell, or, "I'm cold. Put on a sweater!" or "Bring a jacket!" or, "His brother's a doctor," or, "I wouldn't if I were you . . . but it's your life," or the perennial favorite, "Why bother?"

Benji had gotten the scoop as to Penny's whereabouts through Jenn Tile, an erotic actress who managed to move freely between coasts. After a few month's yeoman's work filling gaps dancing in clubs, Penny had found her way back to Milton, changed her name to Cali, gotten the requisite bleach and boob job, then married Papa Bear in a quickie ceremony in Las Vegas. (Benji and Penny having never legally wed; rather, they had declared their vows privately, in a no less religious ceremony in the Ithacan gorges on a black and purploid moonless night.)

Benji entered the restaurant and was hit with a blast of ammonia, not unlike the smell of the porno shops that suffused Times Square. That his life should lead him to this moment, to this establishment, to this confrontation with this clumsy antagonist, seemed at once funny and incomprehensible to Benji. I have been miscast in my own life, Benji thought to himself. And then, as the thought settled and cooled, a sense of great, easy freedom fell over him. You could leave, he thought. You could just leave. Walk out and leave it all behind. A life without history, without consequence, without emotional ties, without friends, without enemies . . . It was then that Benji spotted him. Having not seen Milton in several years, Benji was surprised to see the expression of his face had turned that much deeper, as if an artist had carved the lines out of soft clay with an awl. His beard had turned that much whiter, his girth that much thicker, his taste in clothes that much more garish. (Apparently Milton had entered the flower print Hawaiian shirt phase of late middle-age-dom.) Fully tan, he had the unhappy color of an orange that had been left out for too long. He was eating what looked like a plate of spongy mushrooms floating in a thick, pasty, brown brew, all the while studying his red and white paper chopstick wrapper.

"Question. Why do Jews love Chinese food?" Milton asked, his head in his hand, a meaty palm inadvertently pulling his left cheek, stretching his eyelid orientally. "Answer. Because they're the only ones who haven't persecuted us. Sit down, Benjamin," Milton announced, without looking up or redirecting his attention. "Look at this," he said, passing the chopstick wrapper to Benji, who silently held it between shaking fingers and read:

> Welcome to Chinese Restaurant. Please try your Nice Chinese Food with Chobsticks the traditional and typical Chinese glorious history and cultural.

"It doesn't even try disguising itself as a sentence does it? Chobsticks. It's wrong. In every way, it's just plain wrong. Spelling, grammar, sentence construction. Which is why I love it. Which is why I make a special point of buying them from these Asian illiterates. Now, no one's asking them to do anything so outrageous as learn the language, but still, you'd figure they'd at least try to learn the terminology basic to their business, or, failing that, at the very least have a family member, a cousin, a friend, who, y'know, spoke English."

"Where is she?"

"Which is why—to continue—I buy cheap from the chink warehouse in Chinatown. Because it's a classic lesson you can't repeat to yourself often enough: the entirely wrong is entirely to be expected."

Milton looked up suddenly, and Benji, having forgotten the power of his evil-Oz emerald eyes, had to resist the urge to succumb to hypnosis.

"People are still capable of surprising you, Benjamin," Milton began. "That's sweet. It's endearing, really, it is. But what people do to each other should never surprise you. That's rule number one. You know what rule number two is? The story of our lives: never forget the first rule. Now I know that Papa Bear's no longer your favorite person, Benji, but, out of respect to the student-mentor relationship we nurtured for so long, I feel compelled to tell you—wake up! The girl's no good for you! You got her all wrong!"

And with this, Milton slammed a fist down on the table, crushing a cookie that sat innocently on Benji's side of the table. The fortune lay on the table face-up. Through the testaceous rubble Benji read: "Confucius say, man who play golf, putz!"

"Where is she?"

"You make me laugh Benji, you do. It's over, it's been over, and still you come all the way out here to play Quixote. You're a good kid Benji, but you still haven't figured out that's not enough, have you? Good looks, good upbringing, good heart, good intentions, and it's still not enough. The most obvious lesson of all and you just don't get it do you? You're still angry at the world for working the way it does—as if the world owes you something! Still crucifying yourself over the great unanswerables. Still banging your head over how it's possible to love someone, to live with someone, to make a life with someone, and still get them entirely wrong? But you've been asking yourself the wrong question. The question to ask is how you ever could have expected to get them right? Don't you know that's what people specialize in: getting each other wrong?"

"Milton, just tell me where she is."

"Ooooo, getting a little Lee Marvin-ish on me? It doesn't work on you, Benji. You're destined to play the sap. Goddamn it, I'm trying to teach you!"

He slammed down another fist, unleashing misfortune: "It's too late." For a silent moment the two stared at the decimated cookie.

"You know Gabriel killed himself."

"I know."

"And that Marion died."

"Yes."

"So you're not the only one who's suffered, fuckball," and here, Milton began to choke up a little, or, at the very least, his bearded jowls began to tremble a bit.

"You know the last words I have to say on the subject of my marriage to Marion—rest in peace? We were together fifty-two years. I was with her twenty-six, she was with me twenty-six. Completely separate experiences. No overlap. What do you call that in vision, where one eye sees every-thing a little different from the other?"

"Parallax," answered Benji, schoolboying it.

"Yes, that's right, parallax. Never knew what was going on with the other. Dreams, ambitions, interests, inner lives. Never knew what the hell was flying. You want to know why my marriage with Marion ended?"

"Because you're a sick-fuck pornographer?"

"No, before that."

"Why?"

"Because every fight we had was always the same. Because no matter what it was purportedly about—you forgot to pick up milk, why'd you say that about my sister, why'd you say that to my sister—every fight was the same. Every fight was about the same thing. And you know what it was about? You did this to my life. That's what it's always about. You did this to my life. Everything I'm not I owe to you. You fucked up everything I could've been. Benji, you're a young man, you still got it all ahead of you. I took her off your hands, don't you see? She never would have been what you want-ed her to be. People never are, let alone what you think they are. Take Marion for instance—rest in peace. More than anything, I wanted to see

my wife in a Bo Peep outfit. My big fantasy. Don't ask me why, it just was.
A blue-and-white checkered dress with a bonnet and a shepherd's staff. I
even bought it for her in a costume shop on West 36th Street in the garment district. Put it in the closet for her to discover as a surprise. This
went on for years, my cajoling, her considering, her retreating, my making
amends, her reconsidering. Finally, one night, I come home, I check the
closet, I notice it's gone. She'd destroyed it. Cut it up and put it in the
incinerator. 'I'm not doing it, I'm never going to wear it, and I don't want
it in my house,' she says to me. She wouldn't do it! She would not do it!
Even with the high blood pressure and the gout and the arthritis and the
semi-annual prostate pipe shoved up my ass, still she would not capitulate.
Love, honor, respect, kids, and the rest and still my wife wouldn't do that
for me! It wasn't even part of some sick sex thing, that was over between
us by then. I just wanted to see her in it. Make me happy. Maybe if she'd
have done it, I never would have gotten into this cockamamie business,
who knows? Anyway, that was the end. The end of the compassion. The
end."

Dexterously, Milton manipulated his stainless-steel chopsticks, slid another
mushroom down the shaft of his throat, and waited. Benji, caught up in the
sheer propulsive force of Milton's storytelling, tried to resist but couldn't.

"So what happened?"
"Years later, I hear through the grapevine she puts out a book. She'd always
wanted to be an illustrator of children's books, and, after the divorce, she
managed to put one out. *Lenny the Lonely Lamb* it was called. So I go down
to the bookstore to pick one up. And I'm proud of her. That she managed
to rebuild her life after the marriage ended, after the kids had gone off to
school, after everything that happened, that a woman past fifty with no
real work experience manages to make a life for herself is no small thing,
Benji. So I go buy the book and as I'm paying for it who should I see on
the back cover? Who's there, on top of some hilly fucking mountain with
her arms outstretched like Mrs. Maria Von Trapp? Who do I see dressed in
a blue-and-white checked Bo Peep outfit, accompanied not by one, but
surrounded by sheep? Who? *Who?* People are full of surprises Benji-boy,
but still you wonder how Penny ended up the way she did? With Penny it
isn't even a surprise. Girl tells you she's been in rehab or was molested as
an eight-year-old or has a special friend named Bo Limia, those are some
pretty good warning signs, some pretty strong red flags. But still you go

ahead, still you're not scared off. Naw, not our Benji-boy, not Benji the Brave, not Benji the Blind. No, you see all those red flags going up all around you, all those flags waving in the wind and do you think to yourself, run?! Get me the hell out of here?! No, you see all those flags waving in the wind and instead you think to yourself, look, look at all the flags, look at all the pretty fucking flags. But I got another explanation for you, Benji. What if nothing? What if there were no flags? What if there is no reason? What if it wasn't the drugs or the fucked-up childhood or the industry or circumstance? What if there is no reason for the end of love, Benji? What if there's never any reason at all? Now, I know you're feeling a certain sense of betrayal from Papa Bear, I know you think Papa Bear's been dipping his fingers in your porridge—"

"I don't care about any of that Milton, I just want to see her."

"She's here, Benjamin. She's here. She's been here all along."

And with that, he pointed a snail-slick chopstick to his left, where, a few tables away sat a raccoon-eyed, emaciated, stringy-haired blonde. Alone. Staring.

Benji leapt up, and four thick-armed men immediately surrounded the table, leaving him with the ghostly imprint of her face, like the purple blotch that follows after a flashbulb goes off. Come away with me now. Come away with me and we'll fly to our princedom by the sea, Benji thought, pressing knuckles to eye sockets, as he'd done so many nights before, as if by concentrating hard enough, his thoughts would somehow reach her.

"Not so fast, Punch. You're not getting near her, Benji-boy, not today. Listen, why don't you do us all a favor and go back to New York? I think the sun's doing funny things to your head," and Milton looked at Benji again, only this time, the eyes were milder, their jewel-green liquidity duller, and Milton revealed himself for what he was: an old man, a sad old man who'd spent his life picking the wrong fight.

"Benji, look around. They're all the same," Milton said, pointing around the room to one girl after another. "It's not even her. She's not even here. Benji, look, if it's any consolation, you shouldn't hate her for leaving you. I mean, what would reasonably constitute cheating in this cockamamie business anyway? Chippie runs away with someone else. Happens all the time. Don't get me wrong, I'm not saying not to hate her, I'm just saying if you're going to hate her, hate her for the right reason: a stunning lack of imagination. For her not to have run out on you, that would've been something."

He thought of ripping the pair of chopsticks from Milton's hands and jamming them into his eye sockets (an appropriately Oedipal punishment). He thought of charging the four muscle boys, or at the very least, trying to talk his way past them. He even thought of standing up in the middle of the crowded restaurant and desperately, romantically crying out her name. But in the end did none of those things. Instead, Benji crept silently from the booth, out the door, into his rented car, down to the hotel, to the airport, onto a plane, and back to New York. And never laid eyes on her again.

* * *

For a long time, Art Seymour, Benji's father, believed his son had a successful career in advertising. ("That's mine," Benji would nonchalantly boast about a Wendy's "Where's The Beef?" commercial when they'd get together at his place once a month or so for dinner and a little television.) If this deception originated with Benji, it was maintained by Art with the help of a twin pair of alibis: (1) Benji had an Ivy League degree, and (2) Benji had an apartment in Manhattan, a territory long-mythologized by the Seymour family as "the city."

All of this changed when, as something of a gag, Art's old army buddy Paul took him to Show World, Times Square's premiere smut emporium, in celebration of Art's 69th birthday. A sexually conservative man whose travels through the brackish waters of Eros consisted of imagined couplings with '40s Hollywood movie stars, necking sessions with well-behaved Jewish girls under the Coney Island Boardwalk, procreative missionary-position sex with his wife, and determined abstinence following her premature death, Art had never seen anything like this. Flesh. Flesh stripped of personality and romantic longing, flesh presented as coldly, as ruthlessly as swatches of fabric at a garment district warehouse. In that first moment, Art saw another direction his life could have gone—sex not as procreative goal, not as a reward for being a responsible husband and father, not in exchange for being a good man, for supporting a family and living a good clean life, but sex stripped of love, of family, of responsibility, sex as candy, fucking as light as cotton candy—and it scared him. It was only after Paul managed to cajole his friend into one of the private 25¢ booths that Art—who up until then had been directing the majority of his attention to avoiding stepping in silvery puddles of freshly sprayed seminal fluid—looked up at the video monitor and recognized his advertising executive son penetrating his ex-wife from the rear. Weeks later, when Benji called to wish him an annual, belated happy Father's Day, Art erupted:

"Who took these pictures of you?!"
"Dad?"
"You! You and Penny! Who did this to you?! Who made you do this?! Tell me!"

He didn't understand. He didn't understand that this was something his advertising executive son could have chosen to do and Benji wasn't about to explain it to him over the phone. And so the next day, Benji, son of Art, grandson of Ezra, great great grandson of Abraham, took a train out to Avenue J in Brooklyn, and slowly explained it to him. All of it: about Milton, about Penny's disappearance, about his squalid little life as a porn peddler. And it was only through cataloguing the contortions of his father's silent, shrunken, wizened little head as he absorbed the tale that Benji began to appreciate the absurdity of his situation. The thing was, Benji, who, even at his most self-deceptive maintained an extremely reliable self-monitor, realized that part of him was enjoying his father's shock, his openmouthed pain. Benji enjoyed playing the part of the very bad boy. At times, describing the plot of one of his more successful films, or inadvertently slipping into the puns that came so naturally in his line of work, Benji had to consciously stop himself from giggling. He loved his father dearly—recognized him as a good and decent man, a gentleman—but he also knew that some vital part of him wanted to watch the old man suffer, wanted to bash his skull in, to piss vinegar down his throat for so ill-preparing him for the pain of the world, that there were devilish molecules dancing around inside of Benji that always, always hoped for the worst.

"But why? How could you let this happen to you?" his father demanded with clenched fists. "This is your life, this is your life, the one and only life you have, how could you have made this for yourself?"

"Because I loved her!" Benji singsonged, as if about to break into a musical number. "I loved her, Dad. Dad! Daddy! Daddy! Daddy!" and with that babyword Benji transformed himself into a limp weeping flora, some floppy invertebrate, his helpless father attempting to cradle him in his arms. And at the tentative touch of his father's crinkling hands, with their message that this might be it—this might be the last time his father gets to play dad, that this might really be it before crippling arthritis eradicated touch, before Alzheimer's deleted memory like some demon computer virus, before the inevitable nursing home with their visiting hours and bedpans and vanilla puddings, that this might be it before his last parent died and Benjamin Seymour was left alone, exposed, an orphan in the world—the pitiless, inexpiable reality of that impending, unforgivable, inescapable doom, all this made Benji cry all the more. "Because I loved her dad . . . Anything . . . Anywhere . . . I would have followed her anywhere."

He slept that night curled in a fetal position at the foot of his father's bed, visions of his dead mother dancing in his head.

* * *

He remembered witnessing his mother deteriorate from cancer, turning her body over in bed so she could use the bathroom and seeing the yellow imprint where her body lay, feeling one of her jutting shoulder blades and having to remind himself that this noble, jutting bone held in place his mother's arm, her loving arm which connected to her hand, the warm hand he held on his way to school.

As his mother used the bathroom, Benji thought of the mystery of cancer, the paradox of the disease: how cancer cells, which reproduce with breathless fecundity, would seem to be the healthiest of cells, while normal cells, deteriorating and dying with age, would seem the sickest. If cancer cells were a stock splitting endlessly on the exchange, there'd be a riot on Wall Street. But in the human body that kind of mercilessness leads to destruction. What does this paradigm tell us? That extremity is bad? That mono-mania, in all its forms, is inimical? That obsessional pursuit can end only in death?

Arriving early one night, Benji spied his father holding the form of his mother, her papery hospital gown falling off in the back, the twin wings of her shoulderblades naked, white, exposed. When was the last time he had seen them hold each other? When was the last time he had witnessed any kind of physical affection between them? Yet the way his mother looked at his father, and the way his father silently nodded back, Benji knew they must have been in love. Comforted by this, Benji hung back in the shadowed hallway, unseen. An imagined piece of music came in over the radio, and in the silence of the room the seventy-year-old man and the sixty-eight-year-old woman danced. A little shuffle step to a forgotten piece of music from a romantic night long ago.

"Okay, lay me down," his mother said after a moment, and when his father did, Benji feared her yellow skin would crack and crumple like paper. His mother's skin, which she was so proud of just months ago for being so white and wrinkle-free, had turned thin, gray, and sallow overnight. Her back, once a broad white canvas, now looked ashen, the color of earth. She's dying, Benji thought, as his father turned her onto her back, returning her to her damp puddle, she's becoming earth already.

Benji's overactive literary imagination confronted itself with unwanted metaphors once again as he snuck into Penny's hospital room to see her. What should it be? Cancer? Drugs? AIDS? The disease describes a state of helplessness, defenselessness, which was her effect on him from the beginning. Agreed then. As he stood in the doorway watching her sleep, he pushed through the moment by forcing himself to reconcile that this too would soon be memory. This is it, he thought, the big moment you've longed for and dreaded. We've reached the big death scene Benji, so don't blow it! He distracted himself by counting all the tubes running out of her.

All of the veins in her arm had been exploited and, too thin-walled for needles, had collapsed. The doctors had tried her kneecaps, feet, and the spaces between her fingers and toes, but nothing worked, and so finally they had to attach a direct line to her heart. This too, Benji read as metaphor as some lucent liquid or other was fed to her from a drip bag, hanging like a cow's kidney from a metal stand.

Why are hospitals so quiet? Benji thought, self-consciously silent himself as he stood in the doorway. Why send patients out on pillows of silence? Better to send them out the way they came in, mewling, screaming. Better for them to remember the struggle their lives were while they still have a few breaths left in them.

He continued staring at her. He missed the happy girl Penny was in photographs, the girl he'd never met. He missed the boy he was. How badly he wished he could have introduced those two. How much he wished he could find his eight-year-old self and talk to him, tell him something of the world and its pain.

"I didn't think you'd come."
"I came as soon as I heard," said Benji through dry mouth.
"Come sit with me," she said, extending her hand. A ghost. She's already a ghost.
"I had a horrible thought the other night," she began, sucking water through a plastic straw. "That when I died, the world wouldn't be left a worse place or a better place, but the same. That it wouldn't change at all."
"That's not true."
"Yes," she said. "It is."
"I'll change," he said, choking on the words.
"O, honey."

They were holding hands.

"I was thinking about how the whole thing is set up for us, set up just right. Nutrients in the air for us to breathe, in the food we eat, in the water we drink, in the sun that shines down on us. Someone's thinking about us, Benji. Someone's taking care of us. And our bodies. All the pleasure they can bring. All the pleasure we carry around inside us. I mean, I know it's compulsory, I know we're inclined toward that direction, but it didn't really have to be like that, did it? We could have been programmed to do something unpleasant. Something that keeps us apart."
"Hm."
"Sometimes I think about all the people who've watched our movies. All those thousands of people."

"Millions."

"Millions. They saw, they saw how good we were together. How good we fit. We made people happy."

And in the way she looked at him and squeezed his hand, he knew what she was asking. Her body had deteriorated badly, her skin was bruised, her face was pulled taut, she had lost a good deal of weight, and that, combined with her breast implants lent her the look of a medieval grotesque. Still, looking at her, he knew he loved her more than anything he had ever seen or imagined on earth, or hoped for anywhere else.

"Can we do it without a camera?" he asked.

"Pretend we're back at school, Benji. Pretend we're kids."

"We're still kids, P. Always."

And so, Benji slid off her and quietly searched the hospital corridors for a condom machine before he grudgingly acknowledged that there are no condom machines in hospitals. He rummaged through his wallet, where he found the wrapper of the gold Trojan condom he had lost his virginity with when he was nineteen. Too embarrassed to buy one for himself, he had stolen it from his parents bedside table and even now didn't know which was more unsavory: the thought of his parents having sex, his stealing sexual accouterments from them, or his keeping them as mementos. Also in his wallet was an old, crushed condom, an Italian brand given to him by his Italian friend, Fabrizio. An indestructible elastic with no discernible expiration date, the condom had left a permanent "O" in the soft leather of his wallet. Returning to the room, he locked the door, pulled down his pants, opened the wrapper with his teeth, and rolled it on, getting some hairs tangled in its eel-like, rubbery slickness.

Entering her, he realized this was the first time they'd had sex with a condom since college. He was close enough to breathe her air.

"Shh. Shh," he cooed.

"I never knew. I never knew what you wanted. I'm afraid—"

"Shh. Shh."

Working into a gentle rhythm, Benji felt her crumbling beneath him. Leaves. Her body felt like a bag of dry leaves. Dry leaves covering a patch of mulch. Her innards like soft clay. She was dying, turning into earth. La petite mort. La grande mort. Sex, taking place in the hushed corridors of a hospital, comes crazily close to cradling someone in their death throes. He gently came.

"You are my lamb."
"Go to sleep now."

And in that moment, with her heavy eye at half-mast, closing, did he finally see her? Did he get an answer to the question of her? Did he glimpse her mystery? Was there ever any mystery at all? In the end none of it mattered. She died the next morning.

* * *

There are so many ways she could have died, so many ways he could have killed her, thought Benji, present-tensing it, grinding his knuckles into his temples as he regrouped in front of the Disney Store on 42nd and Seventh. But people do not usually die in emotionally satisfying ways, and this is not what happened.

What happened was this: on the morning of June 16, 1993, Penelope Catherine Pigeon got into her 1988 canary yellow Porsche convertible and drove off one of the cliffs at Big Sur. She did not hit the water as planned. Her suicide note, dated June 15, read simply, tersely, "Words." As for a farewell, an explanation, a clue, a cue, Benji had only words to play with.

10

EXT. NEW YORK CITY STREET — DAY

The 42nd Street entrance to the Disney Store, before which stretches Times Square, Crossroads of the World. A whirling cityscape mist of light and noise, in all directions streets blink on-and-off like pinball machines. Candy corn–colored cones spill billows of smoke into the torpid late afternoon sky where they curl like swirls of cream poured into hot coffee. A grimy hot New York day, the air is humid, saturated with a thick animal heat.

Slowly, through the pixilated crowd, a lone figure emerges, a man frozen in space and time amidst the cyclonic rush. He is Benjamin Seymour, BENJI, thirty-three, sweaty, frazzled, in black. BENJI'S THEME—a lush, circular, romantic string music that never reaches a climax—begins on the soundtrack. Benji's wounded, smoke-blue eyes clear as he pulls himself together and, with renewed purpose, walks forward, toward the store entrance. He pulls open a pair of doors, their silver handles cast in the shape of Mickey Mouse ears.

CUT TO:

INT. THE DISNEY STORE — DAY

SALESCLERKS, dogsbodies in white shirts, beige khakis, and turquoise cardigan sweaters scurry about, helping croaking customers load their baskets with merchandise as blue-blazered security guards, haughty as giraffes, patrol the store on foot. Newborn babes cry out like hungry birds, feral children run amok like small woodland creatures, mothers swat away purchase requests like mosquitoes. A squealing, mewling symphony. A bestiary.

With his first step, Benji trips awkwardly into the store.

                    SALESCLERK
          Don't fall.

                    BENJI
          Already have, thanks.

Benji enters the first room—the palace of the Beast—approaches a pillar, and places a cool hand on its sturdy stone for support. Plastic! Discouraged, he moves onto the next room—Alice in Wonderland's pastoralia—an inviting verdant expanse filled with towels, sweatshirts, mugs, and umbrellas. He touches a delicate-looking taffeta nightgown. Synthetic! He staggers forward to the final room—the Lion King's lair—a black and gold South African veldt. As he approaches a shelf of videocassettes, molecules dance in the Saharan heat and *The Loin King*, *Jumbo*, *The Little Spermaid*, *The Fox and the Mound*, *101 Dominations*, and *A Lad In Me* emerge from the dyslexic blur.

He turns. On nearby shelves sit row after row of lonely, disfigured, bug-eyed crookbacks; figures more closely akin to friendly neighborhood pedophiles than cute and cuddly children's toys. Confused, Benji picks up one of the figures and turns it upside down, unsuccessfully searching out its genitalia. Discouraged, he puts the doll down and approaches a rack of books, scanning over a dizzyingly redundant display: *Disney's The Hunchback of Notre Dame*, *The Art of the Hunchback of Notre Dame*, *Disney's The Hunchback of Notre Dame Big Golden Book*, *Disney's Hunchback of Notre Dame Golden Look-Look Books*, *Disney's The Hunchback of Notre Dame Little Golden Books*, *Disney's The Hunchback of Notre Dame Piano Fun EZ-Play Songbook*, *Disney's The Hunchback of Notre Dame: An Animated Flip Book*, *Disney's The Hunchback of Notre Dame Meet The Characters*, *Disney's The Hunchback of Notre Dame Postcard Book*, *Disney's The Hunchback of Notre Dame: Quasimodo's New Friend*, *Disney's The*

Hunchback of Notre Dame Upside Down and Topsy-Turvy Volume 1, Disney's The Hunchback of Notre Dame Forever Free, Disney's The Hunchback of Notre Dame Illustrated Songbook, Disney's The Hunchback of Notre Dame Songbook, Disney's The Hunchback of Notre Dame With Easy Instructions Xylotone, *Disney's The Hunchback of Notre Dame Topsy Turvy Day Pop Up Pals, Disney's Treasury of Children's Classics From The Fox and the Hound to The Hunchback of Notre Dame Volume 1,* Disney's The Hunchback of Notre Dame Stained Glass Kit Volume 1 . . .

ALICE, a salesgirl, apple-cheeked, approaches.

> ALICE
>
> C'I help you?

> BENJI
>
> Yeah, what's with all the hunchback crap?

> ALICE
>
> It's Disney's Hunchback of Notre Dame, our 34th animated feature, coming this summer!

> BENJI
>
> As in Victor Hugo's Hunchback of Notre Dame?

> ALICE
>
> I don't know about that . . .

> BENJI
>
> As in Quasimodo?

> ALICE
>
> Yes, that might be the one you're thinking of.
> Our hunchback's named Quasi!

From the rafters descend giant marquee signs with flashing neon red lights that read: "WELCOME TO QUASI-LAND!" and "THIS WAY TO QUASI-WORLD!"

A thin, avaricious smell invades Benji's nostrils.

                              BENJI
                        (*in recognition*)
                    Same smell, different shit.

Syncopated SNAPPING is heard. MINNIE and DAISY, two shadowy figures in elbow-length ivory gloves, sable and mink boas, black bowler hats,
and stiletto heels emerge from the darkness and sidle up to Benji. Their
posteriors out-thrust in provocatively soliciting positions, they swing glittering sequined purses between Bob Fosse knees.

                              MINNIE
                Ever wonder why cartoon characters wear minis?

She flashes him.

                              DAISY
                        Or white gloves?

Minnie slips a fastidious finger deep inside Daisy and passes it under
Benji's nose.

                              BENJI
                        (*smelling gleefully*)
                        Ah! Foie gras!

Daisy holds a green and gold zoetrope to Benji's eye.

                              DAISY
                    Give a peep? Just a penny?

                              MINNIE
                    For the new, fully evolved man!

                              DAISY
                        The complete man!

                              MINNIE
                    A pornosophical man!

DAISY
For the man who has everything!

MINNIE
For the man who likes to watch!

Benji presses a hungry eye to the peephole.

BENJI
But I can't see. Is that? And?

Daisy impatiently pulls the magic box away from him and peers into it herself.

DAISY
(as the zoetrope spins faster, faster)
O, he did. Into her. She did. Done.

She tosses it aside.

MINNIE
(pleasuring herself with a magic wand)
It gets so lonely with Mickey away! Always trot-
ting over the globe!

DAISY
(snorting lines of fairy dust off a shard of mirror)
And Donald's speech impediment drives me to
drink!

MINNIE and DAISY caress Benji languidly. The seaweed-and-copper-
penny smell of sex overtakes Benji as duck fornicates with mouse, mouse
fornicates with lion, lion fornicates with pig, mermaid is taken fin-wise by
sea monster, the seven dwarves resort to the Italian solution, Beast and
Beauty do that thing with the cup . . .

Benji feels a great stirring in his trousers. It grows, it grows! The Mickey
Mouse PEZ dispenser escapes from his pocket and ambles onstage, harmonica pressed to plastic lips, spotlight casting it in harsh relief. It speaks:

PEZ

(in a thin, adenoidal whine)
Thank you, thank you ladies and gentleman,
birds and beasts, thank you. I'd like to dedicate
this next song to the ghosts of Times Square past.
This one's called "The Lonesome Ballad of Dear,
Dirty Old Times Square."

The Pez dispenser begins to sing to the rhythm of Bruce Springsteen's "It's Hard to be a Saint in the City":

PEZ
Well the streets of old New York
Man, they sure are really pretty.
But I remember when this town
Was once a pretty shitty city.

So they cleaned up those mean streets
Of every drunkard, every pimp.
And they boarded up the porn shops
Man, on that they didn't scrimp!

All the Disney Store animals join in the CHORUS:

CHORUS
So a neighborhood is gone now
Yeah, and no one seems to care.
That vanished is the place we loved,
Dear, dirty old Times Square.

PEZ
Up went coffee shops and superstores
That're clean, but they're all bores.
Down came a rain that washed away
The junkies, buggers, creeps, and whores.

Asshole, fuck, cocksucker, shit:
Words not considered nice.
So we've replaced the ass and tit

PEZ (CON'T)
With cartoon ducks and mice.

And when the final smut shop closed
St. Disney staked his claim.
'Cause in the eyes of cap'talism, baby
Money's all the same!

CHORUS
So a neighborhood is gone now
Yeah, and no one seems to care.
Forever's lost a paradise,
Dear, dirty old Times Square.

The animals APPLAUD wildly. Out of the crowd emerge, rumpled, a gathering of Dead White Male AUTHORS: Victor Hugo, Lewis Carroll, Charles Dickens, even moldering old SHAKESPEARE himself. They stand in a processional line before the enormous, oversized MICKEY MOUSE, bowing in silent homage.

With great solemnity Mickey anoints each of the authors in turn, tapping them on the shoulder with a strike of his magic wand. One by one the authors are transmogrified into cartoon likenesses of themselves. Their frowns become smiles, their gray dusty clothes turn Technicolor bright, their sesquipedalian words curdle and are foreshortened in the very air of speech. The authors shrink, become small, are sprayed with a noxious coat of fairy dust. Brought down to size, they scamper about like mice, combing out King Mickey's golden flowing locks, tending to the honey-brass buckles of his shoes, tightening his berry-red suspenders. They sing in unison:

THE AUTHORS
When you wish upon a Starr . . .
Makes no diff'rence who you are . . .
When you wish upon a Starr . . .
It's a small, small woooorrrlllld . . .

Except for Shakespeare, who resists:

MICKEY
Kneel!

SHAKESPEARE
(*rigid in facial paralysis*)
Non serviam.

MICKEY
(*sneering*)
Bow to me bawdy bard!

The authors, assisted by armies of animals, attack the noble fellow. They nibble at his ruffles, pluck the whiskers from his beard, tear flesh from divine fingertips, smear wet ink across his famous visage, rip the very paper stuffing from his dress. Time's livid final flame leaps and, in the following darkness, ruin of all space, shattered glass and toppling masonry, the great globe itself shudders and shakes as Shapesphere is brought to heel.

SHAKESPEARE
(*flashing a toothless pitchman's smile*)
Two thumbs up for Disney's McBeth! A bloody good time!
(*presenting a plastic Happy Meal cup to Mickey*)
Collect all four!

BENJI
Fucking rat!
ALICE
Pardon?

Benji, attacked by crippling stomach spasms, waves the girl away. Sweating profusely now, a hand kneading his somersaulting stomach, he approaches JIMMY, a nineteen-year-old sales clerk with a rough-hewn, equine face.

BENJI
Where's the toilet?

JIMMY
(hoarsely)
I'm afraid the restrooms are for employees only, sir.

BENJI
(with a bold, sweeping hand)
Where do all the animals go then?

Plastic and plush rabbits and ducks and mice and dogs and lions and dwarves stop copulating and simultaneously squat and defecate on their respective shelves. A look of dull confusion crosses Jimmy's face. Sacks of gold foil chocolate coins—Chanukah gelt—draw Benji's attention away from him. Benji picks up a pouch and turns the yellow coins over and over through the thin mesh pouch. He looks up. The temple is suddenly filled with moneychangers, exchanging coin of all currency.

BENJI
(bearded, berobed)
I understand, I understand, but you see
(reads nametag)
Jimmy, I was planning on spending a good deal of
money today at the Church of Disney Christ, and
I like to feel clean before I defile myself, if you
know what I mean.

JIMMY
(with a whinny of laughter)
I think so.

BENJI
Good. Good. The toilet, Jiminy! The crapper!
The can! The commode!

CUT TO:

INT. BATHROOM, THE DISNEY STORE — DAY

A single-stall unisex bathroom: Freedom of Choice tampax machine on the wall, full-length mirror behind the door, handicap assistance bar next to the toilet, a pebbled fresco floor.

Benji sits on the bowl, squeezing, as silent, powerful bowel movements snake out of him. A look of satisfaction crosses his face, the profound comfort that comes with the recognition of one's own sweet rising stench. Then concern. Globules of sweat pour from every pore. Forehead veins swell with exertion. Agoraphobic-white skin turns beet-red. Benji tries crying out, but only low, guttural grunts escape.

What's happening is unclear, but it won't stop. He's tapped into the motherload of putrescence. He's losing pounds, shedding identities, shucking off souls. Surely this is no ordinary shit. Several long, woeful minutes pass.

Finally finished with this intestinal ride of the Valkyries, Benji rises and looks down at the BOWL, afraid of what he might find. Dizzy, he sees JESUS CHRIST in his stool.

JESUS CHRIST

Adonai.

He flushes.

BOWL

Hooooooooooooooooooome.

CUT TO:

INT. 2ND FLOOR HALLWAY, THE DISNEY STORE — DAY

Benji stands in a hallway, tapping an impatient foot on black-and-white checkered tile, talking on a payphone. On the soundtrack, we hear an answering machine BEEP.

BENJI

Listen Troy, stupid favor to ask—

CUT TO:

INT. COMMERCIAL URBAN MODELS — DAY

The place is a ramshackle mess. Benji's desk is overturned, papers are strewn about, the television kicked in, diploma smashed, the stuffing of the couch ripped out and exposed like entrails. The hallway looks as if a sledgehammer has been taken to it. In the editing suite, lights blink on-and-off, on-and-off in an electronic state of manic-depression. It seems the only thing left in working condition is the answering machine, currently receiving a message:

> ANSWERING MACHINE
> —but I forgot it was Father's Day yesterday so if
> you're out today and find yourself near a card
> store . . . You know what, forget it, you're proba-
> bly out right now anyway.

CUT TO:

EXT. NEW YORK CITY STREET — DAY

NIGGA LUV, a hardcore rap song, plays on the soundtrack as two burly, mustachioed Emergency Service Unit PARAMEDICS wheel a gurney out of an anonymous-looking building at 337 West 33rd Street. They are accompanied by TROY, a wiry young black male, twenty-five, and a tall, Irish, blond-haired POLICE OFFICER.

Strapped to the gurney is JULES, a large, muscular, young black male, in black. He is badly bruised, his face a topographical map of bruises and cuts, a chronicle of a fight irrevocably lost.

> POLICE OFFICER
> (transcribing into a reporter's notebook)
> So, lemme get this straight, this guy, who you say
> you've never seen before, comes in and tears the
> place up looking for a videotape?

> TROY
> (keeping both hands clearly in sight, palms out,
> the entire time)
> I don't know, officer. Like I said, some strange
> people into this stuff. Maybe his local store didn't
> have it in or something.

Semiconscious but with great urgency, Jules pulls one of the paramedics near and struggles to speak through broken teeth.

> JULES
> *(fading fast)*
> Bantabibblebelta.

SUBTITLE: "Santa's Little Helper."

> PARAMEDIC 1
> Okay, take it easy, pal.

The paramedics wheel Jules into the back of a waiting ambulance.

> POLICE OFFICER
> What line of work you say you were in again?

> TROY
> Me? I'm a list maker.

CUT TO:

INT. THE ED SULLIVAN THEATRE — NIGHT

DAVID LETTERMAN, looking fit and trim in neatly cropped hair, wire-rim spectacles, and double-breasted pin-stripe suit, sits onstage behind his desk, a scaled model of the New York City skyline twinkling behind him.

> DAVID LETTERMAN
> Ladies and gentleman, I have in my hand
> tonight's Top Ten List.

INSERT SHOT: Computer generated numbers BURST across the screen like confetti.

> DAVID LETTERMAN
> From the home office in Beaver College,
> Pennsylvania, The Top Ten Reasons Pinot Is
> Better Than a Woman.

PAUL SHAFFER, bandleader, behind the keyboard in swishy shades, repeats:

> PAUL SHAFFER
> "Top Ten Reasons Why Pinot Is Better Than a
> Woman."

> DAVID LETTERMAN
> That's right, number ten: you can score with a
> pinot on the first date. Number nine: pinot does-
> n't get upset when you look at other pinot.
> Number eight: at least the women in pinot pre-
> tend to have orgasms. Number seven: it only
> costs $2.50 to take out a pinot. Number six: two
> words: "condom, schmomdom." Number five: "A"
> is for anal. Number four: no need to fast-forward
> to the good parts, in pinot, it's all good parts!
> Number three: you only have to spend an hour-
> and-a-half with a pinot. Number two: pinot
> don't sit on the back of no bus. And the number
> one reason why pinot is better than a woman is . . .

DRUMROLL.

> DAVID LETTERMAN
> Pinot can't hurt you and pinot never says no!

CUT TO:

INT. THE DISNEY STORE, MAIN FLOOR — DAY

Elevator doors slide open, bringing Benji face-to-face with a row of seven,
plush, three-foot-tall dwarves. He is transfixed by their faces—old and
bearded, yet smooth, wrinkle-free—and the fixity of their expressions:
Bashful, Sleepy, Grumpy, Sneezy, Happy, Dopey, and Hippocratic.

> BENJI
> (whispers)
> Lonely.

Out of the din of noise MILTON'S MILITARY MARCH—a bold brass beat—is heard. And there he is. MILTON MINEGOLD, fifty-five, thickly middle-aged, bearded, cheshire cat smile, walks triumphantly forward. His dress is dapper—gold-buttoned blue blazer, rich red tie, shiny black boots. On his pinky finger rests a large gold and diamond ring in the shape of a ship's anchor. He could be the captain of a yacht, a seaman. Benji, noticeably younger, trails behind him. They are in a warehouse.

FLASHBACK BEGINS:

TITLE: "1985"

INT. WAREHOUSE — DAY

A huge empty space on the Brooklyn docks. Milton walks toward the heavy open doors. Outside, several trucks are parked. Crates of metal, plastic, wood, aluminum cables, wires, costumes, props, pipes, gels, lights, lightstands, dolly rig, and PVC tubing are being removed from the trucks and brought inside. Two actors—rotund, hirsute JUSTIN CASE, and beakish, balding JUSTIN THYME—carefully carry a 35mm movie camera through the dusty space. Covered in a black hood, the camera resembles the head of an Episcopal monk.

MILTON
(*hoisting a camera tripod*)
Careful with that boys, she's a rental.

TITLE: "BLOW WHITE AND THE SEVEN WHORES"

Begin long-take STEADICAM shot, moving through the warehouse.

BENJI (Voice Over)
It was the day of my first shoot. It was the day I
met everyone. It was the day I discovered the
new world.

BENJI'S THEME begins.

BENJI (Voice Over)
There was Lulu, who only talked about herself in
third person . . .

LULU, leonine in a leopard-skin leotard, her face woozy, raccoon-eyed,
her hair a natural shade of bleach, sits cross-legged, drinking a long tall
glass of Thai iced tea, a meditation book by her side. She talks to no one
in particular, practicing come-hither looks in a mirror.

LULU
They say, Lulu, you look so beautiful, how do you
do it? And Lulu says, I don't know, I'm just Lulu.

She snorts a line of coke off the cover of her book.

BENJI (Voice Over)
And Justin Thyme, who was always bragging
about his twins . . .
Justin, pride emanating from his high patrician forehead, points to his
eight-inch-wide gold belt buckle depicting an adult and two baby whales
swimming in the ocean.

JUSTIN
My kids got it for me for Father's Day. For a
whale of a dad. Get it? For a whale of a dad!

BENJI (Voice Over)
And Ana Rexia, who was always complaining
about something . . .

ANA REXIA, frowning, in a black leather catsuit, sits before a mirror,
applying peach-colored foundation to bruises on her legs.
ANA REXIA
You tell that gimpy bald-headed fag if he can't get
wood, he's not a professional, and I don't need to
work with people who aren't a professional!

BENJI (Voice Over)
There was Marcello, the set photographer . . .

MARCELLO, thirties, boorish, Midwestern, used-car-salesman oily, roams around the warehouse in a pastel baby blue blazer, a slab of pizza crust hanging from his mouth, a 35mm Polaroid camera slung around his neck.

MARCELLO
Smile for your mug shot.

CLICK! The sound of dishes crashing.

FREEZE FRAME: a black-and-white photo of an unhappy Ana brandishing a cat-o'-nine-tails.

BENJI (Voice Over)
And Big Bob, the cameraman. He may have been
big as a bear, but he was as graceful as a gazelle.
BIG BOB, grizzled, red-haired, bearded, flannel shirt Timberland boots type, tiptoes around, inconspicuously taking a light meter reading off Lulu's forehead as she continues practicing her facial expressions.

BIG BOB
Milton, what were you thinking man? This warehouse is throwing shadows around like a motherfucker.

BENJI (Voice Over)
And of course, there was Milton, who strode
through it all like a colossus, like Orson Welles in
Citizen Kane . . .

MILTON
(beaming, slapping Big Bob on the back)
You provide the pretty pictures, I'll provide the
porn.

Milton spins around, the coattails of his blazer opening like a cape, obliterating the frame. End STEADICAM.

BENJI (Voice Over)
It was the day I met everyone. It was the day I
met Milo Pipe . . .

MILO PIPE, five-foot-four, pudgy, with a seventies-style handlebar mustache, stands by the catering table, passing a piece of congealed danish under his snout. He spots Benji standing alone in a corner and motions for him to come over.

Benji approaches, entering the frame.

BENJI (Voice Over)
Milo was only thirty or thirty-five at the time, but
he was already a legend. He was a classically
trained actor who had studied with Lee Strasberg
at the Actor's Studio. He had done soaps, he had
played bit parts in B-movies, he was in the original
Broadway production of *Hair*. The point is, he
had his options, but he liked erotic films. He
actually preferred them to going legit.

Benji and Milo appear face-to-face in MEDIUM SHOT as Voice Over ends.

MILO
This your first shoot?

BENJI
Yeah.

MILO
Look here kid, there's nothing to worry about.
You're working with Milton, so you're working
with the best. But while we're talking here lemme
give you some pointers what not to do.

Milo expectorates a cough-ball of phlegm.

LOUDSPEAKER (Offscreen)
Milo and Lulu, five minute call.

Milo nods, unzips, and fishes his penis out of his trousers. Flaccid, it resembles a pupa in its cocoon, a chrysalis. Milo nonchalantly places it in front of the FLUFFER, a pretty, plump, freckle-faced girl of about twenty. She is reading a book entitled *Handling Your Money*. As Milo sips his coffee, the Fluffer tugs and pulls and tickles his penis, gradually inducing an erection as Benji looks on.

MILO
(*to Benji*)
There's nothing to be nervous about. First shoot, almost everyone breaks down on the set. That's what the fluffers are here for.

The Fluffer looks up from her book at Benji, crinkles her nose, and smiles.

MILO
This one time, I don't remember, maybe I'd been out late partying the night before or something, I don't know, the point is, the wood just wasn't ready. And because of my size, you can't just throw in a stunt dick and expect audiences to buy that. I have my fan base. Audience sees that, they catch on. With all due respect, it's not like in *Cannonball Run* where you see Burt Reynolds jump in a car and they cut to a stunt driver with a fake mustache and a Stetson. My audience knows. They come for Milo cock. They pay for Milo cock. You better give them Milo cock. Anyway, this went on for about an hour and nothing doing. So eventually they bring out this cooler, like you'd bring to a ballgame or the beach or something—dry ice, cold air shooting out the thing. And they pull out this syringe filled with this green stuff called, what'd they call it?

FLUFFER

Prostaglandin.

MILO

That's right, prostaglandin. And they shoot it
into the base of my cock and everything was fine.
So basically what I'm saying is, you have options.
Lots of options.

The Fluffer nods appreciatively. Milo takes a bite of Danish as Lulu passes
between them.

LULU

(to herself)
Lulu's ready for her scene. Lulu's all kinds of wet.

MILO

Used to be catering trucks from the Carnegie
with corned beef and tongue on rye instead of
this crap.

Milo tosses the Danish disdainfully back onto an aluminum tray.

MILO

What's Milton have you doing today?

BENJI

Just straight sex I think.

MILO

(nodding)
Good. Used to be like two, three sex scenes per
film and that was it. Now, seven, eight, ten
scenes per film's not uncommon. And straight
fucking's strictly passé. Like anal. A used to be a
very rare occurrence, something you very rarely
saw. Now, it's almost compulsory. And I don't like
it. I don't have time for it. Like the last time I did
A, I ripped the girl wide open. Which was not

                        MILO (CON'T)
fun. I got upset. But she loved it. She thought it
was fantastic. Which bothered me. My con-
science. And I don't have time for that.

                   LOUDSPEAKER (Offscreen)
Milo, wanted on set.

                           MILO
Ahhhh, that's all right. I can tell you're a good
kid, you'll be all right.

                                                    CUT TO:

EXT. THE BROOKLYN DOCKS — DAY

A cloudless day. Across the East River, the Brooklyn Bridge and buildings
are in bloom. A handful of sailboats loll contentedly about. They all look
fake, out of a Fisher Price play set. Outside, the sun is shining brightly and
the water is calm, but inside the space is gloomy, threatening.

Alone, standing on the docks is a woman, a young girl in a summer dress
of peacock greens and blues. She is Penelope Pigeon. PENNY, twenty-one,
is beautiful, but her beauty is fluid, her compass unfixed. Her back to
Benji, her hair makes gossamer webs in the saltwater air. Instinctively, she
reaches a hand behind her and pulls Benji near. They are standing together now. She looks to him with much love. PENNY'S THEME—a lilting
piano waltz, music for fairy elves—begins. She looks out at the water.

                           BENJI
              Y'sure you want to do this?

Penny nods and squeezes his hand.

                                                    CUT TO:

INT. WAREHOUSE — DAY

Benji and Penny are fucking missionary style. With silent tongues they communicate in ancient languages of instinct and grace. Slowly, the perspective widens to reveal a green frog costume and a glittery gown lying in puddles on a king-sized, sheetless mattress. Then: lights: a movie camera: voices.

MILTON (Offscreen)
Good, now flip the burger, Benji!

Benji pulls out as Penny assumes the canine position. Hot lights bounce off the couple's sweating bodies, casting them in a shiny-slick sheen. Big Bob, bouncing around them like a buoy, swings around to Benji's POV, screwing the camera-head onto the tripod. Light refracts off the lens prismatically, in rainbow-colored hues.

MILTON (Offscreen)
Hold it now, Benji, hold it. Keep stroking it.

As Benji struggles to maintain an erection the Fluffer takes a quick measurement between Penny's flared buttocks and the camera lens. Big Bob takes a light meter reading and makes the proper focal adjustments. The Fluffer snaps up the yellow tape measure, puts on a heavy pair of earphones, slings a sound recorder around her shoulder, and picks up a microphone boom.

MARCELLO
(holding a slate)
Sound.
FLUFFER
Sound.
MARCELLO
Speed.

BIG BOB
Speed.

MARCELLO
Blow White and the Seven Whores, scene twelve, "doggie," take one.

Marcello SNAPS the slate shut and exits the frame. The camera begins to
HUM.

>   MILTON (Offscreen)
>   And action! Say something nice about her ass!

>   BENJI
>   (*tenderly*)
>   You're beautiful.

>   MILTON (Offscreen)
>   Her ass, Benji! C'mon Benji, this is X!

>   BENJI
>   You have a beautiful asshole.

>   MILTON (Offscreen)
>   Good, now Penny I want you to stick that butt
>   out, stick that beautiful butt way, way out!

Penny arches her back.

>   MILTON
>   Good, now spread those fucking legs! What is
>   this Sunday-fucking-school?!

On all fours, Penny grinds her forehead into the mattress, places both
hands on her buttocks, and spreads them apart.

>   MILTON (Offscreen)
>   Now hit it Benji! Hit it big-time!

Benji enters and begins pumping away. Marcello's camera goes POP!

>   BIG BOB
>   That's great, that's great. Just hold that for a
>   minute.

Benji struggles to control the tempo as Penny undulates her torso in waves. Big Bob swivels around to capture the scene from the front, quickly mounting the camera on baby legs.

> BIG BOB
> We're still in focus kids, just keep it rolling, keep it rolling.

The cables in Benji's neck grow distended from the strain.

> MILTON (Offscreen)
> Keep it bouncing Benji

Teeth bared Benji begins to bark.

> BENJI
> Rrrrrffffffff!

> MILTON (Offscreen)
> Good boy!

Penny stares directly into the camera and licks her lips.

> MITLON (Offscreen)
> Oooooooh, that's nice, do that again.

Penny licks her chops.

> MILTON (Offscreen)
> Say something dirty for me. Say "doggie."

> PENNY
> Doggie.

POP! goes Polaroid.

> MILTON (Offscreen)
> Oooooooh, say that again.

> PENNY
> (*low, guttural*)
> Doggie . . . doggie.

> MILTON (Offscreen)
> Good, now Benji, lick your thumb and stick it in
> her ass.

The tip of the boom enters the frame.

> BIG BOB (Offscreen)
> Boom.

> FLUFFER (Offscreen)
> Sorry.

The boom bows out as Benji barrels in.

> MILTON (Offscreen)
> Say, "It's tight."

> BENJI
> It's tight.

> MILTON (Offscreen)
> Say, "You're so goddamned fucking tight."

> BENJI
> You're so goddamned fucking tight.

> MILTON (Offscreen)
> Good, now bring it home Benji. Bring it home
> now anytime.

Benji pulls out. The aspect ratio of the frame widens to take in the entire group. Big Bob removes the camera from the baby legs and perches it on his shoulder like a pirate's parrot. The camera glides over them, around them, between them, beneath them, behind them, beside them. Penny sits on the mattress and turns around on her knees to face Benji, making expectant, challenging eye contact with him. Benji masturbates frantically. Milton sits in a green director's chair, just off to the side.

                    MILTON
          Waiting for the pop shot now, Benji. Anytime.

                    PENNY
          Baby?

                    BENJI
          Yeah?

Benji's compass dipping south.

                    PENNY
              (whispers lowly)
          It's so easy.

                    BENJI
          Gaaaaaaaahhhh!

He ejaculates across her face.

                    MILTON
          And cut!

FLASHBACK ENDS

INT. THE DISNEY STORE — DAY

From across the store, a young girl's voice rises above the tapestry of noise.
FINN, a young girl, ten years old, in black, face smudged with ice cream,
is arguing with a twenty-two-year-old CASHIER.

                    FINN
          What do you mean you don't have it?

                    CASHIER
          I'm sorry, we don't carry Pez.

FINN

But you're the Disney Store!

CASHIER

Yes, I know that, but we don't sell that product.

FINN

But I want a Mickey Mouse Pez dispenser, goddamn it!

A tug of recognition pulls at Benji's face. He spots her.

BENJI

FINN!

Finn searches for the source of the shout. From across the store she locks
eyes with the stranger. They freeze. A look of puzzled recognition crosses
the girl's face. FINN'S THEME—moody, atonal jazz music—begins. She
runs. Benji, tripping over the seven dwarves, pushes his way through the
crowd, chasing after her.

CUT TO:

EXT. NEW YORK CITY STREET — DUSK

Benji bursts forth from the store, scanning crazy-crowded streets. About
half a block ahead, he spots her, racing down Broadway. Benji, raising a
policeman's white-gloved hand, plunges into the street against the light,
blindly navigating through traffic that closes in on itself claustrophobically, like the geometric blocks in the video game Tetris. An eighteen-wheel
truck with a rig the size of a movie screen swerves out of the way as driv-
ers blast their HORNS and PROFANITIES punctuate the air like fire-
crackers.

HORNS

!*******!**!**!*********!******!***!

PROFANITIES

¡@#$%^&*()+:;™?£¢∞§¶•ªº–≠`~<>

The Ghosts of Times Square Past—Tin Pan Alley musicians, *New York Times* reporters, Brill Building songwriters, Irish Cops, bare-chested boxers, Ziegfeld Follies girls, sword swallowers, jugglers, fire-eaters, tightrope walkers, bearded ladies, flea circuses, Hubert's Museum, Gypsy Lee Rose, feather boa-ed hookers, peg-legged Peter Stuyvesant, VJ-Day soldiers, gutter drunks, leather-vested pimps, Travis, Betsy, and Iris—line up and salute Benji as he races past hurdles of families, coffee drinkers, and camera-clicking tourists.

Benji runs down Broadway, past pulsating red and yellow lights screaming Show World, Custom Novelties, Peep-O-Rama, Tad's Steaks, Fun City, Midtown Video, Gourmet Deli, Les Nouveautes, 25¢ Private Booth. Buildings tremble and fall as Starbucks, Rite Aids, Nike Stores, Gaps, and Virgin Megastores rise out of the sticky rubble of fallen porn palaces.

Benji passes the FunTower at the triangle between Broadway, 42nd Street, and Seventh Avenue. Perched atop the tower sits GABRIEL MINE-GOLD, arms outstretched in a position of Christ-like agony. He leaps.

> GABRIEL
> Aaaaaaaaaahhhhhhh!

Darkness spreads across the sky in blue and purple sheets. Distant rumbling THUNDER announces oncoming rain.

> THUNDER
> Bababadalgharaghtakamminarronnkonnbron-
> ntonnerronntuonnthunntrovarrhounawnskawn-
> toohoohoordenenthurnuk!

RAIN falls to the ground in ellipses.

> RAIN
> . . . .
> . . . .

Nearby, a giant THUNDERCLAP triggers a Nexus to unleash a four-pronged CAR ALARM that booms to life as Benji bounds past.

CAR ALARM
Hooooooooommmmmme!
Hooooooooommmmmme!
Home! Home! Home! Home!
Ho-ome! Ho-ome!
Howowowowowowowowome!

On street corners across the city, UMBRELLA MEN magically materialize, hawking cheap black umbrellas from tote bags.

UMBRELLA MEN
(in unison)
Three dollars! Umbrellas, here, three dollars!

The sky turns black and opens like a deadly flower. An electric bolt of
lightning streaks across the firmament, cracking the sky in half. Out of a
godless heaven down pours a tundra of slate gray computers, compact
discs, VHS cassettes, beepers, buzzers, pagers, cell phones, vacuum cleaners, dustbusters, coffee makers, electronic Rolodexes, Palm Pilots, cam-
corders, answering machines, joysticks, headphones, wristwatches, VCRs,
television sets, all tumbling out of the sky, CRASHING to the concrete
street, cords trailing behind like umbilicals.

In a black Sabbath, an orgy of technological copulation, videocassette
finds camcorder, CD finds stereo, Zip drive finds hard drive. One-by-one,
the appliances pair up and make their way to a large plastic ark, operated
on autopilot. Benji, in hot pursuit, is oblivious to it all.

BENJI
FINN!

Just ahead, at 42nd Street and Seventh Avenue, Finn ducks into a darkened subway station, and slides down the stairway banister. Benji follows,
considers taking the stairs by twos and threes. Doesn't. He calls after her:

BENJI
Wait! I just want to talk to you!

CUT TO:

INT. SUBWAY STATION — DUSK

Finn jumps the turnstile. Benji, considering the same, readies himself for the leapfrog, when a TOKEN CLERK calls out to him from his booth.

> TOKEN CLERK
> STOP!

Benji, flummoxed, grinds his momentum to a halt. He watches as Finn disappears down the stairs. A wild goose chase. Benji turns around slowly, smiles, and approaches the token booth. He pushes two crumpled dollar bills under the glass.

> BENJI
> (panting)
> One please.

> TOKEN CLERK
> (taking his sweet, mulish time)
> Smile for the camera.

> BENJI
> Wa?

Slipping a token through the slot in the glass, the clerk nods to the station video camera, mounted behind him. In the camera's placid eye, Benji recognizes his reflected self. For a moment, all is lost. The clerk pushes two quarters toward Benji.

> BENJI
> (snapping out of it)
> Thanks.

Benji feeds the turnstile a token and slowly pushes through.

CUT TO:

INT. SUBWAY PLATFORM — DUSK

A dank, cavernous space lit with syphilitic fluorescent light, the subway platform is empty save an Asian man playing *The Godfather* waltz on a steel drum. Spackled on the walls are posters, peeled one layer at a time, palimpsests of movie seasons past. At the opposite end of the platform, some twenty yards ahead, stands Finn. The staircase nearest her is gated up. There is nowhere for her to go.

Benji, catching his breath, approaches slowly, palms open to the universe.

> FINN
> Listen, mister, I don't know who you are—

Benji takes a hesitant step forward.

> FINN
> —and I don't want to know.

And another.

> BENJI
> *(softly)*
> I'm a friend.

> FINN
> A friend? Whose friend?

> BENJI
> I'm a friend of your mother's.

Finn's small fingers fumble with something. A cigarette?

> FINN
> My mother hasn't any friends. And I, just one.
> *(in full* Hamlet *regalia, skull outstretched)*
> Tobey or not Tobey? That is the question

FINN (CON'T)
Clothes oft proclaim the man. A lawyer you are
not.

They are standing together now.

BENJI
No.

FINN
No, you don't look like you work on the
plantation.

BENJI
The plantation?

Behind Benji, in blackface, appears Finn's mother, KATE WELLAND,
dressed like Hattie McDaniel from *Gone With the Wind*, a shiny pickanin-
ny.

KATE WELLAND
I's done takin' anutha deposition massah! Yassuh,
dat dere's da finest deposition you evah have
seen. An' aftah you done reading it I'm gwine
shove it up yo' white Ivy League ass!

FINN
Just because you make six figures a year doesn't
mean you don't work on the plantation.

Benji nods in understanding. From wet clothes, Finn removes a damp book
of matches. She struggles to light one.

FINN
D'you have a light? It seems I'm poorly matched.

BENJI
Uh uh.

> FINN
>
> Shit!

With that word, a sulfurous Lucifer match ignites. Finn stares into the flame intently, alert to the sorcery of the world. She cups her hands, lights the joint, inhales deeply, and passes it to Benji.

> BENJI
>
> You must be kidding.

> FINN
>
> Take it.

> BENJI
>
> Put that out.

Finn stares him down.

> FINN
>
> Shibboleth!

Benji demurely takes hold of the totem, takes a suspicious look around.

> BENJI
>
> Thanks.

Benji smokes but does not inhale. He passes the joint back to Finn. Deeply, she takes another drag, and for the first time, considers her surroundings.

> FINN
> (to herself)
> City beneath a city. World of things made. World without end.

Finn looks at the grimy, patched-together man standing before her.

FINN
(softly)
Underground man. The messenger?
(to Benji)
So who are you?

Finn exhales, engulfing Benji in a thin cloud of marijuana smoke.

BENJI
Me? I'm in movies.

CUT TO:

INT. THE DOROTHY CHANDLER PAVILION — DAY

Benji, in Giorgio Armani tails, slicked-back hair, sunglasses, cellphone, and discrete red AIDS ribbon, stands at the podium before a golden Academy Award, speechifying:

BENJI
I'd just like to take this opportunity to ask everyone within earshot tonight to divest their holdings from South Africa.
(applause)
And to support bi-lateral weapons bans against
nuclear testing.
(applause)
And to work together to lift the economic embargo
against Cuba.
(applause)
Let's free Tibet and bomb Iraq and feed the children because We Are The World. Free Mumia,
props to Biggee, peace out to Tupac, support the
United Negro College Fund, vote for Proposition
209 in the upcoming referendum, remember
when recycling to remove staples from all paper
products, direct all reparations for Native
Americans to the Starwood Resort and Casino in
Connecticut, save the whales, swim with the

BENJI (CON'T)

dolphins, Luca Brasi swims with the fishes, Star
Kist chunk white tuna in oil, oil and water don't
mix, a watched pot never boils, the pot calls the
kettle African-American, silence equals death,
silence is golden, golden showers bring may flowers, the early bird catches the worm, the early
bird special at the Nebraska Diner, and most
important, I'd like to thank the little people.
Thank you little people, thank you!

STUMPY THE MAGIC DWARF and LARRY LITTLE appear onstage in
full leather bondage attire to raucous APPLAUSE. They do a little dance.
Milton Minegold rises from the audience.

MILTON

So we know Benji wants to be a
filmmaker. What about you,
Penelope?

FLASHBACK BEGINS:

INT. 666 FIFTH AVENUE, 13TH FLOOR — DAY

The offices of Scylla & Charybdis. Milton, in a blue pinstripe suit and
thick green silk tie, sits in a plush leather armchair before a huge oak desk
the size of a pirate's treasure chest.

The tabletop is impeccably neat and clean: an enormous polished surface
covered with writing instruments: an antique Underwood typewriter, an
engraved nibbed fountain pen, two bottles of Watermark emerald ink, ink
blotter. Not a paper is out of place. Prominently displayed on the desk is a
framed portrait of the Minegold family—Milton, Marion, Gabriel, and
Jessica—from happier days. In the corner, a sleek red telescope sits contentedly on a tripod, facing the window, pointed spaceward. Outside, New
York City TRAFFIC doubles for the sound of wavespeech. The light is
good.

Around the office hang framed vintage movie posters. Fellini's sad-faced clown from $8^1/_2$ and Saul Bass' *Vertigo* stick figure mingle with the ebullient Technicolor gang from *The Wizard of Oz*. Inching up around them are stills and framed box covers from some of Milton's movies: Milton dressed in rabbinical garb, lustily devouring a Jamaican beef patty off the naked bosom of a young black woman outside a Newark, New Jersey, Synagogue from *Hiding the Afikomen*; a leering, erect Milton, reclining at the head of the Passover table from *Shank Bone*; yarmulked Milton as Tevye, dancing naked through the shtetl in *Diddler on the Roof* (poster tagline: "How Did The Jews Come To America? Yiddle By Yiddle.") Finally, off to the side, an ancient, yellowing caricature of Milton from his son Gabriel's Bar Mitzvah, his porcine body exaggerated into the shape of a hot air balloon, gas leaking from its corkscrewed piggy knot.

Sitting across from Milton in hard-back chairs are Penny and Benji. Penny is dressed in tight black jeans, white halter top, and purple lace-up Doc Martin boots, her sleeveless shirt revealing a white fleshflower of vaccination. Benji is dressed in a blue and white button-down oxford, beige khakis, and Hush Puppies. The wall behind Milton is paneled with mirrors.

> PENNY
> (*with one eye on Milton, the other consulting her reflection*)
> Call me Penny.

> MILTON
> (*worrying a top-row tooth with his tongue, as if trying to remove a piece of sticky rice*)
> Okay, Penny, what'd you have in mind, professionally speaking?

> PENNY
> Well, for now, I was thinking about substitute teaching.

CUT TO:

INT. CLASSROOM — DAY

A classroom rises before her. MS. PENNY, in glasses and smart pants suit, hair pinned back in a taut-tight bun, stands at the head of the class, ruler in hand.

Behind her on a blackboard, in Bart Simpson block letters: "THINGS I LEARNED IN SCHOOL THAT HAVE HAD NO PRACTICAL APPLICATION IN MY EXPERIENCE OF THE WORLD: THE PYTHAGOREAN THEOREM; THE HYPOTENUSE; SCALENE, ISOSCELES, AND EQUILATERAL TRIANGLES; THE NULL SET; POTENTIAL AND KINETIC ENERGY; PHOTOSYNTHESIS; CHROMOSOMES; ISOTOPES; VECTORS; THE DOPPLER SHIFT; IONIC AND COVALENT BONDS; CHECKS AND BALANCES, THE TEEPEE AND THE TOTEM POLE; CUNEIFORM AND ANCIENT SUMERIA; HIEROGLYPHICS AND ANCIENT EGYPT (PYRAMIDS!); DIPHTHONG."

Ms. Penny stalks the aisles, checking on her students' progress. She stops over the desk of YOUNG BENJI—ten years old, dressed in smart blue and white button-down oxford shirt, pressed slacks, and Hush Puppy shoes, hair combed in a neat cowlick. His right hand is shaking spasmodically.

                    MS. PENNY
          Homework?

                    YOUNG BENJI
               (shaking)
          I couldn't complete last night's assignment,
          ma'am.

                    MS. PENNY
               (raising her ruler high in the air)
          And why not?

                    YOUNG BENJI
          My hand, ma'am.

                    MS. PENNY
          And what's wrong with it?

> YOUNG BENJI
> (groveling)
> I can't say, ma'am.

Ms. Penny grabs his hair and pulls it.

> MS. PENNY
> Tell me!

> YOUNG BENJI
> I shan't.

Ms. Penny slides over and slithers a saliva-slick tongue—slippery as an eel—into the child's ear.

> MS. PENNY
> (breathy, low)
> Tell me.

> YOUNG BENJI
> My evening exertions have rendered the appendage inoperable, ma'am.

She smiles knowingly, releases him.

> MS. PENNY
> O, you naughty, naughty boy.

She begins stroking his head.

> MS. PENNY
> Shall I help you?

> YOUNG BENJI
> (eager)
> Yes, please.

His skin, alert, feels her fingertips approach. Softly, knowing, gentle hands glide over the little boy's torso, softly.

> MS. PENNY
Do you know why you're here?

> YOUNG BENJI
No, ma'am.

> MS. PENNY
To learn things.

> YOUNG BENJI
Yes, teach me, ma'am! Teach me!

> MS. PENNY
To stuff that little head of yours full of knowledge.

> YOUNG BENJI
Yes, ma'am, stuff it! Stuff it in there like a stuffed sausage!

She begins kneading his rising trousers.

> YOUNG BENJI
> *(venturing)*
Teacher . . .
> MS. PENNY
Yes . . . ?

> YOUNG BENJI
> *(drooling dizzily)*
I can see your diphthong.

> MS. PENNY
> *(withdrawing)*
That's funny, I'm not wearing any.

> YOUNG BENJI
Grrrrr. Arrrrrrrrr.

A large moist stain spreads across his lap.

CUT TO:

INT. SCYLLA & CHARYBDIS OFFICES — DAY

                    MILTON
          That's not a bad idea, but you need a degree to
          teach. Education courses. Teaching's not some-
          thing you can just get involved with casually.
          What about you, Benji? What do you have lined
          up?

                    BENJI
          I was thinking I could probably go back to my
          summer job. It's in computer publishing.

CUT TO:

INT. THE AIR CONDITIONED NIGHTMARE — DAY

Stacks of paper rise out of the ground, engulfing Benji who sits at a fluo-
rescent-lit cubicle before a dull gray computer. Around him, the steady
tap-dance of KEYBOARDS CLICKING. Benji turns on his machine to
the sound of an innocuous PING! and reads the following message: "The
computer was not Shut Down properly the last time it was used." Benji
laughs to himself. The COMPUTER responds in a low echoing growl.

                    COMPUTER
          Enough tool! Let the dawn of the new flesh
          commence!

Wires, cables, and cords attack Benji like vipers, strapping him into his
swivel chair. Copper wires insinuate themselves into the skin of his arms,
legs, hands, and feet. Plugs plunge into every orifice: eyes, ears, anus, ure-
thra. Paper clips, staples, and rubber bands riddle his corpus like poison
darts. Benji opens his mouth to scream: out slides a spinning three-CD
changer. He lifts up his shirt: his chest cavity has become a twenty-seven-
inch television screen displaying the color bar code, transmitting the
emergency broadcast signal. A VCR cassette ejects from his navel. One
eye becomes an alarm clock, BEEPING on-and-off, the other, a speedball

mouse. His feet become phones. Twin pieces of buttered toast pop out of his shoulderblades, hot coffee runs out both nostrils. His thumbs become beepers, his fingers pistons, his penis, a plug which he lustily sinks into the nearest electrical socket. Out of his buttocks rolls a FAX which reads:

> "ONE DAY BENJAMIN SEYMOUR AWOKE TO FIND HE HAD
> BEEN TURNED INTO A GIANT APPLIANCE."

                                                            CUT TO:

INT. SCYLLA & CHARYBDIS OFFICES — DAY

                    MILTON
        But all the pens you can steal, dress-down
        Fridays, and a gold watch at retirement, right?
        Medical?

                    BENJI
        After six months.

                    MILTON
        Sounds great, where do I sign up? Look, what do
        you want to do? You want to make movies, right?
        How you gonna do that? What does your mother
        do for a living?

                    BENJI
        She's a schoolteacher.

                    MILTON
        And your father?

                    BENJI
        He sells pool filtration equipment.

                    MILTON
        Okay. Good. Good, honest, hard-working people.
        But not the kind who can make the right intro-
        ductions, right?

                    MILTON (CON'T)
                (*to Penny*)
        And you? You're not really sure what you want to
        do, but you're sort of bursting with ideas, right,
        and you kind of like the idea of seeing yourself on
        camera?

Penny confers with her reflection in the mirror.

                        PENNY
        Sure.

                        MILTON
        How long you two been together?

                        BENJI
        Two years.

                        MILTON
        And in that time you've been entirely
        monotonous?
                        PENNY
        Yes.

                        MILTON
        Planning on getting married?

Penny squeezes Benji's hand.

                        PENNY
        We're married in our own way.

                        MILTON
        Kids?

                        PENNY
        No, we won't be having any.

A look of surprise flashes across Benji's face. He suppresses it.

MILTON

(to Penny)

So what is it? You're a tough bitch, you've seen it all before, is that it?

BENJI

—Excuse me?

Penny is silent.

MILTON

You heard me college boy, if you need to excuse yourself go ahead. You know when people say "excuse me?" When they've heard damn well what the other person said and they don't like it. It's a conversational device used to stall for time. You can't take language like that you got no business being here. Do you know what business we're in here?

PENNY

(unfazed)

What?

BENJI

(abashed)

Gabriel told me you're a pornographer.

MILTON

(angry at the mention of his son's name)

Wrong, Benjamin. There's a war going on out there and you're about to be shipped off to the front lines. Are you at all religious, Benjamin?

BENJI

Not particularly.

MILTON
(*to Penny*)
You?

PENNY
Lapsed.

MILTON
Of course you are. You kids ever think about why
pornography is so important to this great
Christian experiment known as America?

BENJI
Not really.

PENNY
Uh uh.

MILTON
Has it never once occurred to you that
Christianity—one of the primary engines that
drives the world forward—is a religion based on
the denial of animal fucking? Now, I have nothing against Christ. In fact, historically speaking,
I'm inclined to say I rather like the guy. But
why'd they have to bring sex into it? Why'd they
have to get it all jammed up? The denial of sex at
the heart of Christianity makes no goddamned
sense. You're gonna tell me that while Jesus is
experiencing life as a man, that as he's learning to
live like the rest of us so he can redeem our suffering he's not gonna dip the godhead in those
murky waters? Not even the tip?! I say bring on
Zeus and the Greeks—at least their overactive
libidos lend their divinity a measure of psychological credibility. Because if we're here to try to
understand the world around us as best we can, to
learn from experience as it presents itself to our
senses, what better tool have we than sex? In

> MILTON (CONT'D)

what other activity are our highest and lowest motives as dramatically, simultaneously engaged? What else offers such a bitch's brew of violence and grace? Of selfishness and generosity? Yet at the heart of the American experiment lay this Puritanical denial of sex. So when you say to me, 'Papa Bear's in the Pornography business,' I say to you, no, Benjamin, no. We're engaged in a holy war, and every time a black guy takes on two blondes atop a pool table, every time a debutante takes it up the ass, every time an unhappily married man brings an X-rated videotape home to his sweet wet rag of a wife, we've expanded the strictures of battle a degree. We're holy men, Benji, missionaries. Existential missionaries.

> BENJI

Okay.

> MILTON

I need you two to think about these things. I need performers who can invest their fucking with some ideology.

> PENNY

Okay.

> MILTON

Now, I need to know what you will and won't do.

> BENJI

What do you mean?

> MILTON

Sexually. I need to know what's on and off limits with you two.

PENNY
(*looking directly at Milton*)
I don't care, as long as I do it with Benji.

MILTON
A?

PENNY
What?

MILTON
Anal?

PENNY
Yup.

MILTON
You've done that before?

Penny nods. Milton looks at Benji, then back to Penny.

MILTON
You like it?

PENNY
I like it, I don't crave it.

MILTON
Girl scenes?

PENNY
Uh huh.

MILTON
Group?

PENNY
(*still looking directly at Milton*)
Hm.

Milton looks from Penny to Benji, from Benji to Penny, from Penji to Benny. He places his left hand over his heart and raises his right.

                    MILTON
          Welcome to Milton's minions, kids. From now on
          I want you to think of me as your patron, your
          protector, your proselytizer. I want you to think of
          me as Papa Bear. Now, Penny, if you don't mind,
          I'd like to talk to Benji alone for a minute.

                    PENNY
          That's okay. There's an apartment I wanted to
          check out today, anyway. You wanna catch up
          with me later, hon?

                    BENJI
          Sure thing.

Penny extends her hand to Milton for him to shake. He kisses it.

                    MILTON
          Penny.
                    PENNY
              (smiling)
          Papa Bear.

Penny slinks off her chair . . .

                    PENNY
              (to Benji)
          Goodbye, love.

. . . and out of the room. Milton watches her very carefully as she exits.

                    MILTON
          You guys are very much in love, I can see that.

BENJI
Thank you.

MILTON
No, it's sweet. It's sweet to see. But—and no
offense—I think this girlfriend of yours is a bit of
a fruitcake. I mean I can understand the attraction. I've seen girls like her before. I've screwed
girls like her before. She's tough, she can take
care of herself, she's fun, she's physical, and she
fucks. She's the lemon in your lemonade and
you'll follow her anywhere. I understand how
these things work. But you, Benjamin, seem made
of finer stuff. No offense, but you look like the
kind of kid who, if he can successfully fold the
Times on the subway without annoying the person
sitting next to him, considers it a good day. So
before we agree on this, I just want to make sure
you understand the parameters of what it is you're
about to embark on.

BENJI
Fair enough.

MILTON
You do this, it's like you're living in another
country. You won't ever be able to look at things
the same. Everything you see is going to be fil-
tered through this prism, and you may not be pre-
pared for that. Imagine you're standing on line in
the bank in front of a retired army general, someone who's been in the military for thirty years.
An old lady cuts the line, and you let it slide, but
he sees it as an infraction: a sneak attack, a serious breach in rank. My point is, his occupation
mandates that he's going to see the world through
that particular lens, and that's what's going to
happen to you: you're going to start measuring

MILTON (CONT'D)

everything you see in terms of its sexual currency.
F'rinstance, I can no longer go to the post office
without confronting what appear to me to be the
titles of countless unproduced pornographic films:
Oversize Package, Handle With Care, Stuffing
the *Envelope, Mail Slot, Do Not Bend.* Anyway,
the point is, you're gonna see some things. You're
gonna see some things. You'll be amazed what
some of these bitches'll do once a camera is
trained on them. With some women, their relation to the camera is like that of a snake to a
snake charmer. Camera lures them out of the basket, makes them dance, makes them do strange
things.

(*shaking his head back-and-forth*)

Indians are right not to have their pictures taken.
Cameras have magic powers of a not necessarily
wholesome sort. Where's she from?

BENJI

Arizona.

MILTON

Yeah, well, you don't get tushies like that in
Hebrew school. Look, I'll be up front with you,
Benji. You're in a bind. You're in love with a
woman who's braver, tougher, stronger than yourself. Now, that's not your fault, in fact, it may
even be to your credit, but when that situation
arises, only one of two outcomes can occur.
Either you can adapt, and find yourself growing
braver, tougher, stronger through her good example, or you can crumble.

A bearish WORKER in overalls and backward-turned baseball cap enters
the office carrying a box of videocassettes, trailing styrofoam popcorn
across the floor. He hands an invoice to Milton.

WORKER

Where to boss?

MILTON

Send those over the Jersey warehouse.

Milton puts on a pair of green-tinted tortoiseshell glasses and checks over the paperwork as he continues talking to Benji.

MILTON

You're in love with someone you don't know
entirely. And that's just fascinating. Well, I got
more news for you, Benji. You may not trust her
entirely, either. And deep down, you're not even
sure you like her entirely.
    (looking up at Benji over his eyeglass frames)
What's the scoop boy-o? You think with her you
can book passage to some other world? You're
looking for a crash course in human complexity?
I'm gonna be up front with you. It's her I want.
The girl drips sex. Now, if she'll only come
aboard with you in tow, if you're the deal-breaker,
that's fine. We can work with that. But I don't
think you're a natural like she is.

BENJI

Even so, I'd like to give it a try.

MILTON

Listen, there's a thousand new girls pass through
the industry a year, but year in year out it's the
same bunch of guys. We take in maybe two-three
new guys a year 'cause unless you're something
special—a Milo Pipe or a Moishe Pipik—the audience doesn't give a damn about the guy in the
scene. Lemme fill you in on another thing, too.
On a porn shoot, the only person more hated than
Jerry Falwell is some strung out piece of shit B-girl

> MILTON (CONT'D)
>
> comes in off the street you have to lure to the set
> with a line of coke. And the only person more
> hated than her is the boyfriend of that strungout
> piece of shit who's taking a cut of the action. And
> the only person more hated than him, all the way
> at the bottom of the diarrhea daisy chain is the
> suitcase pimp who wants to be in the film. And
> that's gonna be you, Benjamin. Now, after all that,
> if you still want to give it a shot,
>> (he rubs his hands)
> I absolve myself, I wash my hands of it.

Benji takes a moment to take it all in, then:

> BENJI
>
> I see my life as a movie anyway, so what differ-
> ence does it make?

Milton leans back in his chair, satisfied.

> MILTON
>
> Okay, yes, you can be the paunchy, hairy every-
> man with the average-sized deckle that winds up
> with the hot goy. We'll be shooting next Monday
> at the warehouse at Pier 21 in Brooklyn. Be there
> at noon. If, for whatever reason, you should have
> second thoughts and want to cancel, or just want
> to talk things through, call the number on the
> card. Any questions?

> BENJI
>
> C'I see the script?

Milton consults his watch.

> MILTON
>
> Tell ya what, we have some time, I'll go you one
> better. How 'bout a little screenwriting lesson

MILTON (CON'T)

'cause my sixth sense tells me if you stick with it,
you're gonna be working behind the scenes some-
day. Okay, first lesson is, it has to be visual.
Forget prose, forget poetry, when you write a
screenplay, you're less a writer than a tour guide:
look at that building, look at that car, look at this
gun, look at him, look at her. Look! Look! Look!
That's the trick. In a screenplay, if a character
just thinks it, if he doesn't say it or look at it, it's
no good. It won't fly. We have to see it. Next lesson is about formatting. Screenplays are all about
formatting. By nature, they're more architectural
than literary. When you write one, you'll find you
spend half the time formatting the fucking thing,
getting the slug lines right, tabbing dialogue over
to the proper indent. It can be very annoying.
But there's a reason for it, the reason being that,
once properly formatted, one screenplay page
equals approximately one minute of screen time.
So a hundred-and-twenty page script equals a
two-hour movie, get it?

BENJI

Got it.

MILTON

Good. Y'ever hear of the term "high concept?"

BENJI

No.

MILTON

It means a movie whose central idea can be
encapsulated in a single sentence.

Milton points to a poster.

MILTON

The Wizard of Oz: there's no place like home.

Again.

> MILTON
>
> *Vertigo*: man crucified on the cross of his romantic obsessions.

And again.

> MILTON
>
> $8^1/_2$: a portrait of the artist having a nervous breakdown. Movies! An art form whose highest aspiration is to define itself in a single sentence! Horrors! Next lesson: dialogue. Individual speeches should never go beyond six or seven lines. Longer than that and you're writing prose. Which is a shame 'cause people don't talk in little spurts. People like to spiel. I like to spiel. But today's movie audiences won't stand for it. F'rinstance, if we put everything I just told you into a movie script, it'd never fly, we'd have to break it up in some way.

> BENJI
> Why's that?

> MILTON
>
> Because people don't read anymore, Benji. It's becoming a strictly visual culture. That said, the one thing screenplay writing will teach you is concision. And that's the most important thing about them: tell the story straight. Beginning. Middle. End. Don't get fancy. Forget about flashbacks, fantasies, dream sequences, voice over narration. They only confuse things. Get it?

> BENJI
> Got it.

> MILTON
> Good. Any questions?

BENJI

C'I see the script?

MILTON

Sure.

Milton hands Benji the screenplay, one page long, written in a chicken scrawl.

INSERT SHOT: HANDWRITTEN PIECE OF PAPER:

BLOW WHITE AND THE SEVEN WHORES

BJ, BJ-2, Lez Ms., Missionary, Cowgirl, Doggie, Doggie-2, A, Facial.

BENJI

I don't get it.

MILTON

Those rules only apply for movies, Benji. This is porn. There are no scripts in P, Benji, just the title and the formula.

BENJI

The formula?

MILTON

The set number of sexual positions. In pinot, the standard formula is this: seven or more sex scenes per film, the first of which occurs in the first five minutes. At least one of those should be girl-girl, and all guy-girl scenes should end with an external cum shot, preferably a facial. Get it?

BENJI

Yeah. What's with the title?

MILTON

O, lots of pornos use variations on the names of
kid's movies for titles. Isn't that what we love
about sex in the first place? The return to child's
play. Isn't that why you're crazy about her? All
that sex appeal: all that childishness.

BENJI

Huh. Who will I be playing?

MILTON

The bullfrog.

BENJI

Benji The Bullfrog. Huh.

MILTON

You're lucky, Benji. You get to turn into a prince.

Benji smiles at the prospect. Milton looks at Benji carefully, then at the
family portrait sitting on his desk. We ZOOM-IN on the photograph, onto
Gabriel's troubled face, which slowly fills the frame. MILTON'S MILI-
TARY MARCH takes on layers of hidden subtlety, hidden depth.

Milton removes his sculptural heft from behind his desk, cracks his back,
and approaches the telescope.

MILTON

Know anything about astrophysics?

BENJI

Not much.

MILTON

It's what Gabriel's studying up at Cornell.

BENJI

Yeah, I remember.

MILTON
(*stroking the shaft of the scope*)
Interesting stuff. But I have to admit, when I first
heard he was going into that field, I couldn't help
thinking itwas a waste of time. But then I did a
little reading. Brought it down to my level. Found
my way in. And what I discovered is that there
are laws of repetition in nature that strike me as
aesthetic, even elegant.

BENJI
Like Jung's theory of archetypes?

MILTON
Yes, but on an even grander scale. F'rinstance, it
may turn out that the universe itself is encoded
with a cycle of life and death, birth and decay.
Now wouldn't that be something? A universe that
struggles toward maturation and later, experiences
the weariness of age? And this consistency of patterns holds even on a subatomic level.
F'rinstance, the atom, with its clusters of electrons and muons orbiting a nucleus of larger neu-
trons and protons resembles the solar system with
its planets and moons orbiting around the sun.

BENJI
Huh.

MILTON
Even the terminology of human relationships is
the same as the language of cosmic glue: someone
people revolve around, circle of friends, opposites
attract, magnetic personality . . .

BENJI
Makes sense.

MILTON

Well why shouldn't it make sense? I mean, if
hydrogen and oxygen bond covalently to form
water, why shouldn't mama and papa Benji bond
to form little baby Benji? The forces that hold
the universe together strike me as not entirely
dissimilar to familial and sexual bonds.
F'rinstance, there's a theory in quantum physics
that everything is made up of these things called
virtual particles. And that each virtual particl
generates an antiparticle. Now isn't that something? That nothing, not even subatomic particles, are meant to live alone? They need to exist
in pairs. And the comical thing is how these particles and antiparticles have these little Punch
and Judy relationships where they're forever
attracting and repelling each other until they
mutually annihilate. Sounds like most of the married couples I know.

BENJI

Is that what Gabriel's working on, quantum
physics?

MILTON

Last I heard he was studying string theory.

BENJI

That has to do with everything being made of little vibrating strings, right?

MILTON

Yes. It's this new theory, very cutting edge stuff,
that's an attempt to reconcile Einstein's General
Theory of Relativity—the behavior of large
forces—with quantum physics—the inner work-
ingsof the atom. It's what Einstein was working
on up to the time of his death and what that crippled guy in England is still trying to figure out.

MILTON (CONT'D)

Basically, string theory is an attempt to devise a
comprehensive theory of the universe, something
that could encompass both the Big Bang and
electron shells. And that's what they call it:
G.U.T. for Grand Unified Theory, or T.O.E. for
Theory of Everything.

BENJI

Sounds interesting.

MILTON

It is. Anyway, if I ever speak with Gabriel again,
the question I'd like to put to him is this: how
does it relate to us? Not how do they relate to
one another but how do they relate to human
consciousness? Because it seems to me that
human consciousness is the central mystery of the
universe, and, as such, it should necessarily affect
physics, large and small. And I think I have an
inkling as to how it does. Benji, do you know
what the scientific definition of time is?

BENJI

Wa?

MILTON

An increase in disorder, or entropy. Science dis-
tinguishes the past from the future simply as an
increase in disorder. In other words, our lives get
more complicated as they go along. That doesn't
sound like math to me so much as fortune cookie
philosophy. But what if our concepts of space and
time are just crude patterns? What if space and
time don't really exist as such? And what if that's
where we were to come into play? If human consciousness truly is an anomaly in nature, that
would mean God needed us to create time. It
would mean He needed our memories to

> MILTON (CONT'D)
> give a direction to time.

> BENJI
> You lost me. How does any of that relate to what
> we've been talking about?

> MILTON
> Because Benji, film, for all its limitations, for all
> its stupidity, for all its flaws, is capable of doing
> the one thing no other art can do. It can freeze
> time in motion. Preserve it. That's what makes it
> so gorgeous. Film steals fire from the gods twenty-
> four frames per second. Just think: you and Penny
> fucking! That moment preserved, frozen forever
> through all space and time!

> BENJI
> Huh.
>> (*regarding the telescope*)
> Can you see anything out of that thing?
> MILTON
> Nah. Air pollution.

CUT TO:

INT. SUBWAY PLATFORM — DUSK

Twin streams of smoke issue forth from Finn's winged nose.

> FINN
> Movies, huh?

> BENJI
> Yeah.

> FINN
> I don't believe you, narc.

                         BENJI
        I'm not a narc.

                         FINN
        Okay, narc.

                         BENJI
        Would a narc do this!?

Benji takes hold of the joint and takes a massive hit. BENJI'S THEME is
reinterpreted for the sitar.

                         FINN
        Whatever you say, narc.

From the other end of the platform, a policeman, OFFICER CRANLY—
forties, red-haired, vulpine—appears. Panicky, Benji puts the joint in his
mouth. He coughs, jolts, quickly pulls it out and tosses the roach onto
skeleton tracks.

                         FINN
        Hey man, that's my ganja!

INT. SUBWAY TRACKS — DUSK

The roach extinguishes itself in an algae-thick puddle of brackish water.
From a sepulchral dark corner, a fearsomely large rat materializes, nibbles
at the leafy roll, and carries it off into the night.

INT. SUBWAY PLATFORM — DUSK

Officer Cranly approaches.

                         BENJI
        Shit.

                         FINN
        The fuzz.

>   BENJI
>   (*turning around*)
>   Shit.

>   FINN
>   What's that pig coming toward us for, narc?

>   BENJI
>   Sh! Just be quiet and let me do the talking.

>   FINN
>   Sure thing, narc.

Officer Cranly reaches the pair.

>   BENJI
>   (*nervous, rapidly*)
>   Nice night, isn't it? 'Cept for the rain of course.
>   Train coming anytime soon? How 'bout those
>   Bulls?

>   OFFICER CRANLY
>   (*craning his neck forward*)
>   Don't think I didn't see what you just did.
>   Y'know, not only is it illegal to smoke on the sub-
>   way, but what kind of example you hope to set,
>   smoking in front of a girl that age?

>   FINN
>   It was I who was smoking. He only extinguished
>   the offending ash.

Officer Cranly looks confused.

>   OFFICER CRANLY
>   (*to Benji*)
>   Is that true?

Benji shrugs.

OFFICER CRANLY

O, Jesus and Mary, the girl can't be more than twelve years old!

FINN

Ten. Perfect number. Alpha and Omega.

Benji leans in to the policeman, out of Finn's earshot.

BENJI
(softly, conspiratorially)
I was hoping you would come over and put a little fright in her.

OFFICER CRANLY
(to Benji)
Gotcha.
(to Finn)
Y'know miss, I could write this up, have it put on your permanent record.

FINN

Ooooo, not my permanent record.

OFFICER CRANLY

Yes sir, a mark on your permanent record will follow you for the rest of your life, prevent you from getting into some of your better schools and universities.

FINN

Your rules do not threaten me, sir.
(pointing to her forehead)
It is in here that I must kill the mayor and the mother.

OFFICER CRANLY

What'd she say? She say she's gonna kill the mayor?! She just threaten to kill Giuliani?!

BENJI

I think she was speaking in metaphor.

FINN

O, what did I have to meet her for?

BENJI

She's a bit precocious for her age.

Six-foot-tall Amazonian MODELS appear in Victoria's Secret lingerie, strutting down the subway platform runway, each speaking in turn.

IMAN

What if she's not pretty?

FREDERIQUE

What if she's not thin?

STEPHANIE SEYMOUR

What if she's smarter than the boys she dates?

TYRA BANKS

Or makes more money?

THE MODELS
(in unison)
So smart. So sad.
Broke heart. Too bad.

FINN

I imagine there is a malevolent reality behind
those things I fear.

BENJI

I think I can take it from here, officer. After all,
the real parenting begins in the home.

FINN

I will not be returning there tonight.

OFFICER CRANLY
Boy, this kid's got a mouth on her.

A blast of infernal heat informs the air as a downtown TRAIN dopplers into the station.

TRAIN
Bababadalgharaghtakamminarronnkonnbron-
ntonnerronntuonnthunntrovarrhounawnskawn-
toohoohoordenenthurnuk!

FINN
Our chariot.

BENJI
(furiously shaking Officer Cranly's hand)
Well, this is our train. Thanks for all your help officer. Thank you! Thank you!

Stumpy the Magic Dwarf and Larry Little dance around the policeman and carry him off triumphantly, aloft on their shoulders. Benji and Finn step into the subway car.

INT. SUBWAY — DUSK

Subway straps hang in the air like question marks. The train is full, if not quite crowded, with a collection of BUSINESSMEN and outer-borough COMMUTERS. Most everyone is seated. Most everyone looks tired. Some sleep, some read, some just stare off into the middle distance, inhaling the stagnant air of another day gone by. An old, crabby-faced HISPANIC WOMAN knits small colored flowers onto a sweater. Two TEENAGERS—one in a sleeveless wife-beater T-shirt and blue jeans, the other in a blue and orange windbreaker topped with a furry Kangol cap—argue about pro-wrestling:

TEENAGER 1
I seen some shit on the WWF last night—

TEENAGER 2

—Shit's fake.

TEENAGER 1

—So's movies. Long's it's entertainin', yo.

Benji and Finn take adjacent seats of Burger King yellow and orange. A ratty homeless MAN enters the car. He recites the alphabet in a singsong voice as passengers drop nickels, dimes, and quarters into his knit wool cap. He makes his way to the pair.

ALPHABET MAN

W, X, Y, Z. A, B, C, D, E, K, G, H, I, J, K—

FINN

—Stop! I think you got it wrong. Do it again.

ALPHABET MAN

A, B, C, D, E, K, G—

FINN

Yes, you did get it wrong. Where I see ef, you see kay.

ALPHABET MAN

Guess so.
     (holding out his cap)
C'you help me out?

FINN
     (obliviously handing over a crumpled bundle of
     bills)
That goes on your head.

BENJI
     (intercepting the money)
Here, let me take care of that.

Benji reaches into his pocket and ponies up a shiny coin.

ALPHABET MAN
(*moving along, stymied, muttering letters to him-self*)
O, I c!

BENJI
(*furtively separating and counting the bills*)
Thirty-three. Better let me hold onto that for you.

FINN
Doesn't matter.

BENJI
I know but . . .

FINN
A, B, C, D—why are women's bras sized with letters?

BENJI
I dunno.

FINN
It's cruel. As if we're being graded in reverse. I'm a B, but I really want a C!

BENJI
Huh.

FINN
Did you know there are more words in English than any other language?

BENJI
No, I didn't know that.

FINN
It's true. What's your favorite?

> BENJI

Wa?

> FINN

Word.

> BENJI

I don't have one.

> FINN

That's too bad. Everyone should have a favorite word.

> BENJI

Waddaya care so much about words for, anyway? Shouldn't you be playing with dolls or skipping rope or eating candy or something?

> FINN

My father used to teach them to me.

> BENJI
> *(regretting his previous remark)*

O.

Pause.

> BENJI

I do have one.

> FINN

What?

> BENJI

A favorite word. Limpid.

> FINN

Sounds weak-willed.

                    BENJI
        No, it means extremely clear.

                    FINN
        You'd think you'd want your favorite word to be
        something simple, something you use everyday,
        wouldn't you think?

                    BENJI
        Hm. What's yours?

Finn looks at the stranger.

                    FINN
        That one I'll keep.

The train doors open. Some passengers get on, some off.

                    FINN
              (smiling, ebullient)
        I don't think I've ever taken the train before.

Her smile grows.

                    FINN
        I can't stop smiling. I can't stop smiling! Why
        can't I stop smiling?! Help me!

                    BENJI
        It's called "perma-smile." It'll go away. Try not to
        think about it.

                    FINN
              (tugging at him)
        Help me. Help me. I'm not used to this. The
        train is moving! Help me! I'm hungry! I'm
        thirsty! My throat is dry! Help me!

Benji removes the Pez dispenser from his hip pocket and proffers his last purple pellet.

> BENJI
> (*in pontiff's hat, the bells of St. Peter's RING-
> ING behind him*)
> Here. Suck on this.

Finn opens her mouth as Benji the Benevolent places the wafer on her tongue.

> FINN
> Thank you.
> (*savoring the candy*)
> I can feel every pore. Every grain of sand.

> BENJI
> Yeah, well, it's Pez.

> FINN
> It's like remembering what sugar tastes like for
> the first time.

> BENJI
> Easy, killer.

> FINN
> (*appreciatively*)
> What's your name?
> BENJI
> Benji.

> FINN
> Benji . . . You don't know my mother, do you?

> BENJI
> No, not really.

FINN

Then why were you chasing after me?

BENJI

I made a promise to her. I'm . . . I met you earlier
today. I gave you an ice cream.

FINN

I remember. The messenger.

BENJI

Wrong role.

FINN

(smiling)
One of many.

BEGIN MONTAGE:

In quick succession, Benji and Finn appear in a series of costume changes:
Benji and Finn as the Messenger and Medea, as Quixote and Sancho
Panza, Charlie Chaplin and Jackie Cooper, Prospero and Ariel, Lear and
the Fool, Humbert and his girleen, Didi and Gogo, Benji and Finn.

END MONTAGE

BENJI

Why are you running away from home?

FINN

Home? How do you define the word?

Benji looks at her, puzzled.

FINN

Can you locate it? When you can direct me
toward one, I'll go.

They sit together in silence as the subway gently rocks back and forth, like a cradle.

                    BENJI
        Your parents divorced long?

                    FINN
        A year. Once around the sun.

                    BENJI
        Why'd they split up?

                                        CUT TO:

INT. ASPEN SKI LODGE — NIGHT

Kate Welland and MARTIN, Finn's father, sit before a blazing fireplace, arms entwined with champagne flutes, curled up together on a bearskin rug. A framed school portrait of Finn, sad-faced, suspended before a silkscreen of sky, sits on the fireplace mantle surveying all.

                    MARTIN
            (in plummy British tones)
        I adore you darling.

                KATE WELLAND
        And I you.

                    MARTIN
        But the child, Kate, the child.

                KATE WELLAND
        Incorrigible.

                    MARTIN
        Yes, I agree.

In the portrait, Finn's young eyes grow wonderstruck wide. Martin rises, takes hold of the frame and cavalierly tosses it to the flames. In the blazing conflagration, Finn's frown warps into a smirk, and then, a smile.

Finn's eyes grow wild, deranged. She plunges her little fingers into Benji's bicep.

CUT TO:

INT. SUBWAY — DUSK

> BENJI
>
> You okay?

> FINN
>
> I would like not to think of it.

Finn retreats into silence. Benji, bored, looks around the train. His eyes alight on a young woman, a mother, peeling an orange for her child, a boy of perhaps six or seven. In an inadvertent lesson in fractions, she parses the fruit in halves, then quarters, then eighths. She hands a section to her son, and places another on a napkin that she leaves on the empty seat between herself and a homeless man in a crumpled blue cardigan sweater, gaunt as Picasso's guitar picker. Seated adjacent to him is a burly Hasidic Jew in a black fur hat and heavy woolen overcoat, his face obscured by a heavy leatherbound prayerbook. He looks up. It is Benji's father, ART.

> ART
> *(with tallith, long-lighted candle, yarmulke, and
> tefillin)*
> And Terah begat Abraham and Abraham begat
> Isaac and Isaac begat Jacob and Esau and bongs
> begat bells and Benji begat nothing.

> BENJI
>
> Dad?

> ART
>
> Not a card. Not a call.

BENJI

Did I disappoint you?

ART

(stone cemetery plots sprouting around him like mushrooms)

An old man. Father. Dead. Mother. Dead. Married forty-one years. Wife. Dead. How does it work? It spins. It spins. It's over before it begins. Gone in a flash. Benji! The beauty of the world! Breathe. Eat. Sleep. Dance. Enjoy.

He buries his face in the book.

BENJI

Dad?!

But the man does not respond. Benji distractedly bites the NAILS on his left hand.

NAILS

Ow! Ah!

NAILS

The brute!

NAILS

Cannibal!

NAILS

I bleed! I bleed!

NAILS

The pain is . . . delicious.

Benji's attention flits from sign to sign as the train travels between stations, lights blink on-and-off, on-and-off. When you make your choice. If you need an abortion, we're here for you. Nearsighted. Farsighted. 1-800-END-PAIN. 1-800-BAD-FOOT. Visit the Bahamas. Sandy dunes. Ocean.

Palm trees. The sky. The MUSIC of Maurice Jarre is heard.

CUT TO:

EXT. THE DESERT — DAY

Penny, veiled, eyes made impossibly large by dark mascara, bejeweled with toerings, silver, and gold spangles, a beaded bellychain, and gold sash, sits outstretched before WALLY THE CAMEL who is feeding from a nearby fig tree.

Plump olives and almonds, yellow honey, succulent mangos, lemons, limes, and melon fruit are spread out across a blanket, waiting to be eaten. The air is full of fragrance, golden wine, perfumed oils, wafts of incense, curry powder, pomades, and spice. Festoons of camel bells TINKLE in the late afternoon breeze.

Out of the blazing sunlight, a stranger appears on the horizon. Slowly, slowly he blurs into focus. Mounted atop a white stallion, a curved golden dagger at his side, he is fashioned in brilliant white Valentino robes of the finest silk. A gutrah obscures the sharp lines of his face, revealing only a pair of large Occidental eyes. The stranger reaches the camp, dismounts and approaches the cloven-hoofed beast, who kneels down in abeisance to the master, making an offering of his long, noble neck. He strokes.

WALLY THE CAMEL
Hmmmm.

The stranger approaches the harlot, removing the gutrah. It is LAWRENCE OF A LABIA.

PENNY
I have been waiting.

LAWRENCE
(seductively)
Pornotopia is an ocean in which no oar is dipped.

He leans in for a kiss.

PENNY

(sighing)

O, Lawrence.

Slowly, note-by-note, ORIENTAL MUSIC is heard. Benji rises and approaches a FORTUNE COOKIE tree, and PLUCKS one of the treats. He opens it:

FORTUNE COOKIE

(in lilting, obsequious, Oriental tones)

You are a kind and generous soul. You have many talents. You will travel far and wide. You are a popular person with many admirers. Your life will be happy and full. Open your eyes, Benji, open your eyes, open your eyes . . .

CUT TO:

INT. SUBWAY — DUSK

Benji opens his eyes. An advertisement. A pair of hands in handcuffs, open-palmed to the heavens in supplication: "When you have just one call to make, dial 1-800-SHYSTER, 24 hrs. a day."

BENJI

Twenty-four hours. A day.

FINN

A day.

Finn looks down at her wristwatch. It is gone.

FINN

What time is it?

CUT TO:

EXT. SPACE — TIME

Benji looks down at his watch. On the face of it, numbers have been replaced by astrological symbols, swirling in a thick constellation soup. Aquarius, Pisces, Aires, Taurus, Gemini, Cancer, Leo, Virgo, Libra, Scorpio, Sagittarius, and Capricorn spin in the icy blackness, circling cold, coiling interstellar winds in roulette wheel orbits. Flying spaceward, Benji and Finn travel past Mars, Jupiter, Saturn, Uranus, and Neptune, past Pluto's rings, beyond the solar system, across Jackson Pollock Milky Ways, through chimes of time and clockwork gears of nature they slide down double helix strands of DNA. Radiant, the pair push past Planck's Constant; separated, they participate in Pauli's Exclusion Principle; indecisive, they haggle over Heisenberg's Uncertainty Principle. Reunited, they strut-step with string theory, witnessing the Big Bang, the birth of creation where all laws of time and space break down. Bounding into a black hole they pass through the event horizon, heading for the singularity. Time slooooooooooows. Their bodies stretch. Benji's waist returns to college inches, college girth. Finn grows six-feet pretty, six-feet tall. The pair is crushed, regurgitated as radiation. Reincarnated as dark matter, they are deposited back in their subway seats. ALBERT EINSTEIN sits between them.

CUT TO:

INT. SUBWAY — DUSK

ALBERT EINSTEIN
(bemused German accent)
God does not play dice with the universe.

Benji looks at his watch, frozen at a stroke at 6:17.

BENJI
I dunno. It's stopped.

Across from them, Gabriel Minegold appears, arms outstretched in a position of Christ-like agony, crucified across twin telescope beams.

GABRIEL
Time bends. It twists. It doesn't exist.

                    BENJI
But it does. Things begin. They end. They begin
again.

                    GABRIEL
          (bending his body into a Möbius strip)
Live in the past! Forget the present! Remember
the future!

Gabriel points to a subway advertisement: "THE MUSEUM OF PER-
SONAL HISTORY."

                                        CUT TO:

INT./EXT. BENJI'S BRIEF HISTORY OF TIME

Light! Amoebae crawl out of the primordial sludge, Cro-Magnon kills
saber toothed tiger, Homo erectus kills Cro-Magnon, Homo sapiens kills
Homo erectus, the dawn of civilization and its discontents begins as Baby
Benji is born, Moses floats downstream, the pyramids are built, Jesus does
time on the cross, in the third grade Ms. Dubrowsky informs Benji, "Good
Job!" Huns, Goths, and Visigoths rampage through Rome, Benji sees his
first Pinot, darkness falls, the Irish save civilization, Michelangelo paints
a ceiling, Leonardo writes backwards, Galileo takes a measurement, man
gets enlightened, Benji goes Ivy, Gutenberg presses on, Queen Elizabeth
gets a makeover, the bawdy bard invents the human, for his freshman writing seminar Benji writes a paper entitled "Fear of the Other in *King Lear*,"
Benji meets Penny, Newton is hit by an apple, Napoleon forgets to pack
for winter, Columbus miscalculates, tea time in Boston, Union forever!,
Mr. Charles Darwin has the gall to ask, an automobile manufacturer rele-
gates history to the bunk-seat, Benji gets a blowjob, a Spanish painter
imagines a world of French squares, a Viennese witch doctor imagines
Hamlet has the hots for his mom, in Russia the proletariat follows the
money, in Prague a clerk imagines himself a giant cockroach, in Germany
a short, dark, unitesticled art student convinces his countrymen that
Aryans are the master race, six million Jews are exterminated in the death
camps, Benji's mother dies, the Bomb is dropped, Dylan goes electric, JFK
bites the bullet, Martin Luther has a dream, King Richard resigns, Saigon
falls, Benny and Penji profess their love, homosexuals weep, a Republican

President sleeps, Penjamin make a movie, MTV debuts, the Blessed Virgin is reincarnated as a popstar slut, Sony unleashes the Playstation, McDonald's introduces the McRib sandwich, www.worldwidewasteoftime: computers of the world unite!, David Hasselhoff serenades Germany as the Wall comes a tumblin' down, Penny secedes from the United States of Benelope, Penny dies, Benji is cryogenically frozen through all space and time.

CUT TO:

INT. SUBWAY — DUSK

Benji looks at Finn. She stares back in return. Her face swirls in a sea of visages. Her eyelids open wide, the lids pulling back over the entirety of her face until they form lips and fold over the girl, devouring her. Now all mouth, she attempts to hold Benji's hand with her tongue.

BENJI
(pulling away)
Ah! Tongue! Germs!

FINN
What are you talking about?!

BENJI
Back, tongue!

FINN
What's the matter with you?!

BENJI
Back, tongue! Back!

The mouth opens wide, turns black, and inverts itself again, regurgitating a human form from its gaping hole. YOLANDA, the seventeen-year-old black girl Benji pursued earlier, appears.

YOLANDA
It's just grass, baby.

                                BENJI
Yeah?

                                YOLANDA
Oooh, I bet I know what baby wants to see.

                                BENJI
Wa?

                                YOLANDA
Baby wants to see mama take a shit!

Yolanda squats to the ground and squeezes. Out of her asshole emerges a baby carriage. CHIME BOX LULLABY MUSIC is heard. Benji approaches, steels himself, then tentatively peers over the carriage hood with large expectant eyes. In the baby carriage is he.

                                                    CUT TO:

INT. BROTHEL — DAY

Garish red curtains fall around the baby carriage in shards, framing it in the center of a jarring, strangely theatrical setting.
Suddenly, a throng of women appear, swarming about. A harem, a CHORUS, they are: Benji's MOTHER; Finn; Kate Welland; Ana Rexia; Lulu; MRS. FITZPATRICK; BABE, THE FARMER'S DAUGHTER; CORRINE DWARFKIN; WINNOW SCREENLAD; LES DEMOISELLES D'AVIGNON, all the women in Benji's life barring Penny, who is conspicuously absent.

They kneel, ready to cater to any and all of BABY BENJI's whims. All fall silent as Baby Benji, big-headed with curls of dark hair, struggles to form his first words:

                            BABY BENJI
Me. Me. Me.

                    LES DEMOISELLES D'AVIGNON
Oui! Oui! Oui!

KISSES fly through the air, alighting on blushing soft pink babyflesh.

KISSES
Pooh! Pooh! Pooh!

Baby Benji's bare buttocks are stroked with velvet; his curly locks are smoothed with an ivory comb; he is hand-dipped in chocolate; navel, nostrils, and crevices between fingers and toes and licked clean by an army of tongues; he emerges triumphant from a cumulus cloud of baby powder and is passed from hand to hand.

MOTHER
I want to rub Baby Benji's bottom!

CHORUS
The bottom! The bottom!

MRS. FITZPATRICK
I want to give Baby Benji the bottle!

CHORUS
The bottle! The bottle!

KATE WELLAND
I want to kiss Baby Benji's boo-boo!

CHORUS
The boo-boo! The boo-boo!

MOTHER
(cradling the two-hundred-pound baby in her arms)
O, Benji, you were the happiest, most beautiful baby. Never cried. Never complained. I was so sad when you grew up.

DR. ANA Rx-IA
(*in surgical scrubs*)
Technically ma'am, he doesn't have to grow up.
You see, there are certain worlds—subcultures, if
you will—that specialize in the infantilization of
young men. These fields include sports, the arts,
politics, and pornography. And my prediction is
your Benjamin will instinctively gravitate toward
one of them.

CHORUS
Hurray!

Baby Benji is joyously passed from tit to tit.

KATE WELLAND
(*making a fan of her folded law degree*)
His corduroys are so sexy!

LULU
(*snorting a line of cocaine off a dictionary*)
He's so smart, he always has the right word for
Lulu!

MRS. FITZPATRICK
(*stepping forth from a coffin-like grandfather
clock*)
He always has the time for me!

CORRINE DWARFKIN
(*fondling a strap-on dildo*)
If only I could have found a man like him!

WINNOW SCREENLAD
(*in midpenetration*)
Or woman!

FINN
(*tearing a photo of her father in two and consigning it to flames*)
The perfect father!

BABE, THE FARMER'S DAUGHTER
(*carrying two pails of milk*)
The perfect brother!

KATE WELLAND
(*splayed naked across the scales of justice*)
The perfect lover!

CHORUS
Hurray for Benji! Benji the Beautiful! Benji the
Bold! Benji the Brave! Hurray, Hurray!

Baby Benji is deposited before his mother, who looks down at her progeny
wistfully.

MOTHER
(*aging, yellowing*)
Still, it would have been nice to see him grow up
to be a man. To find a wife. To have grandchil-
dren. That would have been nice. That would
have been something to see.

Baby Benji offers up gurgling words of consolation.

BABY BENJI
Guuuuuuh.

ANA REXIA
But . . . there is another baby.

LULU
O, Never mind him, he's not the cute baby. Lulu
loves Baby Benji so much! Lulu leads the lullaby!

CHORUS

Go to sleep
My little Benji-bear
Close your little button eyes
And let me smooth your hair
It feels so nice
And silky-like
I love to cuddle down by you
So go to sleep
My little Benji-bear

Baby Benji, smiling beatifically, closes his eyes. Out of the firmament appear asterisks and exclamation points, starfish and unicorns, kaleidoscopes and the Cartesian grid. They sing to him. They dance for him. The cosmos itself spells out his name across a canopy of stars.

MOTHER

Where is this other baby? Can I see it?

KATE WELLAND

Another baby?

FINN

A brother?

Baby Benji begins to bawl. Murmurs are heard. A rumbling. A swelling of discontent. Uterine walls shudder and disconnect from amniotic sacks. Hoping to silence this potential female uprising, Benji fixes the bitches with a strident masculine stare.

THE MALE GAZE

Heeeeeeeeeeeeeee.

The women stare back with the collective force of universal motherhood and whoredom. Baby Benji befouls himself.

MOTHER

I want to see it.

Ana points a gnarled, elongated finger. In the corner, twitching, trembling, is a baby: a changeling devoid of features: its face, blank: a marmoreal mask: a wax-doll effigy.

> MOTHER
> (through ashen, bony hands)
> But whose baby is this? It resembles no one.

Slowly, the baby's face fills with color luminescence, first, yellow, then gold, then pink, then red, a red which grows darker and darker in intensity, threateningly dark, until the baby shudders and squirms under the force of its unnatural hue, bursts, and slides away. Baby Benji SHRIEKS. The sound melds into that of the subway, SCREAMING through stations.

> CUT TO:

EXT. THE SUBWAY — DUSK

Finn sits next to Benji, staring.

> FINN
> Don't freak out on me, okay mister?

> BENJI
> (sweating, wide-eyed, puffy-cheeked)
> Okay.

Passengers approach in concern, but Finn shoos them away.

> FINN
> It's going to be okay, okay?

> BENJI
> Okay.

> FINN
> It's just herb, okay?

> BENJI
> Kay. I'm okay now.

He looks around the train.

FINN

It's okay. We'll be home soon. Just look at the
signs. Look at the signs.

All other sounds fall away as Benji rests his tired eyes on a subway advertisement.

INSERT SHOT: Barnes & Noble "Poetry In Motion" placard.

"The voice of my beloved!
Look, he comes,
leaping upon the mountains
skipping upon the hills.
My beloved is like a gazelle
or a young stag.
Look, there he stands
behind our wall,
gazing at the windows,
looking through the lattice.
My beloved speaks and says to me:
"Arise, my love, my fair one, and come away;
for now the winter is past,
the rain is over and gone.
The flowers appear on the earth;
the time of singing has come,
and the voice of the turtledove
is heard in our land.
The fig tree puts forth its figs,
and the vines are in blossom;
they give forth fragrance.
Arise, my love, my fair one,
and come away."

Penny rises stark through the floor. She appears cubistically, seen from all
sides. She is naked, her body withered, her hair a tangle of thorns, her
skin, chalk white. Her limbs move in a broken fashion, the strugglings of
a fallen bird.

PENNY
(*with cold-damp breath*)
Hello sweetness.

He opens his mouth to speak words that will not come.

BENJI
(*horrorstruck*)
Wa?

PENNY
I was once the beautiful Penelope Catherine
Pigeon, the girl you loved. I am dead.

BENJI
(*with certainty*)
Penny.

PENNY
Is it so lonely where you are?

A trinity of loneliness appears. Benji's DISHES AND PLATES CLATTER
on the table top:

DISHES AND PLATES
(*in clipped English accent*)
A table set for three
With biscuits, milk, and tea.
But here's the tragedy:
There is no family.

NESTOR THE TURTLE, alone in his tank, ventures to speak:

NESTOR THE TURTLE
(*in heavy Brooklynese*)
An aquarium built for one
None too much in the sun.
Back and forth all day I run.
Not my idea of fun.

A thirty-two ounce tub of JERGEN'S LOTION speaks out of its nibbed dispenser-head:

> JERGEN'S LOTION
> (in dulcet Southern tones)
> We're thirty-two ounces of bliss!
> Good grease for the pole and the fist!
> Parve! L'chaim! To Life!
> Now everyman can be his own wife!

> BENJI
> You came.

Milton Minegold appears on all fours, covered in lambs wool, crying crocodile tears.

> MILTON
> Benji, beware! No one knows anyone, not that well!

MARION MINEGOLD appears, in blue-and-white Bo Peep outfit, holding a shepherd's staff. With outstretched arms she opens her mouth and inhales deeply, ready to burst into effusive song:

> MARION
> Baaaaaaaaaah.

> MILTON
> (relieving himself on her leg)
> Aaaaaaaaaaah.

> PENNY
> This is no place for you.

> BENJI
> I know! Come! Fly home to me!

> FINN
> Home? What makes the word?

BENJI

Show me! Show me the way!

PENNY

O, Benji.

BENJI

I see you everywhere. The sun. The stars. The
sea. The moon. The sky.
(*weeping now*)
Please show me . . . I'd follow you if I knew how . . .

He rushes toward her, desperate to hold her, but sifting like a shadow, she
flutters through his fingers . . .

PENNY

No. Not today. Today you will live. Look . . .

Benji looks behind. He is seated. Beside him sits Finn, asleep, her tiny
hand entwined in his.

PENNY

Warm hand.
From behind Penny unfold two large, feathery wings.

BENJI

There's so much I want to tell you.

PENNY

Goodbye, love.

She recedes.

BENJI

Wait! Don't go!

Blindly, Benji leaps from his spot and pulls the train's emergency brake.
Time's livid final flame leaps and, in the following darkness, ruin of all

space, shattered glass and toppling masonry, the train rockets and grinds to a halt. Darkness. Silence.

> LOUDSPEAKER
> Garble, warble, marble, barbell.

SUBTITLE: "This train is out of service. Please wait for a conductor to escort you to the nearest emergency exit."

The panic of human voices rises out of the dark. Amidst the commotion, the subway car doors open and passengers are led out onto the tracks in two and threes.

DISSOLVE TO:

INT. SUBWAY TRACKS — NIGHT

WHISTLES call and answer. Through the drifting fog, VOICES echo, hang, subside. In the spongy darkness, the pair are passed through a series of hands. Books of matches are distributed and struck—Pfffttt!—illuminating people like shades. In the shape-shifting flames, Finn sees boys and girls dancing, men and women kissing, angels and devils warring.

> MAN'S VOICE
> This way to the light.

> WOMAN'S VOICE
> No, I think it's this way.

> TEENAGER 1
> BROOKLYN! Top of the food chain!

> CONDUCTOR'S VOICE
> Be careful of the third rail.

> OLD WOMAN'S VOICE
> ¡Flores para los muertos!

MAN'S VOICE
Heh-heh.

TEENAGER 2
This shit is repugnant, yo!

WOMAN'S VOICE
I think the train derailed.

MAN'S VOICE
No, just some asshole pulled the emergency
brake.

TEENAGER 1
Yo, don't be pulling at me!

CHILD'S VOICE
Mommy, I don't like the dark.

WOMAN'S VOICE
Is anyone hurt?

CONDUCTOR'S VOICE
No, but it's a bit of a walk. We're smack between
stations.

MOMMY'S VOICE
We'll be home soon, honey . . .

OLD WOMAN'S VOICE
¡Flores para los muertos!

Benji and Finn are deposited in black velvet darkness. Sewage, chicken
bones, tar, and turnip-white filth leak past in liquid lapses of murmuring
streams.

Imperceptibly, Benji and Finn are separated from the others, who recede
into the darkness like footprints washed away by the tide. In the distance,
matches blink on-and-off like fireflies. Benji and Finn hold hands, moving

further and further away from the faint sounds of human voices into col-
laged, newspaper-stripped blackness.

>   FINN
>   Where are we?

>   BENJI
>   I don't know.

>   FINN
>   I'm scared.

>   BENJI
>   Me too.

>   FINN
>   Promise me we'll get out of here.

>   BENJI
>   I promise.

>   BENJI
>   Where are the others?

>   FINN
>   I don't know. I think they're up ahead.

An idiot wind HOWLS through the cavern.

>   FINN
>   Or behind.

In the darkness, the last traces of light fade into invisibility.

>   BENJI
>   We're going to have to find our way out of here
>   on our own, aren't we?

FINN

I think so.

BENJI

Okay. Let's go.

They do not move.

DISSOLVE TO:

INT. SUBWAY TRACKS — NIGHT

Benji and Finn, further along. They have been walking for some time, deeper into the seat of desolation, a place devoid of light, which bellows like the sea in tempest when combated by warring winds. The air bites shrewdly. Hot, cold, moist, and dry, four champions fierce, strive here for mastery. Here sighs, lamentations, and loud wailings resound through the starless air; strange tongues, horrible languages, words of pain, tones of anger, voices loud and hoarse, make a tumult which whirls through the air forever dark, as sand eddies in a whirlwind.

FINN

Is it true there are alligators in the sewers?

BENJI

No.

FINN

Why were we in Vietnam?

BENJI

I don't know.

FINN

Did Lee Harvey Oswald act alone?

> BENJI
> (*rubbing his temples*)
> Yes. I think it's wearing off.

> FINN
> (*eagerly*)
> I have some more if you want.

> BENJI
> No thank you.

> FINN
> C'mon man, it's good shit.

> BENJI
> I have a headache.

Benji removes his Pez dispenser from his hip pocket. In his hands it becomes a giant Swiss army knife. A buzzsaw pops out. He holds it to his cranium. BUUUZZZ! Benji places both hands on the top of his skull and—POP!—off comes the crown. A giant spoon unfolds and—SCOOP!—out come the brains.

> BENJI
> Aaaah, nice to be rid of that thing! All that dead
> weight.

The spoon retracts and out slides a can opener. Benji uses it to cut a valentine across his chest. He reaches in and pulls out his heart—still beating—which he casually discards.

> BENJI
> What a heavy load that was!

> FINN
> But Benji, no heart? No brain?

> BENJI
> And we already know I haven't any balls! Come
> on, Finn, let's go!

They lock arms and dance downstream.

> **BENJI & FINN**
> (*singing*)
> We're off to see the Lizard!
> Gunch looks like turkey gizzard!
> Da,da, da,da, da,da, da,da
> Da,da,da, da,da, da,da

Overhead a Train whistles past, rattling chains and dragon's feet.

> **TRAIN**
> Hoooooooommmmmme.

Finn stops suddenly.

> **FINN**
> (*with certainty, solemnity*)
> Home.

> **BENJI**
> (*to himself, in silent acknowledgment*)
> Home.

> **FINN**
> (*turning on him*)
> You're the adult, can't you find our way out of here?! Don't you have any sense of direction?! Can't you do anything?!

CUT TO:

INT. BENJI'S APARTMENT — DAY

The opening strands of Giacomo Meyerbeer's "Ô, Paradis!" are heard. Benji, dressed in the plume feather'd hat, lace petticoat, dark velvet hose, and silverbuckled boots of a New World explorer, telescope pressed to a hungry eyeball, walks in circles around his living room.

> MOTHER
> *(tacking a glowing report card to the refrigerator*
> *door with a yellow smiley face magnet)*
> Such a good boy. So many things he could do.
> O, his drawings!

A scowling Benji in a white T-shirt, whitewash-splattered overalls, whiskey flask none-too-discretely stashed in a back pocket, cigarette dangling from snarling lips, drips viscous white paint onto an outstretched baby blue blanket.

> MOTHER
> Such a talent!

JERRY SEYMOUR appears on Benji's couch in drag.

> JERRY
> And so compassionate. He was always ready to
> listen to my problems. I always thought he should
> have been a shrink.

Benji, looking severe in tweeds and pointed goatee, phallic pipe thrust between thin serious lips, listens intently to Jerry who lies outstretched on Benji's couch.

> JERRY
> When I came out, he knew just what to say.
> "Jerry," he said, "you're a bullying asshole, and
> just because you're gay doesn't mean I'll ever stop
> thinking of you that way." It was beautiful.

Jerry begins to cry.
ART appears in the middle of Benji's living room floor, splashing naked in an inflatable pool.

> ART
> And his mind. So analytical. I always thought he
> should be a lawyer, make a little something for
> himself.

Benji, in rimless glasses, suspenders, gold watch chain, polka dot tie, and chalk-stripe suit, kneels down to examine the corroded wooden train tracks as crumbling, yellow GORDON NORMAN drops sacks of money around his knees.

> GORDON NORMAN
> That's one million putative damages, fifteen mil-lion compensatory for the distress and anguish caused this smart-assed fucked-up kid.

> BENJI
> *(pocketing a third)*
> Thank you, thank you. On behalf of my client, I'd just like to say—

But Finn is gone. CLOSE UP on Benji.

> BENJI
> Finn?

MEDIUM SHOT.

> BENJI
> Finn!

LONG SHOT.

> BENJI
> FINN!

> FINN
> Yeah?

> BENJI
> Where were you?

> FINN
> Just up ahead. I figured you could have your little episode without me. I think I saw some lights.

Benji notices Finn's pants leg is torn. Her knee is scraped, oozing bright red blood, a trail of droplets illuminated behind her like jewels.

> BENJI
> What happened?

> FINN
> I fell.

> BENJI
> Does it hurt?

> FINN
> (she thinks, then, dispassionately)
> I think so. Yes, it hurts.

Benji reaches into his pocket, hoping to find a tissue, but comes up empty- handed.

> BENJI
> Let me see your bag.

She turns around. He tries to open the BOOKBAG, but the zipper is stuck. At last it yields.

> BOOKBAG
> Wisdom of the world. Words, words, words.

Benji reaches in, pulls out a BOOK, flips through it, finds a blank page toward the back, and TEARS it from the volume.

> BOOK
> Ah!

> FINN
> Hey!

> BENJI
> It's filthy down here. This'll keep it from getting
> infected.

He presses the clean white page to the child's wound.

                    FINN
          Ow!

                    BOOK
          Mm.

                    BENJI
          C'mon.

Out of a pool of scummy water, an enormous, hungry gray RAT appears, following the trail of blood.

                    FINN
               (pointing)
          AH!

The creature bares its spittle-moist lips.
                    RAT
          Hssssssss!

The rat dines on a droplet of blood before disappearing into the gloom. Finn is shaking, shuddering, distill'd almost to jelly with the act of fear. Benji's not doing so hot himself.

                    FINN
          What was that?

                    BENJI
          A rat.

                    FINN
          I don't think it was a rat. No. It was a kitten.

                    BENJI
          It was a rat.

> FINN
>
> Or a raccoon. A bunny perhaps.

> BENJI
>
> A foot long rat.

> FINN
>
> I'm not certain of that. I've never seen one before
> and I'm not ready to commit myself.

> BENJI
>
> A foot-long friggin' rat.

In the darkness, the creature's HISSES echo. It darts!

> FINN
>
> A rat!

And disappears again into the murky muckiness. Benji wearily sits down
in the filth, resigning himself.

> BENJI
>
> I'm not getting out of here.

> FINN
>
> Mister—

> BENJI
>
> In fact, in this moment I think I can see the mas-
> ter's hand.

> FINN
>
> I need you to help me!

> BENJI
>
> An appropriate end.

The paper covering Finn's wound is now soaked through with blood, it
falls away.

FINN

Please!

BENJI

Pit of excrement.

The creature's yellow-red eyes glow in the darkness, greedily assessing its prey.

RAT

Hsssssss!

The animal proceeds slowly this time, provocatively. It emerges from behind a chocolate dark stalagmite and stops a few yards from them, grinning in challenge. The rodent rises on powerful, thickly muscled haunches and bares its fangs. Its tough gray coat is bristling wet, matted down with filth, foodstuff, marijuana leaves, and liquid dung; its jaundiced eyes pinpoints of malignancy; its tail a snaking exclamation point. Plastered across its body are shreds, remnants of a crumpled yellow paper flyer, thrownaway, that reads: "Are You Ready?"

BENJI

This is the end.

Everyone freezes. The earth trembles, the midnight sun is darkened, a screaming comes across the sky, red rails of the apocalypse spin out of every corner, stars all round the sun turn roundabout, trumpets BLARE, golden chariots trample cross the firmament, time's livid final flame leaps and, in the following darkness, ruin of all space, shattered glass and toppling masonry, THE END arrives:

THE END
(in a medley of voices)
Accosted by a malignant pestilence, the pair successfully make their way forth, out of the darkness, to see again the stars: the Champs Élysées: a yellow cab: Superman: television: memory of a giant matzo ball: a letter: efflorescent flowers: around, over, under, in: yes, yes, yes. Begin!

                        RAT
Hsssss!

                        FINN
Vampire!

The rat leaps out, standing now just inches from Benji and Finn. It scowls.
It smiles. It collapses. It rises. It does a wobbly, jittery, herky-jerky little
frug around itself, chasing its own tail. It gets up, bares razor-sharp fangs,
then falls again. Finn, instinctively hiding behind Benji's leg, pulls her
hood strings tight.

The animal rolls onto its back, spreads its arms and legs apart and waves
its limbs. A lolling tongue slides out the side of its mouth. It giggles.

                        BENJI
That's one fucked up rat.

The animal rolls over and snaps out at Benji, just missing his hand.

                        BENJI
Christ!

                    JESUS CHRIST
Home.

Benji retracts, leaving Finn exposed, vulnerable. The rat leaps onto the
girl, digging grinning red claws up her right leg, around her torso, over her
bookbag, beyond good and evil. Perched on her shoulder, it rears back,
preparing to sink bloodthirsty fangs into soft white flesh when—SWAT!—
Benji knocks the creature off the child.

The rat—SQUEALING—goes flying. Finn is frozen, eyes wide shut.
Benji, ready for action, rolls over the ground, commando-style, a bowie
knife clenched between tight teeth. Finn opens her eyes.

                        FINN
A hit! A very palpable hit!

Man and beast circle each other warily, respectfully, surmising each other's secret histories, searching out hidden weaknesses, points of vulnerability. They are joined in a dance. The rat makes its most feral face, and Benji matches it in ferocity.

Benji reaches into his pocket and unsheathes his sword. He holds the Mickey Mouse Pez dispenser before the hungry beast, who is transfixed by the object. Something like love transcribes itself across the animal's face.

                              BENJI
          Here!

Benji drops the totem. Languorously, mournfully, the rat approaches. Haunted, romantic ORGAN MUSIC fills the cavern. The rat sings:

                              RAT
                    (en basso profundo)
          As you wander through this life
          There are things you must avoid.
          Like subterraneous sewers and
          The works of Ziggy Freud.

          But beady eyes and bristly hair
          Don't mean to give you fright.
          We'll feast on filth and listen to
          The music of the night!

The rat, in Phantom of the Opera mask, navigates a skiff through a stream of raw sewage.

                              RAT
          Parlez-vous français?
          Comment vous vous appelez, mon ami?
          The waters are not blue
          But it's a princedom by the sea.

The rat, in curled mustache, black beret, and red-and-white striped gondolier's shirt, cradles the Pez dispenser in its claws.

> RAT
>
> We'll disappear, begin anew
> A single subway fare.
> A paradise beneath our feet
> Dear, dirty old Times Square.

The rat maniacally attempts to copulate with the Pez dispenser from the rear but the object remains placid, inanimate. A look of dull confusion crosses the rat's beady face. The clumsy seducer looks to Benji.

> BENJI
>
> Go. Be happy together.

The animal snuggles next to the object. No response. It rises on powerful haunches and flexes its rot-fed musculature. The object plays it hard-to-get. The rat attempts to kiss the object's enameled head. The Pez dispenser snaps its beak.

> RAT
>
> Eeeeeeeeee!

The animal turns around, forlornly, one last time. No response. He ambles off into the night, dejected. Finn dances, recoups the Pez dispenser, and places it in Benji's hand.

> FINN
>
> You did it! You did it!

But Benji, his exertions having depleted him, is lost, fallen to the ground, staring into the swirling contours of a putrid puddle of water. In the distance, faintly, the sound of PENNY'S THEME.

FLASHBACK BEGINS:

EXT. ITHACA GORGES — NIGHT

A black and purploid moonless night. In the darkness, the Ithaca gorges look like an illustration out of a fairy tale by the Brothers Grimm.

Penny stands in the water. Off to the side, on the rocks, stands fresh-faced, twenty-one-year-old Benji (BENJI I), and behind him, in super-imposition, the somewhat more troubled Benji we have come to know (BENJI II). Penny leans in to touch the WATER, which whispers in response:

> WATER
>
> Seesoo, hrss, rsseeiss, ooos.

The MOON peeks out behind its velvet curtain.

> MOON
>
> Mmmmmmmmmm.

Light bounces off drops of water as they pass through her hand.

> PENNY
>
> You ever feel like you have a split personality?

> BENJI I
>
> No . . .

> BENJI II
>
> Me either.

Penelope squats over the water and pulls down her ZIPPER.

> ZIPPER
>
> (loud)
>
> Zrrrrrruuuupppppp.

She defecates.

> BENJI I
>
> What are you doing?

> PENNY
>
> I have to go to the bathroom. Don't worry, no one can see.

> BENJI I

I can see.

> BENJI II

I still see.

> LEAVES

Wsssssssshhhhhhh.

> WATER

Seesoo, hrss, rsseeiss, ooss.

> URINE

Rrrrrsssssssssssssss.

> FECES

Sccccrrrrr. Blooooop.

> PENNY

Tell me something. Tell me you love me. Tell me
you'll love me forever.

Benji I checks his watch against Benji II.

> BENJI I
> (*blustery*)

C'mon. How many stupid twenty-year-olds say
that to each other?

> PENNY
> (*pleading*)

Then say something original, say something
smart.

> BENJI I
> (*washing his hands*)

Aw, they're just words.

The Moon throws a spotlight on her.

PENNY

Yes, but we have only words to play with.

WATER

Seesoo, hrss, rsseeisss, ooos.

PENNY

Tell me what you're thinking.

Benji I confers with Benji II.

BENJI I

Nothing.

PENNY

C'mon.

BENJI I

Don't accuse me of thinking.

PENNY

Tell me.

BENJI I

You make taking a shit look sexy.

PENNY

I'm serious.

BENJI I & BENJI II

(*simultaneously*)

Me too.

PENNY

You never tell me anything.

BENJI I

You tell me something then.

                    PENNY
         Like what?

The Moon hides again, casting the scene in inky blackness.

                    BENJI I
         Tell me . . . what do you know about light?

                    PENNY
         The light?

                    BENJI I
         Yes.

                    PENNY
              (thinks, then, smiling)
         The light is the light that lights other lights.

The Moon emerges from behind its gauzy gray veil, full-force, throwing sil-
ver-gray spangles across the water, reflecting itself in shimmering pools,
washing away the sadness of rain-slicked walls, crowning the tops of bristling lonely trees, finally illuminating Penny in profile, christening her
limpid mortal beauty.

                    BENJI
         It's gonna be weird going home, huh?

                    PENNY
         Benji?

                    BENJI
         Yeah?

                    PENNY
         You are my home.

The sun and the stars and the sea and the Moon and the sky and the leaves
and the trees and the squirrels and the birds and the worms and the cater-
pillars MURMUR in hushed acquiescence. The couple embrace in the
water. The sky is filled with blessed life.

FLASHBACK ENDS

INT. SUBWAY TRACKS — NIGHT

Benji rises sodden from the caked black earth, the lineaments of his face solidified, adult; his look silent, thoughtful, alert. He reaches a hand out for the young girl.

                         BENJI
              Come. This way to the light.

BENJI'S THEME reaches the resolution it has been searching for as the pair comes forth, toward a great white light, until the stars are visible again.

THREE

| |

The question then, was where had they landed. Having both ingested (via air and nasal passageway) goodly portions of the marijuana narcotic (dried leaves and flower clusters of hemp known to induce euphoria), and sharing temperaments predisposed toward the melancholic, imaginative, easily distracted side of things, the pair had been subject to misdirection. That is, they had taken the wrong train.

Following his dark afternoon of the soul, Benji emerged into pincushion black sequined white Brooklyn night unalarmed. Leaving the Grand Army Plaza subway station, he immediately recognized the intersection of Flatbush Avenue and Plaza Street West for its proximity to the central branch of the Brooklyn Public Library, wherein whose hallowed halls young Benji had spent many an afternoon plagiarizing high school term papers. For his companion-at-arms however, this was an epic journey whose end was not in sight, a pilgrimage which had at present deposited her she knew not where, and Benji, taking for granted his geographic comprehension for her own, did nothing to clarify the situation for the girl. He did, however, offer a hand to hold and an arm to cling to, as Finn, who did not yet have her sea legs back, was still a bit weak-kneed. "Here, lean on me," Benji said, and led her on accordingly.

Side by side then, physically close, mentally apart, together the pair made their way through blind blueblack night along curving tree-lined cobblestone streets, across an empty seven-lane parkway, onto a desert island atoll where they were greeted by a disembodied memorial bust of one John F. Kennedy, 35th President of the United States, cut down in his fighting prime in 1963, the year of baby Benjamin's birth.

Staring into hollowed dark Irish eyes, Finn thought to herself, yes, all must go through it, princes and kings included. And in that moment, she felt very near to her creator, realizing as she did with certainty, as certainly as she drew her next breath, that life is but a blink twixt a sleep and a wake. Chilled, she was forced to acknowledge that even the intellectual imagination may prove a meager defense against so mysterious, so ineluctable an offense. Still she did her best not to pursue such thoughts and let such thoughts gain ground, instead focusing on the warmer, more material realm at hand, moving her eyes first from Benji's fingers, intertwined with her own, up his sleeve, on toward the shoulders, past his neck, to the unresolved jigsaw puzzle of his face. Kind of looks like him, Finn thought, mapping a physical resemblance between prince and pauper. Maybe if he had a shave and some sun and lost a few pounds. Not at all bad looking, really, once you peel the grime away. And then she retraced the previous few hours, reminding herself who she was, who he was, and of all the journeying which had led them to this particular pocket of space and time.

They moved inward. In the center of the isle was a sculpture, rendered in the neoclassical style, bathed, as it was not, in a dried up scummy pond. With traffic noises providing somnolent swooshing sounds of the sea, together they stood in silent appreciation of the oceanic collage consisting of smiling tea-green Poseidon, ornamental shells, frogs, serpent's fins, and mermaid and merman, perched atop the sculpture like a barnacled bride and groom, held together in a slippery embrace. As if to better appreciate the work by framing it in a darkpolished rectangle of lacquered night sky, Finn released herself from Benji's grip and took several steps back, in the process tripping over the topsoiled roots of a stubborn old oak. Recovering her balance, she turned around to see what it was she had stumbled upon.

The tree was huge. Thirty, maybe forty feet in the air and slanted like a giant spiral staircase, the oak was clearly king of the plot, dwarfing all nearby competitors. With its wrinkled grooves of deepdark bark and glowing electric leaves hanging against the night sky like a lantern, the physical fact of the tree gave the girl pause. Ineluctably rooted to the earth while reaching forever, majestically upward, tearing the ground below asunder while cracking the night sky into a thousandpieced blueveined mosaic, the tree spoke to the midnight child as something ancient, organic, remote. With its decrepit knobby knots and moss-filled pubic corners, in its orneriness and dewy raunch, through the youthful twist and torque of its thickheavy spine and the learned gentle fretwork of its tender limbs, strumming the night air with a hundred wooden fingertips, the tree offered the girl some insight into the unresolved, dualistic, expressive possibilities in nature, for surely this tree was as complex as any character she had encountered either in worlds of fiction or the world at large. She pressed a hand against it and felt a variety of sensations pass through her. Rough. Cool. Soft. Warm. It was at this moment that, for no reason in particular, the man stepped forward, and with a mighty hand and an outstretched arm, ripped a leaf from it.

"Don't," said Finn, who up to then had said nothing whatsoever of any kind.
"Wa?"
"It'll bleed."
"O."
"That tree."
"Yeah."
"It's really."
"Yeah."

It was then that from above the treetop she spotted it. With a gasp of air Finn removed herself from the scene and made her way forward to a clearing where she espied in full view the great bronzerustgreengold memorial arch, resplendent with spear carriers, trampling chariots, and winged, triumphant angels, all luminous in lemony sodium vapor light.

"France!" Finn exclaimed, blindly sailing into the sea of the street.

Now Benji, having grown up in Brooklyn and possessing a loose familiarity with its landmarks, recognized the memorial arch framing this fine boulevard as not the Arc de Triomphe of the Champs Élysées, but rather, a municipal job entitled, "The Defenders of the Union 1861•1865," which marked the intersection of Flatbush Avenue, Prospect Park West, and Eastern Parkway, along whose border spread, in a not unpoetic juxtaposition of Eros and Thanatos, the springing seedlings of the borough's Botanical Gardens just adjacent to the mildewed Egyptian mummies of the Brooklyn Museum.

All of this and more flew through Benji's mind as he stumblingly chased after the girl, who had thrown herself into the traffic-filled intersection with abandon, an endeavor whose outcome would prove in the most lucid of circumstances tentative at best, as said intersection was tentacled, pentapod, and impossible to navigate. But even putting aside the persuasive powers of invulnerability that night and narcotics will induce, the child was jung and not easily freudened.

What followed was a moment's worth of vehicles led aswerve, brakes applied and squealingly stretched to a halt, and bright bouquets of hot, wickedtongued language directed against the elfin child. Once (terrified) guardian and (oblivious) charge were safely reunited under the protective shadow of the arch, Finn turned to Benji, who was slightly asthmatic and breathing heavily, and beamed, "You did it! You did it! I don't know how but you did it! France! France! Merci beacoup! Merci beacoup!" And there was much parleyvoo talk and can-can revelry from Finn who showed a surprising facility for high kicks.

With respect to the English-language street signs and black kids dressed in the latest baggy pants hip-hop fashion, Finn proved oblivious. But Benji, appreciative of this other, playful side of the child, which until then had been turned away from him and hidden like the dark side of the moon, indulged her, rationalizing to himself that if Brooklyn was not in fact France, it was still, in some critical respects, Ye Olde Country.

"Picasso! The Moulin Rouge! Escargot! Merci beacoup!" the girl sang, with Benji following, basking in her musical glow.

"Mademoiselle," Benji said, extending a hand for her to hold. And so it was with a good deal more trepidation than displayed on previous occasions that the pair crossed the street. With minds traveling in opposite trains of thought, the duo arrived before an old gray government building framed with a pair of greatheavy doors adorned with simple Doric columns, doors embroidered with goldpainted figures of legend and myth. There was Aphrodite on the half-shell and Moses off the mountaintop, there was Pegasus and Neptune and Theseus and Jason and the Argonauts, and even lonely old Odysseus looking for his way back home.

"The wanderer's return," Finn mumbled, mind wandering, returning.

"Hm."

"What is this building?" she asked, sherlockholmesing it up.

"The library. I used to borrow books from here."

"Italian architecture," Finn surmised with a tired unwrinkled face, "bildungsroman."

And they stood for a brief space of time in deference to that world of knowledge, reading the stonechiselled message of the engraved doors halfaloud in unison:

HERE ARE ENSHRINED THE LONGING OF GREAT HEARTS
AND NOBLE THINGS THAT TOWER ABOVE THE TIDE
THE MAGIC WORD THAT WINGED WONDER STARTS
THE GARNERED WISDOM THAT HAS NEVER DIED

And as was her custom when attempting to absorb something of a particularly fine or moving or thought-provoking nature, Finn turned heavenward, as if to file the information away for later use, only this time, her gaze was averted by the spotlight of the moon, blinking down at her through shymisty clouds.

"Looks like a big brie," said the cottonmouthed waif.

"Are you hungry?" asked Benji solicitously, only to be answered, as if by magic, by the far-off sounds of a wobbly white truck, hobbling down the street, announcing the introduction of forthcoming food of the sweet, frozen, dairy variety via chimebox lullaby which took the form of a humming ode to patrimony:

Da,da, da,da,da,da, da,da, da,da
Da,da, da,da, da,da, da

Having grown up on the Upper West Side of Manhattan under the supervision of a health-conscious supermom, the girl was unaccustomed to such sights, and, as a result, was transfixed by the well-behaved line of children that immediately materialized as if by magic before the truck and the seemingly neverending stream of custard issuing forth from the ice cream pump's stainless steel nozzlehead. Where does it all come from? she thought, as one child after another was led away from the vehicle licking, laughing, dripping, happy.

Transporting its precious cargo through darkened midnight streets, Finn imagined the truck the vehicle of a newfangled superhero, a dark crusader, an estranged avenger, a hooded angel emerging from deepest night to eke out his own special brand of ice cream justice, using the dessert to both reward his allies and punish his enemies. She pictured the ice cream truck traversing the hot heavy globe, amphibiously traveling over sleepy meadows and rolling hills, over cracked desert floors and roiling seas. She imagined ice cream armadas of all stripe and size, ice cream sandwiches delivered with the newspaper on Moanday mourning doorsteps, snow cones parachuted to safety out the sides of airplanes, torrents of ice cream shot out of tanks over scorched razed battlefields, ice cream oozing out the sides of tankers run aground off foreign coasts, ice cream force-fed to the criminal element of society, ice cream dripped from hospital plasma bags, ice cream gently spoon-fed to the elderly, the sick, the poor, ice cream ice cream everywhere spreading cold custard comfort cross a cruel weary world. Navigating through the curdled pastures of her fantasy, Finn hardly noticed it was her turn to order.

The driver of the truck peered his head out of the portal. In possession of a red meaty porkchop of a face, the Kustard King surveyed his subject with still anticipation, awaiting her choice. Finn, having been advised by her mother against the mixing of milk and meat products, banished all thoughts of pork from her head and instead concentrated on the menu, printed as it was in ancient pictogram style on the side of the truck.

The black hairs on the Kustard King's regal folded arms were matted down and across his barrel-chested T-shirt stretched a large gray triangle of sweat, and it was only after taking note of this royal expenditure of perspiration that Finn realized that the rain had subsided and given way to a sticky damp summer's night. Finn could feel the moisture in the air. She breathed. And breathed again. And remembering that one needs to breathe in order to live, breathed again, only this time consciously inhaled, held the precious stuff, and released.
"WhatcanIgetcha?"
"Do you have frozen yogurt?"
"No. Just ice cream."
"What's good tonight?" Finn asked, nodding to the nozzlehead.
"Vanilla. Chocolate. Or swirl."

Looking into the man's suspicious, allsurveying face, Finn could feel her pupils contract to the size of pores. The King knows I'm blitzed, she thought.

"Please do not judge me, sir. I am but a lowly squire."
"Huh?"
"She'll have swirl," Benji interjected.
"Cup or cone?"
"Do you have sugar cones?" Finn asked, regrouping.
"Yeah."
"Cone."
"And for your dad?" queried the King.
"Nothing for me, thanks," Benji replied, responding to the misnomer without the slightest hesitation whatsoever. "But could I trouble you for a cup of water and a couple of napkins?"

And so, after paying the King's tribute and wishing him a fond adieu, Benji led the girl away toward an empty patch of park, where he tended to her wound, first wiping clean her knee with water, then dressing the wound with absorbent damp paper cloth. All the while the girl administered to the cone, artificial vanilla and chocolate flavors experiencing the joys of miscegenation in the great lake of her mouth.

"Yes, swirl," the girl said, savoring.
"Hold still," said Benji, bent.
"Duality."
"Wa?"
"Vanilla. Chocolate. Why choose? Divide. Divorce."
And with that final word she took a huge bite out of the upper region of the conehead, frozen foodstuff coming into sharpnerved contact with the rawtender hatchlings of an incipient tooth.
"Gaaaaaaah," the girl cried, spinning around and pressing both hands to her shuddering skull. "God!" she pleaded to a disinterested universe, as the cone, held just inches above her head, baptized her with dual dripping drops.
"No," Benji replied, removing the offending dessert. "Ice cream headache. Bite down. It'll pass."

So she did and it did.

It was then the two noctambules—dirty, dripping, adrift, borne back ceaselessly into the past—beat on, circumnavigating the perimeter of the park on foot. Shadows intermingling, stretching, and contracting over wet ground and silvergreen trees, surrounded on all sides by starless black implacable night, Finn felt she could continue walking on this path indefinitely. Happily. Forever.

"Where does it lead?" she asked, staring below at a ground embedded with winedark stones and oliveshaped pebbles.

"Around. A circle."

"How far?"

"Three, maybe three-and-a-half miles."

"Hm. Lovely."

"Listen, don't you think it's time to go home?"

"Why use small words which make me so unhappy?"

"What word? Home? Home's a good word," said Benji thoughtfully, "maybe the best word . . ."

"If it is, I haven't found it," Finn replied, exasperated, and with that, halted, removed from her pocket a wrinkled plastic bag, reached in, pinched a bit of spice from it, placed it in a smallthin piece of paper and began rolling the entirety into a tight cylindrical shape.

"But it's where your stuff is. It's your roots," Benji said, desperately pointing to a nearby tree by way of visual reinforcement. "It's the one place where . . . it's . . . where you belong."

"We can't change the word," Finn said, none too politely, bringing her third joint of the day to pursed beestung lips. "Let us change the subject."

"No, enough of that," Benji said, lifting the cigarette and the still half-full bag of narcotics from the girl's fumbling small fingers. "It's too easy. Cuts you off from things is all it does. Plugs you into yourself. There's enough of that in the world already . . . Plenty of mystery without it," he said, emptying the bag onto mulchy, stilldamp earth and stamping the contents into the ground.

Listening to this synopsis of things in general, Finn stared at nothing in particular. She could hear, of course, all kinds of words changing color in the prism of her mind's eye, but it was only through a concerted effort that she was able to follow the loose thread of conversation and the spasmodic movements of the man, who appeared to her in the jerky, pixilated spurts of a garden sprinkler. Rather, she focused on the surrounding magnificence

of nature; of a park gouged out of the earth by a succession of ancient gla-
ciers; of the night's effect on the color green in all its radiant varieties, of
the sky spread out overhead like a darkblue blanket, enveloping everything in its velvety embrace.

"Cab!" Benji announced, and in the next moment Finn was pulled into
the street—ground tumbling, sky aswirl—and spirited into a vehicle
which looked suspiciously like the yellow vehicles she was familiar with
from countless morning commutes. Squeakily, the pair sat on seats of Aqua
Velva blue. Then, as if to reinforce the memory of her father's morning
shave, Finn experienced an olfactory hallucination, the smell of the inside
of the cab transforming itself from peppers and garlic and onions to alcohol and butterscotch aftershave. Wonder what time is it over there?
Wonder what he's doing? Could he be shaving now? The digital meter
began but the cab remained still.

"Where do you live?" asked Benji with some urgency, pulling Finn back
into the present. Having been instructed by her maternal ward never to
release said information to strangers, Finn grappled with this question for
some time, then pointed a thin finger to her skull and looked out at the
man with large staring eyes.

"Minds are in bodies, bodies are in the world."
"A street number?" Benji asked with soft rebuking eyes.
"67th and Columbus."
"Not bad," said Benji, impressed.
"Yassum," Finn answered, followed by the cracking sound of a whip.
"Bridge or tunnel?" the cabby interjected in lilting Indian tones.
"The bridge," said Benji. "It'll be more educational."
"Can we have some music?" Finn asked, leaning forward with hot herbal
breath.
"Radio's out."
"Can you sing for us then?"
To this request the cabby simply shook his head back-and-forth and emit-
ted a small sibilant tut-tut between fullcracked lips. He wore a turban on
his head, and the tops of his exposed ears were lined with black hairs of
the finest silk. On the side of his neck a small pink scar in the shape of an
arrow pointed to the road ahead. Finn looked at the driver's registration
certificate. Jamal Sadjawa. They were moving.

Over six-lane highways, through downtown marbled Brooklyn streets, past pizza parlors and parking meters they sped, the wonders of the world streaking past at twenty-four frames per second. After a time, the great webbed net of the bridge appeared, approaching closer, the city spread out below on all sides: glassy, shimmering, atwinkle, awake.

You did it, Benji thought to himself. You promised you would find her and you did. You did it. You're bringing her back. A mother's love. Her love. Outside of his sphere of circumscription, Benji had difficulty remembering the last time he had been in a car, let alone a cab, and that, combined with his dreamily imagined hero's welcome produced an inadvertent physiological response. Modestly, he reached for a section of newspaper left on the floor in front of him and inconspicuously covered his lap. If only my dick could read Braille, Benji thought as the newspaper gently lifted column-by-column, moving across a page of the Help Wanted section line-by-line, discriminatingly dismissing one job after another. Accountant. P. R. Account Exec. Copy Editor. Paralegal.

Finn meanwhile was too entranced by the scenery and her own selfconscious registration of it to notice the pneumatic display taking place beside her. In the jeweled prism of her mind's eye, a variety of forms made and unmade themselves. Kaleidoscopes of sparkling light, reflecting panes of glass and steel, slivers of cobalt water and shadowed sky all projected themselves onto the dilated movie screens of Finn's tired unblinking eyes.

"Qwertyuiop," Finn whispered, surveying the landscape's rising dark cubist pyres.
"Wa?" asked deepblue knight.
"Nothing . . ." the girl growled, drowsily reaching into her bookbag and removing a tattered paperback philosophy primer. "My inheritance," she said, and then, with a dullpointed pencil, scribbled out some words on the blank backpage.
"What're you reading that for anyway?" Benji asked, removing the book from her hands and fingering its crisp yellowing pages.
"Superman," she sputtered as the cab passed through the entrance of the Brooklyn Bridge.
"Wa?"
"Eternal return. The past repeated. With no difference."
"Eh," said Benji dismissively, harking back to Philosophy 101. "Stuff like

that only works in books."

"But could you do it?" the girl asked gloomily. "Repeat everything? As it happened to you? Good and bad?"

Benji, contemplating some grime lodged under the ragged half moon of his left thumbnail, considered this question a good long time before answering firmly, definitively, with finality, "Yes."

"But how?" asked the girl with large expectant eyes.

And here ÜberBenji turned away from the child and looked out his window at the city, dancing in its hypnogogic sway. To Benji, the rising and falling buildings, swooning against glittering black velvet night looked less like a typewriter than a sleeping zoo, a bestiary, a midnight menagerie, a Noah's ark athrong with armadillos, giraffes, and elephants. And it was then that it occurred to him that God—because for all his posturing Benji believed in God firmly, resolutely, and without irony—God must be a prankster because who but a prankster would think to create something as strange as a giraffe. Or an elephant. Or an armadillo. Or the forces that drive us forward. Gravitation. Magnetics. Time. Love. Protean. Inescapable. Unknowable. Everywhere. Nothing. Give a teenager a sheaf of psychedelics and an Etch A Sketch and they couldn't have made a bigger, more beautiful botch of things.

As the cab sped over land and water, Benji thought of some of the things he loved: the city, buttered toast scrambled eggs and coffee, the morning paper, movies, sunsets. Warm towels. Dark hair falling. Sunlight. Trees. Children. He thought of his family and how he loved them. And of the girl he loved many years ago, so clearly the wrong girl yet the right girl and how he loved her, too. And he thought how he wouldn't have missed out on any of it not for a moment. He turned back to the child.

"Because it's what we have," he said, gently handing the volume back to the girl. "Now put the book away."

A long moment passed between them. Searching silent still, Finn finished the poem, her first, then closed the book and sleepily slipped the tome into her bag.

    With vampire smiles

And grinning teeth
Tis what it is
This life, is sweet

"Do you think she's home?" the girl asked.

"I think so, yes."

"Pretty early for the plantation," she said, wearily consulting the bare white band of flesh round her wrist.

"Finn, I assure you," our hero said soberly, paternalistically, "you have your mother very worried."

"Yes . . ." asked the girl with yawning heavyclosing eyes. "And how would you have her?"

1 2

What course did Benji and Finn follow returning?

Starting at Fourth Street and Prospect Park West they traveled to Seventh Avenue through an absence of traffic down Seventh to Flatbush Avenue: then, bearing right on Flatbush they sailed along Atlantic Avenue at reduced speed into increased traffic reaching Smith Street which, after transforming into Jay Street, curvilinearly ushered them to the stony solemnity of the Brooklyn Bridge: then, over the bridge they glided at a scenic pace toward the FDR Drive, gently tracing the contours of the East River before exiting at 42nd Street: then, neatly bifurcating the city from East to West, in dangerous dodgeball fashion they sped up Eighth Avenue, circumscribing Columbus Circle at 59th Street, and continued to climb North until they reached 67th Street and Columbus Avenue.

Awake, of what did Benji deliberate enroute?

Night. Light. The loosening strings of the day just passed. The transience of time. The persistence of memory. Technology. Pornography. Judaism. The animal kingdom. Aesthetics. God. The sleeping perfection of a child's face.

Asleep, of what did Finn dream?

Of winged noble creatures, feathers long and black, flying low over silent hills and streams.

What act did Benji make upon arrival at their destination?

He delivered a fee, $23.00, to the driver.

How was this tariff arrived at?

Through chilly calculation of mechanical meter (the fare) in concord with the passenger's thoughtful generosity (the tip), determined as follows:

The meter (regardless of the number of passengers or stops):

> (1) $2.00 for the initial unit.
> (2) $.30 for each additional unit.
> (3) The unit of fare being:
> (i) one-fifth of a mile, when taxicab is traveling at eight (8) miles an hour or more; or,
> (ii) ninety (90) seconds (at a rate of twenty cents per minute), when the taxicab is not in motion or is traveling less than eight (8) miles an hour.
> (4) $.50 night surcharge for all trips beginning after 8:00 P.M. and before 6:00 A.M.

The fare: $19.30
The tip: $3.70
The total: $23.00

Upon exiting the vehicle, what did Benji see?

Below him: currents of terrestrial water running toward the rotted mouth of an open sewer. Level to him: couples of all races, classes, and ages holding hands and strolling through the humid summertime penumbra; an amazing efflorescence of freshcut flowers swaying outside a nocturnal Korean grocery store. Above him: a blank blackboard of sky; the moon covered by chalky clouds; celestial canopy obscured by milky filth.

What did Benji imagine lay behind?

Quiescent quasars: coiled, unspooling galaxies: cold interstellar winds: the boiling whirlpool of the universe. A design untouched by human hands: the silent apathy of stars.

Away from the light pollution of New York, what constellations were visible on the night of June 17, 1996?

The ten-billion-year-old globular cluster, Ophiuchus-Serpens. On the meridian, the head of the snake, Serpens Caput (a gold-tinted giant of class K, 79 light years, 24.23 parsecs distant). The interstellar beast wriggles from the south across the bottom of a figure resembling a large tent, ending with its long tail, Serpens Cauda (white, Sirian-type star cluster, approximately 130 light years, 39.88 parsecs distant, at a separation of 900 astronomical units). The tent is Ophiuchus, the serpent-bearer; his head at the tent's peak, the star Rasalhague (a white giant of the "Sirian" type, 59 light years, 18.10 parsecs distant, lying in the North Polar Spur).

If the constellation is made reference to in the Bible, list the reference.

> Heaven is beautified by His winds
> And His Hand pierces the fleeing snake.

> —Job 26:13

Did Benji, stargazer, accept as an article of belief the theory of astrological influence upon terrestrial occurrence?

He neither believed nor disbelieved, as such beliefs seemed neither more nor less rational than other beliefs and practices appeared.

If Benji believed in the possibility of extraterrestrial life, what led him to this belief?

A sense of being watched from above, an affinity for almond-shaped eyes, the pyramids of Egypt, the Roswell incident, H.G. and Orson Well(e)s, Led Zeppelin crop circles, tabloid newspapers, the films of Steven Spielberg, the Fox Broadcasting Network, the pinwheeling psychedelia of the heavens, laws of mathematical probability, resolute belief in man's inconsequence.

What led him to disbelieve?

The silent perfection of space: the pervasive loneliness of Earth.

At the end of his journey did Benji receive a hoped-for sign of providence?

Yes. Standing before the building, the semiconscious, chemically-enhanced prepubescent nodded toward a structure immediately in front of them, and the two entered the building vestibule.

What immediately precluded their advancement?

Sitting behind a well-lit desk, watching the pair advance through closed-circuit security cameras, Eduardo, the night doorman, mistook Filthy Finn and Benji the Begrimed for a pair of street urchins, and refused them further admittance.

How did Benji overcome this obstacle?

With open palms and trusting face, softly, gently, equanimitably, Benji explained the true identity of the midnight child to the guard, who, after flipping Finn's features through his mental Rolodex, announced the wanderer's return via intercom to the keeper of apartment 13-A, and sheepishly let the pair proceed to the elevator bank.

Passing down a long mirrored corridor, what did Benji see?

A lumbering man approaching, child in tow.

Who was the man?

The man, moving closer, revealed himself to be he. That is, Benji found he was moving closer and closer to himself.

Scooping up the sleeping child as they entered the elevator chamber, what classical configuration did motherfigure (male) and Christfigure (female) assume?

The Pietà.

Pressing the elevator button, what talismanic examples of the number thirteen undermined Benji's belief in triskaidekaphobia?

The happy baker's dozen: the number of Christ and the apostles: the year of the Bar Mitzvah ceremony in Judaism.

Describe the mechanical means of their ascendancy.

In a modern variation of the classic rope and pulley system, the pair stood still in a vertically rising chamber, positioned between guiderails, suspended by cabled hoistropes, balanced by counterweight, moved and held between floors by grip brakes.

What seeming kinetic paradox did this signify?

The ability to move while standing still.

What Jungian tenet did this exemplify?

Transcendence versus immanence.

If, at the conclusion of their trip, Finn loosened herself and fell from Benji's grip, how did she fall?

32 ft/sec^2 by her known bodyweight of sixty-five pounds in avoirdupois measure.

Did she rise uninjured by concussion?

Momentarily awakened by impact, regaining new stable equilibrium, Finn rose uninjured though irritated, took measure of her surrounding environs, and uttered a single, favorite word.

Name the word.

Home.

As the elevator doors opened, what open-armed apparition awaited them?

Ms. Katherine Mary Welland, who, sobbing, happily relieved Benji of the girl, anointing her face with bouquets of gummywet kisses.

What was Ms. Welland wearing?

A dark blue bathrobe with white trim over long-sleeve blue-and-white striped, 100% cotton Kilgour, French, & Stanbury drawstring pajamas from Barney's Men's Store, embossed with her ex-husband's initials, "MHW."

Why was the host wearing men's bedclothes?

Because the nocturnal vestments were still tinged with the longed-for, sweet-sweat smell of her ex-husband Martin.

How had Ms. Welland spent the intervening hours of Finn's disappearance?

She filed a missing person's report with the proper authorities. She left a telephone message in England for her ex-husband, Martin. She called the Brearley School and spoke to Finn's teachers and supervisors, and Tobey, Finn's friend, confidant, and alibi. She paced. She cried. She spent time alone ruminating on her (perceived) failure as wife, mother, worker, woman.

The parameters of this (perceived) failure?

As wife: inability to keep one's husband. As mother: incapability of instilling appropriate feelings of maternal warmth and familial fortitude in remaining member of clan. As worker: diminishment of spiritual nourishment in a relationship inversely proportional to increased monetary compensation. As woman: indecision over interstices of prescribed roles of wife, mother, worker.

If the guest accepted the host's invitation of entrance, how did he enter?

With circumspection, as invariably when entering an abode, his own or others.

Entering through the threshold, upon what similar occasions did Benji reflect?

Passage through previous portals of discovery: fingerpainted kindergarten classroom doors; Gothic Ithacan ivied doors; Penny's candlelit bedroom doors; antiseptic white hospital ward doors; green whirlpooling Scylla & Charbydis doors; Mickey Mouse handled Disney Store doors: liminal spaces all, each marking one world from the next, beckoning invitation, offering change.

Closing and locking the door behind him, following softly along the hallway, taking note of the accouterments of the dominion laid out before him, what single monosyllabic word encapsulated the sense of economic disparity between guest and host?

Oak.

Entering the living room, what was the host's first action?

With sleeping child wrapped monkey-like around her shoulders and waist, she negotiated her way to the nearest wall, and with half-free hand flipped a switch, filling the room with softly spreading light, spreading softly across the room.

How did it spread?

Dualistically, as wave and particle.

As wave: white light radiating from a source in a straight line traveling electromagnetically with electric fields acting at right angles to magnetic fields through empty space at a constant speed of 186,287 miles per second (300,939 km per second), containing a spectrum of colors of various degrees of vitality (red, orange, yellow, green, blue, indigo, and violet), in a manner such that it can be reflected, refracted, dispersed, diffracted, absorbed, or transmitted.

As particle: responding to relativistic gravitational forces, able to be emitted or absorbed in indivisible bundles of radiant energy known as photons or quanta.

Describe the host's next action.

From across the expanse of living room, Ms. Welland switched off the television.

How was this accomplished?

With the press of a remote control pad button, a silicon chip set off an electronic oscillator, which in turn produced an infrared beam (100,000,000 Hz frequency, 100,000 Å wavelength), which carried a coded signal in binary digits to an infrared sensitive receptor where the signal was amplified and the command carried out.

What did this offhand gesture connote to Benji?

That there is magic in nature: that scientific explanations do nothing to rob natural phenomena of their sense of wonderment: that we live with sorcery in our midst.

What early examples of this (seeming) paradox flashed through Benji's mind?

Sitting in a restaurant as a child, Benji watched as his brother Jerry sucked some soda through a straw and then, calling attention to himself, placed a finger to the open hole. Having thus created a vacuum, the liquid stayed suspended in a quivering state of anticipation until Jerry removed the digit, releasing the stream. At the same dinner, after rubbing knife and spoon together in symbolic gesture of his growing hunger, Benji noticed he had inadvertently magnetized the silverware: head of spoon leading tail of knife around the table in a circular waltz.

What qualities of technology did Benjamin Seymour, technophile, admire?

Its magic, its wealth of information, its ease of access, its democratic egalitarianism. Man's progress: God's speed.

What qualities of technology did Benjamin Seymour, technophobe, fear?

Its inorganic nature. Its refusal to be reasoned with, cajoled, kissed, or fondled. Its demonic plastic arrogance. Its aiding and abetting popular culture in its (easy) victory over classicism. Its gluttony of choice. The blind, ever-increasing velocity of modern life.

Helping mother put child to bed, what prominent features did Benji notice about the girl's room?

A mantle filled with a collection of oversized multicolored coffee cups and saucers, interspersed with a polished assortment of tubular glass and oil kaleidoscopes; a large pine desk atop which sat a vintage black Underwood typewriter missing keys for the letters "M" and "C," a pen and ink set, a blotter, a hand-stenciled bookmark that read, "YOU CAN DO IT," with each letter fashioned out of the bent human form of a court jester costumed in harlequin reds, blues, and greens; a bookcase filled with volumes of all stripe and size, arranged alphabetically according to authors' surname.

Catalogue these books by author.

The Big Strawberry Book of Astronomy, by Jeanne Bendick, illustrated by
    Sal Murdocca (1979)
Benét's Reader's Encyclopedia, Third Edition (1987)
The Uses of Enchantment, by Bruno Bettelheim (1976)
The Western Canon, by Harold Bloom (1994)
The Book of Solo Games, by Gyles Brandreth (1984)
Bulfinch's Mythology, by Thomas Bulfinch (1855)
What Would You Do?: A Child's Book About Divorce, by Barbara S. Cain,
    and Elissa P. Benedek, illustrated by James Cummins (1976)

Alice's Adventures in Wonderland, by Lewis Carroll (1865)

Through the Looking Glass, by Lewis Carroll (1872)

Chess Fundamentals, by José R. Capablanca (1921)

Don Quixote, by Miguel de Cervantes (1605)

The Adventures of Pinocchio, by Collodi (1883)

Basic Chess Endings, by Reuben Fine (1941)

A Pocket For Corduroy, by Don Freeman (1978)

Self-Working Handkerchief Magic: 61 Fool Proof Tricks With 509 Illustrations, by Karl Fulres (1988)

A Brief History of Time, by Stephen W. Hawking (1988)

The Amateur Magician's Handbook, Fourth Edition, by Henry Hay (1983)

Juggling For Fun and Entertainment, by Ron Humphrey (1967)

The Odyssey, by Homer (c. 9th Century B.C.)

Man and His Symbols, Carl G. Jung, editor (1964)

The Seven Pillars of Wisdom, by T. E. Lawrence (1926)

The Chronicles of Narnia, by C. S. Lewis (a seven-volume-set containing the following softcover volumes: *The Lion, the Witch, and the Wardrobe* (1950), *Prince Caspian: The Return to Narnia* (1951), *The Voyage of the Dawn Treader* (1952), *The Silver Chair* (1953), *The Horse and His Boy* (1954), *The Magician's Nephew* (1955), *The Last Battle* (1956))

Frog and Toad Are Friends, by Arnold Lobel (1970)

Frog and Toad Together, by Arnold Lobel (1972)

Frog and Toad All Year, by Arnold Lobel (1976)

King, Queen, Knave, by Vladimir Nabokov (tr. 1968)

The Defense, by Vladimir Nabokov (tr. 1964)

Chess Thinking, by Bruce Pandolfini (1995)

Pastimes With String and Paper, by William R. Ransom (1963)

Nine Stories, by J. D. Salinger (1953)

Franny and Zooey, by J. D. Salinger (1961)

Where the Wild Things Are, by Maurice Sendak (1963)

The Giving Tree, by Shel Silverstein (1964)

Where the Sidewalk Ends, by Shel Silverstein (1974)

A Light in the Attic, by Shel Silverstein (1981)

Hamlet, by William Shakespeare (1600)

King Lear, by William Shakespeare (1605)

The Complete Works of William Shakespeare (maroon, leather-bound)

Caps For Sale: A Tale of a Peddler, Some Monkeys, & Their Monkey Business, by Esphyr Slobodkian (1947)

The Hobbit, by J. R. R. Tolkien (1937)

Conspicuously absent from the room?

Television, computer, stereo, phone.

What worn volume did the guest add to the bookcase?

The Basic Writings of Friedrich Nietzsche, an apprentice poem transcribed on a formerly blank backpage.

What did Finn believe to be the most fun a child can have alone in a room?

Reading.

The most fun two adults can have in a room?

Not reading.

What is a book?

A magic object: a masterpiece of human design: an ancient machine that cannot be improved upon.

If at one time Benji had imagined for himself a career as poet and author, in what practices did he engage in support of this?

He kept a dream journal; he studied the biographies of great authors; he maintained lengthy lists of both the books he had read since college and the books he wished to read; he listened to NPR; he scrupulously followed *The New York Times* and the *New York Review of Books*; he developed titles for immense, plotless, award-winning books.

Such as?

The Aesthetics of Complaint
Complexity
The Great American Lonely
Have No Fear
The Hypnogogue
Megalopolis
New York Times Number One Bestseller
Porno, A Love Story

Were these books ever begun?

No. Never.

What forces rendered a literary career undesirable?

Disapproval of sedentary occupation. Improbability of detached refraction and reorganization of experience. Linguistic leeriness. Fear of mathematical relation whereby successful investigative insight into the human psyche exists in direct proportion to compounded feelings of isolation.

Describe the ceiling of Finn's room.

A crepuscular sky stretching from sun to moon, with stars rejoicing in between. The ceiling, painted by Finn's father Martin, was begun the day after Finn learned to her disappointment that the sun (average 92,955,630 miles, 149,597,870 km away from the Earth) and the moon (average 238,900 miles, 384,400 km away from the Earth) were not following her and her alone as she walked down the street.

What visual phenomenon is responsible for this illusion?

Parallax: the apparent displacement or the difference in apparent direction of an object as seen from two different points not on a straight line with the object.

Did this scientific explanation rob the sun and moon of their magic?

No. The sun rose with Finn, the moon set with her.

What prominent portents of Penelope Pigeon were present about the room?

A full red bank, with the legend, "A Penny Saved Is A Penny Earned," imprinted across the front, a mass of copper coins forming a jagged plateau aligned with the inscription, "Hollywood Vacation," a place Finn always dreamed of visiting; a six-and-a-half inch statue of a golden winged seraphim, awarded to Finn for her for prizewinning fourth grade essay, "Hamlet: Insufferable Mama's Boy," a pigeon planted outside the windowsill, humming, contented with the night's mercy.

Laying her down to darkbed sleep, what infantile memories had Ms. Welland of the sesquipedalian girl with winedark hair?

Finn, nine months old, sitting in a highchair in a redboothed diner. Teasingly, then-united mother and father placed a menu before the still-mute wild-eyed girl, who, after scanning its contents, looked up at the waiter and cheerfully placed her order, a polysyllabic word, her first.

The order? The word?

Hamburger.

What other memories had Ms. Welland of Finn's childhood?

Also in a restaurant: Finn, six years old, jokingly given a sip of her father's Merlot, mounted the table and, showing a surprising facility for high-kicks, broke into a stirring rendition of Irving Berlin's "Anything You Can Do (I Can Do Better)." Ushered out of the restaurant, Finn, unaware that vanished patrons leave money on empty tabletops for tips, peeled the bills off several tables as the group was shown to the door. Once out on the street, Finn presented the stack to her mother and father and the three of them treated themselves to ice cream.

In what position did Finn take rest?

The fetal. Thumb grazing lips, spine a bent spoon, childwoman weary, womanchild in the womb.

Womb? Weary?

She rests. She has traveled.

Drifting deep into nocturnal depths, consciousness unmaking its daily bed, what discrete succession of sensations did Finn perceive?

Cool linen crispness; nearby maternal warmth; strong paternal presence; cozy dozy cove; diurnal disintegration; familial regeneration(?)

Standing at the foot of Finn's bed, what did the guest feel?

The penumbral darkness of the room; the warm glow of the girl's face; a cold poignant pull; an imagined child of his own.

His next action?

In the presence of the host, the guest planted a discreet kiss on the child's forehead, then silently crept into the adjoining room.

After receiving permission from the host, whom did the guest call?

His father, Art Seymour.

Why?

To wish him a (belated) happy Father's Day.

Senior Seymour's reaction?

Disorientation (at being torn from sleep's furry embrace), consternation (at the knowledge that, once woke, he would be unable to go back to sleep), resignation (at pulling himself into full consciousness), happiness (at the recognition of his son's voice), love.

Speaking to his father some thousand miles away, what two memories did Benji recall?

The first: Christmas Eve dinner, twenty years earlier. It was snowing outside. Inside, the Chinese restaurant was empty and warm. Benji remembered his father holding his mother's hand, which was unusual since his parents did not often show signs of physical affection toward one another. He remembered his father tearing up. When Benji asked why he was crying, his father said it was because he could tell his mother was happy, and that in turn made him happy.

The second: At Benji's Bar Mitzvah he had witnessed his father, whom Benji had always taken for a tight, physically cautious man, spend the majority of the affair on the dance floor proving himself a graceful, inexhaustible dance partner.

If Benji had made sure to catalogue these twin memories of equal and opposite importance, what about their respective natures did he value?

The first: the idyllic, the iconic. The second: the revelatory, the unexpected.

Iconic? Unexpected?

He luxuriated in the purity of the first memory, in which people he loved played roles according to plan. He took comfort in the ambiguity of the second memory, proof that someone you know intimately can still be capable of surprise, of kernels of unknowability. That is, he was happy both to know and not to know his father.

Had (reversible) space and (irreversible) time equally but differently obliterated the memory of these reminiscences in either narrator or listener?

No, they had not.

Cradling the telephone, why was the guest (victim, predestined) sad?

Because he knew that his father would one day die and he would be left in the final state of orphanhood that awaits us all.

What did the guest counterpropose to the host's proposal of coffee, tea, or late-night meal?

Access to the bathroom facility adjoining the host's bedroom.

The host's reaction to this?

Relief.

Why relief?

The host did not know how to cook and consequently kept a poorly-stocked kitchen.

In the bathroom, list the guest's actions.

He washed his hands. He wiped gelatinous grease from his forehead with some toilet tissue. He patted down his matted hair. He washed his face and rinsed his mouth out with cold fresh neverchanging everchanging water. He dried them, hands and face, with a soft yellow cotton towel. He ran a forefinger along the valley between underlips, teeth, and gums. He pulled up his socks. He opened and inspected the medicine cabinet.

What did this inspection yield?

Claritin, Midol, Neutrogena Clarifying Astringent, peroxide, cotton balls, Neosporin, nail clippers, Nyquil, Stim-U-Dent toothpicks, Glide dental floss, "sporty-strip" Band-Aids, mini sewing kit, mineral ice, bath salts, unopened vacation-sized shampoo and soaps, yellow and orange razors, Tylenol PM, Nytol, Sominex, Compoz, Unisom, prescription bottles of various heights and widths, aligned like chess pieces, of ProSom, Dalmane, Doral, Restoril, and Ambien.

The guest's next action?

He unbuckled his pants, lowered his shorts, and gave himself a thorough preventative wipe.

Was the guest's underwear devoid of traces of stool?

Remarkably, they were.

What is stool?

Most of the substance known as stool is food residue following the removal of nutrients. Stool usually consists of about 75 percent water and 25 percent solid material. Some of the water is found in mucus, which lubricates the stool and eases its passage from the body. Of the solids, approximately one third is bacteria, one third undigested fats and proteins, and one third cellulose or roughage (undigested plant foods).

Describe the process by which food becomes stool: its heroic odyssey, its noble transformation, its inexorable liberation.

As we eat, saliva produced by the parotid, submandibular, and sublingual glands moistens food, allowing it to be chewed and swallowed efficaciously. The tongue presents food to the teeth for chewing and molds the softened food into a ball, or bolus, ready for swallowing. The tongue positions the bolus into the pharynx, the muscle-lined cavity at the back of the throat. From there, the bolus is pushed down the esophagus in a series of wave-like undulations known as peristalsis.

The esophagus is connected to the stomach, the muscular bag situated in the upper part of the abdomen. The stomach lining produces digestive juices containing acid and enzymes that break food down into a pulp, known as chyme. A ring of muscle called the pyloric sphincter intermittently relaxes, allowing food to pass from the stomach into the duodenum, the first portion of the small intestine. In the duodenum, acid is neutralized by alkaline secretions, pancreatic juice, and bile (bitter greenish fluid used to break down fat globules), which pour into the duodenum via ducts from the gall bladder and pancreas. This thick, semi-fluid mass then enters the small intestine where the food's desirable nutrients are absorbed by the body. With a surface area composed of delicate, 1mm projections called villi, the jejunum is the locus in the small intestine where nutritional elements of food are absorbed. The jejunum leads onto the large intestine, which is divided into four parts: the caecum, the colon, the rectum, and the anus.

The colon moves solid material to the anus, absorbing salt and water delivered to it from the small intestine. The rectum consists of a muscular tube lined with epithelium, which produces mucus that lubricates the stool, making its passage easier. As stool nears the end of its journey, it gradually hardens as the body absorbs liquids and solid waste is pushed into the rectum. The anus is the opening through which stool is excreted. At the end of the anus are two rings of muscle, known as the internal and external sphincters. Normally, these sphincters keep the anus closed, but, during defecation, they relax to allow stool to emerge. The internal sphincter, which is under the control of the nervous system, senses the presence of stool and allows it to enter the anal canal. The external sphincter, however, is consciously controlled and kept closed until a socially convenient moment presents itself, and the stool, butterfly-like, is set free.

Was Benji aware of these internal processes?

No.

How did he regard defecation?

As metaphor.

For?

General transformation from cleanliness to filth: the body's expression of rank self-hatred: society's ineluctable decay.

On this occasion, did Benji feel filthy?

No. Clean.

Reinforcing this sense of cleanliness, what did Benji do next?

He flushed the toilet paper, tucked in his shirt, rebuckled his pants, closed the medicine cabinet, and examined himself in the mirror.

Reflected, what did he see?

A poorly resolved, blurry man, framed by yellow reflecting pools of flowered wallpaper.

Why blurry?

Because Benji suffered from myopia and had neglected to put in his contact lenses that morning (explaining little, though not much, of the psychedelic nature of his visions during the day).

If Benji was generally known to avoid mirrors, why did he avoid them?

Problems of representation: feelings of dislocation: narcissistic repudiation.

How do mirrors work?

Light rays from an object strike the surface of a sheet of glass coated on the back with silver or some other highly reflective metal and are reflected in the opposite direction at exactly the same angle creating a reversed, reflected image of the original object. Since the reflected image appears to be the same distance behind the mirror as the object in front of the mirror, the reflected image appears to have originated from behind the mirror. But there is really nothing behind the reflection.

What object did Benji remove from the bathroom drying rack and place in his pocket prior to exiting?

A pair of plain white cotton panties.

For?

Future olfactory delectation, tactile stimulation, permanent file initiation, post-ejaculatory decontamination.

Upon entering the bedroom, what small religious emblem did Benji notice hanging from Ms. Welland's neck?

A crucifix.

Benji's reaction to this?

Comfort.

Why comfort?

Because his personal sense of it was that Jesus was a nice Jewish boy from Nazareth, and He appealed to him historically, if not necessarily religiously.

What about Him appealed to him most?

His idea that love—and neither money nor material goods—was the answer, the universal balm that greased the human wheel. In this and Jesus' willingness to look for the goodness and grace in the underside of things—in lepers and whores—Benji was reminded, in no uncertain terms, of himself.

If Benji identified with Jesus, had he ever considered conversion?

No he had not.

Why?

Because he also admired the tradition, the practicality, the sanity, the Old World masculinity of Judaism. He was marked a Jew physically, intellectually, and temperamentally, and was decidedly grateful for it.

In support of this belief, in what religious practices did Benji engage?

He fasted each Yom Kippur. He donned a suit and visited his parent's shul in Brooklyn each year to say Yizkor for his dead mother. He kept an electric menorah in the window during the eight nights of Chanukah. He visited his father in Florida with Jerry each Passover for a Seder at Cookies, the neighborhood kosher restaurant.

During his matriculation at Cornell University, on the one occasion during which Passover did not coincide with spring break and he was unable to spend the holiday with his family, what did Benji do?

He organized a small Seder in his apartment for both Jewish and non-Jewish friends alike. Spread out across the floor, Haggadah in hand, guiding everyone through the ceremony, Benji felt very manly that night, different from all others—paternal and wise—as he explained the significance of the shank bone and the bitters. And he never loved Penny more than he did watching her pug nose bounce along a ridge of matzo.

What did Penny contribute to this ceremonial meal?

Matzo ball soup. That is, she opened and heated a one liter can of chicken stock broth and, unfamiliar with the traditional soup, fashioned from a package of Manishevitz Matzo Meal one enormous ball, from which everyone was encouraged to carve an appropriately-sized scoop.

Inside the bedroom, which bureau drawer did the host open?

The bottom drawer, dedicated to assorted esoterica.

What did this unlocked bottom drawer contain?

Three silk Victoria's Secret lingerie outfits (red, black, and white: unworn); cylindrical electronic device (feminine: unused); two of Finn's baby teeth in a medicine bottle labeled "Baby Teeth"; a lock of Finn's hair in a plain white envelope marked "Stephanie, November 19, 1986"; a passport, stamped in England, Spain, Portugal, Morocco, and most recently, "Paris, December 29, 1995"; two photo albums filled with Finn's baby pictures and drawings; her engagement announcement, dated March 20, 1986, printed in gold-embossed letters on Crane's cream white card stock for a ceremony taking place in New Hampshire on June 12, 1985; the little bride and groom that sat atop her wedding cake under a plastic arch of pink and white flowers; the crumbling cork from the champagne bottle she and her husband shared in their honeymoon suite; the white lace nightgown she had worn to bed that night; her teenage orthodontic retainer, a worn Rubik's cube (at rest in the solved position); her complete movie stub collection, kept in one of her father's old cigar boxes, beginning with *Sleeper* (1973) and ending with last week's *Mission: Impossible*; her first grade black-and-white marble-covered notebook; her report card transcripts from Columbia Law School; a wooden yo-yo her grandfather had made for her, its face carved to resemble a buffalo head penny; a folder containing originals and photocopies of Martin's short stories, newspaper, and magazine clips; three groups of love letters, separated and organized in medium-sized manila envelopes marked "Paul, Freshman Year," "Stephen," and "Martin," arranged chronologically within and bound with tape and rubber bands without; a silver watch Martin had given her, a family heirloom permanently stopped at 6:17; her wedding ring; a yellowing envelope addressed to her from Mr. Walter Gelman.

Who was Walter Gelman?

Ms. Welland's eighth grade English teacher.

What, if any, significance did the letter hold?

On the eve of Ms. Welland's junior high school graduation, Mr. Gelman had asked his class to write letters to themselves as they imagined themselves to be ten years from then. He advised that his students think long and hard on the assignment, as this would be one of life's only opportunities for their younger selves to commune with their older selves. The good teacher then promised that if the class took the assignment seriously, he would seal the envelopes, and wherever he was, wherever they were, he would find them and mail the letters to them ten years hence, when his students were in their early twenties, poised on the teetering cusp of adulthood, so as to remind them of who they were and where they were calling from.

What had Ms. Welland written to herself?

"Don't forget, move forward."

If Ms. Welland was known to consult the contents of this letter from time to time, what occasioned these revisits?

Moments of stress, moments of sadness, moments of resignation. When she felt Finn growing up too fast.

What became of Mr. Gelman?

He was killed in a grocery store hold-up late one night, having gone to get some ice cream for his wife, in the seventh month of her pregnancy.

Was Ms. Welland aware of this occurrence?

No. Her name misspelled in her junior high school yearbook (one "l" instead of two), she was kept unapprised of updates and so did not receive the alumni newsletter containing news of Mr. Gelman's death.

Was the teacher then, kept vibrant in his student's imagination, still alive?

Yes.

What item did Benji add to this collection of objects?

A Mickey Mouse Pez dispenser.

Explain the significance of Pez.

Pez mimics emesis, but the product does not reek. Pez dispenses candy, whereas people dispense blood, excrement, mucus, saliva, seminal fluid, vomit, and words. Pez is perfect, but it is only capable of producing one thing, ad infinitum: a single tooth-shaped candy. In this regard, pornography and Pez become almost synonymous: porn Pezes sex into candied pill form.

What exchange of money took place between guest and host?

The former returned to the latter, without interest, a sum of money advanced by the offspring of the latter to the former.

Compile the budget for June 17, 1996.

Debit		*Credit*	
1 Knish	$2.00	Cash in Hand	$37.60
1 Cream Soda	$1.00	Loan	$33.00
1 King Cone		(Stephanie Welland)	
Ice Cream	$2.00		
Phone Call	$ .25		
Subway Fare	$1.50		
1 Ice Cream			
(cone, swirl)	$1.50		
Cab Fare	$23.00		
Loan Refunded	$33.00		
(Stephanie Welland)			
Balance	$6.35		
	$70.60		$70.60

Sitting (tentatively) on the edge of Ms. Welland's bed, what word occurred to Benji?

Firm.

Describe the mattress.

A king-sized (38"x80") extra-firm Sealy Posturepedic Crown Jewel Dual Support System mattress with Syner-Flex™ surface and EverEdge® total perimeter support and Presidential select wool and silk blend ultra plush pillow top, also extra-firm.

Why extra-firm?

To accommodate Martin's bad back, which he had reinjured playing tennis in the months just prior to their divorce.

As his left foot, crossed over his right leg, began to fall asleep, what thought occurred to Benji?

That the bed, purchased for two, abandoned by one, left to the other, was too big for her, and in all likelihood both symbolized and exacerbated her sense of loneliness.

Reflecting on that last word, which Bob Dylan song occurred to Benji?

"Mama, You Been On My Mind" (song four, disc two of The Bootleg Series, Volumes 1-3).

Its final refrain?

> When you wake up in the morning
> Baby look inside your mirror
> You know I won't be next to you

You know I won't be near
I'd just be curious to know
If you could see yourself as clear
As someone who has had you on his mind

Did Benji, teetering on the verge of a flashback, succumb to the warm womb of the song?

No. He pulled himself back from the reverie and the lyric lifted in a flash.

Upon what did Benji concentrate instead?

The mole on the left leg of the woman standing near him.

What did the host see supplicant before her? A fish? A bicycle?

Late millennial Homo sapiens.

Which seemed to the host to be the predominant qualities of her guest?

A courtly, old-world manner in speech and conduct as contrasted by a slovenly appearance in dress. A regal, handsome profile undermined by a sweaty sexual panic.

Which seemed to the guest to be the predominant qualities of his host?

An all-encompassing compassion: a barely-suppressed emotionalism: a charming neuroticism: a furtive sex appeal.

What two temperaments did they individually represent?

The artistic. The pragmatic.

In other respects were their differences similar?

In melancholy, in humility, in altruism, in passivity, in economy, in the instinct of tradition, in sexual conservatism, in poor sleep habit.

What practices did Ms. Welland engage in to alleviate her insomnia?

She nightly drank cups of chamomile tea. She made sure not to eat past nine o'clock in the evening. She watched old black-and-white movies on A&E, and TNT. She took scalding hot baths. She read magazines and romance novels. She masturbated. She tried five different prescription sleep medications.

Did these practices help to relieve her sleeplessness?

They did not.

What proposal did Ms. Welland, somnambulist, mother of Finn, diambulist, make to Benji, noctambulist?

To pass in repose the hours intervening between Monday (proper) and Tuesday (normal) on an extemporized fold-out sofabed in the room immediately adjacent to the sleeping compartment of the host.

What immediate advantages would or might have resulted from such a temporary extemporization?

For the guest: avoidance of late-night transit amidst the forbidding obscurity of night; exchange of damp outer vestment for dry; the potentially ameliorative effects of new nocturnal surroundings on the unconscious; relaxation of painful left foot bunion; sweet surrender to the pull of inertia.

What various advantages would or might have resulted from a prolongation of such an extemporization?

For the host: potential application of firm full masculine active hands to leaky faucet, creaky door, and misaligned shelves; exposure of (positive, masculine) role model to (negative, feminine) child; removal of nocturnal solitude.

Was the proposal of asylum accepted?

Promptly, amicably, gratefully, it was.

Describe Ms. Welland's next action.

She opened her robe slightly, allowing for (masculine) pajama top button to release itself from (feminine) slit, exposing a not unimpressive display of décolletage.

Was Benji witness to this display?

No.

Describe how Benji Seymour saw less.

Three possible explanations for myopia are: (1) the cornea has too much curvature, (2) the eye is too long from front to back, (3) the lens is focusing excessively. In each of these instances, light is focused in front of the retina, meaning that Benji's vision focused at once physically before him, metaphorically behind.

Despite this visual oversight on behalf of the guest, what involuntary action followed?

An ounce of blood rapidly shot to arteries in the erectile tissue (corpora cavernosa and corpus spongiosum) of the male genitalia, engorging it. This engorgement was accompanied by a chemical release in the body of adrenaline, norepinephrine, acetylcholine, prostaglandins, nitrous oxide (laughing gas), and a mixing of secretions from the prostate gland, seminal vesicles, and testes in preparation for eleven mph ejaculation of one quarter ounce of seminal fluid consisting of an average of 500 million sperm, protein, the vitamins C and B12, the minerals calcium (Ca), potassium (K), magnesium (Mn), phosphorous (P), and zinc (Zn), and the two sugars, fructose ($C_6H_{12}O_6$), and sorbital ($C_6H_8O_2$).

What did Benji do to alleviate this pressure/pleasure/pain?

He quietly bit the insides of his cheeks, curled his toes, flexed the muscles in his abdomen, thought fervently of bunnies and battlefields, mentally revisited the triumphant Mets season of 1986, looked to the ground and began cataloguing and studying individual fibers of carpet.

Did the stratagem succeed?

No.

If the guest was afraid, why was he afraid?

Having not engaged in coital propinquity in three years, the guest was nervous, nervousness compounded by uncertainty as to whether or not the host's offer of asylum implied an implicit invitation to engage in explicit course of action. Moreover, if said offer did include implicit invitation to explicit course of action, the guest feared that without the reassuring buzz of technological apparatuses (camera, lights, recording equipment) he would be unable to bring implied, implicit, explicit heterosexual copulation to fruition.

What clinical psychological condition did the guest suffer from?

Scopophilia: a desire to look at sexually stimulating scenes, especially as a substitute for actual participation.

What popular Alfred Hitchcock film diagnoses this condition?

Rear Window (1955), which deposits Jimmy Stewart's broken-legged photographer, L. B. Jeffries, in a wheelchair and surrounds him with a variety of long-lensed (read: phallic) cameras. Cemented to his chair, in an effort to pass the time, Jeffries begins good-naturedly spying on his neighbors across the courtyard, all of whom are conveniently laid out before his open windows like actors on a proscenium stage. In the course of this, he comes to believe he has been made witness to a murder.

Through it all, Jeffries shows almost no erotic interest in his high-spirited girlfriend, Lisa (Grace Kelly), until she leaves his apartment and enters his field of vision across the way. Thus, the erotic relationship between spectator (read, moviegoer) and the object of his longing (read: movie star) is mimicked and approximated through the very design and staging of the film.

Did the guest believe pornography to be an accurate depiction of the physical act of love?

No he did not.

How does pinot miss the mark?

A tactile experience related visually: an interior journey expressed externally: a hallowed act rendered commercially: a private sacrament distributed indiscriminately.

What ameliorative aspects rendered human interface preferable to the technological?

Organic curves versus hard-angled geometry: organismic warmth versus metallic coldness: humanity's talent for resilience, for unpredictability, for unprogramability, for strangeness, for adaptability, for change: the sad heroism of living: the existential quality of every exchange.

Existential?

People can hurt you, people can always say no.

If the host took note of the self-tented trousers of her guest, what was her reaction to this?

Alarm: what was she to do with that? Humor: there being something slavish and stupid about the male erection, resembling, as it does, a dog on its hind legs begging for a treat. Comfort: over the capability of still being able to inspire such hydraulic feats in a man.

What involuntary action followed?

For the first time today, Ms. Welland smiled.

What is a smile?

A facial expression, based on built-in signals called "displays," specific to particular species, that are ways by which one individual informs another individual of his or her intentions. The human smile is an example of such a display, as the response is found in babies across the species, even in those born blind (and thus could not have learned it through imitation). The smile is often considered a signal by which human beings tell one another: "I wish you well; be good to me."

Describe the origin of the human smile.

According to evolutionary biologists, the human smile grew out of the "fear grin," an apparent appeasement display found in monkeys and other primates which usually signifies submission but may also indicate reassurance when directed by a dominant animal to a subordinate.

In an effort to suppress her smile, what habitual action did the host inadvertently undertake?

She began biting her nails.

List the physical imperfections the host was self-consciously aware of.

Assorted fingernails and cuticles (torn, ravaged).
Left hand (nicked).
Right earlobe (torn).
Facial scar (right cheek, 2 cm).
Left leg (mole, protruding).
Right thigh (cauliflower of cellulite).
Elbows (ashy).
Hair (spiderwebs of gray).
Ass (fallen).

The guest?

His smell. His pelt. A streaming abundance of lugubrious globules about the face and neck. Stubble. The sweet cinnamon roll of flab accumulated around his midsection. An invincible planters wart on the third toe of his right foot. A painful bunion on his left. Simian gap between big toe and little toes. Imminent discovery of occupation.

Which of his physical features was the guest pleased with?

Large, emotive, Greek-blue orbs: innocent when downcast, ravaged when directed heavenward, contemplative at rest, puppydoggish when wet, furrow-browed when stymied, bedroom-eyed when seductive, distant-eyed in reverie, in action like an angel, in apprehension like a God.

Ms. Welland's next words?

Thank you.

For?

Finding Finn.

Name two occasions in which Ms. Welland's erstwhile husband, Martin, had lost Finn.

The first: three years previous, having promised to spend quality time with his daughter, the generally preoccupied Martin Welland set aside a Saturday afternoon to attend the Ringling Bros. and Barnum & Bailey circus at Madison Square Garden with his daughter and several of her friends and their parents. Finn, who had a particular distaste for animals (allergies) nonetheless had expressed a rapt enthusiasm to attend, and in particular was looking forward to the grand finale, the Globe of Death: a propulsive display of stunning centrifugal force whereby two customized 75 cc motorcycles perform sixty mph whirligigging loop-de-loops around a sixteen-foot steel sphere in the center of which stands a sequined damsel, distressed.

Did Finn witness the Globe of Death?

No. After suffering through one-and-a-quarter hours of allergic reactions to horsehair and elephant shit, Martin Welland received a page on his beeper. Leaving Finn under the guidance of her friends' parents, Finn's father excused himself to return the call, not to return.

Describe the second occasion.

Halloween, one year previous: Finn, in black, in full Hamlet regalia with outstretched Yorick skull, was trick-or-treating with neighborhood friends dressed as Yoda, Leonardo the Teenage Mutant Ninja Turtle, and the red

Mighty Morphin' Power Ranger, with her father, dressed as Dracula the Vampire, leading the charge. After about an hour, the motley gang stopped by a brownstone belonging to a writer friend of Finn's father. Depositing the children in front of the living room television, Martin—caped, defanged—retired to the other room with his friend, and the evening's festivities were abruptly cut short.

What eleemosynary arrangements did Mr. Welland implement to compensate for these parental lapses?

He made presents of various books and assorted objets d'art: he raised Finn's weekly allowance by an increment of one dollar: he made her a gift of his antique Underwood typewriter: he kept a private stash of sugary cereals and junk food for Finn hidden from the baleful eye of his wife.

Did Finn forgive him?

In word, yes. In the silent recesses of her heart, no.

Had Ms. Welland?

In word, no. In the silent recesses of her heart, yes.

In response to the host's catechetical interrogation of the day's events, what elements did the guest omit from the narrative?

Finn's successful career in mendicancy, her evasion of municipal turnstile, her predilection toward inhalation of leaf-green narcotic, her ingestion of non-kosher non-dietetic dairy product. The pair's musical encounter with a subterraneous rodent, their detour to roughhewn outerborough bog, their blind traversal of cascading intersection. Long-termed proclivity toward self-abuse of a decidedly sexual nature. Appropriation of enticing undergarment.

Was the narration otherwise unaltered by modification?

Absolutely.

What personage of enigmatic significance did neither host nor guest entirely comprehend?

Michelangelo Virelle.

Which person or event emerged as the salient point of the guest's exegesis?

Finn. The protean multifacetedness of her personality: her cleverness, her cunning, her resilience, her intelligence, the depth of her unhappiness.

Listening to the guest recount the day's events what theme could the host detect?

Growing bond between man and child: the goodness of the man.

Ms. Welland's next action?

She sat down on the bed's snakespiral springs and positioned her face such that masculine skiff (tongue) was invited to dock in feminine lake (mouth).

Benji's reaction?

Exhilaration, excitation, anticipation, followed by minor calculation, some deliberation, a moment's hesitation, a final resignation.

Exhilaration?

Assuagement of magnetic attraction of a nonunilateral nature.

Excitation?

Prolific reproduction of physiological reflex response.

Anticipation?

Meditation upon proliferous physiological reflex response held—ritardando—in a concerted effort to prolong, protract, and preserve previously described feeling of pleasure/pressure/pain.

Calculation?

Unsuccessful search for words meant expressly for her first last only and alone whereas anysuch combination of words originated before him and were used elsewhere by others in other times in a series originating in and repeated to infinity.

Deliberation?

To do or not to do? To act or not to act?

Hesitation?

Every person a story of unknowable outcome: a doorway to places unknown: both princess and tiger, harbor and tempest.

Resignation?

Staring into darklonging eyes, Benji was faced with the realization that, regardless of outcome, nothing would surpass this moment. That is, he recognized that every human relationship is, finally, a story of loss.

Did he act?

Host kissed guest kissed host. Spirit made flesh.

Sitting across from each other in restaurant, boardroom, or bedroom, where do two lovers begin?

With a question.

The answer?

13

Yes because he brought Stephanie home to me which puts him above all others especially the British bastard who promised to love honor and obey in goodness and badness and sickness and health in sleeping and wakefulness till death do us part suppose you mean those things when you say them so in a way they're true men love to lie gets them excited like Pinocchio polevaulting out the room only becomes a real human being when he loses his erection that story has a lot to tell us about men is he awake look at the way his chest rises and falls like that how much air they can hold in them that's a sight for sore eyes a man lying next to me the best feeling in the world drifting off to sleep with someone beside you close enough to breathe your air feeling safe and certain sometimes there are infinite nooks of mercy and tenderness in the world like Blanche says in *Streetcar* sometimes there's God so quickly yes sometimes there's God so quickly only sometimes there's not like when I tried talking to ma after the divorce really tried talking to her about what happened all she could say is everything would be fine and things would change for the better and everything would work out unless it doesn't she was horrified when I told her really disappointed in me like how come I couldn't hold onto to him how come I couldn't make it work she was very taken with Martin from the first time they met an accent can go a long way but no one knows what goes on between two people let alone the two people in it and who knows if my parents got married today if they would've made it has he ever been married no ring on his finger but you can't go by that a very sound sleeper so sad watching Martin sleep beside me knowing he was so close and so

far away at the same time early afternoon in England now what's he thinking of at the office or on assignment or called in sick and stayed in bed all
day with Susan the cow we'd do that every once in a while call Stephanie's
school call in sick for her too spread a blanket out across the living room
floor fill it with everything we'd need for the day open all the windows and
pretend we were stranded on a tropical island couldn't get on or off tell
stories to each other eat and watch television all day he had his romantic
side Martin did and everything he said just sounded so smart and funny
everything does in that accent cruel British bastard well every woman
loves a fascist and I loved him really loved him does he think of me from
time to time in quiet moments like this or just a set of memories from a
past life now a name in his Rolodex an item on his list of calls to make at
holiday time the first voice who picks up the phone when he calls for
Stephanie flipping through my phone book the other day made me so sad
to realize these are the people of my life this is the cast of characters of my
life my dramatis personae how many more will cross the stage

Was still in love with him when it ended still young no real money problems great kid and still it didn't work just said his life wasn't working out
the way he'd envisioned New York the writing having a family nothing
was matching up to the way he'd envisioned things threw some awful bit
of Irish poetry at me about dreams and responsibility but what about facing up to things when they don't go according to plan whose life works out
the way they'd imagined it would anyway that was it no fighting no dra-
matics everything well-mannered and sober low voices and the two of us
taking Stephanie to the child psychologist to explain how mommy and
daddy still love one another and none of it is her fault and packing our life
together in corrugated boxes and throwing us away like we're nothing
show a pair of shoes more respect almost wish he had been having an affair
give me a reason to hate him at least that you can chalk up to weakness or
better thighs or a prettier face or a tighter butt or magnetism or electrici-
ty or something chemical like when Linda became convinced Michael was
having an affair kind of fun for us for a while playing detective all those
details to catalog lipsticked collars and strange credit card bills and phantom phone calls and all of us venting our frustrations about our husbands
and marriages on Michael gave a direction for our anger but when it just
dies like that where does it go must change to something else has to con-
servation of energy left with all that anger battling with happy memories
the Spanish Steps St. Peter's standing under the arches in the Coliseum in

the rain first time we tried sushi and sake slowdancing to Nina Simone under the overhead fan in our first apartment in Stuyvesant Town taking him to Nathan's in Coney Island and riding the Cyclone his first American rollercoaster the Mermaid Parade painting the stars on the ceiling in Stephanie's room Stephanie with chickenpox covered in calamine lotion the three of us walking across the Brooklyn Bridge the city laid out open for us like a jewelry box the day he proposed on the boat windy and my hair flying around like crazy and I didn't want him to propose to me then felt so silly with my hair going every which way and he told me not to worry he loved me he loved me more than the wind and out popped the ring and I love you I love you more than the wind always had the right things to say back then good with words always thought before he spoke like you could see he was picking over the right ones to say and the letters he would write me always typewritten because he was embarrassed by his handwriting southpaw I liked that formality that measure of reserve something so courtly and old world in his manner so gentlemanly and fine the early days were nice it was nice being married then different too still a lot of distance between us still surprised when I'd find out he didn't eat a certain type of fish or vegetable or how much mayonnaise he put on his sandwiches or had never seen a favorite movie of mine or always locked the bathroom door or the type of soap he used or that he preferred gray suits to blue so much unknowable about another person still is well you don't fall in love with someone you know you fall in love with something you create in your head then you match it to the person in front of you make adjustments and hope for the best

Wonder if he'll stay till morning suppose it's my feminist prerogative to kick him out of bed and don't let the door hit you on the way out but that was good between us last night what is it Stephen used to say after we'd had sex you give me good love that was it you give me good love he'd say soft and low like a jazz musician come in from the rain true what they say about black men won't ever find out I suppose they are sexy though especially the muscular ones with shaved heads we were young and in college but so what maturity doesn't have the market cornered on emotional integrity what a voice he had so sexy and low smoked because he knew the effect it had on his voice loved it when he used to read to me in bed while he smoked his Marlboro reds always associate that smell with Stephen even now made him wait for it but was glad when we did wouldn't let us have boys sleep over the dorms at Wellesley so we waited until we could drive down to Alice's beach house on the Jersey shore eerie in the middle of winter real Springsteen territory and the town was deserted and at night the place was so silent and desolate only made us more nervous both knew what we'd come there for just to put a good face on it we'd packed all our books and pretended to each other that it would be a good quiet place to study for a weekend before finals at first I was so tight he couldn't get it in and he wasn't even that big so we drank some whiskey and walked along the beach with all the rocks and broken seashells and washed up jellyfish that looked like burst plastic bags and talked about what we wanted from life and how things would change after college and how we'd always be there for one another no matter what and all the things that boys and girls tell each other and when we went back to the house I felt warm down there and knew I was ready there was a big overstuffed teddy bear on Alice's bed the kind you win at a carnival and we were afraid to move anything around that her parents would know someone had used the house and we'd get Alice in trouble so we kept the teddy bear on the bed with us I can still picture its face with those big blank eyes whole thing lasted about two minutes when it was over felt like thanking the bear Stephen was so apologetic that he came quickly until a few minutes later he got hard again and we tried again and this time it lasted longer and it was good and I remember thinking this is it this is sex and tried to stop cataloguing all the sensations inside me and participate a little more and he asked if he could turn me over and I lied on my belly and felt him hot and wet on my back like an eel feels so different from behind looser deeper and more sensitive and he made all these babybites on my neck and back and ran his fingers hard through my hair it was long then and pulling me by my hips and me not knowing what to do with my hips and my legs not knowing if I should wriggle around or just lay still and let him do all the work he worshipped me after that I was the girl he was fucking he was so proud of that only after that he no longer really saw me everything was either talking about how great everything was or planning when we'd get to do it again they never see us whole even now always less than the sum of our parts to them a set of eyes and mouth across a dinner table a pair of hands doing laundry and paying bills a collection of holes and curves in bed beside them so much time spent wondering what we want but they really torture themselves building us up and tearing us down and making religions out of us and then hating us for it even bleeds pretty heavy symbolism that

Still it was 1978 everyone was fucking everyone and not having boys around just made it worse I should have been wearing flower dresses and tripping through strawberry fields I should have been sitting on any boy I could find instead of worrying about being such a good girl and then he was upset because I wouldn't go on the pill like all his friend's girlfriends and how he couldn't feel close to me that one time he lost the condom inside me I didn't feel it and he just kept going couldn't believe he would do that I was so young and afraid of sperm getting in me and swimming upstream like salmon couldn't believe he would do that just keep going and then pulled out and came on my ass like I was a picture he'd masturbated over in a magazine sex makes people do crazy things he said in that voice of his that was so practiced when I was crying afterward trying to make me feel better hated him so much for that could see him clearly then it makes people do crazy things we kill ourselves with our bodies we make weapons of our eyes and our legs and our hands he said and I could tell he loved the way he sounded that he loved the way the words sounded coming out of his mouth that he thought he was getting through to me being all poetic and doomy but the more he talked the more I hated him and it was never any good between us after that

He spent a long time licking my asshole no one has ever done that to me before made me feel self-conscious about what I ate today last time I'd gone to the bathroom how clean I was liked it though he said I have a beautiful asshole made me very wet also made me wonder what a beautiful asshole looks like yes he's a strange one this Benjamin sucking on my fingers and toes and armpits and licking all around inside my bellybutton opposite of every man I've been with working from the outside in and me just laughing the whole time at one point he was sucking on one of my toes and came across a stray piece of toenail and just bit it off and swallowed it a toe job he called it huge space between his big toe and the rest can probably pick things up and pinch people that way and sign his name with his feet what's the word prehensile yeah this is a strange one this Benjamin his belly is sexy it's hard and soft at the same time I like the way it feels I like the way I could feel the sweat trickling down his back I liked how he was self conscious about the hair on his shoulders the salty taste of his neck the heaviness of his thighs on my back the way he tasted going down warm salty seaweed and copper penny taste O I missed that taste jamming it all in like you're drowning and it's an oxygen tank after I was done he turned me over and spread my arms out to the sides like a crucifix and held me there for a while and licked my back and rubbed his face in my hair lapping me up like a kitten no like a painter coating me with his tongue over and over seemed like he wanted to do everything but stick it in me can't blame him really who knows what goes on in there bacteria and yeast like an oven pour in some chocolate icing out pops a birthday cake open system put you in the chair throw your legs over your head see clear to China so complicated still it would be nice to turn it off and just take a man imagine the power that must come with that couldn't handle an orgy though too many thank you notes hahaha but two men at once three men at once must be an awfully full feeling when he handed over that money to me I got so excited like he wanted to pay me for it didn't realize he was holding onto it for Stephanie was wearing Martin's pajamas got so flustered I put the bills down my pajamatop like they do in movies but not in real life because that's the first place they go for prostitution would keep you in shape though meet lots of interesting people that way too I'll bet sailors and cops and firefighters lonely old married men virginal college boys home on break they're so sad men they need us so much more than we need them nothing to tie them to the earth so they wander from job to job and city to city and port to port but always orbiting back to us back to where they came wonder what it's like with another woman must be nice all those curves and passageways to feel around dark turning corners holy land bump in the road difficult to map strange thing even the word is a struggle up and down the peak of that mountainous middle syllable clit tor ris up and down pre present post Martin was useless when it came to finding it firm believer in Freud's mature vaginal orgasm put his fingers deep inside then bring them to my mouth to taste didn't mind but he'd never kiss me after I'd swallowed him loved it when I'd wear high heels leave them on he'd say I want to fuck you with your heels on and I couldn't stop laughing because it reminded me of John Wayne or Alan Ladd or one of those other Western guys who just really really really wants to die with their boots on he hated it when I'd laugh during moments like that but I like to laugh what's everyone always so serious about sex for anyway snarling faces and grimaces he came on one of my shoes once so pleased with himself like a baby staring at his own shit and me just wondering if semen is good for Italian leather strange fetish to have only distances you from what you're afraid of turns it into theatre like you need a costume and a cape to face another person

It was always like that with Martin either a straight silent eyes-closed fuck or blindfolds and feathers and high heels with him cursing like an

American truck driver which was useless since it only made him sound more like the prissy knicker-wearing over-educated prep school boy he really was talk dirty to me he would whisper when his erection would start to flag and as soon as a four letter word came out of my mouth he'd be up again like a hat rack what would I say the usual really no talent for profanity I love it I love it when you fuck me fuck my cunt your cock is so big I love it when you fuck my cunt with your big hard cock just building on the previous words one after the other like it was the words that were exciting like it was the words that were rubbing against each other instead of bodies you just feel silly like what you're saying has nothing to do with what's going on with the bodies down below or maybe the words take precedence it all takes place in your head anyway maybe it's all about the words we say and the stories we tell one another maybe that's the only way we ever really penetrate each other like how molecules never touch no matter how close they get how they get closer and closer but never really touch so even when two people are having sex no one's ever really penetrating the other person I don't know and then after reading that awful book he wanted us to have simultaneous orgasms so that became the goal for a while timing the whole thing out like we were stunt pilots or safe crackers or tightrope walkers just made me tense well every man who can raise it thinks he's the world's greatest lover and every woman who can't come on cue thinks she's the worst

No justice in that but shouldn't look for justice in the world won't find it strange symbol the scales of justice blindfolded woman in a bathrobe both hands occupied perfect to sneak up from behind only a man would have thought that one up who wants justice to be blind anyway open your eyes there's work to be done had problems staying awake in ethics never missed a class though liked school was good at it clever been through all of F. Scott Fitzgerald's books and all that but life isn't like that you can't prepare for it and you're not graded on it or rewarded for getting the right answer still there's something satisfying about taking a test empirical right or wrong miss the clarity of exams saved the biggest for last two full days of constitutional criminal evidence torts civil procedure contracts packed a lunch that day caffeinated Coke and tuna salad instead of turkey because turkey breast has tryptophan in it makes you sleepy call it the bar because that's where you need to go as soon as you're through with it everyone hates lawyers even Shakespeare first thing we do let's kill all the lawyers don't even feel like a lawyer most of the time like today before Stephanie disappeared dealing with Peggy and that actor on the phone for two hours seven million dollars a movie probably twenty for the one after this just a nice clean faced kid wonder what he'll do with money like that buy a PlayStation for every room in the house I would travel maybe try living in Italy for a while or France know how badly Stephanie dreams of going there would that make me happy or do you adjust to that kind of wealth and find things to make yourself miserable about people are resilient that way still can't get a read on Peggy known her for years and have no idea what makes her tick never seen her have a bad day don't really mind entertainment law not the most taxing thing in the world truth be told plays well to the folks back home but that's what people don't understand it's all about billable hours paperwork and filing the whole point is to avoid going to trial how many times have I stood before a jury the past ten years two yes two not what I imagined it would be got into it to be where the action is surprise witnesses gasps from the gallows pounding gavels bailiffs dragging me out by my hair I'm out of order you're out of order this whole court's out of order instead in my office alone most of the time like a cowboy without a horse or a brain surgeon treating a cold the sheets aren't cold anymore they're warm from us our oniony smell is tangled up in the sheets nice and good I like his smell I like him stretched out beside me tall why are New York lawyers all so short anyway I'm a good three inches taller than every man I've dated this past year haven't dated much at all really so depressing anyway let me take you out tell you all about my health club and my mutual funds he's a good height though six feet tall would be my guess if he stood up straight I liked the scratchiness of his stubble between my legs his hands going down along the knobs of my spine the feel of his pants worn corduroy so soft maybe tomorrow I'll go feel some clothes who needs a shrink when you have Bloomingdale's retail therapy I like the feel of clothes cotton and linen especially something light imagining myself in them my skin rubbing up against different weights of material imagining myself in different settings on a cruise ship or at a gallery opening or a grand ball or a nightclub never look the same on you at home as they do on the rack for some reason and those little lingerie outfits forget it consider it triumph having bought them then bury them on the bottom of the underwear drawer still it feels good to buy something nice been a long time since I've bought myself something nice to wear not for work a new long nightgown or a bathing suit or a pair of bluejeans O when I got home from the police station I was just dying to get out of my suit couldn't wait to get into Martin's old pajamas hate the

clothes I have to wear hate wearing dark pants and wool suits and changing out of my comfortable shoes the minute I step foot in the office what's
that line from Prufrock I grow old I grow old I shall wear the bottoms of
my trousers rolled yeah well they even dress us up like men what kind of
victory is that put us in suits and lock us up in a tower why so high up anyway makes people look like ants Harry Lime on the Ferris wheel why is it
the higher up you go the more expensive real estate gets shouldn't it be the
opposite the closer you get to people to things to the ground the worst is
when I have my period and I'm wearing panty hose and a hot wool suit can
tell when the other women have it too in a meeting with all of us squirming around in our chairs trying to be professional and pay attention to
what's going on and as soon as it's over off we go to the stalls religious Jews
make you take a ritual bath afterwards wonder if he's Jewish always been
comforted by my period like a house that's being built every month and
always that hope a tenant will move in until swish no buyers a man's parts
are no better always building themselves up and tearing themselves down
too but always directed back into themselves at least we manage to make
something out of it I like the way my breasts look when I have my period
fuller and rounder and more sensitive not just the nipple looking around
in the locker room at the gym amazed at the personality of bodies sad sagging breasts bright optimistic twins everyone so thin these days rib cages
showing through the skin when did women's bodies get like that the other
day in the gym I saw a girl with what do you call it when the abdominal
muscles protrude like that on bodybuilders washboard abs Joe six-pack yes
bony hipless and hard everything a man could want muscles mustache
deep voice dried up womb like a raisin the gym and the leotard are this
generation's kitchen and apron one cliché replaces another the hardbod-
ied look of a convertible the new squeaky-clean model they want us to
emulate can't win career can't win gold digger can't win slut can't win
prude can't win women's bodies just aren't supposed to look like that and
I don't care I like my hips I like my thighs I like my breasts they aren't as
sensitive as they used to be my nipples are bigger and darker now from
breastfeeding the thirsty little bugger she loved ice cream when I was pregnant remember that's all she wanted to eat vanilla Swiss almond butter
pecan dulce de leche chocolate fudge bet she's got ice cream flowing
through her veins don't let her get at it though so many appliances we got
as wedding gifts I never use juicer professional breadmaker ice cream
maker I used once don't get any real cravings for food anymore his nickname for her was hamburger and I was pickle didn't eat pickles when I was

pregnant though didn't mind being pregnant relieved not to have my period she'll have hers soon she'll be a young woman soon what kind of woman will she be used to wonder what kind of woman I would be and now I'm wondering what kind of woman my daughter will be how did that happen fine lines around my mouth now thirty eight birthday cards that joke about my age thirty eight years old with a great future behind me when I go to the bathroom now I turn on only one light when did I get a woman's face sometimes I see my mother's face when I look in the mirror when did my face become no longer my face thirty eight what kind of face will I have when I'm old will my wrinkles be laugh lines will I be a happy old lady or sad will things pass me by when will I no longer understand what Stephanie's talking about stop listening to her music and watching her movies I accidentally stepped in on her taking a bath the other night thought I could see her breasts starting to develop a little curve where there was no curve a little blush where before there was none I have fine hairs on my lip now soon I'll be the mother of a teenager I hope she doesn't scare boys away no she won't she'll be happy she'll be a June bride wore my mother's nightgown on my wedding night white silk mother to daughter generation to generation ashes to ashes everlasting to everlasting if I must die I will encounter darkness as a bride and hug it in my arms was good with Shakespeare then college drama class so many things that interested me then poetry and wines and horticulture and dance and sailing the world like a basket of fruit pick and choose what to bite was so young then was so young that's all right I'm accomplished I have a child I make $246,000 a year I own my apartment I write depositions for a living I know how to make a vodka martini I have a stationary bike play racquetball once a week am a member of the Book-of-the-Month Club have a subscription to the *New Yorker* floss twice a day took a photography adult education class last summer can make an eggwhite omelet get extended cable went to my twentieth high school reunion have a wedding ring I no longer wear I have a child what would the first baby have been like he was a boy Jonathan we were going to call him began bleeding at the end of the third month stayed in bed for weeks the doctors knew the baby was dead but thought it best for me to go through natural labor so I carried him around dead inside of me for a month it was horrible think I lost Martin during that time too like something was wrong with me but we got pregnant again not too long after that even though the doctor warned us and said we should wait didn't care missed that feeling so much just wanted to have a baby growing inside me again maybe just pride never failed at anything why should this be any different so careful the second time no wine with dinner left restaurants if we saw a lit cigarette don't even think we saw R-rated movies then wanted things to be okay so badly so desperate for things to work out okay this time and then I could feel her fluttering around inside me like a butterfly could see her when I was in the bath fighting to get out like she was punching from within I remember when Martin would come into the bathroom and bathe me with a soapy towel and run his hand over my belly all wet and slick like a seal and sometimes he would be so overcome he would cry Stephanie kicked so hard she kicked the stethoscope out of Dr. Melnick's ears that time after she was born she'd always kick the blankets off her the last few months were the hardest she couldn't wait to get out and start memorizing words and me going to the bathroom to pee every five minutes even thought of writing a book about the best public restrooms in the city hated sleeping on my back like that hot and sweaty all the time even with the air conditioner on full blast up all night wondering who is this creature growing inside me who's of me but not me what will she be like will she like me will we be friends it's strange that men try so hard to get back to from where they came you'd think they'd get out and never look back instead when they crawl on top of you it's like they're babies again like they want to get closer and closer and closer until there's nowhere else for them to go but through you so they pass through you inside you and then they feel bad because they know they don't belong there so they pull out again and then they feel that longing again so they dive back in such a strange act of repetition like we're working at cross-purposes from each other stay go stay go not like pregnancy at all so natural and clearminded and calm they say you forget the pain but you don't really you never forget a minute of it you're just so overwhelmed with love the best of worlds you can instantly pick your baby out from all the others think you recognize each other in some way makes you believe in everything in God in life in love when they brought Stephanie to me after she was born she looked at me and I knew it was her nothing prepares you for that moment everything fades away all the unnecessaries fall away except this girl staring at you and that's one true thing she was born with a full head of hair the nurses combed so excited never seen anything like it before and sharp nails the nurses had to cut the day she was born sharp vampire nails that scratched then bringing her home and feeling this is why we bought the apartment we're a family now with a baby in the next room still a member of your old family but making a new family and not sleeping worrying about her choking in the middle of the night just wanting to be there when she'd wake up crying a pull that keeps you awake even when the baby is sleeping working to get my body back all those hours on the stationary bike all those grapefruits and rice-cakes and dieting and monitoring my stretch marks as they faded from white to silver Martin said he loved the way it felt after that finally knew what sex was about everything prior to that had been adolescent craving he loved the size of my breasts then save a few drops for me over coffee at the breakfast table creepy British pervert

Can't sleep none of those pills work probably bad for you anyway yes throws off your rhythm tired all day can't sleep at night once removed from myself night is a giant eight hours tall never had insomnia until after Stephanie was born some men masturbate before going to sleep come into a sock or a towel just knock themselves out can't do that in bed too sad like doing it in the bath with the mineral salts and the steam and the heat throbbing and slick like to be cold in bed sometimes on hot nights like this I put my sheets in the freezer an hour or so before I go to bed so cold against my skin read somewhere that Marilyn Monroe used to put her panties in the icebox quite a surprise for Art and Joe like drifting off to sleep reading have dreams that take place in the world of the book has to be the right story though like once I went to bed reading contracts for work and dreamt I was filing all the memories of my life in this vast cob-webbed warehouse or that time I went to sleep reading with the television on and dreamt I was on the Hollywood Squares only I was in each of the nine boxes and I was the host and both contestants and we were all com-peting against each other no it has to be the right book with exotic locales and silver jetplanes and jewel thieves and bloodred Mediterranean suns or oldtime romances with men in top hats and canes and women in bodices fountain penning calligraphy letters back and forth to each other to make those worlds live in your head characters more alive than the people in your life that's a wondrous thing when an author can do that makes the world a less lonely place O I'm going to be ruined tomorrow if I don't get some sleep the morning after you've been up all night staggering around all day tired and puffy but energized too like it's drained you and filled you up at the same time see the world through new eyes sunstunned eyes a secret you carry around all day inside like you've pulled one over on the world it takes so little too just a kiss really when we were sitting on the bed together he waited a long time to kiss me then can't really blame him though that first moment so awkward like the pause in musicals right before they burst into song like they're talking about a big new idea they have or the girl they'll marry or the one that got away and then suddenly the orchestra starts in only here there's no music and the words fade and you pass into that silent world of touch and taste and smell I opened my eyes during that first kiss he was looking at me too don't know what's better watching or being watched more intimate than sex even faces so close like a little kid again with butterflies in your stomach and goosebumps on your arm heart going like mad maybe that's why God gave it to us so we could always feel like kids again feeling your way around with your mouth and tongue they say babies first learn about the world through their mouths maybe that's what kissing is God's way of making us feel like babies again still remember my first kiss over twenty years ago took me up to his roof hot summer night like this one so hot and stuffy in his room with his parents watching television in the room next door climbed out the window onto his neighbor's roof and laid a towel out over the tar and I was shaking because I knew he would try to kiss me the stars were out for us that night sounds of traffic coming from the street down below we have an audience he said and I remember it was all so romantic and corny why bring me up to the roof to kiss me like he has to frame the moment why not just grab me in the hallway or on the street or something instead of making a whole production of it but also wanting it to be dramatic and being thankful to him for that he was chewing gum I could tell he was nervous by how fast or slow he was chewing boys don't know what they're doing still don't then he started to say something like I really like you a lot or something equally poetic only he stuttered and I thought O so that's why he talks so slowly that's why he chews gum all the time and I felt so badly for him then I didn't want him to talk anymore so I covered my mouth over his and he stopped me so he could throw his gum away over the side of the roof and we kissed O it's like it happened yesterday when I think of it it's still so fresh in my mind so vivid a kiss makes you magical nothing like it just opening your mouth like that like you're the only two people left breathing in the world locked together in a foreign land surprised I knew what to do with my tongue and my lips and my hands and my eyes but I did know what to do like a spider that just knows how to spin a web and we were kissing grinning young lovers under the stars that was the first time I saw one too all goosepimply and hard like that and determined too with a head like a mushroom cap and hairy at the root like something you'd find growing out of the earth like a flower yes when he sat down with me on the bed and saw all those dried up roses on the mantle O I was so embarrassed I almost died dried up black roses with purple spiderveins like an old widow why not something inviting like fresh flowers from the Korean grocers downstairs must have passed them a thousand times daisies and lilacs and lilies and azaleas and sunflowers and snapdragons and daffodils and roses and irises and orchids and poppies and carnations and chrysanthemums and tulips and irises and dandelions and birds of paradise does the heart good to see how many times must I've passed them and never bought any five dollars a dozen ten dollars a dozen must have a function in nature but seem to exist just to give pleasure God's way of smiling at us smiling down on us first thing tomorrow I'll buy bunches I'll fill the halls with flowers who was it compared a woman's sex to flowers Lawrence *Lady Chatterley Sons and Lovers Women in Love* yes a woman is like a flower pretty when tended to otherwise all dried up I asked him if he thought I was pretty and he could tell I wasn't one of those catty women who are always fishing for compliments but that I really needed to hear that that I really meant it that I hadn't been told those things in a long time and a woman needs to hear those things and he looked at me and said you're a beautiful woman Ms. Welland and then he paused and added you ought to be fucking in hotel rooms O when he said that I thought I'd soak right through the mattress I ought to be fucking in hotel rooms well I should be fucking in hotel rooms I should be eating chocolate cake I should be drinking champagne out of a glass slipper I should be prowling midnight streets I should own a pair of leather pants I should paint my eyelashes black I should be wearing silver bracelets on my wrists and flowers in my hair I should be sleeping in the sand I should be a mermaid I should be fucking in hotel rooms no one had ever said anything like that to me before when he said that I didn't know what to do so I looked down and traced the veins in my hands and thought of how these are no longer girl's hands even though I still bite my nails and then I thought of all the things he couldn't know about me and all the things these hands had done the hours they'd practiced piano and the shoelaces they'd tied and the papers they'd written and the homework they'd helped Stephanie with and the depositions they'd taken and all the times they were wrapped around Martin's back and the dishes they'd washed and the diapers they'd changed and the laundry they'd folded and all the times they'd made this big bed I like my bed in my bed I am a queen still it's nice to have someone here beside me so warm amazing how the body works with all that heat and all those valves opening and closing all the time with all sorts of liquids pouring out of you like a runny nose I can feel myself closing up now I wonder if he can feel that smells like the sea I used to love the ocean when I was a girl it's been so long since I've been to the ocean sand in my crotch pores open to the sun saltwater air sky like a big blue bowl sound of water against the shore just a few more hours and I'll have to get ready for work hate the sound of alarm clocks worst sound in the world just an inhuman sound so many better ways to be woken up someone cooing in your ear or sunlight on your face or the sound of waves maybe I'll take tomorrow off yes maybe I'll take tomorrow off and go to the beach with Stephanie a day off to celebrate summer another summer here already he's warm lying in bed beside me Benjamin is warm beside me his eyelashes are long when he came he closed his eyes and made a little Elvis snarl I have to admit I'm surprised at myself having done this especially after saving myself all these years for prince cartoon on the white horse guess that means I'm still capable of surprising myself just don't get too hopeful hope can be such a sad and dangerous thing in dreams begin responsibility yes that was the line in dreams begin responsibility so he came in handy after all still there's something kind about him I could tell that as soon as he walked into the office this morning something honest and sad about his eyes yes and shy like a little boy he was shaking when he entered me and he was so polite too always asking if he could do certain things before he went ahead and did them and asking how I felt and how did I feel much gentler than Martin yes and he asked could he put it there yes and could I put it there yes a little trouble getting that in there yes because he pleased me greatly last night yes because before when we were sitting together on the bed he said to me you have a good girl in there Ms. Welland an extraordinary girl yes and maybe I could see you and her again sometime yes maybe we could all do something together sometime soon if you'd like and yes I said I would Yes.

ABOUT THE AUTHOR

Born in Brooklyn in 1973, Andrew Lewis Conn has contributed film criticism to *Film Comment* and *Time Out New York*. He is a graduate of Cornell University.